My Brother
is an
Only Child

Il fasciocomunista

© 2005 Arnoldo Mondadori Editore SpA., Milano

ANTONIO PENNACCHI

translated from Italian by
JORDAN LANCASTER

BOOKS

FT
Pbk

REVOLVER BOOKS

Published by the Revolver Group

Revolver Books Ltd, 10 Lambton Place, Notting Hill Gate, London W11 2SH

First published in Great Britain in 2008 by Revolver Books, an imprint of Revolver Entertainment Ltd, Registered Offices: Craven House, 16 Northumberland Avenue, London WC2N 5AP

Translated from the Italian, *Il fasciocomunista*
© 2005 Arnoldo Mondadori Editore SpA., Milano

Translation © Jordan Lancaster 2008

Antonio Pennacchi has asserted his right under the Copyright, Designs and Patents Act, 1988 to be identified as the author of this work.

ISBN: 978-1-905978-06-9

Cover design © Revolver Books 2008

A CIP Catalogue record for this book is available from the British Library

Text design and typesetting by Dexter Haven Associates Ltd, London
Printed and bound by CPI Group Ltd

www.revolverbooks.com

My Brother is an Only Child

chapter 1

At a certain point, I became fed up with life as a seminarian. I went to Father Cavalli and said to him, 'I don't want to become a priest; I want to return to the world.'

'The world?'

'I want to go and see what it's like.'

He didn't want to believe it. He tried everything: 'But you seemed to me to be so sure of your vocation. Let's take time to think it over, maybe this is just a crisis of faith and it will pass. We'll ask the Lord for His advice, let's wait.'

For me, that was it. I was fed up. And then he called my mother – or, to be precise, he called Signora Elide, the only person in town with a phone, who then informed my mother – suggesting that she wait too. But she – Mamma, not Signora Elide – was more adamant than me in her response: 'If he's really going to return, just let him come back, there's no point in stretching this out. Praised be Jesus Christ.'

And so I went home.

Brother Pippo travelled with me. We took a coach from Rome. It was red. I still remember today. The two of us sat at the back, on the last seats. While we waited for the coach to depart, the doors remained open and there was fresh air. Wind on my face. It was the beginning of May and the day was sunny. Brother Pippo fiddled with his rosary and the wide black sash of the Vincentian Order. In front, the driver was relaxing with his feet on the steering wheel, and he had the radio on full volume. Betty Curtis was singing full throttle. And I was going home. Happy and delighted.

But my family was neither happy nor delighted.

*   *   *

The house was already full to overflowing. And, for better or for worse, everyone had already carved out their own personal space; Otello and Manrico in one room, my father and my mother in the other with Violetta and Mimì. My father was an obsessive opera fan: my two oldest sisters were called Norma and Tosca. Every once in a while they would come home too – with their husbands and children – and then everyone would move: these outsiders in the boys' room and Otello and Manrico in the dining room, with mattresses on the floor. What was my father thinking to bring so many children into the world? Seven: four girls and three boys.

Mussolini and Our Lady had made him do it. Mussolini because he gave a prize for every child that was born and – even if after he died in 1945 they didn't give the prize out any more – my father had become addicted by then, and continued to beget children until 1953, when Mamma finally said, 'Enough.' And that was it. Every night was a drama. She would always take one of the children to bed with her – actually, always the littlest one, Mimì, the only one that she ever cuddled, whose real name was actually Turandot – and she would put her in the middle of the bed, right in the middle, so that my father wouldn't be able to get to my mother's side. And this situation continued for years, even after she reached menopause. Not that she continued to take Mimì to bed, but that she wouldn't let my father touch her: 'I'm disgusted by it now,' she said. 'I really can't understand those people who enjoy it.' However, it would seem that my father could.

The other reason was Our Lady. The Church was categorical: every attempt to malign the Madonna was a mortal sin; imagine if my father and my mother were willing to lose out on paradise. And that's how it was: every time they did it, it happened. That's why there were so many of us. Too many of us.

Thank heavens for Father Pio. My mother went to visit him shortly after the war, in 1944. Or rather, it was still wartime, but only in the North. It had already ended where we were. And as soon as it ended – in June 1944 – she went to see Father Pio right away. Down South in Puglia. A haphazard pilgrimage. Riding in the back of a lorry. Everyone seated on wooden benches. All one on top of another. Around forty people. All relatives. On those roads full of potholes from the bombings. Four hundred kilometres there, and four hundred back. Always bouncing on that wooden bench. And she was six months pregnant. With a big bump. Bouncing and bouncing along, as soon as she returned home – after receiving a blessing from Father Pio – she lost the baby. Father Pio gave us a miracle. Otherwise rather than seven we would have been eight.

Anyhow I returned home. I expected hugs and kisses. But instead she didn't even say hello. She was already completely pissed off. She sent Brother Pippo away after a few words. She pretended to ask him, 'Would you like to eat with us?' But he had already understood and said, 'No thank you, I'm not hungry. Praised be Jesus Christ.' He ruffled my hair and he was gone. I found myself there. With everyone staring at me: 'A fine beginning,' I thought.

She took me to the bedroom. She had added a cot: 'This is your bed.' Then she cleared one drawer for me – throwing its contents into another drawer – and said, 'Empty your suitcase here,' and with that she was gone. Manrico arrived – 'So you've ripped off my drawer, eh?' – and right away I understood that he would be my undoing.

He was Mamma's favourite, and I hadn't seen him in years. Our paths had never crossed. If one of us was around, the other one wasn't. When he was ten – and I was five – he had left for the seminary. He was the first one, he paved the way. If truth be told, my father had also tried with Otello, our oldest brother, but he wasn't having any of it. Papà had taken them both to San Tarcisio, a Salesian seminary, and he had shown them the football pitch, the basketball court, the ping-pong tables, and he even bought them a bag of sweets. That evening, at the end, he said, 'Do you like it here? Look how nice it is. Do you want to stay here?'

'Oh Papà,' said Otello, 'I don't like it at all. Take me back home right away.' But Manrico said, 'Yes, I want to be a priest,' and later he would drag me along too.

He went to the seminary. But not to San Tarcisio, the Salesian College in Rome. He went to Siena, to the Vincentians, because they were missionaries and he wanted to convert souls in Africa. He stayed there for five years. And my mother and father were thrilled. It wasn't just a way to pay for his studies. They really wanted a son who was a priest. It was the greatest blessing they could ask for: to give a son to the Lord. That's exactly what they would say. And when my father said it he was so happy and his eyes practically brimmed with tears. Instead when Mamma said it she would be sad and disconsolate. And we – I mean me and Violetta – when we would ask her, 'Mamma, who do you love the most?', each of us hoping to be chosen, you could be sure that she would reply, 'I love Manrico most because he is far away. And because I have given him to the Lord.' It was always about the Lord. What else could I do?

At least my father would always answer, 'If I cut off your finger, which would hurt more, the index finger or the middle finger?'

'What difference does it make? They're all the same.'

'That's right,' he would reply. 'With your children it's the same. You don't love one more or another less: they are all the same.' But neither Violetta nor I ever believed that he was telling the truth.

Then he would show off – my brother – when he would come home for vacation, once a year. Fifteen days. In summertime. He dressed in his cassock. And spoke with a sort of Sienese accent. And as soon as I opened my mouth he would say, 'Little fool.'

'Just you wait until I'm ordained too,' I would think.

My parents would go to visit him at Christmas and Easter, alternating my father one time, my mother the next. They would go to mass in the Termini Station chapel, the one that was under the tracks for the Lazio trains, and they would come back the next day. Once, at Christmas, they even took me along, because by then it had been decided that the next year I would go to the seminary too, so we did a trial run. But when we arrived in Siena, at the seminary – and he ran towards us – as soon as he got close he stopped and went white: 'Why did you bring Accio? I wanted Violetta.'

So the next year I left. I went to the Vincentians too. Because I was supposed to go to convert the infidels. I wanted to go to Africa, to the Congo, or maybe to Molokai. However, there were many applicants at that time, and Siena was full. So the classes for the middle school were moved to Zagarolo, close to Rome, in a property deep in the countryside. It was called Colle Palazzolo. So my father had two gifts for the Lord. One was in Siena, in his last year of secondary school, and the other one was in Zagarolo. And no one was happier than him. 'It's a sacrifice I gladly make,' he said to his friends in the San Marco Chorus. But it seemed to me that we were the ones making the sacrifice. Now it seems like this, naturally, but not then; then it seemed to me that there was no choice; I was going to be a saint, full stop.

The first night I felt homesick, in my bed. I was a little boy just ten years old, and I huddled under the blankets, covering my head well so as not to hear the boys who were crying in the other beds and made me want to cry too. One of them had been brought from the town in a rental car, because at that time there was no other transport, and when the car dropped off the luggage and left again and they closed the gates, he tried to run after it, he beat his fists against the gate, and cried and screamed while Father Cavalli held him. Poloni had been brought by his father, on a Lambretta scooter, from Ascoli Piceno. Two hundred and fifty kilometres. My father brought me too. By train. But my mother couldn't be bothered: 'Mimì is little, who will look after her?' Father Cavalli would. And I began to pray. Hail Marys at the top of my voice, and Our Fathers. 'Dear God, grant me the grace, give me a miracle: make me wake up tomorrow morning already twenty-four years old and just ordained.' Instead, the next morning, I would find myself back at the beginning: alone at the seminary. Actually, right at the very beginning. And I felt disappointed. Not so much because I was there, but because God hadn't granted me the miracle. The night before I would have sworn,

I was sure. In *The Mysterious Island*, when Pencroff opens the Bible at a random page and reads the words 'Ask and you shall receive/ Knock and the door will be opened,' the next day right away he would find the box with all the tools. 'Ask and you shall receive': for me it was God's truth, undeniable. And I knocked all night, even in my dreams. I would dream of my mother and I would say to her: 'You knock too, and knock loud.' But even with her stick it wasn't loud enough.

Anyhow, time passed. The first year, for better or for worse, I managed. Of course it was difficult to get used to. But all the others were in the same position as me. There were about fifty of us. As far as food was concerned, we ate well: first course, second course – at home we never ate this well – and sometimes there was even chocolate pudding made by the nuns with the milk brought by the farm worker. We learned to serve mass, all the prayers in Latin, the songs: 'O via vita veritas', 'O salutaris hostia' and all the others. Then etiquette lessons: how to eat with your mouth closed without making noise, and all these fine things. 'Because it's just not right,' said Father Tosi, 'for a missionary to go around with food stains on his cassock like a country parson.' Every day he would read to us – and then he explained it in detail – an excerpt from the *Galateo* by della Casa, a treatise on etiquette, in the afternoon during a break from our lessons. But he told us other stories too, especially stories about strange deaths. Like the story about a man from his town, when he was young, who had an apoplectic stroke – that's exactly what he said – right after a Fascist Saturday parade. He was at the tavern, in uniform, and suddenly he had a stroke: that's how they buried him, in his uniform. A few years later, I don't know why, they disinterred him; maybe they wanted to move him to another tomb. In any event, they opened the coffin and found him with his bayonet through his stomach. 'He must have woken up,' said Father Tosi, 'and he found himself there. He must have been desperate, he took his bayonet and he committed suicide. Now he's in hell.' Or else the story of the other man who was a sort of saint. He died young, but in odour of sanctity. They had begun the process of beatification and everything had gone well: witness statements, good works and even a few miracles. For the final approval all that was missing was just the examination of the body. So they disinterred him, but when they lifted the cover from his coffin they found him with his eyes open and his hands clawing at the cover of the casket, in a final attempt to push it away. Then they put a definitive end to the process of beatification and nothing more was said about it: 'Clearly he wasn't dead; he woke up and then died like that, in there. But in those moments who knows what he must have thought? Certainly he must have lost faith in God. So they didn't make him a saint after that.' These were the stories that Father Tosi told us. And others like that. He was obsessed, and he made us obsessed too.

In any event, the first year went like that. Father Cavalli taught us Latin. And it was love at first sight. For Latin, that is, not for Father Cavalli. He was the Father Superior, in charge of everything. He became a priest at age thirty-six. Before he was a lawyer. And he even had a girlfriend. At a certain point they decided together, he and his girlfriend: one became a priest and the other became a nun. And they still wrote each other letters. During the war he was a lieutenant, in Yugoslavia. After 8 September the Germans captured him and they put him in a concentration camp, at Wyala Pollawska in Poland. Some evenings, during recreation, we would ask him to tell us the entire story: about the hunger they suffered in the concentration camp, and the time when, before Christmas, they decided to put aside one potato a day and a knob of butter each, starting in November, to make a special Christmas dinner. And on Christmas Day they made a giant portion of mashed potatoes. A feast. But their stomachs weren't used to it any more. They were all sick, and the Germans beat them because the next day they couldn't go to work.

'Father, did you kill anyone in the war?' we asked him once.

'I hope not,' he replied, but he hesitated a moment; he wasn't as quick as usual. 'Once, in a trench, I had to shoot,' he added later, 'because on the other side there were partisans and I was commanding my men. I had to do it. But I pray God that I didn't hit anyone.'

'And your vocation?'

'I found my vocation in Yugoslavia, in a little church, in the mountains. I was demoralised. "Who knows if I'll return home," I said to myself. I saw the little church, not much more than a hut. I went inside. No one was there. I began to pray. I felt such peace that I said, "If I make it home, I'll become a priest."'

Then the troops still loyal to the Fascist cause arrived in Wyala Pollawska, gathered all the Italian prisoners and said, 'Whoever wants to go back to fight for Mussolini, beside the German allies, take one step forward.' And he did. They sent him to a training camp in Germany – Monterosa division, I believe – he put on his uniform again and was an officer once more. But before he left for Italy they made him take an oath. 'However,' said Father Cavalli, 'I had already made my oath to the King and, much as I liked him, I didn't feel that I should do it again for Mussolini.' So he didn't say a word, but lifted his arm. And when they returned to Italy – ready to fight – the first time that the train stopped in a tunnel during an air raid, he took off. And he slowly returned home. To Siena. And then he became a priest. And his girlfriend became a nun.

Probably I didn't look at him with much approval when he told this part. A few times actually, as if to ask for forgiveness, after he told me that every sacrosanct morning, when he said mass, every day he prayed for the salvation of the soul of Mussolini and the King. Every day. But he told me this much, much later. At first I didn't like him. He was choleric, severe. He was obsessed with loyalty: 'There's just one thing I can't stand' – but actually there were several – 'and that is lack of sincerity. Bread for bread and wine for wine, says Jesus Christ,' but it seemed to me that he made a difference. There was a fellow from Siena with us – his name was Panzini – and it was as clear as could be that he was the teacher's pet. They even spoke with the same accent. But he was a really good student, he wrote well and had an accommodating nature; I couldn't dislike him. However, it bugged me that he was a good student, better than me.

One day, in class, Father Cavalli must have admonished me for something that I can't even remember. But he must have gone on for more than a few minutes, in a quiet voice, not very angry; who knows what he said to me. At a certain point he went crazy, all purple and standing on his podium: 'Don't look at me like that!' He shouted like a madman. Everyone was terrified.

'Like how?' I asked him.

'Like that! Stop looking at me like that! Lower your eyes,' he shrieked even louder. And I lowered them. To make him happy. But I swear I hadn't understood at all.

'You were looking at me with hatred in your eyes,' he told me later, when he called me for a private chat.

'But didn't you say that you wanted loyalty?' I replied.

And ever since then I liked him. Even if others began to say that I was the teacher's pet. But I didn't believe it, I just believed that he did things right. Once he became angry because someone had thrown some nut shells under the desk: we had old-fashioned wooden desks, with shingles underneath, to use as foot rests. 'You'll be in trouble if you continue to throw nut shells under the desk. And whoever does the cleaning and finds them must absolutely inform me,' because we would do the cleaning ourselves, according to a rota, for the entire school. Every month they changed the rota: you have the toilets, you have the chapel, you have the classrooms, and so on. One day, after the lessons and before going to refectory, as we were getting up, the boy who sat next to me dropped his pen cap – it was a blue one, from an early Bic. I advised him, 'Pick it up, otherwise he'll go wild.'

'But he said nut shells, not pen caps,' but I knew that he meant pen caps too. He went berserk again. He punished both of us, even if he knew that it couldn't have been me with my Germanic adherence to every rule. 'Who sits here?' was all he asked, not whose pen cap is this. During recreation in the afternoon – while the others were playing in the courtyard – he kept us in the corridor facing the wall. 'I told you so,' I kept repeating to Poloni. And he kept insisting, 'But he said nut shells.' And they couldn't stand each other for the twenty years that Poloni remained in the order. Even now, forty years later, when I speak with him, he still complains, 'That Father Cavalli.'

They say that I was troublesome and always had a point to make. Father Tosi called me Cicero, not just because I excelled in Latin but because, in his opinion, I thought like a lawyer. And the others called me Cicero too. Father Tosi said that when the emissaries of Mark Anthony finally took him near to Formia while he was trying to slip away, and they cut of his head, before he died Cicero allegedly said, 'Causa causarum miserere mei.' According to Father Tosi, this must have saved his soul. Anyhow, so as not to go wrong, I would pray for Cicero's soul too, as well as for Mussolini's. But not for the King. Father Cavalli already prayed plenty for the King.

When Maltoni arrived – it was a few months after the year had begun – Father Tosi made him sit next to me: 'He arrived late and we can't start all over again. You explain the beginning to him.' He was small, short, very dark, with curly hair and he was from Predappio, Mussolini's home town. I adopted him because they were relatives, his mother's name was Rosa Maltoni, and I helped him with all the lessons. He was afraid of having to repeat the year, but instead at the end of the year he passed, and his best subject was Latin. But they kept us together just long enough to cover the lessons he had missed, then they moved him to sit somewhere else. This was another standard rule: every month they changed the seating plan. In the refectory it was the same: every month we would move and change seats – Father Cavalli was in charge of making the arrangements – so that, maybe, they would move you from sitting next to someone you liked and they would put you next to someone you couldn't stand. It took me years to understand why.

Once Father Cavalli told my father that he would prefer to close all the seminaries for such young boys; he was only our principal because he had been ordered to do so: 'If someone wants to be a priest he should come when he is older, not at this age. At this age they should be with their mothers.'

'But I'm happy here. I want to be a priest,' I piped up.

And my father looked at me, and then looked back at Father Cavalli, as if to say, 'Do you see? What else do you want?' Father just patted my head and said, 'Yes, alright,' but the expression on his face read clearly, 'Poor stupid fools.'

Anyhow, the first year went by: in July they sent us home for a month. 'Now you will return to the world,' Father Tosi told us, 'but be careful,' because for him the world was somewhere one should be very careful. And we agreed. The world I found, however, at least on this occasion, was not very appealing. Not at all. I could hardly wait to return to the seminary. As soon as I arrived home I hardly recognised anything: all the fields and the ditch in front of the house, where we used to play, were fenced off with corrugated iron, and they were building everywhere. On the other side of the road they were building the new hospital. I seemed like an outsider. And I didn't stay long at home; just long enough for them to ask, 'How are you? Are you OK?' and then a week in Borgo Montenero, looking after Aunt Agnese's sheep and saying the rosary – kneeling on the ground – more often than we did in the seminary. There was no electricity there either, just gas lights and flypaper attached to the ceiling of the kitchen, which was black with the bodies of dead flies. Then another week in Borgo Carso, with Uncle Menego, and at least there I had fun because he would take me out to gather straw and he taught me lots of Fascist Party songs. I only spent two weeks in my own home, but as soon as they saw me around they would say to me, 'Why don't you go to San Marco?' and I would go to San Marco twenty times a day. I was always serving at mass. That was my job. So, before I left, my mother asked me, 'Are you sure you want to go back? Are you really happy there?' 'I can't believe this,' I must have thought, and my father took me back all happy.

But this last time was painful. Not at the beginning: very slowly, gradually; but every time it was worse. Not the environment, at all: as time went on the environment came to suit me, to fit me like a glove. I was the one who was changing. The environment was ideal. Everyone loved me. Just when they chose teams for football I would be the last to be chosen. When they divided us into teams, the captains – the best players – would choose all the others first, one by one, and I would always be the last one left: no one wanted me, not even gift-wrapped. In actual fact, Panzini, the boy from Siena, was also one of the last to be chosen, and in the end they had to take us simply because Father Tosi told them to. But they really didn't want us. More often than not, Panzini didn't even want to play, he didn't like it. So I would be the odd one out, but I insisted on playing – sometimes in my daydreams I would imagine becoming better than the rest of them and surpassing them all, but I was never actually able to – and in the end they would toss a coin to see who would have to take me, and whoever was saddled with me would complain and want to do it again: 'It's not fair.' They always made me play fullback: 'Don't move from there,' they would order me, 'and if someone arrives with a ball, tackle him.' Father Tosi was the referee, and once when Donati made a bad challenge in midfield – I swear it was midfield – he called a penalty.

'But you can't do that, Father,' screamed Donati.

'What do you mean I can't do that?' Father Tosi replied. 'I just did.'

'But you can't,' he insisted. 'You can send me off but you can't give a penalty.'

'Penalty!' continued Father Tosi. 'And then I'll send you off as well.' And Donati began to cry. Crouched down behind the goal net, with his head between his legs. And he wasn't crying about being sent off, he was crying about the rules: 'He can't give that penalty,' he continued to say in between sobs. Who could have imagined that twenty years later Juventus would win the Champion's Cup in Heysel, with Boniek, for a penalty in midfield? Donati is probably still crying now.

From about fifty students the year before, we were now just twenty-five or thirty: 'Now this is a good group,' said Father Cavalli. 'I'm sure that we'll have a few priests.' They had creamed off the best. As a matter of fact, every once in a while someone would disappear. No one knew anything about it. At a certain point they would assemble us all in a classroom and inform us, 'So and so is leaving. Say goodbye,' and he would appear in the doorway, holding his suitcase, with his father waiting for him in the corridor; goodbye, all the best. No one would know why, even if, more often than not, some kind of insubordination would be suspected. As a matter of fact, the congregation of Saint Vincent de Paul is famous for its three vows: poverty, chastity and obedience. Obedience is fundamental. 'Who knows how you weren't kicked out that time you looked at him?' they would ask me. And I would often ask myself the same question. Another time they threw out two boys on the same day. But they were from the year above us, and we had almost no contact with them. Someone said that Father Tosi had found them together in the same bed.

'Well, what's wrong with that?' I asked.

'Are you joking? It's sinful, you mustn't.'

'Sinful? Maybe one of them had a bad dream.'

My schoolwork went well. Before Christmas I had already read my schoolbooks twice through and I had done almost all of the Latin translations. I could translate from Italian to Latin better than Cicero, and I spoke Latin almost as fluently. Mathematics was the only subject in which I didn't excel, but no one there really cared much about your grades in maths. We studied *The Iliad* in the translation by Vincenzo Monti – 'Cantami, O Diva, del Pelide Achille' – verse by verse, and we committed much of it to memory. The entire class was divided and would take sides: the majority was with Hector and the minority with Achilles; we would even have discussions during recreation. Worse than our football arguments. Panzini and someone else took the side of Ulysses. I was the only one to take Diomede's side. I've never liked to say what the others say.

I prayed whenever I could. The prayers they made us say weren't enough, between morning mass, the prayers at the beginning of lessons, a visit to the chapel before lunch, another little prayer in the refectory, the afternoon rosary, the blessing in the chapel in the evening with the Tantum Ergo, prayers before supper, supper accompanied by a reading from the *Lives of the Saints* and other edifying texts, another visit to the chapel before going up to our dormitory, and a final prayer before turning out the light. That wasn't enough. I would pray on my own. At night. And during the Cuban Missile Crisis I couldn't pray enough. One afternoon Father Cavalli rang the bell and made us interrupt recreation. He brought us together in the auditorium; his face was very dark. 'They must have found some boys sharing a bed again,' said Maltoni. Instead he asked us to pray with all our hearts for Kennedy and for peace: 'Perhaps the Lord will listen to your voices.' He said that the Russians had placed missiles in Cuba and the Third World War was about to break out: 'I've already seen one world war and I know what it means.'

I began to pray even more than before. I would wake up in the middle of the night and go down to the chapel, all alone and shivering. I was afraid that someone might see me, but then again I hoped someone would, because that way everyone would have known how saintly I was. I prayed in front of the statue of Our Lady and offered my life for the conversion of Khrushchev.

Then one day Father Cavalli called an assembly out of the blue and made us watch television when the children's programmes were already long over. Normally, that's all he would let us watch, but that time he showed us the nightly news: the crisis in Cuba was resolved, Khrushchev had thought it over. 'But did he convert?' I asked him.

'Well, no: now you are hoping for too much. But the Lord has heard your prayers.'

'If He heard that prayer, He might just have heard all the rest,' I thought, and I became fixated. Every night, when the others had fallen asleep, I would wake up from my bed in the dark and go downstairs to the chapel: 'Take my life, but convert Khrushchev.' In the end I was dying, but only of sleep deprivation. But when I went back upstairs I wouldn't go to bed: I started washing and cleaning all the toilets scrupulously. One more sacrifice, a mortification of my own self for the souls of all the Russians: 'But how can they be Communists? Don't they understand?'

'It's the Evil One,' said Father Tosi.

In the meantime, Manrico returned home. It didn't really bother me much. Father Cavalli called me and said, 'Your brother has had a crisis of faith. For now he has returned home; we shall see.'

'What's a crisis of faith?'

'Doubts. Regrets.'

'Alright,' but I still hadn't understood. Anyhow it was the same to me. If anyone asked me about my brother, I would say, 'He's had a crisis of faith, he could snap out of it,' but I would say it lightly because I was a bit ashamed. I was ashamed in front of the others, naturally, but as far as I was concerned it couldn't have been better. Not a word was said at home. No one mentioned anything. Two months later, when Papà came to visit me, I said, 'I'm so sorry that Manrico has been sent home. Don't worry,' I stopped him even before he could draw a breath, 'I will become a priest.'

'Well done. What a consolation you are to me.' But the consolation was almost all his own.

He would often come to visit me. Even once a month. Sometimes twice. On Sundays. One month he couldn't make it because he was singing with his choir. So Uncle Carlin and his wife came and spent the entire day telling me how delighted they were that I was becoming a saint: 'Always obey your superiors and remain on your best behaviour.' Mamma could come a few times a year, not more: 'She has so much to do, poor thing,' said my father, but the truth is that he really enjoyed visiting. He would chat for hours with Father Cavalli, they would eat together in the refectory, and then all Sunday afternoon we would walk together in the vineyards which belonged to the order. Every once in a while he would stop to prune, and the farm worker would say to him, 'Thank heavens you come to give us a hand.' I couldn't wait for him to leave, so that I could go back to play with my classmates. But he just wouldn't leave, and kept telling me how happy he was to have given this son to the Lord, and he would take endless photographs of me: 'It's so peaceful here,' he kept on saying. Then he would leave in the evening by train – 'Be honourable' was his goodbye –

and he threw himself back into his own life: the Agrarian Consortium workshop, evening practice at the San Marco choir, and arguments with my mother. He would come to Zagarolo to restore his spirit. Him, of all people.

One afternoon during prep in the big room, Bertini passed close by to me. He was a small boy with glasses, a few years older than me, who was repeating the year. He dropped a note on my desk: 'I love you as a brother. Do you want to be my special friend?'

To tell the truth, I had always treated him much as I treated the others; as a matter of fact, I really hardly noticed him, but I did enjoy receiving the note: 'Someone likes me.' And I said to him, 'Yes, let's become friends.' But he wanted me always to play with him and he would be annoyed if I played with someone else. On Sunday afternoon, while we were watching *Francis the Talking Mule* – there was a big screen in the big room, and every Sunday a lay brother from Rome would come to show us a film – he came very close to me and gave me kisses on my face in the dark.

'Kiss me,' he said. And I gave him a few kisses. On the temples or on the cheeks. I remember that I lost the sidepiece of my glasses. However, I felt embarrassed, uncomfortable. I don't know why, but I wasn't that convinced. Then he said to me, 'Let's meet tonight in the toilets.'

'What for? I go to the toilet in the afternoon.'

'What do you think I meant? You can see the lights from the valley from those windows; they are very beautiful and it must be even more beautiful to look at them together.'

'Alright,' and I went. But then he wanted to move from the window of his stall to the window of mine: 'But what on earth for? You can see the lights just as well from there. And you might fall.'

'You are really stupid,' he said. 'Let me come close to you.'

'No,' and I was out of the bathroom. He came out too, and was all angry. I said to him, 'But what's your problem?'

And he said, 'Just go away!' and then he wouldn't play with me any more and our friendship was never the same. But I didn't care much. Anyhow, he was becoming too possessive. And the next day I had already forgotten about it. But then I sent a note to another boy, a cute fellow with dark hair: 'I love you like a brother. Do you want to be my special friend?' Who knows how ancient this tradition was. A literary tradition. But the cute fellow didn't even reply. Maybe he sent the note on to someone else.

Anyhow, I continued to pray and pray, but something was happening to my body just below my tummy. Suddenly I was growing hair. Long, curly hair. I was horrified. For a while I tried to pretend nothing was happening, then I couldn't stand it any longer, and one night as soon as the lights went out in the dormitory I got up and went to knock on Father Cavalli's door: 'It's terrible, I think I have a disease,' and I started to cry.

'What's happened to you?' he was worried. 'Tell me everything right away.'

I couldn't talk, but then finally I blurted out, 'I'm hairy.'

'Now, that's not so serious.'

'But Father, long hair on my crotch.'

'It's normal. Everyone has that.'

'It can't be normal, Father, it's not like the hair on my legs. This hair is longer.'

'But even I have them.' He was getting angry. 'You have to believe me.' I refused to believe him, and finally he took off his cassock, then his jumper, then his shirt, and he lifted up his vest until I could see his underarms: 'Do you see here? Don't you see that I have them too?' and he lifted his arm so I could see them well.

'But Father, I'm not talking about underarm hair.'

'I realise that. But I can hardly show you down there, can I? Believe me, good heavens, it's normal, everyone has them,' and he smiled at me. He made me kneel down, and made the sign of the cross on my head: 'Benedictio Domini Nostri Jesus Christi descendat super te et maneat semper.' We said a few more prayers, and he sent me to bed: 'You're growing up, don't worry: God's plan for the universe lies behind everything.'

I was quite relieved when I left that time, but I still wasn't absolutely tranquil. And I wasn't convinced at all: 'Who knows if he really has long hair like mine, down there.'

He wasn't my confessor; for that I had a spiritual director. He was an elderly missionary, from Piacenza, who had spent about ten years in Madagascar. He was always around in his little Fiat Belvedere, and no one really knew what he did. He was also the Father economist, the one who looked after the accounts, but the only relationship he had with us was simply for confession. I didn't get on with him particularly well. He was quite cold – or at least that's how it seemed – and that didn't inspire any confidence. He was standoffish. He made me feel uncomfortable. So I asked Father Cavalli if he would hear my confession, but he said, 'No. I'm too close to you, it's better for someone else to be your confessor.' And so I continued with the spiritual director. He was fixated with chastity. And purity. It was an obsession. I was always afraid of falling into sin. When we went to bed at night or when we woke up in the morning, no one would undress in front of the others: first you would get under the covers with your trousers on, and you would take them off there, under the sheets, and you would put your pyjama bottoms on under the sheets. And vice versa. And after I grew those damned hairs it was even worse. I was even afraid to look at myself, because every once in a while something strange would happen a little further down. So I didn't want to shower any more, because I didn't want to look, and I always tried to avoid showering. But Father Tosi was like a rottweiler: he would come to get you wherever you were when it was your turn. And he would stay there outside to guard you: 'Close the door with the key,' he would remind you every time. 'Ready?' he would ask a few minutes later, and as soon as everyone replied, 'Yes,' he would turn the water on. You had to wash, there was no way out. Once I stayed there, pressed up against the door, without getting undressed and without going under the water. I got undressed quickly when he turned the water off. But he noticed: he saw that my hair wasn't wet, and he made me do it again. This time I obeyed, but I kept my pants on. And that's what I continued to do afterwards: I would never take my pants off, and I washed myself everywhere else but there, so that I wouldn't have to look at myself. Then one day, in confession, the spiritual director asked me, 'Do you commit impure acts?'

'Well, I don't think so.'

'What! You don't think so? Do you commit them or don't you?'

I really didn't know what these impure acts were, but I felt that he was a little angry and not so convinced. So I tried to guess what I should say: 'Yes, sometimes,' and right away I could see that he was satisfied with my response.

But he insisted: 'Alone or with others?'

Now I really didn't know what to say. I thought it over for a minute and admitted, 'With others.'

He jumped out of his chair as if he had received an electric shock: 'What? With others!' he shouted. 'Explain everything to me right away.'

And I explained it to him: 'Well, at night, when I get undressed, sometimes I bend over and my bum sticks out. And also in the classroom, if my pen falls to the ground, I bend over to pick it up. And others see me.'

'And these are your impure acts?'

'Well, I think so.'

He was quiet for a moment: 'Are you sure that you don't touch yourself there?' he asked me very slowly.

And this time I was the one who became angry: 'But how can you ask such a thing? Absolutely not!'

Then he hugged me: 'Carry on like that,' and he didn't even give me any penitence. Actually, from that moment forward, as soon as he saw me from far away in the middle of the schoolyard or in the halls, he would call me and he would give me a sweet, and once – when I was cleaning the main hall and he passed by with Father Cavalli – he chucked me under the chin and told him, 'This boy will be our consolation. He will be a great missionary.'

'Eh, I know,' Cavalli replied. But from that moment – ever since that confession – I began to touch myself right where he suggested.

And after that I couldn't stop. It was driving me mad. Like that story of the cute boy with dark hair. In the beginning I had sent him that note like that, because Bertini did it. If he had replied I wouldn't have even known what to say to him. But he didn't reply, and after a few days I gathered my courage and asked him, 'Did you read the note?'

'Yes.'

'Well?'

'Well what?' and he went off to play on his own. And he continued like that, day after day, as if I didn't even exist. In class, maybe, when we were translating Latin he might ask me, 'What does this mean?' but during recreation he would always play with whoever he felt like playing with. And I wasn't even confident enough to say a single word to him. I just couldn't wait for another classroom translation so that we could talk again. He had entered my head. I was in love with him. Or rather: this is a rationalisation that I made later. Back then I could hardly know that I was in love. I just felt that way and that's all. I mean that I always thought about him, not that I thought I was in love. As a matter of fact, I thought that I was ill: 'I must be having a breakdown; it must be a crisis of faith.' But I continued to think about him night and day, and every day more than the day before: 'Why doesn't he play with me?' It had become an obsession. In the end I couldn't handle it any more, and one day, after everyone else had fallen asleep, I went back to Father Cavalli. 'What is it this time?' he asked me, half dazed. He had just fallen asleep, and had thrown on a shabby old robe to come to open the door.

'I'm having a crisis of faith.'

'For heaven's sake, can't you wait for your spiritual director?'

'I'm having a crisis of faith,' I insisted, 'and I want to make my confession: "Estote parati," says the Lord.'

'For heaven's sake,' he said again, and then, 'Wait a moment.' He closed the door again, put on his cassock, then opened it again and let me enter: 'But let's try to hurry, I'm tired.'

As soon as I began to tell him about the situation – I was kneeling on the prie-dieu and he was sitting on his chair with this stole around his neck and one elbow on my prie-dieu, to hold up his sleepy head – he woke up suddenly. It was as if he'd been bitten by a tarantula: 'Explain yourself. Tell me everything. What are you thinking? Thought by thought.'

'I think that I want to play with him. And maybe sit next to him when we're eating or in class. That's all.'

'There's nothing wrong in that. However, try to play with everyone and to treat him exactly like you treat everyone else. Besides that, don't worry: it's not sinful. However, tell me what on earth made you write that note to him.'

I had never really reflected on this, both because we were in confession and because I hadn't seen anything bad, and I told him about Bertini. He went crazy. Purple. The veins on his throat were bulging. He began to pace the room: 'Sweet Jesus, sweet Jesus,' he kept saying when I told him about the stars and the toilet. And then he began to implore me, 'Please, free me from the secret of the confessional,' which is that thing priests have which means that they absolutely cannot reveal or make use of whatever they learn in confession without committing the greatest sacrilege and losing out on paradise. It seems that God does not pardon this: they must defend the secret even if it means losing their own life. What did it matter to me? I freed him. 'Are you sure?' he asked. 'Are you sure that you free me from the secret of the confessional?'

'I'm sure, Father, I'm sure.'

'What a joy you give me,' and then he gave me absolution: 'Ego te absolvo a peccatis tuis…' 'How will I sleep tonight, though?' I heard him say to himself as he shut the door.

A few days later – I don't remember exactly how long – while we were in the classroom, Brother Pippo knocked on the door: 'Bertini, your father has come to see you,' and he left the room all happy. After around an hour he came back dressed in his best clothes, together with Father Cavalli, who told us, 'Say goodbye to Bertini, who has decided to go home. He had been thinking about this for some time, but we wanted to wait and not say anything.' Bertini was smiling and he seemed happy. We prayed, then said goodbye and all the best. When the bell rang for recreation, we went outside into the courtyard. He hadn't left yet, he was close to the stairs, with his suitcase at his feet. His father was still inside talking. We all went up to him and he smiled: 'I've lost my vocation.'

I smiled too, and as soon as the others went away to play I smiled again: 'You could have told me.'

He was furious: 'The little saint!' He was livid with rage. 'You kissed me too, at the cinema.'

'What are you saying? What does that have to do with anything?'

'Tell Father Cavalli what that has to do with anything.'

'You mean you didn't lose your vocation?'

'But what vocation? He's the one who kicked me out, because of what you told him.'

I have never felt so ashamed. And I continued to beat myself up over it until the evening, when I went back to Father Cavalli's room: 'Why did you do it? You sent him away because of me – you shouldn't have.'

'But you freed me from the secret of the confessional. Don't you remember? I asked you about it twice.'

'Yes of course I remember. But you didn't tell me that then you would kick him out: I was talking about myself, not telling tales about him.'

'But you freed me,' and he was again pacing the room, furious. 'Just one bad apple!'

But I was even more furious than he was, and it had no effect on me at all, I was immovable. And he insisted: 'Just one bad apple and they all go bad. I have to defend all of you, and in that way I even defended him, good heavens: it's better for him to be a good family man than a bad priest,' and he tried every way to convince me.

'Perhaps,' I said to him, 'but you made me seem like I was telling tales,' and I left. He seemed sorry, but nonetheless he'd thrown Bertini out: 'It will pass,' he thought about me. But he didn't know that I kept thinking about it, and I still do today. Actually, if I reflect on things, that must have been the first little stone of the avalanche. The second one came from Manrico and Violetta.

They arrived one Sunday afternoon to visit me. I was expecting Mamma: she had written to say that she was coming. 'She wasn't able to, Mimì was running a temperature,' and they came instead. I was happy to see Violetta because she was my blood sister, I mean that when we were little we cut ourselves with a piece of glass and mixed our blood, like the Indians used to do. But Manrico was so tall, wearing new clothes, and he was showing off. The last time I saw him – a long time ago – he was still wearing his cassock. 'How's it going with your crisis of faith?' I asked him.

'What crisis of faith?'

'The crisis of faith over your vocation. Think it over. You're always in my prayers.'

'Well then, stop it, smart-ass, because I don't want to be a priest. It was my decision to leave.' But several years later I actually learned that they had kicked him out. For insubordination, he said, because he didn't get along with the new director: he was disobedient and argumentative, and always sulking. But I think it was a story like what happened to Bertini. Who knows how many notes he sent and received; he was such a handsome boy.

Anyhow, they had a go at me. Both of them. That little cretin Violetta was still in middle school, but she was just as full of herself as he was, and she already acted like an intellectual: reading books, she knew it all. 'Come home,' he would say, 'what are you staying here for? Nothing they tell you is true; it's all a load of crap.'

'What are you saying? God. The good news.'

But they kept at it all afternoon: 'Total crap. The only thing that exists is atomic matter,' they said. 'God doesn't really exist. It's an invention of the rich to subjugate the poor.'

'And the Bible?'

'What Bible?!'

'Who created us, then? Who made Adam from a handful of dust?'

'Cut it out: man is descended from the apes. Come home with us,' they both said when it was time to leave, as we stood at the gate. And they really laughed. Violetta insisted, 'It's been demonstrated scientifically: we are descendants of the apes, forget about Adam and Eve.'

'Go back, Satan!' I screamed at her, and I made the sign of the cross. 'Go away. Go away immediately. I never want to see you again.' I turned and left them there by the gate.

Now they weren't laughing any more, and they came after me: 'But come on, say goodbye to us. Don't be like that.'

'You are like weeds. Satan. Go back!' until Father Cavalli arrived. 'Send them away,' I ordered him. But he sent me away and went over to speak with them. Then he called me back: 'Reconcile with your brother and sister, who love you and who were only joking,' he instructed me. I obeyed, and walked with them as far as the gate, but I was seething. Then I ran back to him: 'They told me that man is a descendant of the apes, that it's not true that we were created by God,' and I expected that he would scream, 'Anathema!' and make the sign of the cross just like I had, and then maybe we would take the thurible and the holy water to go and purify the road where they had walked.

But he was very calm and said to me, 'Well, it actually would seem to be proved that man is descended from the apes. But someone must have created the apes, right?'

'Father Cavalli!' I reproached him. 'But the Bible? Adam and Eve?'

'The Bible has to be interpreted. And things aren't always as they seem. But you will understand later on, there's time, take it easy. You don't always need to understand everything right away.'

But this was precisely the point: I always wanted to understand. And right away. Not later. When, how much later? I have never had time to waste, when I wanted to understand. And you can't come to me and say, from one day to another, 'Look, these are fairy tales; you have to try to understand what they mean.' You should have told me sooner, told me right away, not at the end. I felt taken for a ride: 'Apes, Adam and Eve.' And what else? Just because he wasn't able to do it, then maybe I wouldn't be able to become a priest either. But it wasn't so much the substance of what those two had told me that was upsetting: it was the fact that Father Cavalli hadn't denied it.

Anyhow, even this – annoying as it was – might just have been a little stone and that's all; in itself it wouldn't have been an avalanche, and now I would easily be a priest, maybe even a bishop. But after these little stones there were some boulders, and after that there was no going back. After the advice from my spiritual director I couldn't stop touching myself. When I would go to confession, he would ask me, as a matter of fact, 'Impure acts?' but you could already see from the expression on his face that he knew what my response would be. 'No,' I would say innocently. And he was satisfied.

It's not that I had learned to tell lies – are you kidding? Remember loyalty! – it's just that I hadn't really understood what these impure acts were. I just touched myself, as if it were normal: suddenly I was getting hairy, and right after that this thing just grew. What did I know? They were the ones who had told me that it was normal. Hair down there. I wasn't at all convinced, but I felt that I had to obey. And so I did, thinking that the other thing down there was also part of the 'hair phenomenon'. Was I supposed to go and ask about it again? To make myself look like an idiot again? I just quietly touched myself. But I did worry a bit – 'Is it normal or isn't it?' – even if there was nothing intentional about it, it was a physical fact, existential, like breathing: I always had this big thing in my pants that bothered me. At most it would be OK for half an hour, then it would start to bother me again. What was I supposed to do? I had to touch myself. In the beginning three or four times, then seven, eight, nine and even ten times a day. I touched myself everywhere – I mean, in any place I could find. Once it even happened to me in the chapel, during morning mass: I had to jump up from my kneeler and run to the bathroom. Obviously there were no women around – well, there were two nuns who mended our clothes and cooked for us, but they were very elderly and all wrapped up in those old-fashioned habits with big white hats. I am absolutely certain that no one could ever have committed impure acts thinking about them. In the beginning, if truth be told, I didn't think that women even existed, except for Violetta and my mother. I'd never seen any. It was just a mechanical need that

I felt to touch myself. Although once I became aroused by the statue of Our Lady – in actual fact, the only woman around, even if she was made from plaster – with all her blue robes but that one naked foot that could be seen peeking out from her robes to crush the head of the serpent. That was a provocative little foot.

Then, I don't know how, in the pages of an encyclopaedia I found a photograph of Canova's statue of Pauline Bonaparte. It seemed like she was alive. I fell in love. Crazy in love. I would think of her night and day. Always. Every time I touched myself. I didn't think of her as being alive, or a real person in flesh and blood: I really thought of that statue, in marble, by Canova. And then in actual fact – life is strange – ever since I've always liked women like that, with a prominent tummy and a belly-button that goes deep into their stomach like buttons on an upholstered sofa. I've never liked women with flat abs. I've always been looking for another Pauline Bonaparte, my first true love. Of the female variety. After thinking of her, actually, and once I was placated, I would turn again to think about the cute boy with dark hair. I tried to be friendly to him in every way, but he wasn't interested. I would anxiously await the regular change in seating arrangements in refectory: 'Maybe this time he'll sit near me.' But no such luck, Father Cavalli would always seat him far away. So one night I went back: 'I can't stop thinking about him.'

'I'm sick and tired of you. Now we're going to get to the bottom of this: tell me everything you think.' And I told him again: to play, to talk and to be close to him. 'But are you absolutely sure you don't want to do other things?'

'What other things?'

'Impure things.'

'Absolutely not, Father.'

'Then that's it, don't come back to bother me with these things: there's nothing wrong, ego te absolvo, now go away.'

In actual fact I had never thought that one could do other things. Or that there were other things to be done. It never ever occurred to me. But, as with my spiritual director, after he told me, I actually began to think about it. Now I would think impure thoughts about Pauline with the cute fellow. Or vice versa. Him nude too. On that sofa.

Could I go on like this, dreaming of a statue, and still present myself for ordination? In the end I got fed up. I began to feel – how can I say? – grubby. I began to suspect that this was not very compatible with the status of a missionary: 'How can I go to Congo, among the pagans, with this hard thing under my cassock?' It's not that I lost my faith, or that I didn't want to be a priest any more, to convert Communists. Nothing about that had changed. And I continued to enjoy the liturgy more and more. I could spend hours serving mass, reciting rosaries with the others, and singing Gregorian chant. I went mad for the smell of incense. I would swing the thurible as if I were in a medieval tournament. But that hard thing was there, too. Hormonal swings, they call it now.

At that time – it must have been spring – Father Tosi began to preach to us every day against 'the world'. Who knows, maybe he had some kind of issues of his own. Every day he had a story: 'The dangers of the world! The temptations of the demons! Lascivious women.' In the end I thought, 'What do you know? Maybe this world is full of real living Pauline Bonapartes: I want to see them, maybe these lascivious women are beautiful.' And I went to Father Cavalli: 'I don't want to be a priest any more. I want to go back to the world.'

He was distressed. He wanted to keep me at any price. He thought I would make it, he said. But I was really fed up, and there was nothing to be done. He had to wait a few days to reach an agreement with my mother, and he said, 'Don't say anything to the others, so as not to upset them before you have to. And of course one never knows,' and every day that passed he was ever more hopeful that I would change my mind. But it didn't happen. In the end, seeing as my family had said that someone would be coming to pick me up, but no one ever came, two days later it was decided that Brother Pippo would take me back: 'But don't say anything – even tomorrow.'

The next day I calmly sat through my lessons, and in the afternoon, at prep, I did all my homework and translations, as if nothing had changed. As a matter of fact, I enjoyed myself like I always had. At a certain point a section of my translation was difficult to interpret – whether it would work better with a literal translation or with a more sophisticated variation. So I went to Father Tosi, who was sitting at his desk, and I asked him. He looked at me strangely: 'Are you joking?'

'No,' and I thought that he was referring to the translation.

He replied, 'Do as you see fit, both are fine,' and as I returned to my place he almost seemed to lose his temper. He clapped his hands and said to everyone, 'Let this boy be an example to you all! I can't tell you why right now, but let him be an example to you all.'

'He's nuts,' I thought to myself.

'What did you do?' Maltoni asked me in a whisper.

'I don't know.'

The next day I left. I woke up and went to mass together with the others, and we had breakfast in the refectory. Then, when they went to the classroom, Brother Pippo helped me to pack my suitcase, and we went downstairs. Father Cavalli was waiting for me downstairs and he was sad: 'I am pained,' he had told me the night before, 'but better a good family man than a bad priest,' just as he had said for Bertini. I guess he said it to everyone. He went with me to the class-room and said, 'Say goodbye to Benassi, who's going home,' and he asked them to pray for me.

Father Tosi revealed, 'This is what I wanted to tell you last night: he knew that he would be leaving today, but just the same he did all his homework as if he were coming to class. Take him as your example: do your duty to the end.' I never had the courage to tell him that I only did it because I found it fun. I like translations. It was a passion for me, just like Pauline Bonaparte. And the cute boy.

'Benedictio Domini Nostri Jesus Christi descendat super te et maneat semper,' Father Cavalli said to me as I walked out the door. I began to cry. And so did he. I made the sign of the cross and I left. The world was waiting for me. Or so I thought.

chapter 2

For the first few days I would still wake up early and go to mass at San Marco – together with Mamma and Papà – to the serious disappointment of my brothers and sisters. Not because they were atheists, but because I would wake them up when I went out early: 'Can't you get up without making so much noise?' snarled Otello. 'This pain in the ass is the last thing we need,' said my other brother. But, lucky for them, after a while I soon got fed up and began to go just on Sundays. But every afternoon I would still go to the Salesian parish youth group. My father insisted, and he already seemed to have lost his enthusiasm for living since I came back home: 'At least the youth group.'

It was the beginning of May. Mamma went to enrol me – and even on this point there was no discussion allowed – in the qualifying exams for middle school: 'If I'd listened to that Father Cavalli, I wouldn't have been in time to register you for these exams, you would have lost both years and you would have had to start from the beginning,' and she made me study furiously. I didn't know how to tell her: 'Everything else is fine, I just have a few problems in maths: I don't know how to do the square roots.'

'Go to Uncle Piero,' she said, because he was a surveyor. And so I went.

Uncle Piero was fantastic. He was a real Fascist and he loved me. He was Mamma's youngest brother – there were fourteen of them – the only one in the family to finish secondary school, with the exception of Aunt Pina, who was even younger than him, a primary school teacher. He enlisted as a volunteer at age eighteen. With the Militia.

He hadn't even finished his studies. But for us it was an obligation: what could you do? – with the famine everyone was suffering in the Veneto region – how could you not enlist as a volunteer after Mussolini had given the family land? There's not a single family that didn't send someone. And so it was with Uncle Piero. He was wounded then taken prisoner in Tobruk by the English in 1942, and they put him in a concentration camp in India. They treated them like animals, he would tell us: 'Worse than the Germans,' he used to say. After the Armistice on 8 September they said to them, 'Italian bastards, now we're allies: if you want to collaborate, step forward and we'll send you home, to fight the Germans.' My uncle wouldn't budge. They classified him as a 'criminal Fascist'. And his tortures were worse than before. He returned home in 1946. He was a young man when he left, but when he returned home he was completely bald. At age twenty-four. When he showed up at my mother's home, at the National Insurance office, he seemed like an old man, like a ghost. Then he returned to his studies, he finished secondary school, and he found a job with the National Insurance office. But for the rest of his life he was pissed off. He wasn't a big man, he was actually rather short. And he was scrawny. But he was full of nervous energy. That time that we went with all the relatives to Borgo Carso by coach for Maria's wedding, with a car in front, on the Epitaffio Road; it stopped suddenly and all the youngsters – we had been playing in the aisle – fell down, Uncle Piero got out and began to shout to the drivers, 'My nephews have hurt themselves!' and he loaded them on the car, while his sisters implored, 'Come back, Pierino, they're not hurt.' The nephews, they meant, not the drivers.

Unfortunately, Uncle Piero didn't know any more than I did about square roots. Maybe they just allowed him to obtain his secondary school diploma because he was a war veteran and in Latina that still counted for something. He even tried to look them up in his school books. I remember he was sweating. He asked Aunt Daria, his wife. 'What do I know?' she replied – she taught Italian. In the end he told me, 'Ask your brothers to explain it to you.' I don't think he was completely wrong: one of my brothers, Otello, was good at maths, and the other, Manrico, was in his first year of secondary school. 'They must know,' said Uncle Piero. 'I don't remember much.'

So I returned home. But Otello told me, 'Ask Manrico to explain it to you,' and Manrico told me to go to Otello, and when I complained, 'That's what he said,' my brother became angry: 'Just read your textbook.' So I let it go: 'What are the chances that square roots will be in the exam?' I reasoned. But that's exactly what the test paper was about. And I failed maths. It didn't matter that I'd done well in the other subjects. When they gave me the passage to translate from Latin into Italian, as soon as I saw it, it just took one glance and I confessed right away, 'I've already done this one.'

'What do you mean?' the teacher asked.

'I already did this one at the seminary.'

Then she went back to the podium and spoke with her colleague. They called a janitor to supervise me, and the two of them went to the principal. After a few minutes, they came back with another translation. I looked at it, and I recognised it, 'I've done this one too.'

'It doesn't matter.' They were getting annoyed now. 'Lucky for you. Just do the translation and shut up.'

'I thought you should know.'

'Just get to work!'

I did it in no time. 'Already finished? Then you really did do it already,' and I don't remember if I got a seven or an eight. But one of the teachers, who knew Violetta, told her afterwards that they thought that I was trying to be a smart-ass and I was mocking them: 'Your brother is so arrogant,' they even had the temerity to say. Me arrogant? I was just honest. Father Cavalli had never explained to me that there is a substantial difference between simulation and dissimulation: for him they were both dishonest. The truth must always be proclaimed at any cost. Even if no one asks you for it. Actually, especially when no one asks you for it. Everyone's happy to respond if they're asked specifically.

Anyhow, they failed me in maths. 'You're a disappointment,' said Mamma. 'Why didn't you tell me that you weren't prepared? I thought you went to Uncle Piero.' There was no point trying to explain every-thing to her. First of all she didn't believe that Uncle Piero didn't know square roots, then she refused to believe that those sons of bitches had refused to help me.

'We never did,' they both swore to her.

'You see,' Mamma said, 'you haven't just left the seminary, you've taken leave of your senses: you've already started to tell lies and dis-credit others. Even Uncle Piero.'

So that summer I had to repeat the course. For the entire month of July. At the Fascist boys' club. Then in August they sent me to the seminary camp, at Rio Martino. I didn't want to go back – I'd already been so many times before – and now I felt too old for it. And why did I still have to be with the clergy? But there was nothing to be done. I just had to go, and that was it: every morning I went to San Marco to catch the bus, and then I would spend the entire day in Rio Martino with boys who were younger than me: 'I wish I'd stayed in the seminary.' I felt lost and out of place, I wasn't the same person as before, and the first time I realised this was because of Mimì, shortly after I returned home. We were playing cowboys and Indians in the garden, with toy soldiers. As usual I had made moun-tains and villages with clumps of earth, to hide the soldiers in. At a certain point I got up and said, 'I don't want to play any more.' Suddenly all the fun was gone – as soon as I finished making the town – and I didn't feel like playing any more. As a matter of fact, I knew I didn't want to play ever again, and I was full of torment inside as I killed the soldiers and Mimì implored, 'One more time, I'll let you win.' It was the same thing with Marietto and Gigi. Yes, I still enjoyed being with them, but we didn't know what to do with each other any more. They would horse around with the little girls who lived in the newly built homes nearby. They would play games just to be with them, but usually they would play spin the bottle, to be able to kiss each other. I didn't like it because there was a new boy who always wanted to kiss Mimì. So I beat him up and said, 'We're not playing this game any more.'

Finally it was October and school began. I was in the last year of middle school. In Building M. Boys and girls together. Twenty girls and ten boys. Almost everyone was repeating the year. The boys and the girls. They were all a little bit older than me, and all much more cool. I was still a sort of half-seminarian, and I was awkward around girls. I never tired of looking at them, but I'd do so surreptitiously. When they spoke to me I'd look at the floor and I wouldn't know what to say to them. I was still very small – I had only turned thirteen in January – and some of the girls were fifteen or sixteen. Some of them were quite overbearing, and I felt ill at ease. Once, Melini said that I had taken the wrong book: the newer one was his and the older one was mine. There was nothing to be done. Only after a few hours, when I found his notes in the old book and a receipt from the bookstore, was he then convinced and gave me mine back: 'Don't let this happen again,' he threatened me. He was bigger than me. And then my mother kept on repeating, 'You'll be in trouble if you argue with everyone.' That's what she was like, and even as a small boy I had to play the part of the victim: 'If you hit someone, I'll hit you when you get home.'

'But if I'm in the right?'

'No one is right. If someone is right why would they be arguing? If someone argues, it's because he is wrong, and you've always been a troublemaker.' Me, not Otello, who was really always fighting with others.

At home I don't remember well, but they always said that they didn't like my tone of voice, and they began right away to call me Accio, which meant 'nasty'. I was the only one in the family to have a nickname, with the exception of Turandot, who was called Mimì, but hers was an affectionate nickname, mine wasn't. I was always on my own. I was always sad. My only consolation was when I closed myself in the toilet to read the pre-war Bompiani encyclopaedia, with all the maps of the Italian colonies in Africa. But it also had a history of art section, with a lovely photo of Pauline Bonaparte.

The boys still slept in the room which we later gave to our sisters. I slept on the cot in the middle, with Otello to the left, by the window, and Manrico to the right, near the wardrobe. Otello mostly ignored me. Manrico would annoy me. He really annoyed me. At night he would grind his teeth, and in the morning, when we woke up, he would put his feet on my bed to put his socks on. I told him all the time, 'Don't put your feet on my bed.'

'But they're clean.'

'I don't give a damn, don't put them there.' Nothing. He still put them there. He didn't care what I said. I was younger than him.

One morning I was at the head of the bed, seated to tie up the shoelaces on my shoes. He put his feet down right beside me. I said to him, 'Move,' and pushed his feet away. Then I went back to tying up my laces. He went 'Gotcha!' and I heard him get up to attack me, from behind. I jumped up like a panther. I turned around and made a direct hit. Like a spring. Natural. Instinctive. All he could do was to throw himself back onto his bed.

'Holy Mother of God, what a left hook,' said Otello. 'If he gets you, he'll kill you,' and he dived in to separate us. Then he went on for a few days, teasing him, 'Holy Mother of God, what a left hook.' He had fun playing us off against each other, and he always stole our money. If you saved anything – in the piggy bank or hidden in the drawer or in your clothes – then you would never see it again. But he didn't steal everything – just a part of it. So when you would say, 'You've stolen my money,' he would reply, 'It's not true. You counted wrong. If it had been me I would have taken everything, I wouldn't leave it behind.' And Mamma would believe him.

Anyhow, we were in the room which later was given over to the girls. They had their beds in Mamma's room. But finally the Council came to do the work. Mamma for years had been going every week to complain at the Council offices because the floor was damp. She even took them Mimì's medical certificate that said she had been ill for four winters in a row with a chest infection. In the end they were fed up and they sent some subcontractors. All the builders and workers were Slavs who had escaped from Tito's Yugoslavia and were living in the refugee camps. On Mondays they would never come to work. They were paid every Saturday, and every week it was a drama, because Di Carmine, the site manager, said that he didn't have enough money, and they would begin to scream, 'Pitchki kuratz! Pitchko materina!' and then one would always take the hammer and begin to break down the wall they had just built, and another would grab the pickaxe and run after Di Carmine, who in the end, every Saturday, would say, 'Just wait for one hour while I go to find the money.' They would sit on the ground, or on top of the pile of earth, and they wouldn't move so much as an inch until he returned. Then they would take their money and go and get drunk. They would drink all day Saturday and Sunday, until they had spent every last lira in their pockets. Then on Monday they would feel unwell. They would only show up for work on Tuesday, when they had slept off their drink. And every Saturday night when they returned drunk to the camp there would always be fights between them, Croats against Serbs, and Serbs and Croats against Hungarians. Every Saturday there would be a few knifing incidents. Until the police arrived and beat everyone up.

When they weren't working and they hadn't been drinking they were actually quite nice to have around. Mamma would make them coffee, and they were all kind. They said that they were political refugees, and that they had to escape because the Communists had persecuted them. But Papà was not so convinced, because they were all heavily tattooed. And they had scars, from knifings. 'These guys are scum, they didn't escape,' he would say. 'Tito sent these guys to us with a first-class ticket. He told them, "Go and bother people over there."' In his opinion they were all common criminals. However, some of them were really Ustascia, Croatian nationalists. There was one of them – Mario – who was as big as a mountain. Back home he had been an electrician, and after I told him that I was a Fascist he would always greet me, 'Long live Mussolini! Long live Hitler!' but he said that Hitler was better: 'Mussolini talk talk, no action,' and I would get angry. It was blasphemy.

Anyhow, they turned our home upside down. The Slavs. They tore up the floors and removed the spongy tufa stone that was underneath.

The tufa bricks were all full of water, they dripped like sponges. They absorbed it from the earth – only twenty years earlier, after all, this area had all been swamp – and they spat it out again over the floor, it was worse than the damp. They rebuilt a new stone floor with ventilation. The work went on for a few months, and Mamma was beside herself: moving beds here, moving beds there, cooking in the lounge, sleeping outside. She did the best she could: Manrico, Otello and Mimì stayed at home; she sent me and Violetta away. Every night we would pack a bag and go to sleep somewhere else: I would go to Aunt Amalia and she would go to Aunt Rita. Anyhow, that's how it had always been: all the space problems were always our problems, because we were almost the youngest. *Lebensraum.*

In the end we returned home, and it seemed like another apartment. Mamma had done things with style, and she made Papà take out a loan from the Farmers' Cooperative, to be paid off month by month, and she added the money from the insurance. She installed majolica tiles in the bathroom, which originally just had oil paint, then she added a bidet – the first time I saw it, I thought it was for washing feet – and hot water and central heating. And behind, near the vegetable patch, she added another bedroom – without planning permission – and there she put us, the boys, and the girls took our old room, next to her. It was the first time, one could say, that finally each of us had their own permanent bed. Papà asked for more money from the Consortium, and he bought a washing machine. She screamed at him, 'All that money! And without telling me anything' (and maybe this is what bothered her). Anyhow, he was offended; he changed his clothes quickly and went to choir practice, and when he got on his bike mumbled, 'Oh crap.' Only when he disappeared over the horizon did she lose it and begin to cry.

But they had been two crazy months. All those Slavs around the place. And that wasn't the worst of it. The Italians were the real problem. Anyhow, in the end Papà said, 'We should make a prisoner exchange with Tito.' In two months the firm had gone bankrupt and reopened about seventy times. In the end Di Carmine wasn't even the boss any more; he would drive around in his car – a Fiat Seicento – but it wasn't his, it belonged to the new site manager, who it seemed had become everyone's boss. He was tall, fat and very gallant with my mother. As soon as my father saw him his expression would change. It's not that Mamma flirted with him, but she was very kind because she had asked him to do a lot of the work on credit. Then there was an issue; it happened right in the new bedroom, the one for the boys. Casanova wanted to be paid; I don't know how much she owned. Mamma said to him, 'I've agreed everything with Di Carmine.'

'What's he got to do with anything? Now I'm in charge.' Even if, in actual fact, the one who was always around – and supervising the Slavs – was always Di Carmine.

'This is not your business – get lost.'

'No, I'm not going anywhere. This is still a building site, and according to the law it will only become your home when I have given you the keys. So pay up or get out.'

Otello jumped on him and took him by the neck: 'I'll show you keys.' But he bent down – he was twice as big as Otello – and grabbed a carpenter's hammer from a trestle. Mamma stopped the hammer in mid-air with one hand and with the other she slapped his face, leaving a mark from all five fingers. 'Otello! He wanted to hit Otello with the hammer,' she said whenever she told the story. 'But why didn't she say anything when he tried to hit me?' I did wonder. 'So everything was fine?'

That's what Mamma was like. Apparently, as a young woman, when she first arrived here, once she was going from Borgo Carso to Littoria on her bicycle to the market. On the Epitaffio Road, a couple of young boys – they were from Sezza, I believe – must have paid her a cheeky compliment. She was sixteen years old. She threw the bicycle to the ground, took off her clog and thumped one of them on the head with the heel. She said that he was bleeding, and said to his friend, 'This girl's crazy,' as he was going away. But Mamma insisted, 'Come here and I'll finish the job.' And another time, as they were being evacuated to Pontinia on their bicycles, they saw a dead German in the middle of a ditch: 'Look, Benassi!' (She always called my father by his last name.) They stopped their bicycles – with Otello and Tosca, who was very young at the time and sitting on the handlebar – and she said to my father, 'He's wearing new shoes.'

They could see the soles of the soldier's boots shining in the sunshine. 'Yes, Lina,' my father said, 'and they're even my size. But I just can't do it.'

'I can,' she said, and she gave him the bicycle to hold, and her kids – he was carrying Norma on his back and all the packages from home on his shoulders. She went down in the middle of the ditch, undid the soldier's boots, and pulled them off. She says that it was hard to get them off – 'Maybe they were too small for him' – and at every pull the German's head would move, as if he wanted to look her in the eyes. She even thought about giving up, but my father didn't have any shoes. So she closed her eyes and she pulled blindly. With her eyes shut. With every ounce of strength she had. And my father got new shoes.

Then, when the front broke – at Cassino – and Germans and loyalists moved back north, Papà had already prepared a cart with all their small possessions to follow them: 'Come on, Lina,' he said, 'get a move on, the Americans are coming. Hurry up, the Germans are leaving.'

'Let them go,' she said, 'I don't care. I'm staying here.'

He insisted, 'But there'll be blacks with them,' because it wasn't just the fact that he was a Fascist Party member, since right after Armistice, and he had always been a supporter of the Germans – he was a mechanic, and he said that no one was as precise as them – it's that he was really frightened by the Americans. 'Now what will happen?'

But Mamma was unbending: 'If you want to go, fine, but I'm staying here with the children.'

And he acquiesced. And for the rest of their lives, every time there was a discussion and he didn't give in to her right away, she would always throw it back in his face: 'Shut up, if it weren't for me, we'd all have been hung in Salò. I'd have ended my days in piazzale Loreto. With Clara Petacci.'

'Oh crap, what have I done to deserve this?' he would always say. 'I should have figured it out right away.' One Sunday, when they were engaged, he went to wait for her outside the Tre Ponti church. The mass had already started, and he recognised her bicycle among all the others leaning against the wall. As a joke, he hid it, and when she came out she thought it had been stolen. For a while he pretended he didn't know what was going on, with that vague little smile he used when he wanted to appeal to others, while she became gradually more and more agitated. Then, when in the end he pulled it out, she went berserk. She shouted and berated him in front of everyone, at the top of her lungs. The most polite word she used was 'cretin'. And 'peasant', just because he was from Umbria. From Perugia. And then he tried to pacify her – 'It was just a joke' – and the more her friends and sisters tried to pacify her, the more she shrieked, 'I never want to see him again! Get lost!' and she threatened him with a clog in her hand. He was so embarrassed, in front of all those people, and inside himself he thought, 'You get lost! Why should I marry a harpy like that? I would ruin my life. I'll stay away, far away.' But that evening he was already back, at the fair on the Via Appia, kneeling in front of her to beg her forgiveness and understanding. 'I should have understood right away,' he would always say. 'I was the author of my own ruin.'

In the end, we went home and I was able to begin the last year of middle school in peace. Well, not really in peace, either at school or at home. At home with my crazy family and at school with all those enemies. They were just the same, they only remembered me when it was time to submit their homework assignments – 'Pass me a copy of the translation' – and during recreation, in the toilets, they would let me smoke. HBs. Like this guy from Mesa di Pontinia, who sat near me. They taught me. 'My mother won't let me,' I told him the first time. 'Do you still do everything your mother says?' he asked, and I smoked. At the beginning I didn't like it. But basically the secret was not to smoke too much. They weren't whole cigarettes; it was just the occasional puff – one would be enough for four of us. But one time I was really annoyed – I gave the guy from Mesa the whole translation, but when they were returned to us with the grades I got eight and he got eight and a half. And he even laughed about it. I really wanted to grab the teacher by the shoulders and ask why: 'But I gave it to him.' I'm sure someone in paradise was looking out for me that day, and I controlled myself.

In front of us there were two girls who were repeating the year: they must have been fifteen or sixteen. One of them was called Rosetta and had light brown hair, almost blonde; the other one was Pina and had dark hair. They both had long hair. It wasn't enough to help them with work in class, sometimes I even had to do their homework for them. One day Pina asked me to do research on Spain for her for our geography class, and I told her no, I had too much to do. She insisted: first she asked me nicely, then she offered me 300 lire. Then I agreed. And she was offended: 'But if Rosetta asked, you would do it for her free: everyone knows that you like her.'

'It's not true,' I replied. And actually it wasn't. But I didn't have the courage to tell the truth. 'You're the one I like.'

For two days in a row, at home, as I copied from the encyclopaedia every word it said about Spain, all I could do was think, 'Now, when I give it to her, I'll tell her.' But when I took the report to her she put the money on the desk and she turned away, while on the other side Rosetta turned around and asked me, 'Can you do Russia for me?' and I didn't have the courage to say no to her. Actually I realised – later – that I really did like her. 'I'll give you 300 lire too,' she said.

But I replied, 'No, I want something else.'

'What do you want?' she asked me.

'I'll tell you when I bring it to you.'

But I had no idea what I was getting myself into: Spain was just a couple of pages, the USSR went on for ever: geography, history, cities, regions, economic resources. Pages and pages in my notebook. All copied out by hand. From the encyclopaedia. That's when I got Kerensky on my mind, and he never left me. And when I gave it to her, all she did was say, 'Thank you,' and turn around. While her friend laughed and nudged her in the ribs. 'Don't be stupid,' Rosetta told her.

'About my payment?' I asked her in recreation.

'Oh, yeah. What do you want?'

'I want you to come to the cinema with me some time. It's my treat.'

Who knows what I was thinking? I thought that in the dark, in the movie theatre, I would gradually touch her arm, and then I would kiss her, and maybe, who knows, I might even touch her legs.

'Alright. We'll go some time.'

'When?'

'I don't know; I can't right now. I'll let you know.'

Maybe even she knew what I was really thinking, because I saw Pina lean over and ask, 'What did he say to you?'

'He wants me to go to the movies,' and then she began to laugh, under the table, pretending to cover her mouth.

'So what did you tell her?' the guy from Mesa asked me.

'Nothing – I didn't say anything.'

I had good grades in all my subjects, except for PE. The coach was a man who had worked for the Ministry of Foreign Affairs, under Fascism. He came from Rome, was of average build, a bit rotund, bald. His name was Ferraro, and he was a real Fascist. During the Republic of Salò he had been a second lieutenant in the Ettore Muti Legion. He was nice with everyone. Or rather, with all the grown-ups. I told him I was a Fascist, but he didn't take any notice, partly because right away – the first time that we had PE and he took us to the Fascist Youth gym – I wasn't able to go up the climbing pole. 'What: you don't know how to go up the climbing pole?'

'No, we were never allowed to at the seminary.' And to tell the truth we never had PE classes at the seminary, unless you can count that small amount of football, where I always underachieved anyhow.

'And haven't you ever climbed a tree?'

'No.'

'What kind of a man are you?' Thanks. That's how things went on. There wasn't anything more to do. He put me in front of that climbing pole for a couple of months, time after time. He would try too. He would show me and climb. He even climbed on the rope. Then he would say, 'Now you try.'

Sure I tried. I really did. I was sweating all over. More because of the tension than because of the effort. After the hour was over, I was sweatier than the guys who'd been on the rowing machine. But I was never able to get more than a metre above the ground. He shouted, harangued. Sometimes he was even kind. But when he was kind I could see out of the corner of my eye that he was looking at the others and making grimaces. In the end he gave up – 'You're really a loser' – and he abandoned me to my destiny. He wouldn't even let me play volleyball any more. There was nothing to be done: just once I was able to grab the ball with both my hands, just with my palms, like he wanted. But that time I sprained my thumb. When the ball came, I would always take it with just one hand, with my palm. I would slap it. It was an impulse I couldn't control. He would say, 'You're a girl.' He would say it quietly, to the others, but he knew I could hear: 'He minces when he walks too.' That son of a bitch. 'One of these days I'm going to send you to do PE with the girls – that way you can play with hula hoops.' I didn't say a word.

When springtime came, there were elections. I can't remember what happened first, the strike or the elections. Maybe the elections. They were political elections. Every afternoon, when I finished school, I would drop by the youth group – just to be seen by Don Russo, so that if my father were to ask him he couldn't say that I hadn't gone – then I would go and hang out in the piazza, or at the movie theatre, to listen to the speeches at the political rallies. All of them. For all the parties. I enjoyed every last word. I wanted to understand everything. And I always found something to comment on: something that didn't convince me. In that way – as soon as the rally finished and the speaker left the stage – I would push through the crowd until I could get close up: 'Excuse me, will you allow a question?' Everyone pretended to pay attention to me – 'Let's hear what the younger generation has to say' – and even the local dignitaries, who surrounded them priggishly, would smile. And I would say whatever crap: I asked Saragat, at the Corso cinema, what his problem was with the Fascists – after all, they'd drained the local swamps. And I asked Pastore why they didn't include the neo-Fascist party MSI in their government coalitions. And I asked the same thing of Almirante, of La Malfa – the real one, not his son – Covelli and all the others. I would even go to listen to the Communists, even in the evenings, after dinner, to listen to the closing speeches. Mamma didn't say anything, but she sent me off and was glad: 'Well done, go listen: you can always learn. But stay away from any confusion.'

'Now you're sending him off into the heart of politics?' my father would ask.

'Shut up, he's not doing anything wrong.'

One Sunday afternoon, after mass, I went to the MSI to register with the Young Italy group. There was a fellow there who must have been fifteen or sixteen. I was just thirteen and I was afraid they might not give me a membership card. But they gave it to me right away. I wanted to pay, but they gave it to me for free. I was almost disappointed: it was as if I had done them a favour, not the other way around. I even asked him, 'Now what do I have to do?' I meant meetings, activities, anything.

'What's there to do? You're a member. That's all.'

But early one afternoon, in piazza del Popolo – it must have been 2 or 3 p.m. – I saw a group of men putting up posters who were arguing. There was a fellow from Turchi – he was a mountain, literally: he was bigger than Mario, the Ustascia refugee from Croatia – who had a round brush and was gluing Fascist posters everywhere. A friend was waiting for him in a car – a Fiat Belvedere. They were from Rome. They were those teams that Turchi sent around the area. Around them there were two or three soloists, who were screeching that the spaces were theirs and that they shouldn't cover their posters. There was even the little doctor – at least everyone called him the little doctor, but he wasn't a doctor, he was the assistant at the San Marco pharmacy – very short, skinny, with dark hair and a black moustache, and even he was shrieking, 'Take down those posters.' The Turchi guy just continued to put them up, and then he pretended to throw the brush at the little doctor, who was the smallest one there. The little doctor jumped him: first he gave him a slap, and then he jumped him. People crowded round, a policeman arrived. They separated them. The Romans went off on their own. But people continued to arrive. And everyone who arrived wanted to hear the entire story from the beginning. The little doctor just said, 'These Romans! They arrive here and think that they can boss everyone around.' Then he looked at his watch and said, 'Let me go, I have to open the pharmacy.' One the one hand I was with the guys from Turchi, because I was a Fascist. On the other hand I was with the little doctor, because I had seen him in the pharmacy since I was a small boy and it was my town, but especially he was a little David battling the huge Goliath. I didn't know whose side I was on, through membership or friendship. But I knew exactly what to do, I didn't hesitate. As soon as they started, I jumped in to separate them: 'Don't do that.' I was still a little sympathetic to the doctor, but I got there before his friends did.

Right after the elections – and I don't remember exactly why – everyone in the class decided to strike. Just our class, for some specific reason which only concerned us. I don't remember if it was to do with the teachers, the classrooms or the scheduling – in any event we were a class full of losers, students who were repeating the year. We were the F section, there were another five sections ahead of us. However, I remember that the cause was just. 'So are we all in agreement?' they asked at the end. 'Even you?' 'Tomorrow is the strike: are you sure you won't surprise us?'

'Are you joking?' I replied. And then at home, like an idiot, I told my mother, 'Tomorrow we are striking.' I was still like that: I would tell her everything. Except for Pauline Bonaparte; I hadn't said a word about that to anyone.

She went red with anger: 'Tomorrow you're going to school,' and she slapped me in the head. She still used to hit me then, at least a couple of times a day.

'But I'll look like a fool.'

'Think about how you appear to me and to the Lord,' and then another slap. 'Think about doing your duty, and you'll be in big trouble if you don't go to school.'

The next morning, when I woke up, before I went out she reminded me, 'Look, I'll come to see if you go into the school.' What could I do? The others were all in the road, in front of Bar Friuli, not going into Building M. The guy from Mesa di Pontinia, always smiling and making fun of me, said to me, 'Well done; we were waiting just for you so that we could all go together to the gardens.'

I said to him, 'I'm not coming.'

'What, you're not striking?'

'No, my mother won't let me.'

'His mother won't let him!' everyone screamed, especially the girls. And then, 'Scab. Traitor. Little boy. All the girls are striking and he won't.' 'Go! Go! Otherwise Mamma will come,' they were still shouting from a distance as I reached the school entrance.

I was the only boy in the classroom, and there were just three girls, the smallest ones, who looked at me with an expression as if to say, 'It's understandable for us, but what's your excuse?' What was different about me? 'You have no idea what my mother's like,' but I didn't say that to them; I kept my own counsel. During recreation the kids from the other classes looked at us, all excited by the heroes who had gone on strike, and with disapproving glances at me. Even the teachers. So I started to say, 'I do what I please, I'm not someone who goes on strike because the others tell me to; I have to be convinced of my actions.' But deep down inside I was totally embarrassed: 'This is the last time.'

The next day was the worst; we had PE for an hour. As I've explained, the gym was at the Fascist youth club. We had to leave Building M and walk there. Usually we would laugh and joke along the way. But that day everyone was serious and morose. Then at the gardens in piazza San Marco we ran into Armando, who was in secondary school, and that day had skipped class of his own accord. He had been in their class the year before, but he had already failed a year earlier. He had very dark hair, and was quick-witted, with a leather jacket and a motorbike. Everyone went up to him, especially the girls, especially Rosetta, who began flirting. She smiled at him, she told him about the strike, and pointed to me: 'You say something to him,' I heard her say, as if she was asking him to beat me up. He called me, to show off to them, but then he was nice to me: 'Don't listen to your mother, you're a grown-up now,' and I understood that he felt sorry for me. Pity. He was the only one. 'Never again,' I thought, 'never again.' And I didn't even go to the gym; I stayed outside for the entire hour, alone. The guy from Mesa came over and called me: 'Ferrero has said you have to come inside, or else he'll mark you down as absent. He said that you won't go up the climbing pole.' And he laughed.

'Tell him he can do whatever he wants,' I replied. That's all I needed, now even Ferraro was making fun of me.

Back at home I held fast. I really took my mother to task: 'Never again,' I said to her. 'I will never listen to you again,' I screamed. And she began to hit me. The more she hit me, the more I screamed. And even Manrico and Violetta said, 'You did the wrong thing: you should have gone on strike. What were you thinking? The strike is a sacred duty. You betrayed all your classmates.' Sure, right. Everyone can give advice after the fact. And without Mamma finding out. They didn't say this in front of her, they came afterwards – when she wasn't around – to give their advice. When she was hitting me, they walked on by. Just like their attitude when it came to choosing which secondary school I would go to.

I passed the final exams for middle school with an average grade of seven and a half. In Latin and Italian I had eight. When the grades were published and I took them home, they said, 'You're halfway through.' Thanks. And then I had to choose. I wanted to study at the lyceum, Latin and Greek. But Papà wanted me to study at the industrial school, so that I could find factory work like him. As far as he was concerned, if I wasn't going to be a priest, the next best option was a secure, unionised job in a factory. That year in Latina they had opened an industrial school where you could choose between the course to be a mechanic and the course to be an electrician. 'But if you want to be an electrician, there's a great school in Velletri too.'

'I want to study Latin and Greek,' and it was as if I'd driven a knife through his heart.

'Absolutely not, and no discussion,' said Mamma. 'Manrico is already studying at the lyceum, and after that he'll have to go on to university. In a few years your father will be retired, and we don't have enough money for two sons who want to study for ever. You need to decide on a course that will get you a good job as soon as you graduate.'

'Eh! What did I say?' said my father. 'Be a factory worker!' And then he told me, in a hushed voice, so that she wouldn't hear, 'Afterwards, if you have good grades, I'll make sure you can go on to university: wouldn't you like to be an engineer?'

'But I like Latin.'

'Latin won't put food on the table. And Manrico is already wasting his time with that,' said Mamma (the girls didn't count: they could study anything they wanted, because anyhow their husbands would provide for them). 'It's decided: you can be a surveyor, follow in the footsteps of your brother.' And that's how it went. The two of them decided, Mamma and Otello, the first-born son: now he was in his last year of secondary school. When I graduated, he would guide my first steps in the profession. That's how their minds worked. He would spend every afternoon playing pool at Bar del Corso. And every once in a while he would come home late at night with his clothes ripped and a black eye, and she would get up on tiptoe so as not to wake my father, to make icepacks for him, because the boys from the council estate had ambushed him on the bypass. He was supposed to show me the way. That Nobel Prize winner. As saintly as Don Bosco. He was twenty-two years old and still repeating the last year of secondary school. He thought he was Pier Luigi Nervi. He had wasted four years, and he was still playing pool instead of going to school. Already when he was just thirteen, he would always win. He had failed twice in middle school and twice at secondary school. The last time they failed him, Papà was fed up: he didn't go back to re-register him, and took him along to the workshop, but he wasn't angry with him; he apprenticed him to one of his friends, a bulldog who was in charge of the welders, and all day long Otello would bang his hammer on the anvil and the forge. Then, seeing he wouldn't adapt, and every once in a while would invent some excuse to run away, they made him work as a labourer in construction, at the building site of the nuclear power station that they were building in Borgo Sabotino. He would come home exhausted, whimpering, and Mamma would be there to cluck over him. 'Keep working, keep working,' Papà would tell him.

But he didn't like real work very much. So he applied to enter the airforce, but he needed parental consent because he was under age, and he brought the forms home for Papà to sign. He ripped them up under Otello's nose and blasted him: 'The airforce? Pretty soon they'll be disarming' (it was the period of thaw, after the Cuban Missile Crisis, and it seemed like Kennedy, Khrushchev and Pope John XXIII had fallen in love with each other) 'and then you'll be out of a job. Learn a trade, seeing as you aren't interested in studying,' and he kicked his ass right back to the building site. Then Otello decided he'd rather study, and began courting my mother's approval, until she went back on the sly and re-registered him at school without telling my father. One morning, when Papà was leaving for work and saw that Otello was still in bed, he asked her, 'But aren't you going to wake him up? Doesn't he have to go to work?'

'He's going back to school,' she replied, 'and I don't want to hear a word from you about it!'

Anyhow, this was the person who was going to lead my way in the profession. My parents even thought we should set up in business together. 'You know how much money we can make?' he would tell her. 'I'll tell him what to do, and if he listens to me…'

I tried another line of reasoning: 'Alright: no lyceum because afterwards the university will be too expensive. But at least let me train to be a teacher, so I can carry on with my Latin, and then as soon as I graduate I'll find work as a primary-school teacher,' also because – but I didn't tell them this – Rosetta was planning to study at Teachers' College.

'A school teacher…Do you really think they'll want you? Be a surveyor!'

'But why not a trade?' insisted my father. And he kept on about becoming an electrician: 'It's the trade of the future.'

'But don't you understand that he's not interested? You can't force your children to do a job that they're not interested in just because it's what you'd like. It's not for him.'

'But surveyor isn't my thing either. Latin is my favourite subject.'

'Shut up – what do you know?' said Otello. And my sentence had been passed. I was enrolled in the school for surveyors.

And they wouldn't even let me enjoy the summer. They wanted me to go back to the seminary camp. 'No camp, no!' I begged my mother. 'I'd rather die.'

'So you expect me to keep you in the house all summer? If you don't want to go to camp, you can find a job.' And Papà took me to the sugar factory, where another friend of his from back when they had built the factory – during the draining of local swampland – had become a sort of production manager. They had a certain number of permanent workers all year, but during the summer, during sugar beet season, they would take on around a hundred seasonal workers, almost all of them students. Even Otello had done it for two or three years, and Mamma would fuss over him when he had night shifts. She would prepare a lunchbox for him, with tinned meat, and she would watch over him when he left in the evening with tears in her eyes. I was dying for the chance to eat tinned meat; once I tried to open a can for myself, and she had ripped it out of my hands: 'Those are for Otello, who's on night shift.' So I was happy to go to the sugar factory. My father took me on his bicycle. I couldn't believe I was going to work there. Just so that I could have tinned meat.

My father's friend told him, 'Gladly, it's no problem.' But when he asked for my social insurance number and found out how old I was, he wasn't best pleased: 'But how can I take him on if he's not even fourteen years old?'

Papà insisted, 'Please could you bend the rules – just do it for me?' And when we returned home, Mamma was upset with him: 'You could have insisted more, you never know how to handle these situations.' Then she went to Mrs Visconti, who was the owner of the Hotel del Mare – she lived close to us, but on the other side of the bypass, in a luxury villa – and she asked her if she would take me on. The hotel was new, they had just opened it the year before. Her husband, Visconti, was a building contractor. And they were originally from the Veneto region too, but they were the only immigrants to come down to Lazio with a bit of money saved up; all the rest of us only had the clothes on our backs. And with that money, they made more. Now they had this hotel, which was very luxurious. It was the first real hotel on the seaside, with a restaurant, bar and a private beach below, with changing rooms. The year before Manrico had worked there, and they were very happy with him – at least that's what they said – because he was always clubbable, someone everyone loved. He said that Signor Visconti adored him: 'Manrico here, Manrico there.' He worked at the beach bar, and in the evening when he returned home he would tell my mother all the gossip, and he would show her his tips before counting them and putting them away. He bought himself a little iron safe, with keys and a combination lock, as big as a biscuit tin, but the next day there was always some money missing, and he couldn't understand why: 'But I counted my money yesterday. What could have happened?' he would ask Otello.

'What are you asking me for? You're the only one who knows the combination.' And he would change it almost every day. Security was tighter than at the Bank of Italy.

Then, after the fruitless trip to the sugar factory, Mamma told him, 'Ask Visconti if they'll take your brother on.' But he wouldn't do anything; he was too embarrassed. So she went. Signora Visconti told her: 'We've already got enough staff, and anyhow he's too young: what can I make him do?'

'Whatever you want.'

'But what can I do? It's just an extra expense: what can I give him?'

'Whatever you want, even nothing; I just don't want him around the house.'

'Alright, but I'm only doing it as a favour for you,' and they took me on. I was thirteen years old, and it was 1963; they gave me 500 lire a day. Every day. Seven days a week. Even Sundays and bank holidays. From dawn to dusk.

I started on 29 June. I remember because it was the feast of Saint Peter and Saint Paul, which used to be a huge celebration. They put me in the private parking lot: 'Look after the cars,' Signora Visconti told me, and I looked after the cars all day, under the burning sun. But all I did was look at them. What else could I do? When my teacher Signora Del Nero arrived – the one from the Latin exam, the one I'd told about the translation I'd already done – she turned to her husband, who was the mayor of Aprilia: 'This is Violetta's brother.'

'I wonder if he's as smart as she is,' her husband replied, and he threw the keys to me, because there were no more parking spaces. 'Park it for me.'

'But I don't know how to drive.'

'So what are you doing?'

'I'm looking after the cars.'

'You're nothing like Violetta,' he said. Sure, right, thanks. But he gave me a tip anyhow, and that evening I came home with my pockets full of coins. I gave them to my mother. 'I'll look after them for you,' she said.

'Should I buy my own safe?'

'Give them to me, it's safer.'

But I only stayed a few days at the parking lot. I made a lot of tips, but to tell the truth I didn't do anything: all I did was look at the cars. After a little while even Signora Visconti must have noticed and she made me work in the bureau – they used the French word – at the reception desk of the hotel. I was the porter.

The first few days I went by bicycle – eight kilometres there and eight back – but after that I stopped because Mamma needed the bicycle to go to the market and to give injections (she gave people injections in their homes, she never asked to be paid, always free of charge: every once in a while people would pay her with a bottle of cognac or a packet of coffee). So I began to hitchhike to work. Marietto taught me how the year before, as soon as I got back from the seminary. One Sunday, instead of going to the parish youth group cinema, he suggested, 'Let's go to the seaside.'

'How will we get there?'

'On foot.'

'On foot?' because as far as I remembered the only way to the seaside was by the Rio Marino road or else the other way, through Foceverde. Either way, it was at least twelve kilometres.

'No, there's a new road which goes directly to Capoportiere. Just seven kilometres.' They had built it when I wasn't around. And we set out on foot. Sunday afternoon. Under the sun. Boiling hot. And then after a while Marietto said, 'Let's stop a car,' and I stood in the middle of the road, with my hand up in a Fascist salute, to show the drivers they had to slow down. He said to me, 'No, do it with your thumb.' I even teased him, 'But what do you mean, just my thumb? How will they understand?' But no, actually that's all it did take for them to understand. And another summer Sunday I travelled all the way alone, hitchhiking, from Latina to Capoportiere, and then all along the sea coast as far as Sabaudia, and then I came back the other way, via Bella Farnia and Borgo Grappa. I must have taken seven or eight rides, all for short distances. When they made me get out, I would walk for a while until someone else picked me up. The way back, towards evening, was more difficult: no one stopped. A lot of cars passed – by then even the people from Latina had discovered just how nice it was to spend Sunday at the seaside – but no one stopped. From Bella Farnia to Grappa on foot. Then Uncle Piero stopped, with his Fiat 1100. Zia Daria and the kids were laughing – they were happy to see me. As a matter of fact, you could even say that Marta and

Giannino were proud of me: 'Look what a cousin we have.' But my uncle seemed angry, and he didn't say a word until he dropped me off in Latina. That's when he asked me, 'But does your mother know that you get around like that?' I told him no, and from the expression on his face I could read his mind. 'Alright then: this time I won't say anything, but don't let me catch you at it ever again.'

However, when it was time to send me every day to work at the Hotel del Mare and take her bicycle again, I asked her, 'How will I get there?'

She didn't stop to think: 'Hitchhike.'

What was the point of telling her that maybe Uncle Piero didn't think it was a good idea: 'But it's dangerous.'

'It's only dangerous for anyone stupid enough to pick you up. Anyhow, it's just a short hop from here to the seaside.'

'Alright, I'll do as I'm told,' and I began to hitchhike. All the time. And I spent all summer working. At the reception desk of the hotel. Carrying luggage. Being courteous to the clients. Helping the house-keepers, carrying dirty linen, cleaning the kitchen, emptying bottles. Without once being able to swim in the sea. Always perfectly dressed, with all those women wandering around, not even in bathing suits, in bikinis. My head was boiling. Once, while I was holding a ladder steady for one of the chambermaids – Anna, a married woman with two or three little kids, short and dark – I couldn't help myself: I lifted up my head, looked up her skirt, and I put a hand on her calf, to caress her. She moved away. It's lucky she didn't fall off the ladder. She slapped me and said, 'Don't tell anyone, and don't ever do it again.' According to what I heard from the waiters, though, and my brother and the lifeguards, everyone there was at it like rabbits. I was the only one who didn't see any action.

Anyhow, I worked all summer long, and as soon as I earned any money – even my tips – I gave it to my mother. She told me she was keeping it safe for me. Only once I kept back something – 15,000 – from my first pay cheque. I was very proud that evening, and I invited Violetta out for dinner. We went to the Gallo d'Oro – it was her first time too – and we ordered two pizzaiola chicken breasts. The next day, when I told Anna the chambermaid about it, she practically hit me again: 'You went to a restaurant and ordered pizzaiola chicken?'

But it was the only dish we recognised on the menu, me and Violetta. Did she expect us to order weird stuff? Then another time I took her to the open-air cinema in the centre of town. We saw *Never on Sunday* with Melina Mercouri. Mimì wanted to come too. But I wouldn't let her.

In October I began at the technical secondary school. In the meantime I must have grown. I hit my head on road signs and shop awnings. Up until the day before I had passed underneath easily. And suddenly the next day I couldn't go under them. For years after that I was always banging my head on the lights at the intersection. I had grown – I was over six feet, but solidly built – and even today I still sometimes hit my head. When I went to ask my mother for some money, she told me there was none left: 'I used it to buy your books. And your clothes.' A blue jumper and a turtleneck. She said, 'Choose one,' and when I replied, 'Both of them,' she gave me a dirty look. And a dark grey raincoat, with a waterproof plastic collar. And I wore them for years. Everything else – trousers, shirts etc. – were hand-me-downs from Otello. She also bought me some white jeans, after I really begged her for them. I couldn't wait to throw out my knicker-bockers. I thought I looked cool in the white trousers. But school started right away, and in the design classroom, when I used the ink, I stained them the first time I wore them. I knew I should never have agreed to study as a surveyor.

I never saw Rosetta again. I spent all summer calling her, every afternoon, when people went to their rooms for a rest and things were calmer. Then they would leave me on my own at reception and I would dial the number with my heart in my mouth. As soon as anyone replied, I would hang up. What would I say? That I wanted Rosetta? And then what would I tell her? I was happy just to have called her. I would call three or four times a day. Every day. All summer. Who knows what her family must have thought. Then, as soon as some people returned, I would take the keys of the jukebox and go to the terrace. I would programme thirty or forty discs in a row. Not always the same ones, because the chambermaids would complain. In the beginning I would play Sergio Endrigo all the time, and at the highest volume. Once Anna came down from the third floor without saying a word, went to the jukebox, pulled out the plug and then stomped back upstairs without saying a word. How could anyone not like Sergio Endrigo? I still listen to him today.

chapter 3

The fourteenth of January 1964 was a Tuesday – it's always been my unlucky day – and I was playing the harmonium in the lounge. The house was full: we'd just come home from school and finished eating. Manrico was studying at the big table, just two metres from my harmonium. In an imperious tone of voice, he told me, 'Shut up, I have to study.' I continued to play. The previous evening he had spent hours on the harmonium and no one had protested. Again he told me, 'Shut up.'

I continued: 'Why's it alright when you do it? Now it's my turn.'

The harmonium had arrived just before Christmas. They had to move the practice room of the San Marco choir, and it didn't fit into the new room. So, because they didn't know where to put it, Papà had brought it home: 'Violetta can practice,' because she was studying clarinet at the convent school. She was a Communist – albeit a closet Communist – but she chose to take her music studies in the convent. And Papà was so happy. But afterwards he found out that she would chat with boys on the way home. Anyhow, basically the harmonium arrived in our home and everyone horsed around with it. But we played badly; we had learned a little how to play at the seminary, and before Christmas we had some fun, around the Christmas crèche, singing 'Adeste Fideles' and 'Tu scendi dalle stelle' at the top of our lungs. My father was the only one who didn't join in: 'Dreadful. You can't sing like that, it's an insult.'

Anyhow, I kept on playing. And Manrico got up from the table like a madman, came up behind me and closed the cover of the harmonium with a bang, and if he had been any closer he would have broken my hands: I just moved them away in time; I even felt the gust of air as it suddenly closed. I turned around and began to pummel his thighs with my fists.

There had been another argument at the Hotel del Mare during the summer. A traveller was leaving, and he had given me a 50 lire tip – with one of those silver coins – saying, 'Share it with the others.' How was I supposed to share it with twenty staff? There wouldn't have been anything for anyone. So I decided to share it with my brother: 'Half each.' But instead of appreciating my gesture, he began to take the moral high ground, as if he were issuing me with rules for the conduct of life: 'If he told you the tip was for everyone, you have to share it with everyone.'

'But there'll be nothing left.'

'It doesn't matter.'

'Do you want your share?' I gave him an ultimatum, because I was already insulted.

'No. Either you give it to everyone or not to anyone.'

'Fine, I'll keep it all to myself then.'

'No, you have to share it with the others.' He was scandalised, and began to shove me. He wanted to get rid of the money now at any cost, and look good to the others: I was the horrible one who stole money, he was the good one who gave the money back to the people. I gave him my left hook right in the face, hard, and the waiters had to separate us. He calmed down right away; he was good as gold when Sandro pinned his arms down, his only concern was to explain to them how things were, to show that he was right. Not me, I didn't enter into discussions – anyhow I realised that there was no point. All I could think of was attacking him, and I was able to get him a few more times in the face. Then the next day we made up. Well, sort of made up, because he couldn't forget the blows he'd received, and inside me something died – all the trust. How can it be that I come to share money with you, money I could have kept for myself, and then you vilify me in front of everyone?

Anyhow, to get back to the the harmonium fight, I hit him a few times in the legs, and he grabbed me by the neck. We began wrestling, and were about to crash into the dining-room table. Violetta and Mimì – Mimì had been playing a duet with me – started to scream, and Mamma and Tosca arrived from the kitchen. Tosca had been staying at our house for a while with her husband and children, sleeping in the girls' room. So we had to move all the beds: in the evening it seemed like living in a refugee camp, with mattresses on the ground or piled on chairs standing in a row. And as if it wasn't enough that she'd occupied our home, she was bossy too. She'd always been bossy. She was a know-it-all. I didn't think of her as a sister, she was more like a teacher. And she would hit us too. So to go back to my story, they came into the room. Tosca in front, my mother behind. Tosca was holding her youngest child in her arms, and they didn't come in saying, 'Stop, what's going on? Tell us what happened.' No, they came in saying, 'Shame on you! It's always your fault!' to me. Tosca grabbed me and began to hit me, with her child in her arms. With one hand she held the baby, with the other she hit me: 'It's always your fault, it's always your fault, shame on you.' And she hit me. My mother was hitting me too: 'It's always your fault, nasty Accio, you'll be the death of me.' And they kept hitting me. They didn't do anything to Manrico. I tried to explain. Nothing. They didn't want to listen, they had already decided that it was my fault before they entered the room. But at least try to listen to me, ask what's going on, try to understand. No. 'There's nothing to understand,' screeched Tosca, 'it's always your fault!' 'Always your fault,' echoed my mother.

So I got the bruises. And the blame. And that's what upset me the most, not the bruises: I was used to them. I spent some time in the easy chair, trying to study, then, when the apartment was quiet, I went out. 'I'm going to the youth group,' I said.

'You can go wherever you want,' replied my mother. But I just went there because it was better than staying at home. As soon as I arrived I felt nauseous. I made sure Don Russo saw me, and disappeared right away. I didn't know where to go. 'I'm going to Nettuno.' I didn't have any friends. The only one was this guy from Nettuno, who came to school with me and who was always chatting. He played in the youth division of Rome Football Club. We sat next to each other.

I went out and hitchhiked to Nettuno. He told me once that his grandmother had a corner shop on the main street and that he was always to be found there. But he wasn't: 'He's training, who knows when he'll be back. Can I help?'

I bought ten Nazionali cigarettes – she put them in a bag for me, like they used to do then – and a box of matches. They were the first cigarettes I'd ever bought. I went along the seaside to smoke: 'I'll wait for a while, then I'll go home.' As I waited I started walking towards Anzio, always along the seashore. In Anzio I said, 'Anyhow he won't be in,' and I thought fleetingly of going home. But this thought bothered me right away. By then I'd walked through Anzio. I was already north of town. So I said to myself, 'I'll go to Genoa.' And I started hitchhiking.

You may well ask, 'But what made you think of Genoa?' Genoa just came to me. Along the coast, along the sea, I thought I would eventually arrive in Genoa: what does it take? Just follow the sea and you can't get lost, then in Genoa one can take it from there, find a boat. Maybe I could join the merchant navy. Then I'd travel to America and make my fortune, and return home when I'm rich. I'd return home with a big car, lots of money, and I'd even give some to them. I'd show them my superiority. Once I had taken my decision I felt better – 'Anyhow, I'm going to Genoa' – after all that discomfort I had struggled with during the afternoon, and especially there, between Nettuno and Anzio, after I couldn't even find this one loser of a friend to talk to. It was January, the sky was as dark as lead, and that road in the middle of the buildings – totally empty, still wet from the morning rain and all the shutters on the buildings closed – only increased my dark mood. 'Enough is enough, I'm going to Genoa,' and I was happy as a bee in clover.

It must have been four or four-thirty in the afternoon. It was still daylight in Anzio. I began to hitchhike north. But in the meantime I walked. A few people took me for short journeys, one or two kilometres: Lido de Pini, Lavinio. I would hop in, then get out and start walking again. Between Lavinio and Torvaianica, I think the sun went down. I kept walking. Alone, in winter, through all these shanty-town homes on both sides of the road. I began to feel distressed again. Darkness. Total darkness. And every once in a while a dog would bark. Behind the shacks I could hear the sounds of the stormy sea. I had always been afraid of the dark, and especially afraid of dogs. I began to feel anxious, and I thought of my mother and I wanted to see her again. But at the same time I was angry, and I was offended because once again I had been judged 'without a fair trial'. First they find you guilty, then – who knows? – actually forget it: you were just guilty, end of story. What was the point of going home? They would have hit me again because I was late for supper: 'Alea iacta est.'

To keep myself going, every once in a while, from far away, I would see the glow of a lamppost, and until I got there I would enjoy my walk. As soon as I walked further I was anxious again, as I gradually walked away from the illumination. When I got to Torvaianica I found a shop open and bought a mortadella sandwich. I ate half of it, the other half I kept in the pocket of that dark grey raincoat with the plastic collar. Now all I had left, after the sandwich, was four or five hundred lire: all that was left from my summer tips. I continued to walk and to hitchhike. A Fiat 1100 stopped, the driver was going to Ostia. He must have been about forty years old; he seemed like a trustworthy family man. He was a man of few words; he didn't seem interested in chit-chat. But I was. He only asked me, 'Where are you going?' and I was off. I told him I was sixteen years old and I was going to Genoa to visit my father, because he worked there but had been taken ill. He was in hospital, and I was going to see him. My mother had given me money for the train ticket, but I lost it all playing poker and so I was hitchhiking. You might ask, 'But what possessed you?' I'll tell you what possessed me: I thought I had to give him some kind of explanation, to tell him the why and wherefore. If someone is good enough to give you a ride, you should at least explain your journey in repayment. You have to say something. So I invented this crap. I don't know how I thought it up. I must have been thinking of the adventure books I read. The poker game was my own addition, a classy way to show off that I really was sixteen years old. Just like the cigarette I was smoking.

He took me to Ostia, then made me get out: 'But are you really going to Genoa?' he asked me. I insisted that I was. But it was pretty obvious that he wasn't at all convinced: 'You should have taken the via Aurelia.'

I didn't even know what it was: 'I'm following the seaside route.'

'Then you should go to Fiumicino now,' he said, but it was on the other side of the Tiber (the airport wasn't even in the preliminary planning stages back then).

I wandered around Ostia. I went into the cinema, hoping to see some hot women and relax a little after all my worries. All that was playing was a sort of western – *The Puppy Dog*, I think – and the audience was just little kids. When I got out, I asked which way to Fiumicino. It was incredibly complicated. So I decided to take a bus, at least that far. 'After that it's easy,' I thought. 'I just have to take the road to Fregene.' I had had Fregene on the brain ever since I was at the seminary: there was a postcard I'd seen with an image of the centre of Fregene and it looked rather similar to Latina. 'One of these days I'm going there,' I had always thought. This was my chance. But instead, from Fiumicino I took a road along the final stretch of the Tiber right up to the end of the port, thinking that sooner or later I would find a road which turned to the right, and then I would have found the seaside route again. No way. I found another cinema, with posters of women with hot bodies, and I almost thought of going inside again. But it was late, and even the last show was about to finish. I asked someone else about the road to Fregene, the seaside route. 'But there's marshland between here and Fregene. You can't go along the seaside.'

'Then what should I do?'

'Well, you should go to Ponte Galeria, and from there you take the Aurelia again.' It was past midnight. There wasn't anyone around. I took the road from Ponte Galeria. I almost regurgitated my sandwich.

Another cigarette. Surrounded by darkness and barking dogs. But what else could I do? I put one foot in front of the other. I sang to keep my spirits up and to show the dogs that I wasn't afraid of them. For about fifteen kilometres. When I got there I was dead tired. I thought I'd reached the town, but there was just a train station. I went inside: 'I'll take the first train for Fregene.' There was no one there. I lay down on a bench and slept. I couldn't believe that I was away from the darkness and the barking dogs. When people arrived in the morning to take the first train, I woke up. There were men going to work and children going to school. So many people. I asked for a ticket: 'Fregene.'

'Maccarese,' he replied. There wasn't even a station in Fregene.

'Alright.' And then I had a stroke of genius. 'Discounted youth fare: I'm under fourteen,' because I remembered that Mamma had asked for tickets like that one time. At the end of the day, I was still young enough, if only by twelve days. I took out my Young Italy membership card. It was the only form of ID I had, but to me it seemed very authoritative. The vendor didn't even look at it: he gave me my ticket and I took the first train. As soon as I climbed on board I fell asleep again on the wooden seats, because it was warm, surrounded by all the confusion of the commuters. In Maccarese, the first stop, I had to get off: I woke up suddenly as soon as the train came to a halt. And I was groggy because I was so sleep-deprived, and I hardly had the strength to start walking again. Then I thought it over – anyhow, the train wasn't expensive, especially with the reduction – and I bought another ticket as far as Civitavecchia. During the night, in Ponte Galeria, I had taken a good look at the map of Italy on the wall: after Civitavecchia it was impossible to go wrong, you took that road – the via Aurelia – and then went straight, more or less along the seaside, until you got to Genoa; even to France, if you wanted. I slept again on a bench, in the waiting room, and when the train arrived I fell asleep again right away on the wooden bench. I would wake up at every stop; I'd look at the station sign, stretch my legs a little to let people pass as they got on and off, and then I'd fall into a deep sleep again. Finally in Civitavecchia I had to get off.

It must have been nine or nine-thirty in the morning. I walked through town, past the port and the power plant. I ate another sandwich with mortadella. I reached the edge of town, on the via Aurelia, and I started hitchhiking again. People would pick me up. Short trips. Sometimes a bit longer. I would get out, walk, and as soon as I heard the sound of a car coming behind me – it wasn't like it is today: back then cars would only drive by occasionally – I would turn around and stick my thumb out. At this point I was already near Orbetello, the sun was beating down. In winter. It was January. The sky was totally blue, without a cloud. The Aurelia was a wide road, surrounded by excavated earth, with steep hills. I felt on top of the world. A Fiat 600 stopped. Two old fogeys. They made me sit in the back. It was a specially built 600 for the disabled. The driver was missing an arm (or a leg?). There were small iron bars attached to the stick shift connected to the pedal of the clutch. The old fogeys didn't inspire confidence. I don't know why, but I was sure they were sex maniacs. They didn't ask me any questions. With everyone else I would always tell the story about my sick father, in hospital in Genoa, and the money I had lost playing poker. These guys didn't give a damn. They spoke between themselves. Every once in a while they would turn around and look at me.

We got to Grosseto, I walked through town, and I began to hitchhike again. One ride after another – even a few big lorries – and I found myself in Cecina. Then Livorno, Pisa, Migliarino. I can't even remember any more all the details of getting into cars and out of cars and the portions of the trip I walked. By now it was late afternoon. In Viareggio I was picked up by a big, new car: I can't quite remember if it was a Giulia or a Fiat 1500. Or a Ford Taurus? The driver must have been thirty or thirty-five years old. He was tall, with dark hair. He looked just like my French teacher, who was also a solicitor and everyone said he was gay. He was effeminate. And when he walked around the classroom he minced. This fellow looked just like him: his hair, his face, his nose, his kind and affable manner, but also the limp wrist. 'He must be gay,' I thought.

But he didn't touch my knee or anything else. He made me talk, he pretended to believe me. I talked about politics, about the merits of Mussolini and Fascism. He said that he was a Social Democrat, and that he had some reservations about Fascism. When I told him about Genoa and my father in the hospital and the poker game he asked me, 'What did you have, a full house?' I didn't even know what that was, so he changed topic so as not to embarrass me.

He drove slowly. Everyone passed us. At the beginning it annoyed me – 'When will we arrive?' – but I liked our chat too much. He encouraged me, and the more he encouraged me the more I talked. It was starting to get dark. 'Where will you sleep tonight?' he asked me.

'I don't know. Anyhow, I'll keep going, we'll see. Maybe I'll make it to Genoa tonight.'

'Why don't you spend the night at my place? Get a good night's sleep, and tomorrow you'll start the day feeling fresh as a daisy. There's space at my place, I live alone.' But he didn't put any pressure on me, he was nonchalant. Just as nonchalantly, I said no.

'Don't tell me you're afraid,' he said.

'What's there to be afraid of?' I parried. I was as tall as I am now, but I was still scrawny. But anyhow I was tall, and I must have had a determined expression, a bit like a nutter. Maybe I really did look older than my fourteen years, maybe I looked sixteen, and I told everyone that I had done boxing. 'It's because I don't want to be a burden on you,' I explained. He didn't insist.

Then he had a suggestion: 'Shall we stop for a drink?' because I had told him that I hadn't had a bite to eat since that morning.

'Alright, but let this one be on me.' I wanted to be elegant.

'But why? We're friends.' And so we stopped. At a shop across the street I got another mortadella sandwich. I ate half and put the other half in my pocket. We sat down at the little bar table, there to one side, but he insisted on paying for our beers. We left as friends and kept on chatting. At a certain point he was silent for a while. 'Tell me the truth,' he asked in a quiet voice. 'Did you run away from home?' And I said yes. Not right away. For a while I was uncertain. But he insisted, insinuating, in a delicate way, without giving up. Then I told him everything. He stopped his car at the side of the road, he turned towards me, and he began to take my parents' side: 'Just think how worried they must be right now.'

'What do they care? One less person to worry about.'

'And your mother? She gave birth to you. She's probably going out of her mind right now.'

'My mother? She couldn't care less.'

Then he started on about my father: 'He must be looking for you. He at least must love you.'

'Him? But it's as if I don't exist for him. An unknown stranger. He can't stand me. All he wants is for me to go to the parish youth club.'

'They love you,' and he kept on going for a while. In the end he convinced me. He made me see it from my parents' point of view. They must be distressed and worried.

But I didn't give up right away, I was indignant: 'But now, if I go back, it will be even worse: who knows what they'll do to me. And you know I was in the right. But that's how it works at home: everything is always my fault. Just imagine what it will be like now.' I even tried telling him, 'Alright,' because anyhow it was getting dark, 'I think on reflection I will stay at your place. Let me sleep on it, then tomorrow is another day.'

But he said, 'No, that doesn't seem like a good idea to me,' and he looked at me with kind eyes. 'You have to go home. Your mother is worried.'

'Alright, now I'll get out of the car and run back. But it would be better for me to rest first,' and obviously this was an attempt to gain time. I didn't want to give up. What kind of idiot would I seem if I went back? A man must be true to his word, not always changing his mind. I should go back and beg forgiveness?

But he was insistent about my mother. He convinced me to go to the police: 'They'll let your family know right away. Half an hour later, she'll be out of her misery.'

'Alright.' And he started up the engine, and he took me to Massa and dropped me near the police station. Not in front. He stopped some distance away.

'That's the one there.'

'Why don't you come with me?' I asked him. I was anxious about pitching up there on my own.

'Better not, it's best that they don't see me.'

'Why?' But he avoided my question and said his goodbyes. 'Can we at least shake hands?' And he grasped my hand with both of his. I got out of the car and started walking. He waited there, watching me. When I was in front of the door, he left.

I told the police officer sitting there on guard duty, at the top of the external stairway, 'I've run away from home. I'd like you to inform my mother that now I'm going back.' That's all. Nothing else. Going back, obviously, was my business. I thought that I would have to give him my name and address: full stop, thank you and goodbye. I had already turned to go. He grabbed me back and took me upstairs to the serious crime unit. Outside it was getting dark. 'These guys are going to make me waste time,' I thought, but already on the stairs he began to chat with me. He was a corporal, Neapolitan, older, kindly. As soon as we got to the office, he left me there – he had already turned to go back downstairs to his post – but the others told him to stay, because they could see that I was at ease with him. I didn't like the look of the others at all. In the meantime, they were checking details. They found the alert that the Latina police had dispatched, and they replied. The Neapolitan policeman kept talking to me; he asked me the details of all the stops I had made since leaving home. When I told him about the guy who looked like my French teacher, he said, 'We know him, we know him. I know who you mean. What did he do?'

'Nothing.' Then they took me to the cafeteria: I ate two bowls of minestrone. Then he took me back upstairs. With his superior officers – the detective and a lady police inspector who had arrived in the meantime – he was very deferential. When those guys had to ask me something, they made him ask me. Obviously I was cold with them. Then they took me to sleep in Marina di Massa, in an orphanage. We drove there in a Fiat Giulietta, the Ferrari of the day. The nuns took me to a dormitory. There were lots of tiny beds, with children sleeping. Mine was a bit bigger. The Sister who made my bed asked me where I was from. 'You're from Latina? Then we're practically neighbours; I'm from Mondragone.'

'Neighbours?' I felt like saying. 'Latina's nowhere near Mondragone. It's almost as far away as Naples.' But I kept my mouth shut.

'Tomorrow they'll take you home,' the Neapolitan policeman said as I got into bed.

'You mean you're not taking me?' I began to worry.

'No, the lady inspector will.' His shift had been over for a few hours, but he'd stayed with me anyway. His name was Antonio.

'I'd rather go with you.'

'I know, but I'm not in charge. This is a matter for the lady inspector.'

I slept like a log. I dreamed of my mother and the via Aurelia.

The next morning the Sister from Mondragone woke me early and made breakfast for me in the kitchen: as much coffee and hot milk as I wanted, with bread and marmalade. And she was chatty too. So I explained to her that Mondragone was actually quite far from Latina. 'It doesn't matter,' she replied. 'Here in the North we Southerners have to stick together.'

'But what do you mean Southerners?' I said. 'My family is from the Veneto.'

'Alright.' But when the Ferrari arrived and she was saying goodbye to me on the stairs she said, 'Give me a kiss.' Then I felt badly, and conceded, 'At the end of the day, we are neighbours.'

'No, no, you're from the Veneto,' she replied.

We went back to the police headquarters, and from there to the train station. There had been a change of plan: now Antonio was coming with the lady inspector. Neither of them were in uniform, and it seemed strange compared to the day before, when I'd seen them in uniform. He was all happy, euphoric, and kept thanking the lady inspector for having interceded and allowing him to come along. 'I did it for the boy, he likes you.' I didn't understand exactly how it worked, but somehow this trip allowed him to take two or three days off afterwards, and he would continue to Naples to see his family after not having seen them for a long time. During the train journey I told them my entire life story – and the entire life story of all my family members – but every once in a while I would worry: 'Will they hit me?'

'Don't worry, they won't hit you,' he reassured me.

'Will you tell them not to?'

'Of course we will, but there's really no need.'

'No need? You don't know my mother.' And then I talked about Fascism and how Mussolini had drained the Pontine marshes. I spoke for hours, and then I had nothing more to say, and he started. He didn't want to, it was my fault, I bugged him for the entire trip: 'Have you ever shot anyone? Have you ever been afraid?' And so it came out that when he was young he served in Milan, with Nardone, and he participated in violent clashes with the Volante Rossa, a group of former partisans who, after the liberation, didn't consider their resistance to be over. Actually they thought it would only end with the establishment of a Communist government. He didn't seem to think that democracy – especially the Christian Democrats – was exactly a fantastic result. It was worse after the liberation: they felt like they were still under Fascism, only worse, and they started fighting again. They would break in and execute people in the homes of former Fascists. He even showed me a wound, on his side, from once when they cut them off in a car chase – the Volante Rossa – and began a shootout. I was shocked: 'Those Communists.' He was a little less shocked. Actually, he seemed to respect them rather than fear them.

The lady inspector asked him, 'Were you really with Nardone?' She couldn't believe it. She thought that he had invented the stories for me, like a sort of Little Red Riding Hood. She was only convinced when she saw the wound. Then she seemed even more interested than

I was: it seemed like this Little Red Riding Hood fairy tale was being told just for her benefit: 'Who would ever have imagined? For years I've seen you there on guard duty, always so courteous, but I would never have imagined.'

'Eh, ma'am…lots of times we see people, but we don't know their stories.' And then he became quiet, silent, as if he had other things to say but he wouldn't speak about them. From that moment she changed. Until Latina and when we said goodbye, she treated him with more respect and a little bit of admiration. It's not that she had been rude before, but she treated him with a sort of paternalism, as if it was more than obvious that she was the one in charge. But now, there, he was truly the one in charge.

We arrived in Latina in the afternoon. As we got closer I began to feel ill. I felt like running away again: 'What a fool I'm making of myself. I didn't even make it to Genoa: I was almost there, I was just a short distance away.' I was filled with regrets, like Judas, and the closer I got to the police headquarters, the more my repentance increased. In the road, as I walked, with every step I took my heart felt a pang. Antonio realised, and told the lady officer, 'There's no hurry: let's get something to drink.' They made me drink Aperol, for the first time in my life, and the waiter prepared it precisely, in every detail, adding sugar to the glass and a twist of lemon. Then he said to me, 'Bottoms up,' and he began to laugh. I begged them again to tell my mother not to hit me.

I expected to find them there, ready to attack me as soon as I turned the corner. But they didn't come: 'We told them to wait at home. We'll advise them when they can come,' and another hour passed, taken up with paperwork and files. Antonio left: 'I have to run, or else I'll miss the train for Naples,' but if I needed him he would stay. He said goodbye, but his final words weren't for me: 'So can I go, ma'am?'

Then that lot arrived. But they didn't even shout at me. They didn't make a peep. Very normal. As if nothing had happened, as if we'd just said goodbye five minutes earlier. 'Did you see?' I said to myself. 'These guys don't give a damn.' Mamma, Papà, Manrico and Otello came.

The chief of police of Latina encouraged us: 'Try to get along.' And then they kicked us out. Violetta and Mimì were waiting outside. Mimì was the only one who came up and gave me a hug. Then, as we walked home, Manrico came over and asked me, 'But where did you sleep at night?' and he laughed.

'Aha, now you're laughing: you're not angry about the harmonium any more.'

'But what do you mean angry?' and he kept on like that, about my travels. 'How did you manage? What did you eat? Where did you go?' Then we gradually moved apart – in the beginning we walked next to each other and we took up the entire road – and now we were walking in pairs.

'And Tosca?'

'She's gone back home.'

'What do you mean, she didn't even wait for me?'

'That's what her husband told her to do.'

In the meantime my father slowly came close to me and allowed all the others to pass ahead of us gradually, then when everyone else was in front of us and the two of us were alone, just me and him, at the back of the line, he asked me in a very quiet voice, 'My son, what did we ever do to you?'

'You didn't do anything, but they did.'

'Your brothers and sisters? For such a small thing you ran away from home and caused your mother and me so much pain? You could have said something!'

'Who was I to tell – Mamma? She's worse than they are. She's unjust.'

It was as if I'd blasphemed: 'How can you say that about your mother?' And such was the enormity of the thing that he raised his voice: 'But she would give her life for all of you.' Because he had raised his voice she heard him, then she turned on me like a wild animal and began to scream in the middle of the road, just a hundred metres from the police headquarters. But she wasn't screaming at me, she was screaming at him: 'We said we weren't going to say anything! We're not supposed to say a word!'

'But I just wanted to know what we'd done to him.'

'Eh, I'd like to know a lot of things, too. Didn't we say that no one should ever say anything to him? That's enough!' He was silent, crestfallen. Obviously he wanted to understand. The others had already understood far too much.

Then Mimì came up to me: 'The police told them that they aren't supposed to say anything to you,' and I felt a little reassured. No one mentioned it again for years. All the neighbours came over as we approached the house. Signora Loreta, Signora Elide from upstairs. And they said, 'Shame on you,' but they were smiling as they said it. 'You had us so worried.'

It seems that they began to worry right away, as soon as it was dark and I hadn't returned home. My mother held it together for a while, but after dinner my father began to go mad. He wanted to know what had happened, but I don't think he got much of an explanation: 'Nothing, don't worry: he went out and said he was going to the youth club.' And they even tried to keep this farce up with me: 'You were fine when you left the house.'

'And the argument?' They'd forgotten about that.

'That was more than an hour before.' Do you understand? They were in denial – 'You'd hardly leave home for that' – as if it had never happened. And then my father went to the presbytery at ten at night to wake the priests up. Don Russo told him that he had seen me in the early afternoon: 'But he ran off almost immediately. As soon as I turned around, he was gone.'

Then he went to the police, and after that, throughout the night, he looked for me all over Latina: at the public gardens, at the market, at the bus station. He didn't get home until four in the morning. Mamma said to him, 'You'll see, he'll be back in the morning: as soon as he gets sleepy,' and, for better or for worse, they tried to sleep too. 'When he gets back I'll beat him till he's black and blue,' said Mamma.

But when they woke up in the morning I still wasn't back. And then all of them really began to worry. Otello went to school, to my classroom, to find out if anyone had seen me. The boy from Nettuno mentioned that I had been there, that his grandmother had seen me. 'In Nettuno? And what was he doing so far away?' Papà asked. 'This must be serious,' and the search widened. They went that far with a friend of Otello who had a car. They were looking for me everywhere, in every road. At the beginning my father was optimistic: 'We'll find him right away,' but the more time passed, the more he lost hope. They even went to look for me at the seaside, beyond Anzio, and at a certain point they found a bundle of rags in the midst of the waves. My father threw himself into the water with all his clothes on – and Otello told me he was crying – to go to get the bundle. They thought they were my clothes, that I had drowned. But when he brought everything to the shore and dried it out, inside there were potato peelings and other trash that must have been thrown from some ship. He even had trash all over him (and even years later, when Otello would tell this story, he would laugh about that and tease him, and the entire family teased him). Then he was convinced that I was dead. They returned from Nettuno while all our friends and relatives searched for me around Latina: 'He must be nearby. Where could he have gone?'

'There's nothing to be done,' my father would say. 'He's killed himself.' And he kept asking my mother, 'What have you done to him?'

'But what do you think I could have done?' and apparently even she was crying.

They began to breathe again when the police arrived in the evening to say that they had found me in Massa Carrara. 'In Massa Carrara? And how did he get there?' asked my father.

I went back to school two days later. I was ready to go back right away, but Mamma said that I had to take it easy. When I arrived they treated me like a hero. They all said, 'You're crazy,' but with an envious smile, as if to say, 'Good for you for being so courageous,' and in the bathrooms, during recreation, other boys would pass me a cigarette butt to smoke without me even asking them. Until the day before I'd been a loser; now I was a celebrity. What can I say? I was pleased.

Formally, things at home continued like before. Every afternoon they would send me to the youth club, I would make sure Don Russo saw me, and then I would leave. I was always at the public gardens, with a group of friends all a bit older than me. We would smoke, we would talk about women, and we said a lot of swear words loudly, especially when old folks passed and any adults. The old ladies would turn around: 'You rude boys!' And then we would walk around the Standa discount shop, always around the same aisle. 'Peppe's route', it was called. I never understood who this Peppe was. We would meet girls from the middle school. They would look at us and smile, nothing more. By seven-thirty we were all at home. When I ran into Rosetta she would pretend not to know me. One time I waited for her near to Building M. I spent an entire week trying to find the courage and the determination to speak to her. My friends chided me, 'You went all the way to Massa Carrara and you're afraid to speak with Rosetta?'

I confronted her: 'We were supposed to go to the movies.'

'I don't remember.'

'What do you mean, you don't remember? What about the research I did for you on Russia?'

She cut me dead: 'I have to go home, it's late.'

'So what about the cinema?'

'We'll talk about it some other time.' Thank you and goodbye. But I never again had the honour of speaking with her, and after a few evenings I heard that she had started going out with that guy Armando, and my friends started calling me the Stag. Meaning someone tall and dark. And the more it bugged me the more they called me that name. I wanted to beat him up. Actually, when I was alone I would always think that I would beat him up. In my day dreams. I dreamed of beating everyone up. I would be the world heavyweight champion. I would even beat Cassius Clay, and I would become very rich. And all-powerful. They would elect me Duce – or maybe even King – and I would win back the empire. I could go on dreaming for hours, for days. I would interrupt if I was distracted by outside events – if someone called me, or if I had homework to do – but as soon as I finished I would start exactly where I had left off. I started from now, age fourteen, and I would go on until I grew up. Beautiful women. Each more beautiful than the last. And Rosetta would come back and beg me on her knees. Then I would start all over again, and every once in a while I would insert some variant, but in the end I always became the Duce – or the King – and it was a real life, I wasn't imagining. I was really better off living like that. It was the sudden recall back into this world that was the truly dysfunctional fiction. Once when I was arguing with Otello, who had been domineering with me yet again, it slipped out: 'I'll show you when I become...' and I just managed to shut my mouth in time.

'When you become what?' he asked me right away. And he was laughing.

I couldn't reply, 'When I become Duce.' I pretended not to hear him.

However, Massa Carrara had now changed my status. When I was with my friends, I would say, 'I fight here, I fight there,' and I saw that they listened to me. They believed what I said. They believed more than I did: 'He beats people up.' I liked the fact that they took me seriously, but I was worried: 'Sooner or later I'll have to really beat someone up; it's not enough just to talk about it.' And I got into big trouble. One time these friends of mine decided to go on strike. They would go to school in the afternoon shift because there weren't enough classrooms for us all to go in the morning, but they were fed up with the schedule, and they asked me to help them. I did. They were all agreed on the strike, the entire class, but one boy, after we left, tried to be a smart alec and went back. He was there long enough to be marked as present on the class register. We found him in the road as he was returning home. He pretended not to know what was going on: 'Anyhow, they sent me away too.'

'Yeah, right, but you're marked as present, and we're marked as absent.'

'It really doesn't mean anything; I just did it to keep my father happy.'

We were all pissed off. He had to be taught a lesson. So I punched him in the face a couple of times. But they were big swings, starting low and making a wide circle, with my arm way out. He gave me two back, but straight and close, and he got me just above my nose. I was about to return his punches, but the others stepped in and pulled us apart: 'That's enough, make friends.'

I pulled myself away. For me it wasn't over, far from it. But there was nothing to be done: they got in between us, until everything boiled over again and he got me in the balls. He won because my nose was bleeding and he didn't have a mark on him. I had lost. This is what pissed me off, not the blood from my nose or the crusts that coagulated in my nostrils for a week. My mother noticed right away, as soon as we got home. Not my nose, but the buttons on my shirt. When you're in a fight, the first things that go are the buttons on your shirt, and then the strap of your watch. And she finished what he'd started: 'You're always getting in trouble,' and she hit me on the head and on the shoulders. And this after I'd lost.

So I decided: 'I have to become a boxer.' And I went to the gym, which was under the basement of Building M. The coach asked me, 'What's your job?'

'Student.'

'This gym is for working men,' and he gave me a dirty look. First – as soon as he'd seen me – he was all happy. 'You're skinny, but it doesn't matter, you'll become more robust with age.' Now he was coming up with a thousand excuses: 'You're too tall and too skinny. Basketball would be better.' He really wanted me to go away. In the end he said I needed parental consent: 'Bring your father here and I'll speak with him.'

When I told Papà, he almost fainted: 'With all the sports in the world, why did you have to choose boxing?' When he was a boy he'd been mad about football and cycling. And cars: 'If there are two sports I can't stand, they're boxing and horse racing.'

'Alright, but what do horses have to do with it? I'm not asking to become a jockey, I want to box.'

'Precisely: boxing and horse racing. I've never been able to stand either.'

'But what do horses have to do with it?'

'Are you still going on about this?' And then he was pissed off: 'I'm trying to explain it to you. I'm against it. I won't give you my consent.' And then he went on for days trying to convince me to go to football camp. He even told me – seeing as I was always going around with his bicycle or my mother's – that I should buy myself a racing bike. When I first left the seminary every Sunday afternoon – when the San Marco choir didn't have a concert – he would take me to Latina Scalo to visit his father, my grandfather, who was at the Belladonna farm. We would go by bike, two girls' bikes, black, pre-war Bianchi. I didn't want to, but he made me go. And then my grandfather would always give me 500 silver lire. Along the road – it was totally straight – not a single car would pass by in those days. And every once in a while he would say, 'I'll race you from here to the second field: go!' and he would take off, because when he was young he'd even done some racing. He had come here to Agro Pontino on his bicycle, from Umbria, and that's how he always got around. At the time of the draining of the marshes he would sleep at Casal delle Palme and he would leave at four in the morning to go ploughing – with Motomeccanica tractors – in Borgo Hermada or Borgo Montenero, which were on the other side of Agro. He would win every time. I would try to make an effort, on the pedals, but he would always win.

A short while after I came back from Massa Carrara one Sunday he said to me, 'Let's go to grandpa's.' I didn't want to. 'He'll give you 500 lire.' I still didn't want to go. 'I'll give you another 500.' So I went. It was eight kilometres. Just after we left Latina, right near the central dairy, he said to me, 'From here to that field: go!' and he began to hit the pedals. I still remember him, with his elbows out wide, bent over the handlebars. At the start he had a few metres on me, but I wouldn't let him get away and I stayed on his tail. When I saw that I was making it and I was right behind him, I began to feel confident, I realised that I could do it. I kept pushing. And he began to fall back. I gradually moved forward a few metres. I passed him. And the more I pedalled, the more I laughed. But I wasn't laughing at him. I was laughing for me. I was laughing with joy, and I kept pedalling. Then he stopped, he gave up trying to catch me. I waited for him at the field: 'I slaughtered you,' I said to him, thinking that he would be happy; I really did. But he was furious.

'I had to stop: my chain fell off.' And then, 'That's enough, stop it now!' he said when I continued to tease him. And when I suggested another race, 'From here to that field,' he said no. We didn't do any more sprints, and we never again went – together – to Scalo. He took me a few other times to visit my grandfather, but we took the bus. I sometimes went on my bike – but alone.

But this time when I asked him for permission to learn boxing, he told me, 'I'll buy you a racing bike, brand new, like I always wanted for myself.'

'What am I supposed to do with a racing bike?'

'Cycle.'

'But I want to be a boxer; cycling's not my thing.'

'What do you mean, you beat me that time?' Aha, so that story about the chain wasn't true after all then. 'That time I thought right away that you had a talent for cycling.' There was nothing to be done; I didn't want a racing bike. In the end at least I convinced him to come and see for himself. I told him that it wasn't to learn how to fight, it was more about working out: 'They do weights and gymnastics.'

He came. He wandered around the gym. He looked at the guys pummelling the bag and the guys playing in the ring with their gloves. He spoke with the coach: 'Where are the weights?'

'What weights? Here the only weight we're interested in is the one on the scales where we weigh the boxers.'

When he came away he was furious: 'I don't want to hear anything more about this: I've never been able to stand boxing or horse racing. All those men fighting with each other. What did I bring you into this world for, to go out and get beat up?' he said as we walked down the street. 'This is not good for you.'

For a while I continued to go to the gym in the evenings and watch the others training. I began to make friends with the younger guys. Then one time the coach asked me, 'So what about your father?'

'He said OK.'

'Fine, start tomorrow,' and the next day I started. My mother gave me one of Otello's old knapsacks, with clothes to change into – a shirt, shorts, a towel – but she said, 'Leave it there; don't bring anything home, otherwise he'll notice.' Sometimes I would bring my towel home on the sly, to have it washed. Months and months of working out always with the same clothes, without ever washing them. But even the others – the ones who didn't need permission – didn't seem to change their clothes any more often. Just the professionals, the oldest ones. Everyone else smelled sweaty like me. The showers and the changing rooms were at the back, but you could smell the sweat as soon as you entered – and as soon as you went down the stairs – with just a slight hint of camphor from the massages.

But the coach always considered me 'the student'. He never wasted too much time on me. He left me for months working on footwork – one-two, one-two down the corridor – backwards and forwards, in front of the mirrors, just to learn how to do uppercuts. He never had time to put me on the punchbag: 'I'll let you have a go next week.' Then the next week a new guy would come along, really built, already a middleweight, and maybe he would be a builder or a butcher, and he would have big hands, and then the coach would send him to the punchbag right away, and he would give him tips, and the next week he would put him in the ring to take and receive punches.

However, I never became demoralised; I knew that I had it in me. 'I'll become a champion,' I told Sergio when we went out. He was my best friend. He must have been seventeen. He was a gentle person, good. Sensitive. He was a builder. In his family they were five boys, all Communists. I tried to convince him: 'But how can you be a Communist? You're such a nice person.'

'It's a family tradition,' and he wouldn't be moved. He was really crazy about boxing. He had technical skill. He was the best one in the gym, the one who – according to the coach – had the most talent. He already had five or six matches under his belt, as a novice and as an amateur; he'd won on points but without being enthusiastic, and some he had tied. But in the gym, in training, he was amazing for his technical ability, control, speed, power. He had all the punches, not just one: the direct, the jab, the hooks, both right and left. The coach made him use professional gloves, a sparring partner. Celio Turrino – a heavyweight, 120 kilos, who had even fought for the Italian title – only wanted him. And also Mario Libertini, who had gone from being an amateur to being the European welterweight champion. He was a featherweight, 63 kilos, but he was better than Cassius Clay in training. In matches and in competition he would get emotional. He would become stiff, unbending. He lost speed. The things that came to him naturally in the gym, he would forget in the ring. The coach had to shout at him from the corner – 'Give him the jab. Turn around. Give him the hook' – and he would do as he was told. But with a delay, as if he was advising his adversary before starting. It was painful to watch. Every time you would wait for it: 'Now Sergio's going to let rip.' But he never did. He would only get into his groove in the final minute of the third round, when the match was about to finish, and then in some way the verdict was balanced out. But up to that point it would be painful to watch. The coach would say, 'He's hard to fuel up, he needs the third round. When he becomes a professional (the matches are longer) he'll knock them all out.' But he didn't knock anyone out, just a couple of KOs, then he stopped. He tried and tried again, but then he would stop. Even as a professional he only got into his groove at the very last minute, even if there were six, eight or nine rounds. He would just make it at the end, when there was nothing more to do, as if at that point he was saying, 'I have nothing more to lose,' and only then could he start to really give his all. Until that point he would be blocked: 'It's the emotion,' he said, not the punches. He had never in his life fought anyone outside the ring, he had never even argued with anyone; but that's because he was kind, gentle. He wasn't afraid of anyone, and when once, by accident, he knocked his adversary out in the first round, in a tournament in Sermoneta, he threw himself to the ground with him as if to help him up, and after the match he was incredibly considerate. 'Is it better now? How do you feel?' and the other guy had to reassure him: 'Fine, fine. Don't worry.' He gave his best when he met a real fighter: he lowered his guard and let him go for it, without fear; then he got out. So he wasn't afraid of getting hit, just of looking bad.

Anyhow, the summer arrived and I had finished my first year of high school. With good grades in design and maths, even. My mother, when the grades were released, said, 'You've done half your duty,' and sent me back to work at the Hotel del Mare. This year I was a bit bigger, a bit more with it – even if I felt exactly the same as the year before – and Signora Visconti gave me 750 lire a day, every day, 30 days, 22,500 lire every month, plus tips. I spent all summer at the seaside in long trousers, looking at the others swimming and sunbathing, and having fun with the girls. All in their bikinis. I never swam; I didn't even know how to swim. Or, I should say, I would jump in sometimes, but I mostly stayed on the shore like a little child: I was terrified of the water.

The gym was closed for a while. When it reopened, the coach sent us all home anyway – 'Come back in October' – because Sandro Mazzinghi had to meet Cecil Mott for the junior middleweight world title match in Terracina, and he'd asked to be able to train at our gym. The coach was proud, and in order to have space he sent everyone away. He only kept on the professionals and the very best amateurs, to allow them to practise with Mazzinghi. He always wanted Sergio. I would go to watch some evenings – the gym was full of spectators – and I showed off that I knew my way around. But no one took any notice of me, except for the coach. Actually, just Sergio and Mazzinghi, who said 'Ciao' to me every once in a while. So in September – when the hotel had shut at the end of the season, school hadn't yet re-opened, and the gym was still closed – I had a little time to myself. I spent every day out and about with new friends. We would go to the seaside in the beginning, then we would go farther afield hitchhiking. There were three of us. Paolo was on the ball: we would go to the discount store, he would look around, we covered him on both sides, and he would put something – anything – under his shirt or down his trousers: records, swimsuits, T-shirts, perfumes. Then we would share the spoils. Once he took a pair of flippers for me. In a shop in Terracina he was able to lift a snorkelling mask. What can I say? I was scared to death. I would tremble. Before we went inside I would say, 'There don't seem to be many people: they'll see us.'

'Are you afraid?' he would ask.

'No,' and I would go in to guard him. Then we shared. Either the stuff or the money from what we were able to sell on. We would even shoplift to order. People would tell us, 'I need this and that,' and we would go to Standa and lift it. We were practically professional thieves. We continued throughout the winter.

In September, at the seaside, they would jump in wearing masks and they would swim far out, but I stayed on the beach, because I was afraid of the water. Paolo would tease me, 'What does it take? Just jump in and swim.'

In the end I was fed up, I said yes. I could hardly continue to be a scaredy-cat, and we went to the wharf of the nuclear power plant. We got right to the end, more than a kilometre from the shore, where the ships docked. I sat on the wharf with my legs hanging down. Federico jumped first, then he waited for me. Paolo pushed me in and then he came too. From the quay to the top of the water must have been eight metres, and the water was probably just as deep. The jump only took a second, I didn't even feel it; the fear beforehand was worse. But when I touched the water and I began to go down, I thought I would die. Paolo had told me, 'Move your hands and you'll see … you'll come back up to the surface.' But I moved my hands and I kept going down. I started to panic: 'Alright,' I thought then. 'Anyhow sooner or later one has to die,' and suddenly I stopped going down and I slowly came up. Everyone applauded me, and I began to move the flippers and we went back to the shore; and I wasn't afraid any more. But I was still afraid of stealing. Let me explain: if I had been certain that no one would ever catch us, I would have continued to steal all my life. What blocked me was just the fear that they would catch me, not the act of theft itself. I didn't see anything wrong with stealing. As a matter of fact, one evening, seeing as we didn't have any particular requests, I took a piece of smoked cheese from the Standa food counter. I took it specifically for my mother, as a gift. When I went home and gave it to her I was really happy. She was happy too that I had thought of her, and she wanted to reimburse me. I refused. She insisted: 'But come on, how much did you pay for it?'

'Nothing, nothing.'

'But what do you mean nothing? You must have paid something for it. Where did you get the money?' So I told her: I told her that I had taken it for free, there was no need for her to reimburse me. It looked like she was about to pass out. She didn't scream, she didn't make a scene. She just went white and gave me a look that when I remember it today still makes me feel ashamed. She wouldn't let it go: 'How long has this been going on?'

'But no,' I said, 'what are you thinking?'

'Promise you'll never do it again.' And I promised.

But when I told Paolo he was upset: 'What about the money? Don't you like having the money?'

'Yes,' but finally – with the excuse that I had promised my mother – I was able to rid myself of that awful weight. I was scared out of my wits in the store, although I have to say that when my mother told me, 'What a shame, what a shame! Imagine what would happen if they caught you,' I strongly suspect that even for her, the worry wasn't that what I was doing was wrong, but that she was afraid that they would catch me.

By then the gym had opened again. The Tokyo Olympics were in full swing, and when I went out with Sergio and the others we would stand in a line in front of Andreoli, on the high street, to watch the televisions in the window, in black-and-white, when there were boxing matches. The Olympics were fantastic, Italy won so many gold medals: Arcari, Atzori, Pinto in the mid-heavyweight category. And we would act out the moves on the pavement, in front of the window. The coach finally let me use the punchbag and even the punchball, and every once in a while he would even spend some time with me. I think it was Sergio who once told him, 'Coach, you have to train him too,' and he put me through some moves to make him happy. I even went into the ring with gloves, but never with Sergio. The coach put me with some novices and a couple of amateurs. I could defend myself well; I had good instincts, intelligence. I dodged. I feinted. I took some good shots. Especially the long left swing: I would feign a jab – short and direct – inside the adversary's guard, but then I would pass below, turn my arm, and give him the long wide left on his face, on the other side, bypassing his guard. It's true that I would leave myself uncovered like that, but the surprise effect always worked.

I wasn't bad. I thought I was OK and so did Sergio, but I wasn't strong enough. I was a lightweight, sixty-three and a half kilos and over six feet tall: a matchstick, I simply wasn't strong enough. I would dodge, I would jump, I would set up the shots. But when I took the shots, they had no effect; my adversaries didn't even feel them. But I really felt it when they hit me. They were builders, carpenters, welders. Well proportioned in height and weight. With calluses on their hands and muscles on their arms. When they hit me it hurt. But this isn't what worried me; it was the coach's face that worried me: I wanted his approval. He never gave it to me. Sergio would say, 'You did well, today,' and so would Michele, who had been the regional novice champion and had just become an amateur. When I boxed with him I saw right away that his punches didn't go deep, he didn't want to hurt me, and when I put him in the corner and he closed his guard and his abs went rock-solid, I heard him say to me in a low voice so that the coach wouldn't hear, 'Hit me now. Give it all you've got.' I didn't though, and not just because I couldn't, but because it seemed wrong. For me, maybe it was just a question of keeping my guard up; I didn't feel like really fighting someone. Then one night he put me with a bantamweight. The coach said that he was the best, and he really believed it, he had to show me. He began dancing, jumping. He swung his punches, he swung them with all his might, but he didn't do anything to me: he didn't know where to aim, but I knew where to take them. He seemed to be mocking me, but it was still a good match: he never broke down my guard, but I caught him out a few times. I was happy, and then when the assistant, Giorgi, helped me take my gloves off in the end, I modestly told him, 'I didn't do so well,' certain that his response would be, 'What do you mean? You were excellent.'

But no. He said, 'We all have our different talents.' It was like a knife through the heart. Then he came into the changing room when he saw that I went quiet. To console me. And then he added, 'You're a good student,' as if to say, 'Lucky you.' I never went back.

chapter 4

My second year of high school was not off to an auspicious beginning: I had a new Italian teacher. The teacher from the previous year – Miss Valentini, who was the daughter of our local doctor – made me write. Essays weren't enough for her; she wanted us to write short stories. She had a little publishing company – they produced local-interest stuff – and she would say, 'Who knows? Maybe one day we'll publish your stories.' She was especially fixated on Manzoni's historical novel *The Betrothed*: she would make me rewrite passages, setting them in the present day. I enjoyed it. I would type my work on a portable typewriter that a missionary had given to Manrico as a gift before they kicked him out of the seminary. When I typed as he was reading, he would scowl, 'That's a load of crap! You don't know how to write.' But my teacher would show my work to her colleagues. He would say, 'Miss Valentini doesn't understand shit. If she were any good, she wouldn't be teaching at that technical school.' As a matter of fact she had told my mother, 'I don't understand why you didn't enrol this boy at the lyceum.' To my mother, of all people. Why didn't she tell me? In the afternoons, at home, I would still translate Latin passages for pleasure – this time for Mimì, who was studying Latin at middle school. I kept on doing them for her right through her studies at the lyceum.

She was a socialist – Miss Valentini, not Mimì – but nonetheless she would listen to my opinion, she would let me say anything that came into my mind. She would never become angry when I interrupted or took positions, and the most she would do was to smile when I became really opinionated. I would interrupt and give my own views in almost every class. I even had controversial opinions about geometry. My classmates would laugh, but the teachers were never angry with me.

But the next year Miss Valentini left to teach at the lyceum after all, and we were given another teacher for Italian. Miss Valentini was tall, blonde, rather Rubenesque, with wide shoulders, but she was one lady who really knew how to carry herself: like a princess. She was thirty-five or forty years old, but her voice was warm and gravelly. She was never shrill. She would speak softly, but you could hear her even down the hallway, because others would be silent when she spoke. I was in love with her, and whenever she entered the room the boys would fight over the front seats, because when she crossed her legs, it was to die for. For an entire year, she took the place of Pauline Bonaparte in my heart.

The new teacher was younger. She must have been about thirty. She was married. Neapolitan. Short, ugly and overweight. You couldn't say a word for fear that she would give you an acidic look. At the end of the year, she failed me. I flunked Italian. The other teacher had wanted to publish my short stories, and this one flunked me, just because I wrote that I didn't give a hoot about the Tree Festival. She always gave us boring essay topics: 'Speak well of goodness'; 'The virtues of peace and democracy'; 'All's well that ends well' – it didn't take long for me to be completely repulsed. I wanted to write about things that aroused my passions. Not her, she just wanted to hear banalities. Whenever she would assign an essay – with Miss Valentini I would be just dying to put pen to paper – it was worse than doing PE. Like that stupid climbing-rope exercise. What the hell does it mean to speak well of goodness? All I could possibly think of to say had already been said. Hard as I tried, I just didn't know what else to add. And then let's think about it: but if everyone has already said all there is to say, then why are you asking me my opinion? If you ask me – I would think in sheer desperation every time she assigned one of these essays – obviously it must be because you want my personal opinion. And that's what I gave her.

The day before they had taken us by coach to Sezze for the Tree Festival: one do-gooder windbag after another got up on to the podium to speak, then a priest gave the blessing and four rustics pretended to plant two miserable fir cut-outs: a total bore. And the next day at school she had the nerve to inflict on us the torture of an essay entitled 'The Tree Festival'. I wrote that I didn't give a damn: all this scare-mongering about the fact that one day there might not be enough trees didn't mean anything to me, even if someone predicted that, given current deforestation, life on earth would be impossible in a hundred or a hundred and fifty years: 'So what?' I concluded. 'I certainly won't be alive then. There shouldn't be any problems during my lifetime. The problems will occur later. Therefore I don't care about the trees.'

But she did give a damn. She went berserk. She didn't laugh, she didn't appreciate my irony, and she didn't even seem to notice the fact that my ideas – although they were divergent from her own – were expressed in good Italian, which, at the end of the day, was the whole point of the exercise. No. She simply went berserk: 'How dare you express such opinions?' and she sent me to see the principal.

To tell the truth, when he and I were alone, he laughed about it, he teased me: 'You'll make a fine surveyor! You're supposed to be designing the relationship between man and the environment, and you don't give a hoot about trees? We're off to a great start.' But he was laughing.

'It was just supposed to be witty,' I explained.

'Ah, so you come to school to be a joker?' He started preaching for half an hour. In the end he went serious, and told me, 'You can't play the joker with your teachers,' and he was right.

She was there waiting for me, when I returned to class, with a vindictive glint in her eyes, and she had to know what had happened: 'So? What did the principal have to say to you?' What did she expect – that I would return to the classroom in tears?

'Nothing, he laughed.'

And she went even more berserk than before: 'I'll fail you. Just you watch, you'll fail the year.' And when my mother went to the parent–teacher meeting – she was as punctual as a Swiss watch, she never missed once – she told her, 'He's disrespectful, arrogant, presumptuous. He never shuts up and he always tries to have the last word.' And she told me the same things in class: 'You don't know your place.'

My mother crucified me: 'You've offended her, go to beg her forgiveness or you'll have to repeat the year,' and so I did. I asked if I could speak to her alone, and I apologised.

'Ah, now you're coming to me to apologise? I had more respect for you before, now you've really made a fool of yourself.'

'You bitch,' I thought to myself, 'What the fuck do you want from me? First you tell me I don't know my place, then when I apologise, you treat me like dirt? I hope one day you'll pay for this.' But I persisted with my apology, hoping to get back into her good books. I was also scared to death by my mother and the fact that, if I failed this course, I would lose my scholarship for the next three years. I told her so. It only made matters worse: 'So that's why you've come to me,' and she even went to tell the rest of the class. What a bitch. That's where all my problems started. I ended the year with an average of seven and a half: I had sevens and eights even in design, chemistry and maths. But I failed Italian. I became fed up with school. Not just the technical college, but education in general, teachers, and basically all of humanity: 'Never trust anyone and never bow down to anyone: when you bow down, you're finished.' She was even a Social Democrat, the bitch.

So I went back to the Fascist movement. You might ask, 'What does that have to do with anything?' Everything. I had nothing to do, no pleasure in life. The remainder of the school year was already ruined, no matter what I did, so at this point all that was left was to change society. So I went back to Fascism.

I had spent some time at the Fascist club the previous year with my friends, shortly after coming back from Massa Carrara. There were about ten boys my age. The provincial youth secretary was a guy called Gianfranco, and he was studying at the science lyceum. We would go to party headquarters in the afternoons to play ping-pong on the table in the main room. Once or twice the chairman would look in and smile at us. Nothing more than that. This was the full extent of our political activism: playing ping-pong. One time the chairman gave Gianfranco some funds. He and the others decided to buy us a Monopoly set. 'Are you joking?' I tried to ask. 'We're supposed to be planning a revolution, not playing Monopoly.' No one listened. Once or twice we prepared a poster, the ones that were put up on the town notice board in the main square.

But even with these posters I found myself in conflict with everyone. They wanted funny one-liners and caricatures of the bourgeoisie 'to make people laugh'. I became angry, I wanted to tell the story of Fascism, how the swamps were drained. Not them. And Gianfranco told me, 'I'm the secretary.' 'He's the secretary,' the others echoed, as if to say, 'If you don't like it here, you can get lost. One less person playing ping-pong.' And so I left, but I was furious. That night, at home, secretly, I made my own poster. It said that as well as playing ping-pong they had ripped off an Easter egg that the chairman had left in his office. I signed it 'an anarchist', and I posted it on the notice board in the piazza del Popolo. Thanks for the memories. For me, it was over.

But then, a short time after the Tree Festival, I ran into Gianfranco, who told me to come back. They'd all left. They were fed up with playing Monopoly and ping-pong. The ping-pong equipment was in bad condition, and apparently at the Christian Democrat party headquarters everything was brand new. So I would go sometimes in the evenings. There would be three or four of us, nothing more. There was Gianfranco, his younger brother, me and Wolf, who was at art college and about my age (his real name was Filiberto, but we all called him Wolf because he was a bit rough and ill-mannered; he was a huge fellow, tall, well-built, short black hair in a brush cut, a unibrow like Bergomi, and he always had a surly look on his face). There was also Piermario, who was also at art college, and he seemed to think of himself as a sort of intellectual, or so it appeared to me.

Naturally, I was the only one who thought so, and I didn't like this Piermario guy much. Not Gianfranco: he was the secretary, and therefore his authority wasn't up for discussion. He had been invested by the chairman: that was enough; anyhow we certainly didn't have any elections, it was like Fascist times; you followed the chain of command from above. And rightly so. Moreover, Gianfranco always agreed with me, he never tried to prove that he knew better. All he cared about was that his authority should be respected, and I always did respect him. But we only went there sometimes, not every night; as a matter of fact we didn't go at all for quite some time.

We went back again at the beginning of June. School was winding up, and the season at the Hotel del Mare hadn't begun yet. The party headquarters seemed like a battlefield. They had given the work of re-painting to a firm that evidently hired Communist painters. The floors were covered with a layer of paint. They hadn't even bothered to sweep up. Before they left, the painters must have specially prepared the overflowing rubbish bins. They threw garbage everywhere.

The grown-ups – the chairman and two or three others – looked on us like manna from heaven. Not just on the political-strategic front, because there weren't any other young members, but from an actuarial-hygienic point of view: they could no longer enter the office; they would stay downstairs by the main door in the evening. They would have meetings in the bar. They made us clean up. At the end of the day even Mussolini had always said that the Fatherland is served even guarding a tank of petrol. And we were all happy. Me, Wolf, Piermario, another guy called Andrea. Not Gianfranco: he had already gone to San Felice for the summer, 'Because my mother says so.' We got cleaning. We were on our hands and knees scrubbing the floors. We didn't even have proper brushes, but we made do with what we had been given. We laboured by the sweat of our brows for about ten days. Every afternoon we would be on our hands and knees scrubbing, then we would tidy up and give the place a mop. Forget just guarding the trash cans. The chairman and Bompiani came in the evening. They would look at the progress we had made and say, 'Well done, well done.'

When we reached the main room we decided to stop: anyhow, we'd done the essentials. But the secretary general passed by, a book-keeper for the Finance Ministry, whose wife had just recently died: 'Would you please be so kind and clean this room for me?'

We had never seen him before, and we didn't even like the look of him much, maybe because he didn't get along too well with the chairman. But we felt badly for his wife, so we said yes. 'But let's be quick about it,' said Wolf right away as soon as he left. It was sheer torture scratching all the filth out of the Venetian flooring. We used so many buckets of water that it seemed like the Polesine flood, and then we got mopping. As we threw the buckets of water onto the floor we laughed, as if to say, 'If it makes him happy.' But in the end it was as bright as a mirror, the paint melted away, and it was easy-peasy to clean. It took us less than an hour to finish. Nothing like the other rooms. Wolf had so much fun he was almost inclined to do it again.

As far as we were concerned, Fascism had started with Benito Mussolini, who had drained the marshes and established the towns we lived in. So we were born here, not in Marzabotto up North. If we'd been born in Marzabotto, it would have been a different story. Talk is cheap: in every street in town you can hardly take a step without finding a manhole cover with the Fascist insignia and big lettering: LITTORIA. Not Latina. For us every stone – from the church of San Marco to the Town Hall – had been put here by Mussolini, and he had drained the marshes himself, alone. When we saw scratches on the marble of the buildings, memories of the liberation, it seemed to us like blasphemy, when his words and the symbols of the regime were erased and wrecked. They tried to cover them up on the council houses, but they reappeared right away, and from a mile away you could see the words 'We shall win', and especially the two biggest graffiti, 'The plough traces the furrow but the sword defends it', and the other one, which always sounded in my ears as a warning, even as a very young boy: 'If you are not willing to die for your faith, you are not worthy of professing it'. Every time that I passed underneath, since I was a small boy, I always renewed my promise.

Then we gradually rectified and added a few ideas. The enrichment of our ideological heritage occurred gradually, inexorably, evening after evening, as we listened to the stories told by the chairman, Bompressi and Livio Nastri. Much had been done during the first twenty years of Fascism, but that was nothing to what would be done later: it was the Fascism of the social republic that mattered. If the republic had won, Italy would have become a paradise. What Mussolini did for his people had never been seen before, not even in Russia: labour papers, pensions, summer camps. And the socialisation? In the National Labour State the workers had the right to participate in the management and in the profits of companies, there was no class warfare. That's what the NLS would have done.

'What does National Labour State mean?' we asked once.

'It's late now,' the chairman looked at his watch, 'and then it's complicated, it will take a long time to explain. Let's talk about it another evening.' But we liked the war stories best of all. They really knew how to tell them well, adding all the actions. They made us feel like we had even been there, and when we left there was a strange sensation of power that stayed with us, mixed with remorse: '125 submarines. What the fuck have we missed out on?'

Anyhow, at a certain point I returned to work at the Hotel del Mare. One afternoon, as I was walking past her house, Signora Visconti stopped me: 'So are you coming back to work for us?' Right then and there I said no. I had my labour book at last, and this year, finally, I wanted to go to the sugar manufacturing plant. Tinned meats aside, it seemed like a more serious option: you do your work and you go home, and you don't have to be anyone's servant. But she persevered: 'To the sugar manufacturing plant? As a factory worker? But that's dirty work. Come back to us, we need someone trustworthy: you're like one of the family.'

So I went back. But I made my conditions clear. She gave me 1500 lire per day and one day off a week: 'As long as it's not Saturday or Sunday,' agreed Signora Visconti.

So I started work. In the most special role. At the beachside bar. It was special because there I was responsible for the cash register, as well as serving fruit juices and ice creams, but especially because I had to keep an eye on the lifeguards. They never trusted the lifeguards. Signora Visconti more so than her husband. When she got up in the morning, she would look out onto the balcony of the room and she would begin to count – one by one – all the umbrellas that were open on the private beach and all the sunloungers. Then she rushed to the bar to check if I had taken the right number of ticket stubs and the subscriptions for the number of open umbrellas. She was convinced that the lifeguards were renting them out on the side and pocketing the money. She was certain. And she was even upset when our controls showed that nothing was amiss: 'Sooner or later I'll get them. I have to understand their game.'

I sided with the Viscontis, because I've always been a bit of an idiot: if someone is kind to me I become their faithful puppy-dog. So at the end of the day, when I closed the cash register and added up the takings – I kept the tips in a separate drawer to one side – if I found any irregularity, I would blame it on them: 'I must have made a mistake in entering some item. Perhaps I forgot to include the ice creams.' Wasn't I part of the family? But honestly, at a certain point it seemed that they were going too far in persecuting these lifeguards, and I tried to defend them: 'Look, Signor Visconti, I can assure you: they are two very decent men.'

'Two decent men? They're two sons of bitches. Do you think that everyone is like you? They'd steal anything that wasn't nailed down.'

Anyhow, things went on for almost a month. I was happy. The pay seemed good, and with the tips at the bar I almost doubled what I took home. There was just a bit of trouble about the day off. Every time there was something. They had to find someone to take my place. The Signora tried to convince me: 'I'll pay you extra,' but I needed that day off like I needed the air to breathe. Hell, it was my summertime, too. Then she began to postpone it: 'You can go the day after tomorrow.' The day after tomorrow, the day after tomorrow, it never happened. At a certain point I got fed up: 'Tomorrow I want my day off,' but I wasn't able to find her to tell her I'd be away: she would always take off somewhere. So I told her brother-in-law, her husband's brother. He would make us all double over with laughter. He was nothing like his brother or his sister-in-law. I told him, Signor Federico, and he replied, 'Alright, stay at home. Maybe I'll look after the bar,' and I took the day off.

In the end it wasn't even anything special, I woke up a little later than usual and I went to the seaside. I even went by the hotel, to go for a swim and exchange a few words with the lifeguards. But when I returned the next day, Signora Visconti was ready to declare war. She didn't hold back, she screamed like a fishwife: 'Who gave you permission?'

'Signor Federico.'

'And who's Signor Federico? Here I'm the one in charge.'

He swore to her, 'He decided it all himself. I told him it wasn't possible, but he insisted he was taking this day off. What could I say to him?'

What could I say? I didn't say anything. It wasn't his fault: she was a harpy. She began shrieking at me: 'I never want to see you again. That's no way to behave, after I took you on as a favour to your mother.'

At that point, I lost it. I must have said something to her; probably about the sugar manufacturing plant, and that my mother had nothing to do with this. And she kept on going, but she changed her tune, from imperious to simply threatening: 'Don't raise your voice! Is this what you've learned from that holy woman who is your mother? Wait till you see what I tell her,' and the more she mentioned my mother's name, the more furious I became. I was unyielding; I looked at her with an expression worthy of Father Cavalli. And I left. Fired. They gave me my money and I left. With everyone standing around and telling her she was right. They consoled her for my impudence. If I had kept my mouth shut, if I had apologised, if I had promised not to take another day off they would have taken me back. They would have forgiven me. Signor Federico came up to me on the sly, to see if I was angry with him. Was I angry? I was furious. But I didn't feel like making it weigh heavily on him: 'It doesn't matter.'

Then at home my mother had a similar meltdown. She wanted me to run after Signora Visconti and apologise. 'I've had enough of this apologising,' and I shut the door as I left the house.

'If you want, I'll go,' she shouted after me. Naturally, I didn't allow her to go.

I would wake up early in the morning – at around six – and I would go to the public weighing-station, with Wolf. That's where all the Neapolitan market traders met when they came to weigh their lorries for the watermelon campaign. And all the pickers would meet there too: the Slavs from the refugee camp and the unemployed of Latina. By now it was too late to go to the sugar-processing plant, and the only available work was watermelons. It was a terrible job. In those years, no one still planted the classic Italian watermelons, the round, black ones. They all planted Charlestons and the American varieties, big beasts which weighed between fifteen and twenty-five kilos. We would hand them to each other in a human chain from the fields, behind the picker, making piles here and there. Then the lorry would come down the dirt road; it couldn't come down into the fields because otherwise it would crush the watermelons that weren't ripe yet. We would make another human chain from the pile to the lorry and then load them. Because I was tall, they would always put me just next to the lorry to throw the Charlestons up. I earned more money than I would have as a waiter, but they certainly weren't giving it away, I sweated for every lira. There were even fights to find work, every morning the same thing: as soon as a trader arrived, an unruly crowd would form around him. They would choose you as if it were a cattle market, or the slave trade. They looked at your muscles, your height, and they especially liked ready-made teams, because they knew you would work well together. Sometimes you would be left behind, no one would take you; and you would continue to bivouac in front of the weighing station, smoking Nazionali and fighting with the Slavs until eleven or even midday. Sometimes there would be a little lorry of small, broken ones, the leftover watermelons that no one wanted, which were loaded to send them to Germany: 'They'll eat anything there.'

So you would make do even with working just for 2000 lire; other times there was nothing to be done and you would just have to go home. Then the watermelon harvest ended. One day, suddenly, there were no more Neapolitans at the weighing-station. They had all disappeared. They'd gone somewhere else. For the harvest of another fruit. And this work was over too. There was nothing more to be done. And the entire summer stretched ahead: 'Verrà/lo so/verrà/la fine d'agosto,' sang little Tony on the radio, but for now we were still at the beginning of the month. You might say, 'But a month isn't really that long.' Now. Back then it seemed like eternity.

So I began hitchhiking again. In the morning I would go to the seaside, and during the afternoon I would explore here and there. First I went to San Felice Circeo to visit Gianfranco, the youth secretary. Then I started going to all the different towns in our area. I would look for the Fascist Party offices. They would always be closed. I would ask for the secretary. I would go to visit him at home. I would ask if they had a youth group. But there wasn't anyone anywhere. Practically nothing. But then gradually I found a few believers: one in Roccagorga, a couple in Sonnino, one more in Terracina. In the evening I would write up my notes: 'Nothing in Sezze. The secretary in Maenza is an asshole,' and so on like this. Every once in a while I would go back to San Felice and report to Gianfranco. I spent hours under the blazing sun waiting for someone to give me a ride. And I would walk endlessly, looking for people, house by house. And the results weren't that great: just in Roccagorga, as I've said, in Terracina, Fondi and especially Formia did I find people – when I was finally able to locate them – who were happy to see me: 'Finally, a comrade.' But usually they were just annoyed: 'I have a lot to do.' But I didn't give up; I was always on the road one day after another: 'I want to meet these young Fascists.' I went everywhere.

Gianfranco would say, 'Sure, go for it, tell them that I sent you,' but no one had ever heard of him. He seemed to know about everything, even about the Fascist Party in Rome, about Michelini and Almirante, and especially the Avanguardia Nazionale. I didn't know anything about Rome, and I thought that everyone in the Avanguardia was big and tall. He said that if you weren't at least six feet tall they wouldn't take you. All these guys did was beat people up, they never spoke: they just sent around fighters. They were all friends of his, and sooner or later he would introduce me to one of them, who was on holiday nearby. Every evening when I left, he would insist, 'Do come back, let me know. We'll talk about it.' In actual fact I went there to talk about politics, but we never really did: I would go to his house looking for him – he would make me wait outside for at least fifteen minutes, he never invited me in – then he would come out and we would go together to see these friends of his; but they were just friends, like my friends from the public gardens. All we talked about was girls. Once he even said to me, in a very low voice, 'Don't talk about politics, because that guy's a Communist.' He would keep me there, with one excuse or another, until it got dark. Then he went home for dinner: 'Ciao.' I would go back to the road and head for Latina. In the dark. Everyone knows that it's harder to hitchhike at night than in broad daylight. Miles and miles on foot. In the end, I got fed up with going to San Felice: 'Why should I?' But the strange thing is that this thought came to me precisely the evening when he finally introduced me to the guy from the Avanguardia. He was tall, yes, but he wouldn't hurt a flea. He told me that he had never been in a fight, and that their leader, Stefano Delle Chiaie, was barely five feet tall.

'So what exactly do you do?' I asked them in the end.

'Nothing. We hang out at the bar in piazza Tuscolo and we chat.'

Of course I must have made an expression like someone who had just found out that Santa Claus doesn't exist, but when I had to leave Gianfranco gave me a lift on his scooter to the main road to hitch-hike. Then he stopped and said to me, 'Tell the chairman that I'm not the secretary any more. Tell him that I nominate you.'

He jumped around like Rintintin. He found me one evening when I was typing up the notes from my travels, and he started reading. He found it amusing, especially when I said that someone or other was a jerk. 'Look at this, look at this!' shouted Bompressi. 'You've hit the nail on the head.' However, he didn't want me to continue hitch-hiking. He thought it was undignified. He wanted to give me money for bus fares: 'It's petty cash.' I refused. It wasn't about the money, but really because I didn't like bus travel in general. I preferred hitch-hiking. That's the real reason I went out exploring; the inspection was an extra, almost an excuse to go hitchhiking. But he made a big deal out of it: 'You'll see,' said Bompressi. 'I bet we can start up a youth club again.'

They thought that a youth club was more than just having three or four boys hanging out in the offices and putting up posters at election time. A real youth club should be like it was in '56. That's all they talked about, when the secretary was Arnaldo Grazzi and they arranged meetings, conferences; they had a presence in every school and they even had a voice at the national level, and when events took their course in Budapest there were fights with the police in the piazza. Now Arnaldo Grazzi was in Potenza working as a clerk at the National Insurance office, and he wasn't a youngster any more either. The others had all lost touch: thanks for the memories. The moment had passed.

I was so envious, I would have given anything to have lived through those times, but at the time I was only six: 'When will it ever be like that again?'

There was nothing to be done; all I could do was to continue travelling through the area – hitchhiking – looking out for any young Fascists that might be left. So I would be quite tired when I returned home in the evening. Eight-thirty, nine. When I would go to San Felice, sometimes I would even get back at ten. They complained at home, but nothing much really happened. They were used to it by now, they had stopped putting the brakes on me. Gradually, after Massa Carrara, they began to resign themselves. Not in the beginning, though, especially not my father. One time Manrico was late home. He had gone to Rome with some of his friends, and they had rented a car. But on the way home it broke down, and Manrico didn't get back until 1 a.m. Otello and I were already in bed; we heard the door to the apartment open and he tiptoed towards our room. Suddenly there was a fuss, as if someone was banging the bathroom door and the bedroom door at the same time. Then Manrico came into the bedroom, and Otello asked him, 'What happened?'

'Nothing. Papà tripped going into the bathroom.'

He hadn't tripped at all. He'd been waiting for my brother there, in the hallway, and he beat him up in the dark. Without saying a word. Only at the end did he say, 'Serves you right.' He took it, without fighting back. He didn't react at all, not even to defend himself, not even to shield himself from the blows. I'm sure my father was preparing himself for another night like Massa Carrara, and when he saw Manrico come home he lost his mind.

My father hit me once too. One of the cots had broken. They were always breaking. Every year he would repaint them with metal paint, but every once in a while the weld on a joint would break. Then he would take them to his shop, at the Consortium, and he would re-weld them.

So one time I was taking them to him, but against my will. When he saw me arrive he must have been in an even worse mood than mine: 'What do you do at night that these cots are always breaking?' To tell the truth, I must have had a guilty conscience, but that was a cheap shot. I didn't appreciate it, and I must have given him a dirty look, and in front of his apprentice. Then he started to work on welding them, but he couldn't wait to get rid of me and get back to his own work. He barked orders – 'Come here! Do that! Hold this!' – as I held the cot and attached the clamps. What do I know, at a certain point maybe I wasn't quick enough in carrying out his commands, and he hit me, over the cot, right in the chest. With all his strength. He left a mark, the sign of his fist, dirty with diesel, on my shirt. I was horrified. He even said to me, 'You see, I can fight too.'

'But I didn't say anything,' I wanted to reply, but couldn't say a word, my throat was choked.

And he looked at his apprentice as if to say, 'Did you see that?' And the apprentice looked at me. I looked at my feet. If he'd hit me for Massa Carrara or for all the times I came home late, I would have understood him. But this time I really hadn't done anything, it was just that the apprentice was watching – maybe that's it. From that day on I couldn't stand him.

However, I must say that he didn't physically abuse us. Just those two times. But we were very much afraid of him, as children, especially me and Violetta. Mamma would always say to us, 'Wait till your father gets home,' but he would never hit us. He would just say, when he had really reached his limit, 'Look, I'm taking off my belt,' but he never did take it off. Just once, when we had no intention of going to bed and we were jumping on my parents' bed – we must have been five or six years old – Mamma said to him, 'But don't you know how to shut them up?' He came into our room, and that time he took his belt right off. He showed us, and that was enough, and that's how it was throughout our childhood. We were still afraid of him, even if he had never touched us. But my mother would slap us around two or three times a day. She kept on hitting my head until I was a grown man. She only stopped then because I had become too tall and she couldn't reach: she would still hit me on the shoulders with anything that came to hand: shoes, slippers, wooden spoons. And then she would say, 'Wait till your father gets home.' So it's no wonder we were all afraid of him.

Things continued just as they had before. Or rather something had changed, but it was difficult to discern. Manrico and Otello had finished school. Otello had begun to work. He should have left for his military service, but at that time there was an exemption for a family with three sons, according to which one – either the first or the third – could be exempted. It was either him or me. But no one even discussed the matter, not him, not Mamma. They automatically decided to exempt him. As far as I was concerned, too bad. Anyhow, he started looking for work, even if his principal activity was still playing pool at Bar del Corso. In the beginning, he went to work for an architect, but the pay was pretty bad, and then he worked with a firm that provided furnishings for shops. He looked after contracts, designed, met with clients.

Manrico enrolled in law at the university. Whenever Papà went to town, he would tell everyone he met that his son was studying law. And he really studied hard. He would take the train every morning and go to the university. He took his exams. After his first exam – natural law – he came home with top marks and Mamma cried. But she dried her eyes right away and told him, 'Keep it up.' He was handsome, good-natured, young and strong, like a heroic figure. On Sundays, whenever the San Marco choir was giving a concert somewhere, he would go with Papà, wearing a dark suit and the choir tie. He was the master of ceremonies. Before each concert began, he would introduce the pieces to the audience. He was the life of the party, everyone loved him. He would always wear a long, white scarf that he wrapped twice around his neck, allowing the ends to fall back over his shoulders and down his back to his waist. When he walked, he had the deportment of an actor. And he worked too, keeping the books for poor Glauco, who had a liquor sales business. He would go there in the evenings after dinner, and Glauco thought he walked on water too. I was the only one who didn't share this opinion, but it wasn't my fault; it was his, really. All this desire to be likeable had to have a counterweight, a release, just like a pressure cooker. He wanted to be loved by everyone in the world except me. He would always be a jerk to me, acting like a know-it-all.

He was an anarchist. Like Proudhon. He maintained that ownership is theft, while I was dreaming of becoming rich one day. During high school he joined the Young Socialist Federation. He said that I didn't understand anything, that Fascists were the supporters of the ruling class, enemies of the workers. As a child, he had been a Fascist too. In our family, everyone was a Fascist – and all of our relatives too. Most of them would vote for the Christian Democrats, but in their hearts they were all Fascists. Papà was the only true Christian Democrat. Uncle Carlino said that Aldo Moro was a Communist. Even Violetta held right-wing views when she was small – I mean in primary school

– and during the election campaigns we would collect pamphlets and pretend to make our own elections: the Monarchist Party would always win. She and I were ardent Monarchists. Or rather, I was a Fascist and a Monarchist, she was just a Monarchist. We wanted the royal family to return from exile. Now she was a Communist, but she didn't declare herself at home, she would just say, 'I support the left.' She studied from dawn to dusk. Always philosophy books. She would only leave home to go to the Socialist youth club. My father was opposed: 'They're all Communists,' he would say. But my mother defended her: 'She's not doing anything wrong; they just study and do theatre.' He couldn't disagree, but he still didn't like it. The Socialist youth club was always his pet peeve. Communists. The Devil.

She was always studying. She would put her nose to the grindstone and study. She even took clarinet lessons from the nuns, to throw others off guard. But she was a leftie. 'I think even the nuns must have become Communists,' said my father. She was always studying and she was always sickly. Every evening she would run a temperature, and Mamma would look at her as if she were Our Lady of Lourdes. I couldn't say a word: I couldn't raise my voice with Mimì, I couldn't sing, I couldn't slam a door. 'Be quiet, Violetta is studying,' every hour of the day and night. Occasionally she would emerge from her room with a suffering, mummified expression on her face. She would whine. All she did was study. Every once in a while Otello and I would burst into her room suddenly to scream at her, 'Garibaldi was a son of a bitch' or 'Togliatti is a criminal.'

She would screech, 'Maaama!' She couldn't stand me any more. 'Fascist,' she would whisper as she walked by me. And she said it with scorn, as if it were a dirty word.

'I'm proud to be a Fascist.'

'Well done. You must be proud of the Holocaust.'

'What does the Holocaust have to do with it?' Because I said that it was all untrue, that the Americans had invented everything, it was just propaganda: 'Can you really believe that one human can exterminate six million Jews?'

'There's documentary evidence.'

'That's right, those films. But they were made in Hollywood. Those guys are so good at historical films, how difficult do you think it is for them to make one about so-called concentration camps? It's all make-believe, or do you think that Clark Gable really dies in the final scene?'

She was good at trying to make me believe in concentration camps, and anyhow, just to be sure, every time I would add, 'Anyhow, everyone knows that the Jews are part of a worldwide conspiracy, they control global finance and they killed Fascist Italy just like they killed Jesus Christ.'

It's not that I was still so wrapped up in defending Jesus Christ, but it was a good argument to throw on the table, something that she couldn't reply to. But she still wouldn't shut up, she would start to shriek. And then I would close the door to her room, I would slam it, worse than when I made those Togliatti and Garibaldi jokes, and I would leave her there screeching on her own: I would have the final word and slam the door. She could say whatever she wanted; I wasn't interested in her opinions any more. But the worst thing about Violetta was how long she spent in the bathroom. There was just one bathroom in the house for all of us, but when she went in, you had to make the sign of the cross. She would never come out. To encourage her to hurry, whenever she went inside I would go right away to the door handle and start shaking the door. 'Mammaaaa!' she would scream.

Anyhow, the school year began again. I was in my third year of high school. I took all my repeat exams in September, for Italian. The bitch was all nice and conciliatory. The written exam went well, and at the oral exam she was almost cordial. Her tone of voice seemed to say, 'Now that you have learned your lesson, we can even become friends,' but friends according to her way of thinking, with her on top and me subservient. 'Not even if you shoot yourself,' I thought to myself.

In the third year we began our specialist professional courses. The first two years had been more general. Now we had to study topography, estimates, construction science. I was never able to stand topography and estimates. Construction science, yes, I liked it right away, almost as much as Italian and history. Especially the statistics problems: how do buildings stay standing, balanced, even under tension. The moment of greatest traction of a beam. The safety point. The fracture point. The bending, the cut, the torsion. Pressure and traction. This is how man builds, and builds so that structures remain standing. Only after many years did I understand why I like it so much. Statistics and the science of construction don't only concern bridges and houses. They are important to everything. Even social relationships, love relationships, poems. You can't load a body with a weight greater than that it can carry. It breaks. And it doesn't break suddenly. First it weakens. If you look closely you will notice. It weakens. Once, twice, three times. Then it breaks. Nor should you build something with disproportionate dimensions in relation to the load it will bear: a mountain to carry a mouse. It doesn't make sense. It's a waste. And waste isn't just immoral, most of all it's ugly, anti-aesthetic. This is why *Inferno* is a masterpiece, and Dante Alighieri is Dante Alighieri: everything is strictly built according to the dimensions of what it has to say. There isn't one extra word, not one syllable. It seems like everything is held together by a miracle, the bare minimum, not even a T-beam. Only small beams that go from one side to the other, they lean and they cross each other; everything is calculated to the most minute detail, but put together they form a grid structure which is indestructible. A biological structure. Life. Not like *Paradiso,* where everything is oversize.

Anyhow, it was soon November. The year before, Papà had retired, but they had kept him on at work. He could stay there until he was sixty-five, and he always continued to work ten hours a day; the two hours of overtime he kept for himself: for his choir and his photography. There was a bit more money at home. He took home a full salary as well as his pension, actually even more than that, because they didn't take any deductions any more. Then it was a good deal to draw a pension and continue working, not a crime like it is today. That's when we got a phone and bought a refrigerator and a television. And the television was my ruin.

At the beginning of November the television began to say that the government had finally reached an agreement with Yugoslavia. The disputes that had gone on since after the war had subsided. Aldo Moro was the Minister for Foreign Affairs; he hurried off to Yugoslavia to sign the definitive cession of Zone B: the Trieste question was resolved. Zone B went to them, and in exchange they didn't consider us their enemies any more. The television continued to tell us this every day, and they didn't announce this news with pain or with any expression of shame: 'What can we do? That's the way it went.' No, they were proud of this news, it was a success story. And no one said anything, not even the papers, not even the Fascist Party, Movimento Sociale Italiano. 'Maybe they haven't realised,' I thought. 'Maybe they haven't realised that it's important. Now I'll make them understand.' It was 15 November 1965. Moro was supposed to go and sign one or two days later, to definitively transfer this Zone B. I was fifteen years old. I organised a strike for all the schools. I thought it would be relatively straightforward: all I would have to do was go there and say, 'We're on strike!' and everyone would have participated enthusiastically.

'But those guys don't give a damn about Zone B, they don't even know what it is,' the others at the party offices complained.

I insisted, 'All you have to do is say it's a strike and everyone will participate. There hasn't been one for a long time, it's an excuse to skip class.'

'That's hardly fair,' said Piermario. 'We have to explain our motivations, they have to be convinced. We can't just stage a strike so that everyone can cut class.'

'What do we care? All we care is that they go on strike. Then we'll give them an explanation,' and I wasn't interested in hearing any excuses. I imposed the strike on everyone. Well, 'everyone' is sort of a figure of speech, seeing as there weren't more than about ten of us, but we were strategically distributed. We covered almost every school. I was at the surveyors' college, there were another two or three at the industrial college and the scientific lyceum, three or four at art college – Wolf, Piermario, Andrea and someone else – so we were more than enough: indeed, all you needed were two or three there, the others would have gone to the classical lyceum. That was it: 'Go on strike,' I told them that evening. Piermario wasn't so sure.

The plan was simple. Back then the students didn't go in one by one like they do today, everyone going in and out as they please. People would arrive and group together outside the secondary entrance. At 8.25 the gates would open. Everyone inside. At 8.30 they would be closed. If you were there, you were there, and if you weren't, too bad, you would have to go in through the main entrance and explain yourself to the headmaster: preaching, reproaches and late notes. So the best plan was to arrive at eight, announce the good news to the first ones to arrive, and take them away from the school gates, around the corner. In that way, no one would have been tempted; it would be easier to convince those who were recalcitrant, and the janitors would be unable to threaten or cajole us. How easy was that? I had the most difficult job, because at my school there were two main doors, one for the surveyors and another for those studying bookkeeping on the other side of the building. Art college was our point of strength. There would be no problems there, Wolf had told me. We even agreed that as soon as the operation had commenced he would send a detachment to give me a hand. In any event, I was already organised. I had found two or three classmates who weren't Fascists, but, just as I had imagined, they liked the idea of a strike. Especially Peppe Palermo – he was of Sicilian origin, short, blond, with blue eyes. His family had emigrated to Argentina, and they had just come back: he was the life of the party, high-spirited, jovial, Catholic, semi-socialist. He was convinced right away about Zone B. He wasn't a Fascist, but Trieste touched his heart. What do I know? Maybe it's because he'd been an emigrant.

And then 15 November 1965 was finally upon us. I couldn't sleep at all the night before, I hardly closed my eyes. My stomach was tight with anxiety: 'But where did I get this idea?' I deeply regretted it: 'I'm always like this. I talk too much. And then I find myself in trouble and it's too late to get out.' I even felt like getting up and going to call it all off: 'Everyone stop, we're not doing it after all.'

And I would have left, I was about to do it: I could go to Wolf's place, all I had to do was knock on his shutters, he was on the ground floor. But everyone else? Could I go in the middle of the night to ring their doorbells? There was nothing to be done, the die had been cast: 'What a fool I'm making of myself,' I thought, as this was the real question: the fear that I wouldn't be able to do it, they would have buried me alive at school. Would anyone listen to me? Who would support us? There were more than a thousand students, all afraid of the headmaster, of the teachers, and of their mothers at home. Were they going to listen to me? Two school entrances. What had I been thinking of?

I woke up very early. I ran to the party headquarters (the chairman had already given me the keys some time previously). Wolf, Piermario and the boys from the scientific lyceum were all there. Everyone took the boxes of fliers – two per school – that we had prepared the night before: 'Hands off Zone B'. The posters were in boxes, without handles. I told Wolf, 'I don't think I can carry this.'

'Don't worry, come with us.' Everyone was waiting to meet in the piazza.

At the moment we left – under the main doorway, when I was almost left on my own – an idea came to me. I ran back upstairs. I took the official emblems from the party headquarters and the youth club. I detached the insignia. I just took the metallic flagpoles with their brass tips. I attached two tricolour flags; I knew that they were kept in Bompressi's drawer. Wolf took one, I took the other one to my school. As I ran – with my furled flag, along viale Mazini – I knew that I was going to my defeat: 'It's the last time,' I said. 'The next time I won't get involved,' and I couldn't wait until it was over.

At the entrance to my school, though, there were no problems at all. The first to arrive said yes right away: 'Go to the bookkeepers' institute, there are enough of us here.' I ran there with Peppe Palermo, and we were already on a high: there were enough surveyors, our honour was saved.

'But now we have to give it our all, we have to make them strike, even by force,' said Peppe.

They were grouped around the main entrance. They were shouting at the janitor: 'Open up, open up!' Especially the girls. They were afraid we'd convince them. The janitor was just about to open early. He was fiddling with his keys. I jumped into the crowd, between them and the gates: 'Go away! Go away! This is a strike!' Obviously I had to shriek like a madman, because the girls were afraid and the crowd gradually moved back, three or four metres from the gates. Even Peppe shouted. He screamed, 'Hands off Zone B!' Trieste belongs to Italy!' but he screamed in a gentle way, in order to be heard, to convince everyone, to make them understand. Someone – who before would have stepped over my dead body just to get in – said, 'And what does it take? All you need are some good manners, like him,' and pointed to Peppe.

Anyhow, they moved away to the other side of the street. The janitor opened, and said to me, 'Get lost and let them in.'

'You get lost,' and I must have been persuasive. He went back up the stairs. When he opened the gates, though, a little group formed on the pavement to go in. They were two or three metres from me. 'Now you're playing for big stakes,' I thought to myself. If they went in, everyone would go in. I went to meet them. I didn't wait for them. I lowered the pole of my flag and I went forward. I pushed the point of the flagpole against the stomach of one of them, in the centre of the group – he was stocky, big, he must have been repeating a year, or maybe from the senior class – and I pushed hard: 'I'll flatten the first one who tries to enter.'

They backed off right away. I heard the big guy justify himself with one of his friends, as soon as they made it to the pavement on the other side of the street: 'He's crazy,' he said. But I only pretended to push, it was all theatre. And then it was just a decorative flagpole, with a brass tip. It would never have hurt him.

In the meantime, the surveyors arrived. Now they were all convinced and the majority were there, around the corner from the school. They were waiting for me to decide something. 'Now what do we do?' asked one of them. To tell the truth, I hadn't thought that far.

The night before, as I tossed and turned in my bed, I hadn't thought it through to this point, I only got as far as the strike: once that was done, I didn't think any further; I thought that everyone would go on their own way, happy to have a day off school and hanging out at the public gardens. I could never have imagined that they would be waiting for me.

'Now what are we going to do?' Peppe asked me.

Right then Wolf arrived, together with Andrea. I felt somewhat better: 'Well then?' I asked them.

'Nothing, we weren't able to do it. We came here quickly just to let you know; now we have to rush back to school, or else they'll mark us down as absent.'

I could have killed them. So they stayed. 'Now what are we going to do?' Peppe asked me again.

'Let's start by taking everyone away.' I replied, 'Take them to the piazza, where the others are,' and I told Wolf to give them a hand. But my real worry was getting them away from there as soon as possible: the battle hadn't been won yet, the situation was still very risky. Things could change from one moment to another; it wouldn't take much, as long as the door was still open, the final word hadn't been said. I continued to oversee the entrance, and I screamed at the janitor, 'Close these gates.' Now the janitor was really getting scared. It was about time for him to close them, but there was a little group of teachers looking on like vultures.

Gradually the crowd began to move. Wolf's flag was at the head of the crowd, waving in the wind, and Peppe was blowing a horn. He had brought along a cow horn, he said that it was made by the Indians of the pampas, a souvenir of Argentina. The bookkeepers and surveyors lined up in two columns. It seemed like everyone had made up their minds. There was already around fifty metres between the school and the students. The janitor started to wrestle with the gates, and I began to move on after the demonstrators. At that point – from behind the corner – the assistant headmaster appeared. He came from the main entrance, from his office. He was a sort of mafia don. He thought he walked on water. He taught some aspect of bookkeeping, I don't know what. He was also a well-established chartered accountant and had something to do with the Christian Democrats. He always wore the same facial expression, as if to say, 'Everyone else can go fuck themselves,' even with the teachers, even with the engineers and architects who taught topography and construction. Everyone sucked up to him. Even the headmaster, practically, was careful not to walk on his shadow.

'Where are you going? Come here,' he called after the stragglers. A group of girls – they must have been from one of his classes – slowed down, then stopped, then almost turned around to go back.

'Follow the group!' I shrieked at them, and they started walking again.

So he raised his voice: 'You can't do this!' and he came after me. We were on a public roadway.

'I'll do as I please,' I told him.

He took me by the arm. I slipped away from his grip. I pushed him away. It's not true – as they said later – that I punched him. Do you think I would have pushed him, banged him against the wall? It's not true, it's a legend; or anyhow I don't remember. He took my arm; all I did was break free, that's all – OK, maybe with some force. He turned into a little sheep, he put down his pens, he wasn't angry any more. He whined, 'You can't do this,' as the other teachers came to his rescue.

'Just fuck off!' I said to him, and I ran after the demonstrators.

'Bravo, well done!' said the girls from before, the ones who had been recalled by him and had just about gone back, like Lassie.

Now everyone was crazy for Zone B. They were furious. There wasn't one of them who thought about taking off to hang out in the public gardens. Everyone was for Zone B. Maybe the day before they hadn't even known what it was. Trieste, yes, of course, and that was all. They all seemed more upset about it than I was, and as I made my way to the front of the group – Wolf had come to look for me: 'Now where should we go?' – everyone called out to me. I ran to get to the front, but they all stopped me, everyone had something to suggest: 'Let's go to the police headquarters;' 'Let's get the other kids from school;' 'Let's go to the offices of the newspaper.' I wanted to get a move on, but I had to stop and talk with everyone, to agree with their suggestions, listen to them, pretend to smile. Everyone knew me, they all knew my name, and I can't hide the fact that I did like it. Especially with the girls.

I got to the front. We were in piazza Dante. People came out from the market to look at us. Peppe honked his horn. Wolf and I waved our flags. Then someone took mine, they wanted it. I told them, 'Be careful with the flagpole, don't lose it.' We didn't shout slogans, and we didn't even have any banners, we were amateurs. Who knows where the fliers had gone. But the crowd was vocal, rowdy. People were shouting and talking in loud voices in order to be heard.

We arrived in piazza del Popolo. I expected to find it full of students from the scientific lyceum. There wasn't a soul. Just us. Wolf was relieved: 'They didn't make it either.'

I was even more angry: 'Let's go and drag them out,' and the word went through the crowd: 'To the lyceum.' In front of the Town Hall the employees looked out at us, and everyone in the square stopped to look. We shouted a couple of times, 'Hands off Zone B,' and we continued to the lyceum. At that time it was just a short distance away, where the old hospital used to be, where everything has been torn down now and they've built a parking lot. The road became narrower, and the demonstrators became more densely packed in – just like in hydraulics, when the section of the piping becomes narrower, the water increases in power at a dizzy speed – and it was like a giddy dance: the students were massed together, there was very little space, and we moved more quickly. We were already in front of the old hospital. The outer fences were closed.

It just took a moment. We heard sirens, and two small vans arrived. They went through the crowd at full speed, without slowing down. They stopped in front of the gates, braking suddenly. The police officers – they were all old men of forty or fifty, some even with beer bellies – jumped out waving their truncheons. Everyone stepped back. I threw myself forward. The crowd moved up behind me. Two police officers took me by the arms and threw me into the back of the van: 'Get in!' one shouted at me, with a nasty expression. He had a tight helmet and was holding his truncheon under my neck. He was tough and ferocious, but he was trembling. They pushed me in, and when I was about to get in, bent over, they gave me another shove and I banged my head on the front. I stood up again, on the van, almost as if I was about to address the crowd. I was radiant. The crowd shouted, 'Let him go!' I only just had time to tell Wolf, 'It's alright,' when they pulled me down, turned the sirens back on, and peeled out of there. The unpleasant policeman took off his helmet. He was all sweaty. 'Look what I've had to get into,' he said to his friend – obviously he was used to taking it easy in the office – and he slapped me. I felt like Damiano Chiesa. In that moment that I had clambered onto the van, I could see all of those screaming students. One thousand two hundred. And on the other side, at a safe distance, normal people and shopkeepers watched us with concern. Down at the end of via Emanuele Filiberto, there was a lady in front of the fruit and vege-table stand. When she looked at me, she dropped her shopping bag. Oranges were rolling on the ground, and she didn't even attempt to pick them up: she just stared at me. It seemed like Signora Elide, the lady who lived one floor up from us, who had always had a telephone. 'But it can't be her,' I thought. 'Surely she doesn't come this far to shop?'

As soon as we arrived at the police station, they took me to the special-branch unit on the ground floor. They took my details and made me sit in the hall. 'Aren't you going to take me to via Aspromonte?' I asked, because that's where the jail was. They looked at me like I was some kind of idiot. I sat there, but I felt bad, I felt like jail would have been a badge of honour, a medal of merit. I mean, even Mussolini had always said – I'd read it in his biography written by Mino Caudana – that a man was only a man once he'd done at least a year of prison. I'm not saying I wanted to spend a year there, but I was up for a taster.

It must have been nine or nine-thirty in the morning. Every once in a while I would hear sirens and vans coming in and going out. After a while they brought in another student, then another again. Finally there were five or six of us, but they didn't take down the details of the others, they left them sitting on the bench in the hall with me: 'When the guy from the political section arrives, they can deal with them,' said the detective.

The other boys were all from year four and year five. The first one had also been picked up outside the lyceum, and he kept on saying, 'But I am a free citizen, I have the right to demonstrate. They can't do this to me,' and the others who came after him said the same thing. One had been picked up in piazza del Popolo, another in front of Standa, others in the piazza in front of the police station. These ones said that the police had shot tear gas. I didn't believe them, I thought they were exaggerating. Then the political section arrived. It must have been eleven-thirty or midday. Until then they had been with the demonstration. The sirens had already been silent for some time, and no one else joined us. They brought my two flags in under their arms, with the brass-tipped flagpoles.

As soon as they arrived, the detective told them, 'You take them.' I jumped up and indicated the others, saying, 'They're not involved. I assume all the responsibility.'

They looked at me as if I were an idiot. Even my friends. One of them said, 'But what are you assuming? Here we're all responsible for ourselves. Now I'm calling my brother,' who worked at the Town Hall.

They took us upstairs, to their offices. They didn't mistreat us. They took our details, wrote us up, read the articles of the criminal code we'd breached – seditious meeting, non-authorised demonstration, disturbance of public order, resistance to public officials: all in all, we were looking at four or five years of jail time – and they gave us fatherly advice. Every once in a while someone would raise their voice. Then they made us go outside again and wait in the hall outside their offices. At around two in the afternoon they let us go: 'Go home, but keep your wits about you.'

I tried to answer back: 'Aren't you going to take us to via Aspromonte?' but they weren't interested in listening. Even I had to leave. But first I asked if they would give our flags back. Warrant Officer Gibino said, 'Now let me at him,' and even raised his hand.

The detective stopped him: 'Tell your chairman that he can come back himself to claim them,' and his tone of voice seemed to say: 'I'd like to have a word with him.'

'It's nothing to do with him,' I complained. 'I took them.'

'Not you again!' growled the detective, and I went home.

To tell the truth, I walked slowly. I was excited about my adventure, but I was also worried about getting home late: 'What will she have to say?' Basically, it wasn't such a huge problem: it was only a little after two in the afternoon. If I hurried I would only be about twenty minutes late for lunch, I could tell her that I had dawdled on the way home and stopped at the public gardens. What was she to know?

I hadn't even shut the door when she jumped at me from the kitchen. She attacked me with the wooden spoon. I covered my face and she hit me on the shoulders: 'But what have I done?' and I even tried to brazen it out. 'All this fuss because I'm a few minutes late?'

'A few minutes late?' she echoed. And she hit me even more furiously with her spoon: 'You'll be the death of me; I curse the day I gave birth to you.'

I had seen correctly: it really was Signora Elide. She didn't even bend over to pick up her oranges, because she was in such a hurry to rush home and blab to my mother. Whenever there was gossip or bad news you could count on her to be the first to tell. She ran through the entire town. She lost her shopping. And as soon as she arrived at the corner of our street, just off the bypass, she started to scream like one possessed: 'Signora Lìììì … they've just arrested your son,' so that all the neighbours could hear. Mind your own fucking business. She never did. And even Mamma – much later – said that the thing that upset her most wasn't that they had arrested me, but that Signora Elide had screamed from the corner of our street: 'She loved every minute of it, that bitch.'

She and Signora Loreta – our neighbour on the ground floor who was like a sister to her – had heard the police sirens in town all morning and the noise of the tumult: 'I wonder what's going on,' they asked each other. 'I could never have imagined that it was actually my bloody son.' However, when Signora Elide screamed, 'They've arrested your son,' she said that she didn't hesitate for a minute: all of us were out, there was no one at home, no boys or girls, but she knew immediately. The other neighbours – Signora Loreta, the lady who lived across the road, Signora Zannella, even a few people leaning out from their windows – at least asked, 'Which one?' Not her. She knew right away that it was me.

'You are crazy. You'll be the death of Mamma,' reproached Manrico and Otello. But even they, and even Violetta and especially Mimì – after Mamma stopped hitting me with the wooden spoon – began to ask questions, wanted to know all about it. Some of them had seen the vans, some of them had heard rumours of injuries, but I knew less than them.

'To prison! They took you to prison!' cried Mimì, filled with shame.

'Well, sort of,' I replied, but quietly so my mother wouldn't hear.

Anyhow, I had lunch, and afterwards I wanted to go out. But she wouldn't let me: 'Now stay here, don't go out any more. Do you want to go out and cause more trouble? It would have been better if you'd just stayed in Massa Carrara. As far as I'm concerned, it would have been better if you'd stayed.'

However, after a while I began to receive visits. First Wolf, then Andrea, then Peppe. They all would come to see if they had released me. And they all had tales to tell. They would ring the doorbell – 'Who is it this time?' sighed Mamma. 'Send them away, come right back inside' – and I would go out, we would sit on the garden wall. I was still pissed off about the lack of success at the other schools, especially at the art college: 'What went wrong?' I was indignant with Wolf. 'You were so strong, the strike should have been as easy as pie.'

Wolf said it was all Piermario's fault. They had begun to picket on the road, and at the beginning it was successful, even if Piermario was hesitant, wasn't convinced, was defeatist: 'But what do we think we're doing?' Then the situation worsened when Ferraro arrived, the one who had taught me PE at middle school, the one with the climbing rope. Now he'd moved on to the art college, and he was their spiritual leader: he'd fought for the Republic of Salò, a font of wisdom and knowledge. And Piermario hung on every word he said. Ferraro told him right away, 'What are you doing? Go to your classrooms.'

'But Zone B...' began Wolf.

'Trieste,' said Andrea.

He replied that there was no one more patriotic than himself, but that they had to return to class: 'You don't send people unprepared like this. Then in the end it's always the young who pay the price' – it seemed like he had a problem with the MSI and the chairman – 'I know it only too well.' So he convinced Piermario. But according to Wolf, Piermario was looking for an excuse anyhow. And Andrea thought that the headmaster had actually called Ferraro over near the main entrance and that they had spoken in conspiratorial tones for a while, before Ferraro left to convince Piermario. There was nothing they could do.

Piermario began proselytising: 'You can't play with the sentiments of young people, you can't send students without a plan,' and so everyone was convinced, even our most ardent supporters: 'If Ferraro says so,' 'If Piermario says so,' and they went back into their classes. At least, that's what Wolf and Andrea said.

A more objective eye might have understood that perhaps it hadn't gone quite like that: there was something that didn't quite make sense; maybe they hadn't really tried so hard. But what did I care? Piermario had been getting on my nerves for a while, not to mention this hero-worship of Ferraro, the master of the climbing rope. And then he always had something to add, he was always argumentative. He was undisciplined, he didn't respect the hierarchy; it seemed as if he didn't submit to my authority. So I was happy with the version provided by Wolf and Andrea, I didn't say a word: the Holy Bible, everything perfect, it all made perfect sense. And they promised me that it was all gospel truth: 'He disobeyed orders: a nay-sayer, an opportunist, a traitor.' I had already begun to compose his letter of expulsion in my mind.

Every once in a while my mother would poke her head around the door: 'What's up?' I would have to send my friends away and go back inside. Fortunately – when Papà came back from work – she had a moment of conscience: 'If I tell him everything as soon as he gets in and you're hanging around, who knows what will happen,' she must have thought. And she told me, 'Get out. I can't stand the sight of you.' I raced out of the house to the party offices.

Everyone was there. People spilled out onto the stairs. From every school. From the lyceum, the bookkeepers, even from the teachers' college. They all wanted to join the party. About a hundred people. Even the bullies from the piazza. Even that guy Armando that Rosetta liked, who had been so awful to me when we went on strike at middle school. Everyone was waiting for me: 'What are we going to do to-morrow? Let's attack here, let's attack there.' And then Bompressi, the chairman. I hadn't seen so many people since the last time Mussolini addressed the public at the Teatro Lirico in Milan. It seemed as if there had really been tear gas that morning. The demonstration didn't even make it as far as the scientific lyceum, so in the end they all returned to the piazza. Wolf wanted to go to the other lyceum, but those in front – a few surveyors and some bookkeepers – preferred piazza della Libertà, in front of the police station. But the police didn't seem to appreciate their gesture. Vans were driven into the crowd. The demon-stration broke up; some of the demonstrators went to the public gardens near the fountain. The vans made it as far as there, to drive them away. One turned a park bench over, and it stayed like that for twenty years. Two vans crashed into each other. But people didn't want to break up, and in the end some of them sought refuge under the porticoes in the centre of town, and the vans even followed them there, breaking a shop window: it was worse than a wartime bomb raid. And now they were all back here calling for a vendetta: 'That was just the appetiser; the main course will be better.' Then they threw tear gas, and the demonstrators gradually went away. It was much more than 1956. But I didn't waste time with chit-chat, and I sat down at the typewriter to compose a letter to Piermario. Then I called him aside and gave it to him: 'Here you go. You're expelled.'

All he said was, 'We need to talk.'

'Whenever you want,' and I went away for a celebratory drink.

But that asshole Bompressi – first, when I arrived, he had a radiant smile – came after me all pissed off, and took me to the chairman: 'What happened to the standards?' He had only just noticed that they weren't there any more, standing behind his desk. I even breathed a sigh of relief: 'Let's hope they believe me.' But my worst suspicions were confirmed: 'And the flagpoles? Where are the flagpoles?' When I told them that they could be picked up at the police station, he could hardly contain himself: 'What's wrong with you? Those are expensive! And who gave you the authorisation? What gives you the right to take things without permission?'

'But we needed flags,' I replied with a tone of voice I thought conveyed resolve and justification.

'You could have taken two small ones. Who gave you permission?'

'Are you still banging on about permission?' I began to get angry. 'So what am I, just a pretend youth secretary?'

And then the chairman began to laugh. He said, 'Alright, come on, it's nothing,' and in the end I convinced him.

'I turned the city upside down, and he's thinking about flagpoles,' I shouted in the hallway, so that the others would hear me – Wolf and the rest.

'That's right, just leave it,' said the others.

In the meantime – I can't remember who told me – the news arrived that I had been suspended from school. The teachers had met in the afternoon and had given – only to me – a five-day suspension, with a warning: 'Then we'll see,' they must have said to each other. They were threatening. I was a little worried, but tried not to show it: 'Let's prepare for tomorrow.'

'Be careful,' the chairman admonished me.

Everyone wanted to go on strike again right away, but I said no, I didn't want to relive the art college fiasco: 'This time we have to be sure.' But everyone insisted. First I'd had to drag them along kicking and screaming, now it seemed like I was the nay-sayer. 'Tomorrow try to convince your classmates. If they're in agreement, we'll organise a really big strike, a good one, with flags and wooden flagpoles.'

'Alright, see you tomorrow evening,' and the guys from Bar di Russo went away with a look of dissatisfaction on their faces, as if I had pulled back.

As we closed the party offices and were going down the stairs, Bompressi came over to reconcile with me: 'But the chairman moves quickly. Now I have to go over to the police station to get the flagpoles back.'

'But they said they want to speak with him.'

'Yes, but instead he's sending me to submit to Caffé and Gibino, damn you and your Zone B.' But he was smiling. And the next day, in *Secolo d'Italia* I finally saw, on the front page, 'Hands off Zone B', and inside the paper there was an enormous article about the strike and the demonstration, and it gave my name when it mentioned 'intimidatory and repressive measures' taken against demonstrators, as well as news of my 'commendation from the National Youth Leadership'. Since the situation in Hungary in 1956, no one had received a youth citation. In time of war, it would have been worth a medal for valour. But I wasn't able to truly enjoy it.

chapter 5

The news of the suspension made it home. Papà returned at 10p.m. from choir practice, but they must have already told him. He didn't say a word to me, just, 'You were such a good boy when you were little; have you forgotten all the teachings of Father Cavalli?'

'Are you still on about Father Cavalli?' I thought to myself. But the way he looked at me, I took pity on him, or rather anyone else would have taken pity on him. I was just annoyed. I could never stand whining: I would slap whiners on the head until they stopped. So they had no choice but to stop, at least if their mothers weren't around. You'll be saying, 'Good God, were you attacking little children?' Talk is cheap: when those little monsters followed me around, they would come right into my room, close to me, to whine. I would tell them, 'Get lost!' or 'Shut up!' But to no avail. They wouldn't leave me alone. And they wouldn't shut up. So what do you expect me to do? I had to hit them. It was the only way to get them to shut up.

Anyhow, before he came back there had been a family meeting. Well, not really the family: just Mamma and Otello. Manrico was her favourite, but when she wanted to give orders she preferred Otello, her first-born. The fact that he was a ne'er-do-well, that he never studied, that he just played pool and had always stolen money from everyone else in our home didn't matter at all; he was her first-born son and that was enough for her – Julius Caesar, King of France – and she didn't do anything without consulting with him. She loved Manrico more, but in terms of pecking order he didn't count, a bit like our father. Now they decided that I needed to make a change: 'Tomorrow you're going to Norma's house' – in Santa Maria Capuavetere. 'You'll stay for a week.'

'But I have stuff to do tomorrow.'

'Precisely.'

There was no way to discuss the matter: 'What will people think?'

'Precisely,' they continued, ever more convinced that it was a good idea. In actual fact, my mother was the only one who spoke. Otello just nodded, because as soon as he tried to open his mouth I became rigid, as if I'd been placed in an electric chair.

'What do you care? You don't count.'

'He's your older brother,' said Mamma, but she understood right away that she had made a mistake, and she made a sign to him to be quiet, otherwise we'd still be there.

Anyhow, the next day they put me on the bus and sent me to Santa Maria Capuavetere. I said, 'I'll hitchhike,' but they wouldn't let me. They were afraid I wouldn't leave right away, and I'd hang around in Latina. They purchased my ticket and made me get on. I got out at Terracina and began to hitchhike. I didn't feel right about going by bus, I was ashamed. I arrived safely in Formia. A car dropped me off, and another one picked me up; the most I waited was fifteen minutes. I got as far as the Gianola junction, a bit before Scauri. I stayed there for quite a while. No one stopped. It was a nice day, it was sunny, it was early afternoon. A red Volkswagen stopped, a Beetle. I'd seen it coming from far away, but I didn't even bother to put my thumb out. There was a woman driving, alone: 'She'll never stop,' I thought. But I kept on watching her. She watched me too, as the car approached. She was staring at me. When she got close, she turned her head towards me on the side of the road. So at the last minute, I lifted my arm, I put out my thumb. She only saw me at the last second, when the car had almost passed me by. She slammed on the brakes and stopped about thirty metres further on. I ran there, almost out of breath, clutching my bag of clothes. My heart was beating more than it had even during the strike: it was a woman, the first woman for me.

You might say, 'What, had you never seen a woman?' No. Not that close up and not in a situation like this; it had never happened to me. Actually, to tell the truth I didn't even know what a woman looked like close up. My only idea was something like Pauline Bonaparte. Beyond that, women were a vague concept, always present in my mind, but in a nebulous way. Like fairies. Or the immortality of the soul. Plus it was everyone's fantasy that a woman would pick you up when you were hitchhiking. But in actual fact it never happened. Yet now I had one waiting for me thirty metres away. I was there in a flash, my heart working overtime.

The car was beautiful. Volkswagen. Red. Brand new. With Genoa plates. Or Turin. She said, 'I'm going to Naples.' She laughed, leaning out of the open window.

'I'm going to Capua: it's along the same road.'

'No, I'm taking the other route: it's faster.'

'Don't worry, that's fine,' I said. 'Take me as far as Garigliano,' and I hopped on board. Of course it would have been better if she could have taken me as far as Capua. 'But at least I'm in the car,' I thought.

She must have been about thirty years old. She had red hair, sort of long, curly, in a ponytail. She was wearing glasses. A pair of white jeans, tight. A suede jacket and a green striped top, with a V-neck. And I don't think she was wearing anything underneath. You could see her neck and part of her throat, the top of her breastbone. She was wearing a little gold chain, but not really a chain, it was heavier, thicker. As she drove, every once in a while the sleeve of her suede jacket would ride up and you could see her delicate wrists. Small-boned. Thin. She had freckles. On her wrists and on her face and on her breastbone. She was a woman, a real woman driving that Volkswagen.

She put the car into gear and we left. She offered me a cigarette. She began to chat. Me too. I told her the story of my life, for around ten miles. Then she told me hers. She drove slowly, but the slower she went the happier I was. She smiled. 'We'll be in Garigliano soon,' I thought to myself, 'then we say thank you and goodbye.' I tried to suggest that it would be faster if she took the other road: as soon as she got to Capua, she could go on to the motorway. It would be a better route.

She wasn't convinced: 'Isn't that longer?' She stopped in Garigliano. I was about to get out. Then she said, 'Wait. I need to buy petrol,' and she left the road for the Motel Agip service station. We went to the bar. She paid. When it was time to say goodbye she said, 'Alright, we'll do as you say, I'll go through Capua.'

'This is it,' I thought to myself.

She had explained to me that she was originally from near Naples, but she had moved to Turin when she was small. Now she started talking again, and she said that she had reflected that if she drove through Capua she would see the places of her childhood again: it was almost as if she was rationalising it to herself. 'What do I care?' I thought. 'The important thing is that she took my road.' She kept offering me cigarettes. She smoked Peers. At the Motel Agip she had taken off her suede jacket, and she placed it on the back seat. It was sunny. It was November, but it was warm inside the Volkswagen. She pushed up the sleeves of her striped top. Those long thin arms with the freckles drove me mad. And her neck. And her breastbone with the gold chain and the crucifix that bounced up and down on her top, just between her breasts.

I held back as far as Sessa Aurunca. On the curves just before we got there she always kept her hand on the stick shift: gearing up and gearing down. Whenever she changed gears she would brush against my knee. I moved back on purpose, but she didn't seem to notice: she kept changing gears. I said to myself, 'This is it.'

After Sessa Aurunca – actually, after Cascano – I put my hand on her leg, just above her knee. We had just passed a major curve, in a straight section of road where the mountains rose up along both sides. No one was around. It was sunny. The Volkswagen was moving very slowly. I put my hand on her leg without saying a word, with nonchalance. Then she asked, 'What are you doing?' What did she think I was doing?

I didn't have time to reply. My hand slid further up, in between her thighs, and began to squeeze her white jeans. Just for a moment. It's not that when she asked me, 'What are you doing?' I didn't want to reply or to provide explanations; actually I was more than ready to if she had given me time. All I had done was to move my hand, then I was about to speak. She didn't give me enough time: 'You've misunderstood.' She began to scream, 'Move your hand,' and she brought her hand down on mine with force. I gripped her thighs even more and kept on going, to the centre of the universe. She clamped her thighs on my hand so I couldn't go any further. Yet she didn't stop, she kept on driving: as a matter of fact she even accelerated, but she didn't shift gears. After the hills you could hear the motor as loud as a tank: all she did was accelerate; I think she was still in third. And she kept on grabbing my hand to get it away from her thigh. She really knew her stuff.

I can't remember what I said to her. But I jumped on her. I took my left hand off her leg and moved in with my right hand. I pulled her into an embrace, and then I was on top of her. I kissed her on the cheek, on the neck, I pulled on her ponytail, and with the other hand I grabbed her thighs. I moved further up, and could feel between her legs, then I moved up her body to her breasts, and I grabbed them. Then I went back down and lifted her top.

She tried to get away from me, and kept on accelerating. She began to sound the horn. She was driving in a zig-zag. The cars that passed us – thank heavens there weren't many of them – sounded their horns back at us and kept on honking after they'd passed us. I heard them as if from far away.

I continued. She didn't have anything on under her top, just her skin. I pulled it up. She tried to push it back down, and sounded the horn. She was wearing a white bra. I began to bite her bra and kiss her belly-button. I tried to open her jeans. I even kissed her there, on top of her white jeans. I could just see the elastic on her panties. She shouted, 'Stop! Don't do that!'

Now the road was passing through a flat section of countryside, in the middle of arable land. I kept holding her and kissing her. She kept on zig-zagging. And she honked her horn. And she screamed. The other cars honked back at us. I don't know how long it went on for. At a certain point she said in a decisive voice, 'Look, I'm on the left.' She was driving on the wrong side. She was driving on the left, like in England: 'If you don't stop, we'll kill ourselves.'

'What the hell do I care?' I thought, and I kept on at my work. 'She's not crazy: as soon as someone comes along she'll move.'

But she didn't move: 'Look, I'm not kidding,' she insisted, and then I looked up, to see what was going on. In actual fact we were on the left and someone was coming towards us, and she didn't seem to be moving away, we were about to hit him head on. He stopped. She didn't, she actually accelerated, it seemed like she was going straight at him. The other driver began to honk.

I moved both my hands as if I'd received an electric shock. She jerked the steering wheel, and we missed him by a hair. We were both silent. But she didn't stop, she kept on driving, albeit more slowly. I moved back to my side, right over near the window. I've never felt so embarrassed. We were both silent. For quite a while. She lit a cigarette. She offered it to me. I said no. She insisted. So I took it and said, 'I must apologise, I don't know what came over me. Please let me out.'

'No, I'll take you like I promised.'

Then I insisted. I wanted to get out; I wanted to end this excruciating situation: 'Let me out here.' But she wouldn't, she kept on going, and she began to preach: it just wasn't right; I was a nice lad, why did I do it? She didn't want to let me out. I prayed silently, 'Let's hope it's not far to the Capua exit.' But even at the junction, there was nothing to be done: 'No, I'm taking the road straight through to Capua,' and she couldn't be persuaded otherwise: 'I'm taking you to your destination.' She seemed disappointed that we would have to say goodbye, so much so that I thought, 'So what does she want then?' And I spent the final miles meditating, 'Should I try again?' until the end, until she stopped and let me out near my sister's house, and the expression on her face was almost tender, as if she was sorry for what had happened. 'I really should have tried again,' I would think for years afterwards. Who knows, maybe if I'd tried harder, she wouldn't have resisted.

My stay with Norma was the worst thing that could have happened to me. Obviously I wasn't in the right frame of mind from the beginning, always thinking about how ashamed I'd been in the car and yet regretting the missed opportunity. At least if I'd been at home I could have consoled myself with political activism. But here there wasn't anything else to do except think about the Volkswagen and run to the bathroom six or seven times a day.

Things were really impossible. Norma was sweet; she was always the sweetest of all my sisters, maybe the only one who was truly sweet. But her husband couldn't stand me. The feeling was mutual. He was a socialist. The house was full of copies of the left-wing newspaper *Avanti!* It's not just that he disliked me because I was a Fascist. He simply didn't like me, and that was it, ever since I was a small boy, and I felt the same way about him, without either of us even trying to hide the fact. But the children loved me: there were two boys and a girl. Only they got up at five every morning. Really: at five they were all up and running around the house. They would wake me up: 'Uncle, come play with us.' I would hit them on the head so hard that I'm sure they still remember. Once their father told me, 'Try to treat the children better.' They were always crying, but they loved me. As soon as they finished crying, they would come back to me: 'Uncle here, Uncle there,' and I would have to hit them again to make them shut up. 'Sooner or later they'll get fed up and they'll send me back home,' I thought to myself.

Fortunately I hardly ever saw my brother-in-law, only at lunchtime. He was always out working – he was in insurance – and in the evening he went out to Socialist Party meetings. After the first few days I stayed with them he stopped even coming to dinner: he said he was too busy. He would come home late in the evening, hoping that I was already asleep, but I would still be up with the light on in the lounge, reading (he had a lot of books). He wouldn't even look up to say hello to me. I would hear him sigh and go to his room. 'When is your brother leaving?' I would hear him ask my sister. If I had stayed any longer, he would have moved out. In the afternoon or the evening, when I went out, I would go to the local Fascist Party office. Everyone knew each other there, and I wanted to meet like-minded friends. He couldn't stand any of them, not just because of political differences but also for personal reasons. In small towns that's how it is, everyone knows: you make friends and enemies in childhood, and that's how it continues. When you grow up, if your enemy becomes a Communist, you become a Fascist. And vice versa. There are a lot of people who would have been completely different if they had been born in a different town. Like if we'd been born in Marzabotto. Or maybe if one time, when my brother-in-law was a young boy, he hadn't had a disagreement with someone, then who knows what he might have become. So when he came home in the evenings he would say in a low voice – but I still heard him – to my sister, 'He's even hanging out with that cretin De Domenici,' who was the Fascist Party secretary. In the end my sister sent me home – 'I think one week is enough' – but it's hard to say who was happier – me or her. He was over the moon. The last day he was even nice to me. He smiled at me at lunch and gave me advice: 'Don't get into any more trouble,' but he didn't say it for my good, he was thinking of himself. The children were the only ones sad to see me leave.

I left after lunch. He wanted to take me as far as Capua. They wanted me to take the bus from there. But I refused: 'I'm hitchhiking;' deep inside I hoped – who knows? – to find the Volkswagen again. Maybe she would be going back, perhaps – who knows? – she had been spending the past week driving back and forth on the off chance of meeting me again. So I insisted they take me to the outskirts of town, but that wasn't enough for my brother-in-law: he stopped just past Volturno and waited in the car: 'Show us how you hitchhike,' cried the children, and then, 'Too bad!' when cars drove past, or else they would inform me, 'Uncle, there's another one coming, another one is coming!' They really were idiots. Finally some loser stopped. I ran, I waved goodbye to them, and jumped in. My younger nephew started to cry, and even my brother-in-law looked at me with kindness. 'Come back whenever you want,' he told me. But if I had really taken him at his word he would have been horrified, he would have drowned me in the Volturno River. I never saw the girl in the Volkswagen again.

Anyhow, I went back to Latina. When I arrived it was afternoon. From far away, as soon as the car dropped me off, I realised that construction of the war memorial had been completed in my absence. When I left it was still covered by scaffolding. Now, from the traffic lights, one could see the white rectangle of travertine marble in the middle of the public gardens. It was beautiful. But I was sorry that they had finished it when I wasn't there any more, it was a shock. You'll say, 'But what does it matter, it wasn't your work.' I didn't make any of the other town squares either, but I was there when they were built. I was there when they excavated the foundations, I was there watching. Before everything was countryside, there were only three or four buildings when I was born. They built all the rest later, while I watched. There was so much space: fields, meadows, bushes. We would play in the middle playing cowboys and Indians, we built forts. There were even paths between the reed thickets and the bramble bushes. One day they arrived and began to put up fences, then they started digging. They laid foundations and began to raise walls. I remember as if it were yesterday when they built the building where Neri's shop is. We were all in a line – adults and children – in front of the only open spaces, and we looked at the bulldozers as they excavated. They were early bulldozers; before then excavation was done by hand. We supervised; I must have been five years old. All day I said, 'Look how fast they work.' In less than two days they had excavated down thirty feet: 'It used to take weeks.'

Someone else said, 'Yes, but think how much work they've taken away. How will people put food on the table?'

I was with Manrico, who was supposed to have picked me up from kindergarten, and was about ten years old at the time, but he was already a know-it-all. He replied, very seriously, 'Well, now the workers who used to dig can go to build tractors and excavating machinery.'

The guy didn't know how to reply: he mumbled something, but Manrico insisted firmly with his point until the other guy finally said,

'Take a look at this boy,' and left. We went too, and I was very proud.
But I hadn't really understood.

I tried to ask for an explanation: 'Once they've built the equipment,
then what will they do?'

'They'll build more.'

'And what will we do with all this machinery? We can't be excavating all the time.'

'That's progress,' he replied. 'One thing leads to another.' Anyhow
– one building leads to another – the town of Latina grew up all
around me as I watched. And I was proud as it expanded; I would
stand around and watch the carpenters who built scaffolding from
wood, because there were no pre-built metal structures then. It was as
if I had personally built every house, the city grew with me, we grew
together and everything went perfectly, according to the natural order:
it didn't worry me, I consented, I accepted it, whereas I'm still unable
to accept the buildings they constructed in front of our home while I
was away at the seminary. I wasn't there, I came back and suddenly
found them, they were strangers to me. And strangers they remained.
But not the war monument: no, I liked that.

After I dropped my things off at home I went to the party offices,
but even there things had changed. Nothing was as it had been before.
Everyone was waiting for me, the federation was full of young people,
and I was their leader. Bompressi and the chairman greeted me with
smiles, only Livio Nastri commented on my defection: 'You deserted
us. There was a battle raging here, and you abandoned your watch.'

'But my family…'

'Your family, what about your family? When the revolution breaks
out, do you go and ask your family for permission first?'

But Bompressi didn't agree. It seems that they had already spoken
a few days earlier, that's just the way Livio was. 'Don't listen to him,'
Bompressi told me. 'They were right to send you away for a while,'
but deep inside I thought Livio was right: he had run away from home
to join the Republican forces, and he still continued to talk about
building the revolution and planting bombs.

Bompressi, on the other hand, didn't even seem like a Fascist: he was calm, moderate and gentle. He was even a bit of a nuisance, because he was always at the party offices, and he was the one who worked the most. We talked about our interests and concerns, then suddenly you would see him come around the corner to give his opinion, and sometimes we were suspicious: 'Does he listen in on us?' He would always have something to say: 'Don't do this, don't do that.' He was especially obsessed with respect for the rules. He didn't want us to stick up posters where it wasn't permitted: only on the Town Hall notice board and the places where it was allowed. 'But what kind of Fascists are we?' we asked ourselves.

'Fascism is respect for the law,' he replied, 'and we've all accepted democracy.'

'That's not democracy, that's Christian Democracy,' Livio Nastri opined. They couldn't stand each other, and yet they were always together. They spent a lot of time with the chairman, and they always complained about each other. Or rather Livio Nastri complained about Bompressi, but it's not that Bompressi really did the same, he would just make a face whenever Livio Nastri's name was mentioned. He didn't say anything, but still we understood. They competed for the chairman's approval, and he would tell each of them separately, 'I like you better.' When they were together, he would say, 'I like you both the same. What would I do without the two of you?'

Bompressi was from La Spezia. He was short: much shorter than me. With curly hair. He was always smiling and always busy. He was quick, almost hasty. Anything he did, he rushed. He had heart problems. He had already had one or two heart attacks. He worked for the Engineering Corps. This is why he had come to Latina. He said that his heart had suffered during the war, in Garfagnana, with the snow. He was in the San Marco Division. He wasn't a volunteer, and he hadn't run away from home either, but when the Graziani competition was published for obligatory military service in the Republic of Salò, he went to enlist. He said that a lot of people didn't show up in La Spezia. Even the first nights in the barracks, together with his schoolmates, all they did was argue, and as soon as they had a free day out, a lot of people didn't come back, they ran off and hid. He and his friends, though, stayed with the San Marco Division, and they fought close to home, in Garfagnana, against the advancing Americans. During the winter of 1945 they were in trench warfare, in the snow. They were young and strong, he said, and they defended the honour of Italy: 'We also defended the company from stupid people,' he said, because at night sometimes when they were on patrol they would go out with tins of paint and would sneak over to the American bunkers and write slogans: 'What was the point?' he said now. The only point was to show it to your friends the next day through your binoculars, that's all. And while they went there they were scared to death, but afterwards, dragging themselves back, they were laughing and happy. You think that's nothing? This was Italian honour, and they risked their health in the snow and the damp.

His wife didn't want him to be involved in politics: she would say to him, 'Think about your children, with what little strength still remains in your heart.'

'Don't worry about my heart! Politics is good for me, that's what keeps me going.' And he really acted as if he was perfectly healthy. He wasn't against violence because he was sick, that's just how he was, he thought like a Christian Democrat. He said that if we hadn't lost the war, Fascism would have arrived at democracy by itself: 'That's what Bottai said.' He was in favour of corporatism because it was the only way to truly defend the interests of the workers, against all the powers being nominated from above. They had to be elected from below, and the ideal was specifically a social republic, anti-capitalist, for the workers, with their participation in company profits and management: 'We offer true socialism,' and he was even anti-American. But there they were all anti-American, even the chairman and Livio Nastri: 'The Americans made us lose the war.'

'So why are we on their side now?' we would ask sometimes.

'Because that's what politics is like. We're against the Communists, and so we have to be with the Americans even if at the end of the day our ideology is actually closer to that of the Communists. We have to be on their side, but don't think even they want us.'

Sometimes Wolf would say, 'I don't understand.' Even I didn't understand sometimes. But what we learned there was now clearly impressed upon us. The Communists were our principal enemies: there was no discussion on this point. Visceral enemies: the Communists and the partisans, who had killed thousands of loyal Republican forces after 25 April. But maybe they were enemies because they were competitors. We were the real defenders of the proletariat masses: didn't Mussolini say, 'Italy belongs to the proletariat and the Fascists'? As far as respect, ethics and morality were concerned, there was no comparison: the Communists were better than the Christian Democrats. These guys were just corrupt. Bourgeois and corrupt. They had an ideal; it may have been collectivist, but it was still an ideal. These guys, the Christian Democrats, were all about scandals and corruption. You could even see it at the youth level: the Communists' world vision disgusted us, but it seemed perfect, ideal even, to the collectivised masses. You could see that the Christian Democrat supporters just thought about making money and business when they grew up: not like us and the Communists, who wanted revolution.

We couldn't stand Bompressi. He was always a nuisance, urging us to be more moderate. 'I want to be a Fascist, not an altar boy,' Wolf would tell him. But he didn't listen. He had to know about everything. He asked us to tell him about the roads that needed repair, broken fountains, anything that didn't work in town. But we were interested in the bigger picture, the dangers of Communism, the unfairness of democracy. And then he always wanted us to clean the party offices, he always wanted to see us cleaning. He would go crazy when we put out our cigarettes on the floor, sometimes he would pick them up himself. 'Worse than at home,' we thought to ourselves. In the beginning I didn't listen to him, because when he worked at things he was excellent. Once he organised an exhibit under the porticoes of the piazza del Popolo. He worked on it for almost three weeks, with all the black decorations. He did the writing with wax crayons, in beautiful handwriting. And then he attached photos of the draining of the marshes and the foundation of Littoria, which no one wanted to think about any more after the war, in Latina, as if the city had been born on its own: you would think that the Christian Democrats had established it, not Mussolini. He cut photos out of the *Illustrated History of Fascism* and then he attached the decorations. When he finished, and the next day, Sunday, he went to put it up in the piazza, he asked us to give him a hand. But underneath he had written 'Fascist Youth Club', as if we had done it, and everyone complimented us on the work. On that occasion, it has to be said, he behaved himself.

But it all ended between us on the trip to Predappio, when we took the bus with all the party members to visit the tomb of Mussolini. We spent the night on the bus; it was before the motorway was built, so we had to take the windy old road, up and down through the mountains. Our only stop was along the way in Umbertide, where we queued to take a leak. There were mostly old men, and just about ten guys my age, and, turning around and pointing out the house, the chairman said, 'There, down that ridge, that's where the partisans came. I was there below, with my family. I said to them, "You'll be in trouble if you shoot before I give the order." We would have given anything to have been there. Then on the bus, someone else began to remember when they were in Bir el Gobi, and everyone began to sing Fascist anthems: 'Giovinezza', 'Battaglioni del Duce', 'Preghiera del Legionario'.

But when we arrived just outside Predappio, in the morning, there was a police blockade and we couldn't enter. There were discussions back and forth for two hours. We were there, standing still in the road, with two more coaches – who knows from where – and our chairman, along with the other group leaders, went back and forth to speak with the police captain in charge of the blockade: 'Maybe now they'll let us pass.' They spoke, and every time, just like officers of opposing armies, with all due respect, the training and formality of the battlefield. The chairman had pins on his lapel which commemorated his campaigns and military decorations: the bronze medal for military valour and the German Military Cross, second class. You could hear their heels clicking on the pavement. Back and forth, back and forth: 'There's nothing to be done: Rome has said that we have to go back.'

Everyone was furious, the older men said, 'Let's charge through,' but they looked at us, they weren't moving.

The chairman slowed things down: 'Let's stay calm.'

Even on the other coaches a few of the younger members were getting excited: 'Let's charge through,' but this was said to us like a request. They weren't moving, and they said it politely because we were the first coach, and especially because we were from Littoria, Mussolini's own city. (When we arrived, they would shout, 'Here's Littoria!' all together, and they all made way for us, lifting their arms in the Roman salute, and some of them took their hats off: 'Littoria has arrived!') So at a certain point I told my boys, 'Let's go,' and I came up behind the chairman – I was about twenty steps away – when the police captain called him over again. I said, 'Let's go!' to the older members too, but they pretended not to hear me. Only Livio Nastri came running: as a matter of fact he ran past me and went to the front, so as to be the leader of the pack. All the young members came from the other coaches, then behind them I even saw Bompressi. I was surprised, I didn't expect it: if he'd stayed back, I would have understood. His face was dark, and he thought for a minute, but then he marched forward. I was unsure, and I even worried: 'Now I should tell him, don't come, you have heart problems,' but it was too late.

In the meantime, the chairman had stopped in front of the Captain, who was standing in front of a cordon of ten officers. Naturally I had brought some supplies: 'One never knows,' I said before I left, and in my bag, with my sandwiches, I placed a tyre iron from my father's cupboard, one of the biggest ones, a 24 or a 26. Now it was in the back pocket of my trousers, covered by the same old dark grey raincoat I had worn to Massa Carrara. I came right up to the chairman; I was less than a yard away. I went straight for the police Captain. He was tall, big. I reached into my raincoat and I felt the tyre iron in my back pocket. I don't know who hit me on the back of my head. Right then and there I didn't understand – 'What's going on?' – because my enemy was in front of me. And I felt someone grasp my wrist so that I couldn't reach for the tyre iron. I looked back to my group, who were going back instead of forwards. Wolf was looking at his feet. Then I understood, when I saw Bompressi grab my hand – the one with the tyre iron – and he held it strongly, so that the police wouldn't see. He hit me. He slapped me on the head. Instead of attacking the police, he attacked one of his own. And all my comrades, even Wolf, were meekly turning away. I didn't have time to say anything, not even to think. I saw the chairman turn around with a strange look, and the police captain asked, 'What's happened?'

'Nothing, we were joking,' said Bompressi, and he began to laugh and play with me. 'This is my son,' he said, and he pretended to hug me. I was red with shame; I didn't know what to do: 'Should I hit him?' I wondered to myself. Afterwards they let us pass, and we went on to Predappio, but the ignominy stayed with me for the entire trip, until we got back. He came up close to me a couple of times on the bus and he said, 'I did it for your own good,' and that's what all the others said, all my group, even the chairman. Only Livio Nastri said, 'If I were you I would have killed him…' I thought that perhaps he was right – Bompressi I mean – but that wasn't the way, he could have told me in a kind way, there was no need to embarrass me like that.

'I wouldn't even allow my own father to do that,' I said to him when he came to sit near me, 'If you do it again…'

'I was so shocked when I saw the tyre iron,' he said. And he laughed. And he hugged me. I moved away. After that I still respected him, but the relationship was never the same. I have to say, he was always very fond of me, and he even held me up as an example to his own son, the oldest one. He wanted us to be friends, and he found every excuse to make me go to his home – to pick up posters, materials, various things – and even to make me play with his younger son, who he said looked up to me: for him I was a sort of hero. But I never got over that slap on the head.

Livio Nastri, on the other hand, was completely different. He was chatty, and you never tired of listening to him. Now – after the strike over Trieste and the exile in Santa Maria Capuavetere – we spent every night together. I didn't go to school any more. I had gone back again right after the suspension, but now it wasn't possible any more: I'd changed, but so had they. I was a sort of hero: the girls looked at me, and even the biggest boys greeted me like a friend. There were a few teachers who treated me in a light-hearted manner, especially those who were politically active, the Communists, but all the others looked at me like a public enemy. In class no one said anything to me any more. I could do whatever I felt like: sleep at my desk, get up and walk around, come and go without asking for permission. They didn't care about me at all: as far as they were concerned judgement had already been passed. I thought they would have been happy with the suspension, but no, they said that at the end of the quarter they would give me five out of ten in deportment, which at that time meant – even if there had been a miracle, if I had walked on water and shown the stigmata – that at the end of the year I would have seven in deportment. That would mean a failure, and I would have to repeat the year.

The only person who reassured me was the construction science teacher, a Communist: 'Take it easy, we're not in the business of ruining peoples' lives,' and so I continued to go to school more or less until December, the Christmas holidays. But instead they really did give me a five: they had decided that they wanted to annoy me. 'There was nothing more I could do,' the Communist told me.

When school started up again, after the holidays, I couldn't show my face again. It was all pointless – why should I allow them to make a mockery of me? I didn't go back. Without saying a word to anyone. In the morning I would get up, have breakfast and leave the house with books under my arm. I would go to the party headquarters, and I would stay there until it was time to go home. In the beginning I would open the window shutters, but later I stopped doing that, because one day Bompressi dropped in: 'I was passing by and I saw the windows open: what are you doing here at this hour?'

'I'm preparing a poster.'

'And what about school? You should be at school.' He wasn't paternal, like Wolf said, he was worse than my mother. So I didn't open the windows again, I shut myself inside until the time to go out. I went out to wait for friends outside various schools, and then home to eat.

'How's school?' asked my mother.

'Just fine,' I replied, and so it continued. It was like a sort of ball-room dance, a tango: every day some kind of argument. With anyone: my brothers, sisters, all it took was one person opening his mouth and the fireworks would start. They said it was my fault, but I thought it was theirs. Anyhow, fortunately the result was that when I went out no one said anything to me any more, not even my mother. As a matter of fact, they couldn't wait until I went out, and I didn't even need to show my face at the parish youth group; my father was resigned to things as they were.

So I would go to the party offices in the morning and stay there with the shutters closed. I would read. I would sleep. I would work on our youth journal (*The Bunker*). Sometimes I would clean the offices, sweeping and mopping the floor, and then I would read again and sleep again, and I would masturbate looking at girlie magazines. And I would plan our evening expeditions.

After the strike for Trieste we had to move forward, we had to build the revolution – we could hardly go back to playing Monopoly. So in the evening, after dinner, we would go to put up posters or to write graffiti. There were never more than one or two of us, because then no one could go out in the evenings. As a matter of fact I was on my own more often than not, especially for writing graffiti, because there were always police cars on patrol, and writing on the walls was a crime. But that's precisely why – the crime gave us an orgasmic thrill. If it had been allowed, what would it matter, who would want to do it? But walking through the night acting as if nothing untoward was happening, with the spray can hidden furtively under my raincoat, and then tiptoeing into the shadows and rushing up to a facade of travertine marble and rapidly writing out the words 'Long Live Mussolini' made me first frightened – before I did it – then afterwards filled with satisfaction, especially the next day, when I would go back and look at it with the others. Like Bompressi in Garfagnana.

So I would go out in the evenings, and at home they couldn't stand it. It's not like I would ask their permission – I would just go out, and that was it. I waited for the others to go to bed. The key was always in the lock of our front door, at all times. When he went to bed, my father would take it out and place it on the credenza in the kitchen. I would put it back into the door and be off. The only problem was that when I came back in the door squeaked, and then my father would wake up, but before he got out of bed and put on his slippers, I would already be in bed, pretending to sleep. It's not that they didn't realise what was going on, especially my mother, but more often than not she would pretend not to notice. Sometimes the door would be locked from inside, but then you could try the window.

I would go out every evening at around eleven, and go to Ghersevich, the rosticceria, to wait for Livio Nastri, who would arrive from the cinema after the late show. Ghersevich was a refugee from the formerly Italian city of Fiume, which was now Rijeka in Yugoslavia. After the war, when Tito took over, the Italian community had to leave. Many of them came to Latina, because there was a refugee camp, and they built a new neighbourhood just for them called Vilaggio Trieste. They had this rosticceria, where one could eat in cheap and cheerful surroundings. He had also fought for Mussolini's Republican forces, and in the evening, late, three or four other refugees from Pola and Dalmatia would meet up there; they had all fought together. His wife was highly strung: she couldn't stand it when they got together. He would let her complain, with a half smile: 'Don't pay any attention,' he would whisper.

Livio Nastri would head there at midnight. He must have been thirty-six or thirty-seven years old, nothing more. He had been born here – in Quadrato, which later became Littoria – during the clearing of the swamps, and he ran away from home in 1943, at fourteen, to sign up to fight for the Republic of Salò. He worked as a dental technician, making braces. He was very thin, with dark curly hair. Until a few years previously he had been an actor, a comic actor, with an amateur theatrical society. He had a compelling way of speaking, unstoppable, with sparkling metaphors. He would play on the absurd, the grotesque, and it was a pleasure to listen to him – he was better than the barber. Once Almirante had said to him, 'Nastri, with you around it's better for me to just shut up.' He always spoke about the revolution, and they would speak about the war; he said that since he had been a boy, a Balilla, they would stand guard in front of the party office, and when the leaders passed by they would salute them and he would stamp with his foot on the platform, because there was a prize for the first person to break it. Once he won.

The leaders walking past him were of course Fascists. 'Can you believe?' he said, 'I saluted Pedretti,' who at that time was the vice chairman, and is now a senator for the Socialist Party, and Cinquanta from the Socialist Party and Tasciotti and Rossetti from the Christian Democrats. 'They taught me,' he reminisced, 'how to be a Fascist, and then when times were tough they were the first to change allegiance. I went to the North, with my mother crying, and they stayed here to get fat with the Americans.'

Once Pedretti even reproached him for his uniform not being in perfect condition: 'What kind of a Fascist are you?'

'Can you believe this, when I've risked my life for Fascism?' He shook his head. He also told me that when we made the revolution, he would go and get him personally: 'I want to put them into an electric meat grinder, like butchers have, and I want to see the sausages they turn into. And I want to be the one there to press the button: like that,' and he showed us how with his finger. I was dying of laughter, and he insisted, 'I swear to you: I might have pity on some Communists, but for those traitors …'

He also said that he had fought at Monte Cassino with the Germans, and a bomb had exploded near him – he still had the shrapnel in his bones. When the weather changed his leg would hurt, and he said he could tell when it was about to rain. Then he got better and returned to combat duty. He was in the Black Brigades, the National Republican Guard and Decima Mas. Sometimes I thought that he must have done too much, too quickly and too young. One time Wolf actually said, 'He's telling tall tales' – and Bompressi, from the other room, nodded yes – because it seemed to us that every once in a while he would be confused on the details: once he told us about a friend who had been shot and killed by the partisans, when they were in the Decima Mas, another time when they were in the Black Brigades. But he said that's how things were then, it wasn't so rigid, people moved from one regiment to another with relative ease, depending on where you preferred to serve, and – I have to say – it appears that all the historical sources do confirm this mobility within the Republican forces. Moreover, it is a fact that another friend of his – Giuseppe Bonanni – ran away from the council estate together with him and never came home again, killed by the partisans somewhere in Northern Italy. And another fellow from Latina – Mobili, who was a lieutenant in battalion M – said that he had seen them together around Milan one evening in the winter of 1945. He was on leave and he suddenly heard a voice in the street calling, 'Mobili, comrade!' He turned around and these two young men – the last time he had seen them they were wearing short trousers on the council estate – were fully armed, with semi-automatic weapons and Republican Guard uniforms. Then Bonanni never came back, and if Livio Nastri was embellishing his story now, what did it matter? A story is just a story.

He came home just after his seventeenth birthday, and shortly afterwards left again to do his military service for the Republic of Italy in the airforce, and again there, in training, a grenade exploded close to his leg, the same one he'd injured before. And the shrapnel from this incident mixed with the shrapnel from the other, but this time he got a pension for his trouble. Nothing for the Salò injuries. He said that he'd served in the police for a while, in Rome. He really looked up to the carabinieri, Italy's military police force, like all of us in the Fascist Party. They were better than the regular police forces: the state police – especially the political section – were infamy itself, people not to be trusted, always ready to support the strong against the weak. 'Look at Warrant Officer Gibino: he was originally in the Italian African Police, the most Fascist of any force, and now he is more of a Christian Democrat than Aldo Moro, and if the Communists took power he would become a Communist. He's a sleazy cop.' The carabinieri were at the top of the hierarchy: anti-Communist and nationalist to the end, men of honour.

Then he told us he had spent time in Rome, he had participated in the foundation of the MSI, and even earlier he had supported the Fascist Revolutionary Party and the Mussolini Action Squadrons, right after the war. He told the story of when he had taken the radio transmission centre one night in the Monte Mario neighbourhood of Rome: they tied up all the staff and played Fascist anthems on air. And other actions like that: writing on walls, putting up pennants around town – paper bombs; just to prove that we still existed.

But those were difficult times, when the Communists didn't just shoot people with the Red Squad in Milan, but also in Rome. A comrade from Torpignattara – he told us that the men of Torpignattara were the toughest – had been found dead in a boat on the Tiber, with a gunshot wound to the head. But they weren't entirely sure that the Communists were responsible. There were so many infiltrators, spies, that no one trusted anyone else. At that time it was almost a crime to still be alive after the liberation of Rome. It's almost as if everyone asked each other, with nothing more than a glance, without speaking openly, 'But how did you manage to stay alive? Either you deserted or you must have collaborated with the partisans.'

Moreover, it is a fact that Mussolini died alone. There was no one left around him to defend him. But this is a point that everyone at the party offices preferred to gloss over: they all said that they had been captured by the Americans, but historical sources don't support this. There would have been too many for the Americans to capture all of them. And back then they were always worried about spies, and every time someone in the party offices took a different position, there was always someone who would murmur, 'He was always a police informer.' And Livio Nastri even said this about the national secretaries, even about Almirante and Michelini.

'Who are you kidding?' I asked.

'No, you're kidding! You really are naive.' Once he saw Bompressi speak in front of Bar Mimì with a police officer from the political section, and later that evening he whispered, 'Didn't I always tell you that he was an informer?'

When Ghersevich closed, we would walk the streets of Latina by night. Sometimes I would show up with the spray can and he would start by saying no, then gradually, 'Well alright,' and he stood on guard for me while I wrote 'Long live Fascism' on the walls of the police headquarters. Sometimes we would also put up posters, always looking out of the corner of our eye for a police patrol car to come around the corner, me and him, with the bucket of glue and posters rolled up under our arms. He didn't really enjoy all this kind of 'action', as we called it, but then he would come along to show that he was courageous, that he wasn't afraid. But he was a maniac, especially with the posters. I always preferred fast action – in and out. Action has to be swift. I might think it over for hours before I started, but when you're there there's nothing to think about, you have to move quickly: then things happen as they happen. If something goes wrong you don't have time to fix it, so the posters are sometimes crooked, but you keep on going, you continue with the plan, otherwise that's where everything goes wrong and they get you. But he was obsessive, the poster had to be perfect: you were in trouble if it was only slightly crooked, you'd have to take it down and start again.

'But the police will catch us,' I complained.

'It doesn't matter, the poster has to be straight,' and he would start fiddling to stretch it properly if there was some air bubble or ripple. He would make it perfectly smooth. I would be frightened to death, I would ask myself, 'But how can this be? The cops will be here any minute.' In the time it took to put up a poster with him, I could put up twenty. But I had more fun when we were together. I would get home at around three. He would ask me, 'What about school?'

'Everything's fine,' I would reply. 'I don't need much sleep.'

'You're just like me. I was the same, ever since I was a youngster I've always slept very little. It's because we both have the same nervous disposition.' And the next day he would go to work. But I would just get up, leave home, and go back to sleep at the party offices, with my arms crossed on the desk and my head resting on them. In actual fact it's not that I had already decided not to go to school any more. Every day I would say to myself, 'Tomorrow I'll go back,' but then tomorrow never came, I wouldn't think about it, and that would be that. In the meantime I was writing all this graffiti, putting up posters, and we even set fire to a left-wing mural put up by some artsy professor type. Politics wasn't all he illustrated: sometimes he added poems he had written, one about Sputnik and another one about Brigitte Bardot. We burned them both. The first time he did it again under the title 'Serious attempt on freedom of speech'. The two of us – me and Wolf – even burned that, and then he stopped.

We also ripped down *Republican Voice* posters, and took them away to burn in the public gardens. When Bompressi found out, he was furious – 'We don't do these things' – and he wanted the chairman to suspend me from the party. Deep down I felt badly, I thought about that poor loser writing poems about Brigitte Bardot and spending money to make his mural, just for us to burn it. I felt badly, but what was I to do? That was my career, I was a revolutionary leader: I had to show the others that I was capable of leadership.

One Sunday morning we went to a Communist Party meeting in the grand hall of the Chamber of Commerce. It was all full of Communists. There were only seven or eight of us. When they stopped talking from behind the table they asked, 'Are there any questions?' I raised my hand. As I went up to the table I could see everyone looking at me. Old men with red bandanas around their throats. One of them said, 'Ah, great, let's let the youth speak out.' Then when I began to talk I don't remember what I said, but I remember only that my last words were, 'Long live Mussolini, long live Italy,' and I raised my hand in the Fascist salute. They went wild. Everyone shouting. An old man – the one who had spoken out before – poked his finger into my chest and shouted, 'Apologise to the assembly! Apologise to the assembly!' while two or three others carried me out. But no one lifted a hand to me, they just took me outside. And then, outside, I lost it with my team: 'You should have thrown chairs.'

'Just thank God that they didn't attack you,' said Wolf. 'If we had started throwing chairs, they'd have killed us.' But Wolf stayed to the end – he only left after I did. The others had run away as soon as I said, 'Long live Mussolini!' without even waiting to see how it ended.

When I told the story to Livio Nastri, he could hardly believe it: 'Were you really so courageous?' And then, 'Really, they didn't try to hurt you?' I don't know, but it almost seemed like he was disappointed. To tell the truth, when I saw all the people around me – an old man who had really picked up a chair to throw it, and the other one who kept shouting, 'Apologise to the assembly!' – I did feel a bit afraid. I almost laughed, and I replied, 'Why should I ask for forgiveness?' But I should have said, 'What's your problem? I was just joking,' and I asked myself, 'How did I get into this mess? This is not what I wanted: if I get out alive, I'll never do it again.' But of course I did.

What else was there to do in Latina? Every once in a while I would hitchhike to Rome, sometimes with Wolf but more often than not on my own. The main thing was to get as far as EUR, then we would take the subway to Termini train station. From there, we would walk down via Nazionale and turn right along via Quattro Fontane to the national headquarters. Or else we would take via Firenze to the national youth centre. Every once in a while we'd find someone to chat with, someone who seemed even crazier than us: who had fought with the Communists the day before, who had been in a fight the night before. They were all tough, and they would say, 'Lucky you, living in Littoria.' 'Lucky you living in Rome,' we would think. 'At least you have fun.' But more often than not we wouldn't find anyone: the offices in via Firenze would be closed, the national headquarters semi-deserted. But we got to know Arturo, the porter in via Quattro Fontane. Someone had told him the story of Zone B – probably me actually, I don't remember: 'They're the guys from Littoria mentioned in the minutes' – and then he grew to like me. 'If only they were all like you,' he would say. I was told that at the time of the Republic of Salò he was one of the most enthusiastic supporters, unstoppable. This is why he was now head porter. He was always on the door, and he didn't miss a trick: leaning on the door jamb, with one foot in the entrance and another on the pavement, he would look into the eyes of the policeman on his beat across the road and memorise everyone who passed by. He would stand straight, as if at attention, when party officials came in or went out in their cars. He would greet everyone with a salute, 'Sir!' and they would smile back at him, 'To us!' Everyone said that he was a guard dog, and he was very fond of me. He had been in the Black Brigades, and then in the Ettore Muti legion. 'Here' – and he meant in Rome – 'there wasn't anyone left you could trust.' But no one in Rome had heard of Livio Nastri, for better or for worse. Anyhow, Arturo was the only person at the national headquarters who was really happy to see me there so often, even if sometimes he had to tell me, 'There's no one here.' I would go upstairs anyhow, and I would find the usual executive, at the youth headquarters, stuffing envelopes. He would look at me sadly: 'You again?'

Only one time did I find all the party officials. There was the MP Delfino, the national youth secretary, and then Bellissimo, president of the Giovane Italia youth association, and other famous leaders – at least famous for us – Anderson, Cerullo. They were all older, they were at least thirty or forty, and to us they seemed ancient, even if Bompressi would say, 'They're still youth directors at their age? I'd be ashamed.' But Bompressi's opinions carried no weight with us any more. We studied Andersen's booklets as if they were the Holy Bible. We even knew some parts by heart. What I liked best was the part about hierarchy: 'Nothing is more more unfair than democracy. People are not all equal. From birth we can see very evident differences in their potential, their intelligence and their virtues. Thus hierarchy is a state of nature, and a social organism which seeks to give life to a harmonious State must be built like a pyramid, according to healthy principles of hierarchy.' The intelligent people must be leaders, and those who aren't as gifted must be followers: what does it take to understand this?

Anyhow, when I saw all of them in a room, all busy, I made a step backwards, so as not to disturb them. But Delfino called to me, 'Come over here,' smiling. 'You're from Littoria, aren't you?' and he made me tell the story of the Zone B strike again. Then he asked me suddenly, 'How many people could you bring to Rome?'

'It depends what for. What do I know? If we hitchhike, they won't pick up too many of us. Three or four at the most.'

He started to laugh: 'Three or four is just fine,' and he looked at the others happily. 'But you don't have to hitchhike. Aren't there trains in Latina?'

'Yes, but they're expensive,' and he took a 10,000 lire note out of his wallet, at that time worth a lot, like two or three hundred thousand today. So I said, 'With this much money I can bring a dozen guys.'

They laughed again, as if they didn't believe me: 'Two or three is fine,' they said. And they asked me, 'Are they committed?'

'What can I say? Guys like me…'

'Then that's fine.'

'…but there'll be around a dozen.'

'All we need are two or three,' and they gave me an appointment. But it wasn't a specific appointment, because they still hadn't organised fully. 'How about here the day after tomorrow, in the afternoon, around this time.' And then – when I made an explicit request – they told me that I didn't have to bring receipts: 'What do we need those for? If it's not enough you can ask for more…'

'No, that's more than enough.' I might have been crazy, but I was still honest. And I went right back to Latina to organise the troops. I began to go around asking this person and that person. I had hundreds of members, but some said they had to study, some said their mother wouldn't allow it. I had to work like a dog to put together a team of eleven guys, and up till the last minute I was afraid that someone would let me down: 'I'll look like a fool.' But in the end I dragged all of them to the station. With most of them I had solemnly promised that we would be back home by eight, otherwise their mothers would fuss. Of course they all asked me, 'But why are we going?'

'It's a demonstration for Vietnam. We're going to beat up the Communists.'

At three-thirty we were in Rome. At that time the train tickets cost about three or four hundred lire each. We felt like VIPs with what was left over. We smoked like mad. A couple of the boys had brought along wooden batons rolled up in their newspapers: 'I want to break open a Communist head,' but it really looked like they'd come because the others had come. And they were all encouraging each other: 'You get him from behind, eh?' But what did I care? All that mattered was that they were there, I had the numbers. Then we'd see.

We walked one behind the other from Termini Station to via Quattro Fontane. To the headquarters. But there was no one there: 'Delfino came this morning,' said Arturo, 'but I don't think he's coming back.' We waited and waited. At a certain point he advised me, 'I don't think it's worth you waiting.' So we moved on. They had said that the demonstration was at the Eliseo theatre, so we went there and stood in front. Nothing here either, and not the slightest evidence of a demonstration: the theatre was closed tighter than a drum, and there were adverts for some comedy.

'Are you sure you're right?' my friends began to ask me.

'Of course I am. Where do you think I got the money?' and that stopped them in their tracks. We moved off in a line, one by one, walking along, some of us holding batons. We went first to via Firenze, to Giovane Italia. That was closed too. We spent another half hour on the pavement – 'Sooner or later someone will come' – some of us seated on the ground. Then we started off again: Roman headquarters, in via Cavour. No one there either. So we returned to the national headquarters (along the way some of them started to leave their batons on the side of the road: 'I'm fed up'). Nothing, so we returned to the Eliseo theatre: nothing there either. Via Firenze: worse than if we'd shown up at midnight. The national headquarters again: 'Anyone been by?' Not a soul.

A couple of my group began to complain: 'That's enough. Give us back our tickets and we'll go home.'

The others agreed: 'We want our tickets.' They were all hot and sweaty and tired, after having walked back and forth in the hot sun.

Even Wolf began to complain: 'Give us back our tickets – you can't hold us here by force.'

I was about to give them back when Arturo suggested, 'Have you tried Prenestino?'

'No.' I didn't even know what was there.

'Whenever something big is going down, that's always where they start,' and he told me this in a low voice, as if it were a party secret, that I had to keep to myself. We had already spent two hours, and walked I don't know how many miles. And then just because it was me, and he trusted me; otherwise I'd still be in the dark. It seemed that the top brass was to be found in Prenestino: 'I think Torpignattara is there.' But Arturo gave me a strange look.

We headed off again by tram: to Prenestino. The office there was a sort of shopfront. We saw the party symbol with the tricolour flame, the shutters were open, but the glass was opaque and we couldn't see inside, though the door was ajar. We went inside: 'Hello?' But there was no one there. It was dark. We tried again: 'Hello?' a bit louder, but no one replied. Then we heard voices. We saw in a corner a spiral staircase, made from iron, and we all began to go down it together. We found an enormous hall, almost empty and illuminated. There were two guys drawing posters. One was short and thin, dark with curly hair. The other was tall, heavy-set, dark also but with straight hair, and he was older – around fifty – with a flat face, like a Mongolian, square, with a large mouth, a square chin, a flat boxer's nose and slitty Chinese eyes. It seemed like his face had been hit by an oncoming train.

As soon as they saw us coming down the stairs – actually, they heard us before they saw us, with the sound of all of us on the iron staircase – they froze for a moment, their paintbrushes in their hands: right away they jumped to grab two truncheons, and then turned towards us like guards. 'Who are you?' shouted the shorter one.

It was difficult to explain that we were from Littoria. 'From Littoria?' they asked, and they didn't want to believe us. We had to show them our party membership cards; they kept their truncheons in their hands. The shorter one – he must have been about thirty years old – they called Muriatico, the other one was called Nero, even if he looked more like Genghis Khan. Then another one arrived, big as a wardrobe like the others. His name was Pietro, and he couldn't have been much older than twenty. They were angry with him because he had left the door open.

'I went out for a sandwich.'

'And if they'd been Communists?' insisted Muriatico.

Anyhow, to make a long story short, they told us that the meeting time was in front of the Eliseo theatre between seven-thirty and eight. It was already after six, and it had started to get dark. 'If you stay here,' they said, 'some of you can come with us in the car, but we don't have room for all of you.' I preferred not to split up – both from a sense of responsibility and because at this point it seemed to me that we made a good effect all together – so we decided to go by tram: 'We'll meet you there.'

'We'll meet you there,' replied the guys from Prenestino, and they were happy to have finally met the famous Littoria troops, ready for battle, next to them.

On the tram the discussions began. It was late, it was dark: 'They're not starting until eight; you had told us that we'd be back by then – my mother will be furious.' I couldn't insist. At the end of the day, at least now we had been seen, they would say we'd been there. So I gave them each their ticket, also because something might happen and we could get separated: 'If anyone wants to go home, they can – the others can come with me.'

'Alright, but now we're hungry.'

'Alright, whoever wants can come to Termini Station and we'll get sandwiches. The others can go home to eat.' We continued our discussions during the ride on the tram.

When we got to Termini three or four of them took the train home, looking downcast: 'If it weren't for my mother I'd stay with you guys.' The others resigned themselves: 'Well, it's late now, my mother's already upset.'

We took our time over our sandwiches and orange soda. We even tried to remember where we'd left our batons. We got there happy and relaxed, to find that the others were assembled. There was a large group: thirty, forty, maybe fifty people at most. We seemed like the largest team. Muriatico yelled at someone in front of him: 'Wait, the guys from Littoria are coming,' as if it were some big deal. But they were all older than us: twenty-five, thirty, forty years old. We were younger: sixteen or seventeen.

They began to run. We were behind them. On the other side of the road, on the pavement, you could see the illuminated entrance to the Eliseo stalls. They began shouting, 'Losers! Losers!' and throwing eggs. They passed us some eggs. One guy had a big box of them, with several layers of cardboard holders. We took these eggs and threw them everywhere, hitting as many targets as we could: heads, faces, windows. We threw them like grenades, and we started laughing, we weren't afraid at all. The others – the enemy – as soon as they saw us coming they ran into the stalls to hide. First we were there on the pavement chatting in little groups, and then – when they saw us, this little group around the cars started clambering onto the hoods and roofs of the cars – they ran into the theatre, climbing on top of each other in the rush to get in. There were more of them than of us, but on their side there were several women dressed in furs and wearing jewellery, and maybe we frightened them, because as we were on our way there, approaching from via Nazionale, one of the guys ahead of us threw a paper bomb into the stalls, it was just very noisy. And then we began to shout, 'Losers!' and throw eggs at them.

There was a guy there called La Pira who had just returned from Vietnam. He was the Mayor of Florence, a Christian Democrat, but they said that he was practically a saint. He had taken a vow of chastity, he had visions of Our Lady, he spoke with God in his sleep. He was a mentor to Fanfani, and he got along with the Communists. Apparently he had a dream in which God told him to go to Ho Chi Minh and other world leaders. God had given them a mission of peace: 'I'm with you, you'll see, people will listen.' And then he left, he went to Hanoi with the Communist Party: 'You're one of us.' Then, of course, the war went on for another ten years, but all the left-wing intelligentsia were there waiting for him at the Eliseo theatre. And so were we.

We were behind the glass door to the stalls, pushing to get in. We continued to shout 'Losers!' and every once in a while the pushing started from the back of the crowd, like a wave. They were pushing on the door from inside too, to keep them closed and because there was too much of a crowd and they couldn't all fit in the hallway: every once in a while the door seemed to open in our direction, as if they wanted to get out. Every once in a while someone would even put their foot out, and then they would quickly rush back into the crowd. Once the eggs were gone, we continued shouting 'Losers!' and pushing.

That's how things continued for half an hour. Three or four of my team began to complain, 'It's late,' I told them. 'Fine,' and they left. In the end only Wolf and I remained, but it seemed almost as if everything was over.

The guy who had been in front at the beginning – to whom Muriatico had said, 'Wait, Littoria's here' – remained off to one side, away from the rest of the group. They called him Bava. Every once in a while he would nod to someone and tell them something. At a certain point – on his orders – we stopped pushing and moved back a few yards.

When we moved back and stopped pushing, their pushing erupted: the door opened and a little group spilled out, just like milk overflowing

on the stove. In physics this is called the 'break point': they suddenly
exploded out, and it seemed just as sudden to them. The first one was
small and blond, with a receding hairline. I had noticed him earlier,
when we found ourselves looking at each other from opposite sides of
the glass and – more than once – he shouted, 'Fascists! Fascists!' as if
to me personally, as if I'd done something to him. When he found
himself outside – he was the first – he looked angry, and he swung his
fists in our direction, towards me. He got me on the neck. On my left
side. With his right hand. Right away I gave him a one-two in the face
– left-right – and then I went again on the other side with my left. I
was about to start again, but I couldn't see him: he had stepped back,
bent over, then slipped. But as he slipped, one of the Cataldo boys
broke his fall, the bigger one. He held him by the neck with his arm,
and with the other hand he punched him over and over again. Even
I felt sorry for the guy. I looked for someone else, but I couldn't
find anyone. There were groups around us that moved back into the
shadows. Quick fists. Even one or two of our own against one of
theirs. As soon as they could they ran back inside. It didn't last more
than one or two minutes. Cataldo was still alone with the blond guy.
And he was pummelling him. Someone got close to hit him too. His
people had forgotten him. Bava went to pick him up. He dragged
him onto his feet and took him back to the stalls door. And he kept
shouting, 'Fascists! Fascists!' My neck was starting to hurt. But then
and there I didn't realise, and I had reacted well, but now it was
hurting. 'Come outside!' we shouted menacingly.

Then we heard sirens and saw the flashing lights of the police
arriving. Bava said, 'Let's go! Take it easy!' and we moved back to
the other side of the street. At that exact moment, they came out
from the stalls and lined up along the pavement. There must have
been fifteen of them, in a line, big guys, all quite young, around
twenty. In the middle – but one step forward – leading them, we saw
Pajetta. He indicated with his hand how they should line up, and
then made them advance. His hair was white – what little he had –
and he wasn't wearing a jacket, just shirtsleeves. His voice was

guttural. 'Come forward,' he taunted us, and they were already half way across the road.

Muriatico was about to start again, and we were right behind him, but Bava took him by the arm: 'What are you doing? Let's go!' and he made a gesture to the others, as the police sirens drew closer. We began to run along via Boschetto. Gradually some people arrived. Wolf and I went behind Muriatico. We got to a Renault 4. Nero was there and someone else. When they saw us they asked him, 'Where can they go?'

'We can't leave them here,' said Muriatico, and somehow they got us on board. He put me in the boot, like a piece of luggage. I still remember the sound of metal as the car bounced. My neck was killing me at this point. The car belonged to someone called Sirio, and he was also impressed that we were from Littoria. There was even a newspaper photographer, and he said, 'I've taken an amazing picture of you.'

Muriatico insisted on going somewhere to celebrate: 'A cappuccino at least.' But it was getting late, and my neck ached. They took us to Termini, and we just caught our train. We found the others on board: 'We lost you.'

'You should have stayed,' we told them, because they got there just as the previous train pulled out. Wolf told them everything, in detail. And I told them more about the blows I'd taken than those I'd given, also because by now I was holding my head in a funny way and they were teasing me. But it was a glorious teasing, as if they were war wounds.

'But that poor guy...' said Wolf.

I agreed with him: 'But what could I do?'

'Not you, Cataldo,' and I agreed. Especially when he told me he was wearing brass knuckles. He didn't just go for his face, he went for his head. He really gave him a working over. With the brass knuckles. And with every blow there was blood. He made holes in his skull. On his bald head. Wolf was there, he could see everything. I felt bad, but what could I do? War is war. And I had behaved myself, even if –

I have to be truthful – when they were all lined up and Pajetta went, 'Come forward,' I was sort of worried and I felt butterflies in my stomach: 'What am I doing here?' And when Muriatico wanted us to advance but Bava held him back, I breathed a sigh of relief, and as we ran away I prayed God that they wouldn't catch us: 'I never get myself into this kind of mess,' I said to myself. But they must have breathed a sigh of relief too when they saw that we were going away. I also wondered about the leaders: Delfino, Anderson, the others. None of them were there: 'Why make me go if you won't be there?' Just Bava.

Wolf said, 'But are you stupid? The leaders can't expose themselves!'

'I guess,' I thought.

The next morning I ran to buy the paper: 'Vietnam and youthful idiots. Fascist youth demonstration.' And there was a photo on the front page, in the centre, of me getting punched in the neck, taken from behind. I displayed it on the wall, and that evening, when we went out, I took the girls to look at it: 'That's me, on the front page.'

'But it's taken from behind,' they all said.

But Wolf said, 'I don't think there's much to be proud of. All you can see is that you're being beat up.' Maybe he was envious.

However, it took a week for my stiff neck to go. 'It must have been the cold,' I told my mother. 'What about the buttons on your shirt?' she asked.

chapter 6

One day, after having spent the entire morning in the party offices –
sleeping on the youth secretary's desk, reading Anderson and Nietzsche,
sweeping the floor, masturbating over saucy photos in a magazine – I
went out just in time to go to the teachers' college and wait for a girl.
She saw me from far away, and left her girlfriends to come running
over to me – finally I returned home, and my mother asked me, just
as I sat down in front of a bowl of minestrone, 'How did it go today?'

'Fine,' I told her. 'What do you expect?'

'But did you go to school?' she asked innocently.

'Of course,' I replied as I pulled up my chair.

'You disgraceful boy! I went to see your teachers today, and they
told me they haven't seen you for two months.' Total meltdown. She hit
me on the back with a wooden spoon. She was like someone possessed,
and I couldn't move because I was wedged into my seat at the table.
She stopped when she just couldn't go on any more: 'You'll be the death
of me,' she cried. And then she went to lie down on her bed. 'I thought
I was going to die. I was so shocked, I even called Dr Valentini.' It really
seemed like someone had died. Everyone looked downcast, no one
said a word. They just looked at me.

'You'll be the death of Mamma,' said Mimì. Now even she was on
my case. She wasn't nice to me again until she needed help with her
Latin homework.

'What do you mean?' I replied. 'She was trying to kill me.'

'Shame on you!' screeched Mimì. 'You think it's funny? She almost
passed out when she got home.' Mamma was always feeling unwell:
her heart must have been in tatters from all the times she thought she

was having a heart attack. Anyhow it was better like that (not that Mamma would have had a heart attack – because after all it didn't happen, and she was standing up and screaming and bossing everyone around shortly after) with things out in the open. I couldn't stand the anxiety any longer, the constant fear of being caught. It couldn't go on for ever. So the next morning I didn't get up at all, and I kept on sleeping in my own bed. It didn't seem real to me, so much better than the desk. But my mother began to harass me. She was on the attack. Every five minutes she would come into my room and shout – she said that she'd reached an agreement with the teachers, she said that I had to go back to school: they were waiting for me with open arms.

Sure, open arms: 'Look who's here,' they would say. Or else, 'Look what the cat dragged in.' In any event, there was just no way. More than two months had passed, and they had moved ahead in every subject. Now I didn't understand anything and I didn't even care that I didn't understand anything. Logarithms, iron beams, girders. What did I care? I didn't want to have anything more to do with it all. It was my mother's choice to make me into a surveyor. Like Otello. Now what did they want from me? I was fed up. So one morning I stayed in bed.

'I don't care what you do,' I told her, 'I'm not going back.'

'I'll kill you.'

'Kill me,' and I rolled over. She kept screaming, but I didn't even hear. As a matter of fact, I fell asleep again before she finished.

Finally she gave up: 'But it's not over,' she menaced.

'OK, fine, close the door for me, please,' and that's how the best days of my life began. I would sleep every day until one or two in the afternoon. Then I had something to eat. Then I would go back to sleep for another hour, and then I would go out. I was always here and there. I would hitchhike to Rome, or I would go to the party office. In the evenings I would take a walk in town or court some girl. I'd drop by home for dinner and some TV. Then at ten-thirty I'd go out again to put up posters, spray graffiti, or hang out with Livio Nastri until 3 or 4 a.m. Then I would read until six or seven. What a life. It was too bad that every once in a while something would happen to ruin everything.

'I provide every meal for you,' my mother would fling in my face. 'Aren't you ashamed?'

'And I go work to support you,' my father reminded me. 'Don't you feel badly? You were such a good boy when you were small. Don't you ever think back to Father Cavalli?' They still wrote to each other, even now that he was the Superior of his religious order in Siena. Then one time my father wanted to take me to the family doctor: 'There's something wrong with you.' But the others stopped him, my mother first of all, and then they teased him about it for years: 'You wanted to take him to the doctor,' and they would all laugh, rather than realising that he was completely mad. When he couldn't get help from the doctor, he turned to the saints: 'You must be possessed, this house is cursed.' And one evening, or rather at dawn, when I came home, I couldn't get to sleep because he had put thorns into my pillow. And I could feel something in the pillow, and started to examine it, incredulous – 'What's wrong with this pillow?' – so much so that my brothers woke up.

'What's wrong with you? What the hell's wrong with you?'

'What do I know?' and I kept on taking the thorns out. In the end I put my hands into the pillowcase and I felt something hard. I turned the light on.

'Are you crazy?' they asked me, but then they burst out laughing, because two holy cards with pictures of Saint Giovanni Bosco came out of my pillowcase, two laminated images that were stopping me sleeping.

And the next day my father acted as if nothing was out of the ordinary: 'Well, so what? A father can't commend his cares even to Saint Giovanni Bosco?' After which, when even this final hope left, he turned nasty: 'Why don't you go back to Massa Carrara? Who says that we have to support you? I regret looking for you. I thought that you had died, and I cried all the way from Anzio to Nettuno. Go back and stay away.'

'Ah, that's what you'd like, is it?' I said to him. 'I'll leave when I feel like it. I didn't ask to be born. You brought me into the world, now you have to support me.' To tell the truth, this time I was joking, I spoke in a jovial tone, but he went mad – we were in the entrance, between the door to the kitchen and the door to the lounge – and he tried to hit me in the chest, furiously.

'You already saw that day at the shop that I can flatten you.'

When he said that I lost it too. I took his hands off my chest, grabbed his arm and pushed him until Mamma intervened. He had made a fist, and was about to lunge, and so was I, but she got between us, and I only managed to hit his shoulder. She shrieked and we moved apart. But from the other side of the door, in the entrance, I taunted him, 'Come here.'

'And why should I?'

'Get out here and take your glasses off, don't use her as your shield.'

He went white and began to scream. Then he spoke to me in a gentle tone, as if he was teasing me, but his voice was barely audible: 'Why should I take my glasses off?'

I didn't say another word.

'Explain to me why I should take my glasses off, tell us what you're going to do,' and my mother was very small, she didn't say a word, she just massaged my father's shoulder. Then I went out, and a few days later he told me, 'As much as I love you, I hope your son never makes you go through what you've put me through. I truly hope not, son. But you would really deserve it.'

Then there was the issue of the university. Paolo Rossi had died in Rome in front of the Faculty of Humanities. There had been some incidents with scuffles during the university elections, and there had been a fight at the entrance. The guys from New Republic started it, and our guys had helped them. But it was just punches and shoves, nothing more. It's just that a commotion occurred between the main door and the terrace in front, and a boy from the left fell down – three or four metres – and he died. Then they occupied the university – all of it, the entire campus – and all the newspapers and television could say was 'Fascist murderers'. The television programmes showed meetings in the university classrooms, banners, posters, demonstrations, popular indignation. It seemed like we'd gone there just to kill the poor guys, it seemed like that was all we thought about: 'Fascist? Murderer.' Could I remain aloof from all of this? One morning I woke up and went to Rome.

The university was closed, locked. You could see the students behind the gates – the reds – going here and there. 'No to Fascism' was written everywhere. On the pavement, on the other side of the street, a small group of young people gradually formed. Every once in a while someone else would come along. The bus stopped, people got out, and they wandered here and there, but someone stopped by to look at the university from the other side of the street, as if by chance. 'What happened?' 'Who are those people?' 'Really, even Fascists...' 'Those Fascists!' It was us, we found ourselves again. Soon there were thirty of us, maybe more. All university students. They said it was an accident. They started, and then someone shoved. Blame the terrace without walls, just a sort of ledge – it doesn't take much to fall off it. I'm sorry for the poor fellow who died, but why all this fuss? We began to say, 'Let's punch our way in.'

A short guy approached. He asked, 'Where do you want to go...'

I looked at him priggishly, as if to say, 'What's it to you? Let us do our work.' But he kept on talking. He had a deep voice, and you could see that he understood us. We found out that he was Stefano Delle Chiaie, the founder of Avanguardia Nazionale, and when I realised I was moved. But he had taken a liking to me, and we spoke for around an hour, he explained more things to me – about corporativism and the social nature of Fascism – than I'd learned from our chairman in two years. Anyhow, now there were about fifty of us and we were starting to make a noise. We shouted to the people unrolling their banners on top of the entrance portico of the university. Among them there were even some lads who were clearly right off a building site: 'Do you see?' we asked each other. 'They're Communist workers, it's not just a student demonstration, it's being manipulated.'

Some of the police, who were standing near the gates, crossed the street and stood in front of us. We began to push. A plain-clothes officer was issuing orders: he was stocky, about forty. He said to us, 'Get back on the pavement,' because we had spilled out onto the road. Delle Chiaie made us get back. 'We're just here to watch,' he said to the plain-clothes officer: 'Can't you see that there are only a few of us? Even if we wanted to do something, what harm could we cause?'

Then there were some pushes and shoves, and two guys took me away to the guard position that they had created in front of the entrance. Including me, in about fifteen minutes they brought another six or seven guys. Then the police officer and Delle Chiaie arrived together – but they were calm, chatting – and he whispered in my ear, 'Don't worry, I'll look after things.' He had come to negotiate our release.

They said to him, 'Come inside and let's speak calmly,' and they made way for him. 'Please take a seat,' they said to him, like perfect hosts. I guess they didn't reach an agreement, because at a certain point Delle Chiaie got up to leave. But they wouldn't let him go. 'Are you joking?' he asked.

'No, you're under arrest.'

'But what's going on?' Delle Chiaie asked me.

'Be careful what you say,' the other menaced.

Then they brought in a couple more. There wasn't room for us any more in that cubbyhole, and they brought a paddy wagon. But before they loaded us in they loaded ten more directly from the road. Ten of us. It must have been one-thirty in the afternoon, and it was hot. They took us to San Vitale, the central police station. There must have been twenty-five or thirty of us. We didn't do anything, but in the evening they told TV news reporters that they had arrested thirty activists under Delle Chiaie's command: 'Who knows? Maybe one of them is Paolo Rossi's killer?'

To tell the truth, I didn't mind at all – actually I only minded later, at almost ten at night, when they released us. I thought that at least this time they would have taken us to jail, and this time it wouldn't have been via Aspromonte, but the high-security facility at Regina Coeli. But no, they just kept us all together on the terrace, under the hot sun, after having taken our details one by one. Then we sang our Fascist songs, and time passed under the midday sun, and some of us worried: 'Now what will I tell my mother? She expected me home at lunchtime.' Even Delle Chiaie was sweating, but he never took his jacket off. He only removed it later in the evenings, when the temperature went down. And he kept on talking, with his persuasive voice and convincing reasoning. He was someone who tried to see things from the perspective of others. He would look at an argument from every point of view. Sometimes he would reason like a Communist: 'They have some valid points,' he tried to convince me. He respected them. He hated Christian Democrats the most, and especially the MSI party leaders. He said that they had nothing to do with Fascism: 'They're all on the Confindustria payroll; they're the White Guard of this regime.' Years later he was incriminated for alleged terrorist activity. They said that he was even in covert agreement with the secret services. For many years he was on the run abroad – apparently he was an adviser to Franco's regime in Spain and then to reactionaries in South America, Argentina and Uruguay. What can I say? Now I don't know what he really did but – as far as I knew at the time – Stefano Delle Chiaie seemed to me like a fine individual.

That time I just caught the last subway train to EUR – otherwise I would have had to stay in Rome overnight – and I stood by the pond to hitchhike. But at night it's much harder than in the daytime. It took for ever: three came and went. When I finally got home, I put some water to boil on the stove, and I cooked some pasta. My family didn't leave anything out for me to eat, but there was always some sauce in the fridge, and at one or two or three in the morning I would make myself big plates of pasta.

The next morning I got up, but I didn't go to Rome: I stayed in bed sleeping long after lunchtime. I went out in the afternoon and paid a visit to the party offices, but my news was already out of date. On the radio they had heard that Fascists had forced the side entrance of the university and had got inside. There were one or two hundred, maybe more. They were lead by Delfino – the national youth secretary who made us go to the Eliseo theatre and didn't show up – Gigi Turchi and Caradonna, but they only got in by a few metres. The police were waiting in the alleyway to the side of the Humanities faculty, and loaded them into paddy wagons without pity as they came in from the gate. They were outnumbered by the police. The radio said that Delfino shouted, 'I'm a member of parliament! I'm a member of parliament!' but they didn't give a damn, and went at him with their truncheons. Then they had to take a step back. The news had reached everyone. Others said, 'Dirty Fascist squads.' The right said, 'Well, at least someone is opposing the Communists,' and then – but only later – I realised that this is why Michelini, the secretary, would let us do stuff every once in a while. It wasn't really a plan to start the revolution – it was just to remind people of our existence, to demonstrate his point to his chums. Delle Chiaie was right. But so was Bompressi, actually.

Anyhow, now the radio was saying that Delfino was in a serious condition. They thought he might have a cerebral haemorrhage. He was in an oxygen tent in a private clinic paid for by Trombetta, a local councillor in Rome who had a lot of money; he was a doctor and had his own clinic. According to the radio reports, we were on the verge of big things: 'Now's the times to start the revolution. If Delfino dies, it will finally happen.' And we were all preparing ourselves to mobilise and leave for Rome: 'Who knows what's going on there.'

'But what do you think will happen?' Bompressi insisted. 'He's in better health than I am.'

'How dare you say that? He's in an oxygen tent.'

'Sure, at Trombetta's clinic… Why didn't he go to the Polyclinic if he's so ill? He made it all the way to Trombetta's place! This is all a game of smoke and mirrors,' and in the end he convinced all of us. 'He just got one truncheon blow, he took it and now he's pretending to be a martyr. Why didn't he go to the Polyclinic if he's so near? He went to Trombetta to go into the oxygen tent. If he'd gone to the Polyclinic they'd have told him the truth: don't waste our time, they'd have told him.' And only two of us went: me and Piermario, the other guy they'd expelled because of Zone B.

He came to the party offices one afternoon a few days after his expulsion. It was early afternoon, and he was alone. He entered the main room and said, 'I need to talk to you.'

'Talk.'

He started up again, saying that it was wrong to send young people out unprepared, and his voice got louder and louder. I think I was shouting too, but he was really inflamed. I was calm. We were both standing in front of the desk, and at a certain point he gave me a wide punch on the temple, really hard. I grabbed both of his wrists. I didn't react. I grabbed his wrist, and I held him steady: 'If you want to fight, let's go outside.'

'No. Let's fight here.'

'Not in the party offices. Let's go downstairs.' I don't know why I had this obsession, as if the party offices were a sacred place – like a church – that could not be profaned. Downstairs was fine, up here no.

'But no one will see us here,' he insisted. I don't know, maybe this is what convinced me. In the end I held fast and he calmed down. But they didn't withdraw his suspension – Livio Nastri said that it was the right thing to do – and before he left he said to me, 'Time will show which of us is the more committed Fascist.'

'Just imagine,' I thought, and for a few months I didn't see him again. Actually when we passed each other in the street on the evenings he didn't even say hello to me. Then one time he must have heard that there was a sort of conference about corporativism where Livio Nastri was speaking, and he came. He arrived a few minutes after we'd begun. He didn't sit down, but leaned on the desk at the back. He had a face that seemed to challenge us, as if to say, 'I've been expelled but I'm still here.' In the end he asked if he could speak. Livio Nastri didn't want him to: 'He's expelled,' he whispered in my ear. But I let him have the floor with a smile on my lips, without any apparent rancour. And without any apparent rancour we started hanging out together again.

The two of us went to Rome. Hitchhiking. Convinced that we would find the city under siege. But everything was calm. The Communists were inside the university and there was no one outside, just police officers. All the party offices were closed, there wasn't a soul anywhere: national headquarters, via Firenze, Prenestino. 'How can it be that no one's preparing anything?' And we went to Colle Oppio. This was another famous party office, run by former Avanguardia activists. They were all strange, sub-proletariat types: people who lived locally, builders, the unemployed, some rough sleepers from Termini Station. But there were students too. When we arrived there were three or four of them, they were on guard at the party offices because they feared an attack. We had to show them our membership cards to convince them, and they took us inside under escort. Later, one of them recognised me: 'Weren't you with us at the Eliseo theatre?'

'How's Delfino?' we asked.

'He's fine.' Bompressi was right after all. He just took one blow from a truncheon and then he ran off. All the others had been attacked too, including Turchi and Caradonna.

'We don't believe it about Turchi,' these Colle Oppio guys said, because he had a lot of money and his father, Franz, was a senator, and during the time of the Republic of Salò he'd been in charge of La Spezia. He was an elected official, but they all treated him like a sort of idiot: 'If he didn't have money...' But this time, at the university, he had done well: 'Giggino Turchi, I couldn't believe what I was seeing,' Calabrotto kept saying. They knew about Caradonna. I don't know what his health issues were, big as he was: he needed two crutches to walk, sort of two sticks – but he always gave his utmost. Actually, because he couldn't walk, the police had taken it out on him, but he defended himself with his crutches.

'We got lost,' Piermario and I said. 'We always arrive too late.' And we had to content ourselves with spending the night with them, guarding the Colle Oppio party offices. We stayed sitting outside until midnight, waiting for the Communists to arrive, then some of our comrades went home, and another few went inside to sleep. We stretched out too on the wooden benches, and used some old posters as mattresses. The place was either lugubrious or picturesque, I can't say which. You came through a door and it was like a cavern. There was a little hill above with flowers, trees. And we were underneath, in this room with arches, all underground.

'This is where Nero lived,' Calabrotto told us. We didn't ask any questions, we thought he was joking, but afterwards – years later – I discovered that we really had been inside the Domus Aurea, Nero's famous golden palace. There were all these brick walls and Fascist standards and symbols with the ubiquitous flames and portraits of Mussolini. I slept badly, turning over constantly trying to find a comfortable position for sleep. But the worst was my head, without a cushion. That's where I started sleeping on my side, with an arm under my head to keep it comfortable. I would dream of Nero surrounded by black standards, with golden Fascist insignia and Communists attacking us.

I woke up with a bad back. My entire body ached. Piermario was the same. We went together to Calabrotto and his friend, who was a bit shorter than him, he must have been about thirty years old. He was wearing a dark brown suit with a tie, but it was all wrinkled. He looked like a dirty old man. He had a few days of beard growth. As we walked towards Santa Maria Maggiore, he walked in a lopsided way – who knows why? – with one foot on the roadside and the other one on the asphalt, like kids do, so much so that I asked Calabrotto, 'Is he lame?'

'No, the pummelling he got yesterday still hurts.'

Every once in a while he would say, 'Trust me to come without my car,' and Piermario and I laughed, 'This guy's an idiot.'

Then Calabrotto said, 'Treat us to breakfast,' and he replied, 'Do you think I'm a bank?' and he continued limping along the pavement in front of us, and the other guy said to us, in a low voice, 'He's rich, he's loaded.'

Apparently he really did have a car, a Fiat 1500, and he owned a fabric shop. He looked more like a tramp than Calabrotto, who was a true member of the sub-proletariat. But a short while later he thought it over, and he did pay for our breakfast at the bar, a brioche and a cappuccino, and he even asked kindly, 'Would you like anything else?

If you want anything else, just say so.' He told us that he had fought for the Republic too. He was a young man, but he said that he was the last to shoot, on 28 or 29 April: 'I fired the last volley. The only reason they didn't shoot me is because they felt sorry for me, I was too small. Everyone else with me was taken out.'

We arrived at the Roman party offices to see if anything was going on, but obviously everything that needed doing had been done the day before. It even seemed that during the night Delfino had felt better and returned home already. 'Think how happy Bompressi will be,' said Piermario. And we returned home too.

Then one evening at the party offices someone who sold linens dropped by. He was a salesman for a firm in Rome. He showed Bompressi and the chairman a whole host of letters of presentation from Almirante on headed party notepaper. His name was Nino. He wanted the list of party members and another letter of presentation for the offices throughout the province of Latina: 'For every bundle I sell I'll give 2000 lire to the local office.'

They agreed, and said to me, 'You go with him.'

I didn't want to: 'Now I have to sell sheets and towels door to door?'

But Bompressi insisted: 'You monitor him and you'll earn some money while you're at it.'

We wandered throughout the entire province. With the fact that I was there, the local secretaries trusted him more, and we sold a lot of merchandise. There was even a set of embroidered towels with the Fascist symbol, the tricolour flame, in the centre, and it could also be embroidered onto tablecloths: people loved them. We went every-where in his estate car all day long – it was blue. I had to get up early in the morning too. He gave me 2000 lire a day plus breakfast and lunch, always sandwiches. A couple of times we would stay in modest hotels. I was bored, because selling linens isn't easy, and it's time-consuming. Every sale takes several hours, you have to intoxicate people with your words, you have to roll out the sheets and show them twenty times, you have to unfold the tablecloths. And then you go here and there, looking for this person and that person: someone is out, come back in an hour, come back tomorrow. Then, in some towns, word would pass between relatives and friends. We sold mountains of linens, even to Communists...even to Protestants. I didn't even know there were so many Protestants living in the mountains nearby. I thought they were all up North. But we arrived there and the local secretary told us, 'I can take you to meet some of my relatives, but they're evangelicals. You'd better not show them the tablecloth with Fascist embroidery.'

We went to a town called Sonnino. There was a girl my age there, with long red hair. She was beautiful. She was also sweet with me. We went back a few more times, because her mother wanted to take us to her friend, and to someone else. Her name was Anna. We spent hours talking on her doorstep, in front of the kitchen, while we opened up the tablecloths. In 1966 it was still a mountain village, there were donkeys walking around, and they had one too. She looked after it. And she talked and talked. Well actually, she was quite taciturn. To get her to talk, you had to ask her specific questions, but I asked her so many that she talked quite a bit. She said that her family had been evangelicals since the beginning of the twentieth century. They got along with the Catholics well enough, almost always. In 1948, there had been a purge, the Catholics wanted them out, but the Fascists sent them into exile first. They respected God and Christians: 'Turn the other cheek. Don't do to others what you wouldn't want done to yourself,' and they spoke in dialect. Even when she spoke Italian you could hear the local accent, with this red hair. I wanted to know everything about her, about them. I even dreamed about her at night. She had strong calves and she wore short cotton socks. She had a serious, wise way of talking.

I was fascinated: I don't know if it was more about her or about them. I was sincerely distressed about the 1948 massacre, the persecutions, and also the Fascist exile: 'But how could this be allowed? And why did you agree to it? Didn't you rebel?' I wanted to convert, I wanted to be a Protestant too, and evangelical, and marry her and vindicate their community once and for all. But I didn't tell her anything. I just tried to feel the situation out, to see if there was any opportunity. There was some hope, because as soon as she saw me she would smile: it's just that after a while she would begin to be serious, when we started to discuss things. She seemed like a theologian. Speaking in dialect. And she treated me like someone who needs to be saved, a little lost sheep: 'That's why I'm here,' I said, but I took things easy: I didn't want to make the same mistake as I did in the Volkswagen. One evening, before we left – as Nino refolded the tablecloths and the donkey outside neighed – I told her, 'Anna, for you I would even convert to Islam.' She smiled and didn't say anything. 'That's it,' I thought. 'The next time we're in Sonnino I'll close the deal.'

But the next day there was a demonstration in Rome for the electoral campaign – we weren't voting in Latina, it was municipal – with Almirante's meeting in piazza Esedra. So we worked hard in the morning and a few hours in the afternoon. By 6 p.m. we were in Rome: me, Nino – with his estate car full of linens – and Nino's boss in a Fiat 2300, the guy who received those letters of recommendation from Almirante. That's where I met Sirio – he drove the car when we left the Eliseo theatre – as well as Calabrotto and a couple of other guys from Colle Oppio: 'Are you coming to put up posters later?' they asked me. Could I tell him no? I had an appointment with Nino next morning: 'We'll leave straight from Rome,' and I went with them to put up posters all night with a van, a yellow Ford Transit. We didn't finish until five. I slept for a few hours in the van, on top of the posters, and then I met up with Nino. We drove all around Latina and the surrounding area to sell linens. That evening I returned with him to Rome because I had another rendezvous with those guys. And that's how things continued for two or three days. I would sleep for a few hours in the van in the morning, and then in Nino's estate car, with my head resting against the window, as we drove around. As soon as I got into the car, I would fall asleep.

'You can't go on like this,' said Nino. 'I'm worried for you: a little bit of politics is alright, but you have to think about your health.'

Nonetheless, I liked putting up posters: I had become something of an expert. That year the municipality had put up new display spaces for posters, made from metal, and it was a true pleasure to put up the first virgin poster. I was very fast, four strokes and they were up. Sometimes we would compete, and I was the champion of my team. I liked the fact that they encouraged me: I felt like someone, and I was more energetic. Sirio was a decent guy. He was tall, blond and decisive, but also sensitive and direct. Like a medieval knight, a crusader. The others were all from Termini Station. One night when he saw that I was completely sleep-deprived, Calabrotto said to me, 'Take this and you'll feel better,' and he gave me a white pill. It did make me feel better for a few hours. Then I asked him for another one. And another one. And so it went on. Finally he said, 'Now that's enough, you're becoming an addict,' and he laughed with all the others. Then he gave me some more: 'But now you have to pay for them – I can't support you for free.'

A few days later Nino said, 'I'm sorry, but I've almost finished selling linens in the Latina area. There's nothing more to be done, the market is saturated now.'

'What about Sonnino?' All I wanted was to return to Sonnino and become a Protestant.

'Nothing in Sonnino either.'

I didn't want to ask any questions. I was upset because I felt like I'd been given the brush-off. He and his linens could go to the Devil, partly because he said to me, 'Before it was different, you worked hard, you helped me out. Now all you do is sleep and think about the posters.'

So I asked him, 'Is the market saturated, or is this about the posters?' He pretended not to understand. He preferred not to respond, and he kept driving. I hit his arm. Hard.

'Both,' he said.

'Ah, both,' I replied with derision.

From that moment I didn't have to go back and forth between the mountains and Rome any more. Of course I was sorry for Anna – and also about the money, which had been useful, especially for the pills

– but I had to think of politics. So I started hanging out with others from the party, even during the day. In actual fact there was a whole group of them – the guys from Colle Oppio and the youth club from the Roman party office – and the leader was one of the Cataldo brothers, the youngest one, not the one who'd been in that fight at the Eliseo. Now I practically lived in the van, surrounded by posters. Every once in a while I would wash up at the party offices at Colle Oppio. It seemed like my suit was holding out. It was hot. I didn't wear the dark grey raincoat any more, instead I always wore the Prince of Wales suit that my mother had made me get: 'Wear this,' she had said. 'You'll make a better impression selling linens,' and so that's what I kept wearing.

Then one evening, at the inauguration of a new office in piazza Bologna where Michelini was present, as we were coming away and I was already going towards the van, Bava came up to me, the guy who'd been in charge at the Eliseo theatre. 'What are you doing with these guys?' he asked me, but it wasn't really a question, it was a comment of disgust, and I didn't understand if he was more disgusted with them – I mean 'these guys': the Cataldo brothers, Calabrotto, the Colle Oppio guys – or with me, because I hung out with them. I tried to say, 'The electoral campaign,' but that was even more difficult: 'You're a provincial youth secretary, you can't hang out with these guys.' He didn't even give me the time to ask, 'Why, what's wrong with them?' He just ordered, 'Come with me,' and he went on, without even turning back to check on me. And I followed him. Without complaining, without even understanding. Exactly like Luke and Matthew when Jesus told them, 'Leave everything and come with me,' and they replied, 'At your word, Lord.' I couldn't even respond. Christ himself at least stopped for a moment, so that the disciples could respond. Not Bava. He spoke, and he turned on his heel and left. All I could do was follow him.

There were those guys from Prenestino – Muriatico, Pietro, Nero – and a couple of lads from Genoa. The guys from Genoa slept in a little pensione. They took me with them: 'The others are coming tomorrow.'

I hadn't slept in a real bed for more than a week – maybe even ten days. It felt like a dream come true when I stretched out, but nonetheless I found it hard to sleep, I kept turning over and over. I wanted a pill. By the time I finally fell asleep, the sun was coming up. It was already coming through the shutters.

The next day the others arrived: a couple of guys from Genoa, a couple from Pisa, one from Pistoia, some from Massa and one from Catania. We moved to a pensione in via Quattro Fontane, just a few steps away from the headquarters. It was called Albergo Zara, and the owner was an exile from Dalmatia. There must have been around fifteen of us. Then there were the people from Rome, from Prenestino. There were always four or five, but when necessary there could be as many as twenty. We were the MSI Volunteers, a new organisation that Bava had established.

He had returned to the MSI a short while before, just a few years, and he was a legendary figure from the earliest days of Neo-Fascism. He had fought for the Republic when he was a boy, and he had done what the others did. He never spoke about it. But in actual fact he never even spoke about what happened later on, he never had a bad word to say about anything, or at least about anything that concerned him. He was tall, well built, blond, half bald, and he had a low voice that sounded like the bass notes of an organ. But it was a warm bass, decisive, communicative; the sound was melodious, and you felt it everywhere: he would be speaking in front of you, but before his words entered your ears, they went all around your neck and came up from behind. You could hear the authority, the gravitas. What little I know I found out from the others, a few words here and there, and when I asked him expressly – even in the moments of greatest relaxation, when we were driving, sometimes on the motorway, and we had hours to chat about this and that – 'Tell me about the bombs at the Communist Party headquarters' (there were a couple of them) he would change topic right away. 'What are you trying to talk about?' and he would go back to the previous topic. He wasn't one of those people who keeps their mouth shut for prudish reasons, or because of some mafia code of silence. Well, maybe there was some of that, but these were all stories about twenty years ago, time had passed, and anyone who'd been sent to jail had done their time by now. It's just that Bava was modest: he didn't like to show off. He was solid as a rock; he didn't need to demonstrate anything to anyone. He did what he did because he thought that it was right, that's all, but he didn't like to talk about it: 'We do things, we don't talk about them.'

At the time of the Republic he had been like all the others – at least that's what Arturo, the porter at the national headquarters told me: 'Who would ever have imagined it then? He was just a boy' – but when he returned home he went mad. When he saw girls offering themselves to the Americans, to blacks, for a bar of chocolate, when he saw his neighbours in San Giovanni who all used to be hardcore Fascists, more than even his own father, who just worked and kept his head down, had become anti-Fascists, Communists, Christian Democrats. They disapproved of him because he'd come back from serving in the Republican forces, and one night they attacked him as he was going home: 'Fascist!' they taunted him, these neighbours who'd been wearing black shirts practically until the day before. So he became a clandestine anti-Fascist with the revolutionary wing of the party. At the takeover of the radio station – there must have been seven or eight thousand participants if you listened to everyone who said they'd been there – Bava was really there. This all happened in 1946–47, when you were risking your life. And then there was the assault on the Communist Party headquarters, in via delle Botteghe Oscure, where Gionfrida lost his hand from a paper bomb that exploded as he threw it.

In 1956 he went to Hungary with some of his other supporters to participate in the riots. He was a rabid anti-Communist. For him – and naturally also for all of us – the Communists were oppressors of liberty, they exterminated people, and most of all they were against the Fatherland, because of the international character of their movement, following Russia, against Italy and against the concept of nation itself, against God and the family. It seems that they had gun battles against the Communists in Hungary, where they had gone to give a hand. Our boys were only just able – with the assistance of the Swedish embassy – to move around the Soviet tanks and get home by the skin of their teeth. Then he left the MSI – when it became obvious that they weren't interested in revolution, they just wanted to take part in democratic life, together with the Christian Democrats – and founded his own little group. There were several of them in Rome, each competing against the others, because every group thought that it was representing true Fascism and that the others were Michelini's police informants. (The chairman said that Rome was the worst aspect of the party: 'It's like a tumour on our nation, it's the centre of corruption. The body of the party is healthy, but Rome corrodes it, it's the epicentre: the divisions and propaganda all start there.') He had established a group of 'green shirts' and had made contact with other groups to work with. Then he must have realised that the revolution wasn't going to happen, or, as he said, 'that the road is rather windy', and he returned to the MSI. Now he was in direct contact with the secretary, with Michelini: he responded directly to him, and he set up this Volunteer Sector, with experienced people, people he had known for years, who had done a lot with him. The ones from Genoa were really hardcore. I was the only new member.

After a couple of days he took me in his car and drove me home. 'What are we going to do?' I wondered. He insisted on going, it wasn't enough for me to call my mother in front of him: 'Hello. I'm still alive.' So he loaded me into his car and he took me home. He even bought me a new pair of shoes before we left, because the old ones were pitiful – no heel, the soles coming open – because I was always walking around, never taking them off, and at night I would put them back together again with glue: 'Aren't you ashamed to go around dressed like that?'

He took me home, and my mother seemed all reassured, she literally hung on his every word. He spoke with that low, gruff voice: 'He's with me, now. I'll look after him. If you prefer, he can stay at home, but otherwise I'd like him with me for the electoral campaign. I'll look after him, you have my word, and when he comes back he'll hit the books again. Isn't that right?' he asked me.

'Of course.' What else could I say?

My mother prepared lunch. She'd made pasta e fagioli. Manrico listened to him; every once in a while he would try to say something, as if to provoke him, but Bava would respond drily – with courtesy, almost with a condescending tone, albeit nicely – but drily, without leaving room for sophisticated rhetoric. Manrico asked me in a low voice when we were alone in the lounge for a moment, 'Who is this guy?'

'Bava.'

'Ah! He seems like Al Capone to me.'

Only my father seemed resistant. When Bava had said, 'If you want, I'll leave him with you,' my blood ran cold, but my mother gave him a look. Bava had won her over. She trusted him: 'Let Accio stay with him,' she said to my father. It wasn't like that time when Livio Nastri came to the house. She had injured my head that night. There was an argument, I can't remember why, around nine or ten at night. We were watching TV. Carmine was there too, Violetta's boyfriend. He was a sociologist, he'd worked as a lawyer, but now he taught philosophy, he was a Southerner, a socialist. He was another political fanatic, but nice, good-hearted. Every once in a while he'd stay over at our place, because he lived in Rome. Well, the argument started, and at a certain point she took a chair and hit me on the head with it. She got me really close to the eye. I put my hand to my head, and I saw that it was full of blood. 'Sooner or later this will dry,' I thought, but the blood kept flowing, there were rivers of it. I went into the bathroom to take a look in the mirror. In the meantime she had gone back to sit calmly on the sofa in front of the television. Everyone was silent, fearful that she'd hit them, too. In the bathroom, I could see that the blood wasn't stopping, and there was literally a huge hole in my head above my eyebrow. So I went back to the lounge – holding a handkerchief to my eyebrow – and I said to Carmine, 'I need someone to take me to the hospital,' because as a minor I needed someone over eighteen to sign for me. Carmine got up from his chair, but my mother said, 'No, tell him to go on his own,' and when Carmine – thinking that she was joking – started to put his coat on, she screamed at him, 'You'll regret it if you go with him, I won't let you ever come back to this house.' So he sat down, he gave me 500 lire, in case I needed anything, and he looked at me as if to say, 'Sorry, what can I do?' And I went out, as Mimì attempted to plead on my behalf: 'But Mamma…' And my mother screamed, 'Shut up! What are you bitching about?' So I went looking for Livio Nastri, at Ghersevich's rosticceria.

As soon as he saw me he went white: 'Did the Communists attack you?'

'No, my mother.'

'My God, she's worse than mine,' and he went with me to the hospital, but first he needed to drop by my house.

'Why do we have to go there?' I asked.

'Eh, no, we have to: they're your parents. If they ask me about it at the hospital, what will I tell them?'

He rang the bell. My mother came out. It must have been eleven at night. She asked him, 'What do you want?'

He replied, 'You have to come with this boy.'

'As far as I'm concerned, it's fine if he dies.'

'Signora, are you joking?'

'No I'm not joking, actually, I'm angry. Who are you, what do you want, who called you, how dare you interfere? It's rude to disturb decent folk at this hour!'

He tried to be tough: 'Signora, you risk being reported to the police: you can't just attack your son with a chair.'

'I'll attack you with a chair if you don't get lost right away with that other miscreant,' and she ran inside to get another chair, while in the meantime Carmine and Otello came outside.

Livio Nastri knew my brother, because they played billiards together, and he said to him, 'You know me: she can't do this.'

And then she came came out and shouted, as the rest of the family tried to hold her back. Papà was running here and there not understanding anything: he had just come back from choir practice, and he was asking everyone, 'What's going on?' Then he looked at me, with all that blood, and he asked, 'What's happened to my son?' and everyone reassured him, 'Go inside, we'll explain later.'

She kept screaming, 'Tell him to go away! Tell him to go away!' to Livio Nastri, waving her chair in the air, 'or I'll knock his block off too!'

'Do you hear what she's saying?' Livio Nastri asked Otello.

Otello replied drily, 'Just leave.'

'At least come with us,' Livio Nastri pleaded.

'You're in trouble if you go with him,' said Mamma. 'I'll break your head open too.' So I ended up going to the hospital with just Livio Nastri, and they gave me four stitches, and we told the police officer on duty at the emergency ward that I'd hit my head against a window.

'You can't report your mother to the police,' said Livio Nastri, and then, as we came away with my eye all bandaged, he congratulated me. 'Your mother is disturbed. She really is worse than mine,' and he kept on saying this, as long as I knew him, but he said it almost with envy. Every time that my mother heard his name mentioned, she would go wild. She would be ready to go after him again with a chair.

But for Bava she made homemade pasta: she'd prepared it in the kitchen as he watched, and then cut it into little shapes as he talked on and on. Smooth as a radio announcer. I never heard him speak as much as he did that day with my mother. He made jokes, he laughed, and he even told my father how right he was, no matter what opinions he expressed, even when during lunch he began to speak highly of Andreotti: 'Well, on balance,' said Bava.

And Manrico whispered to me, 'There was no need to invite him for lunch. You can't just invite in everyone who passes by,' but he was envious. In actual fact Bava had even won Manrico over.

Violetta kept her distance, though. She popped out of her room just to take a plate of pasta, and then she went right back: 'I have to study.'

But, despite his grumbling, Manrico didn't leave even for a minute. 'I like him too,' said Bava afterwards, in the car, as we returned to Rome 'What a nice family you have. And he looked good with that white scarf' (Manrico was still wearing that scarf). Bava added, 'But after this is over you really have to go back to school: you need a diploma, otherwise what sort of life will you have?'

So I began working on the electoral campaign. With the MSI Volunteers. Bava bought us black cotton jackets and made us special membership cards with photos. We put up posters, we wrote graffiti on walls, we went around in cars with the flame symbol attached to overhead luggage racks, and used the megaphone to spread our message: 'Vote and get others to the polls! Movimento Sociale Italiano! The tricolour flame.' And then we acted as guards at the party meetings and all public demonstrations. That's the only time we wore our jackets, naturally, when we had to be recognised and add to the effect of the evening. Bava would be angry if he saw us with the jackets when they weren't required: 'These are expensive – I didn't get them for free.' And we were really in trouble if we wore them when we put up posters: 'They'll be stained with glue.' In actual fact they were our dress uniform. And it must be said that we looked good in front of the podium, all lined up with our black jackets: old men would salute us, raising their arms. When there was nothing to do, we would hang out at the national headquarters. Michelini would always smile at us when he passed by. I was the youngest, and he called me 'Benassi of Littoria'. So did Almirante.

There were no major incidents. But it must be said that Bava didn't look for trouble. He wasn't someone who needed that kind of thing, actually he did all he could to avoid it. If he had a disagreement with someone in public, as he was driving or parking, he would always remain calm, he never lost his temper, and he was always the first to apologise. The boys from Genoa were quite the opposite, they had very short fuses. But he didn't like that, he expressly ordered them, 'Don't make problems.' But then if problems did arise, or if the *raison d'état* so required, he would deal with any issue that arose with attention and calculation, like an accountant.

There were always tensions with the others – the guys from Colle Oppio and the party office. Once we went in the car of the guys from Pisa to via Cavour – I don't know what for – and they were standing together in a group in front of the party offices. They came over to the car where I was sitting, and they started provoking me, but speaking between themselves, from a distance, until I understood that Calabrotto was annoyed with me: 'This turncoat: first he was with us, now he's with them.'

I hadn't really understood, and they outnumbered me, but nonetheless I asked them, 'What's your problem?' I was worried, but I got out of the car.

One of the Cataldo brothers, the younger one, came over and reassured me, 'No, no, we're not angry with you.'

But when Calabrotto saw that Cataldo was ready to separate us, he began to shout, 'Yes, yes, I am angry with you.' So all the others came over, and my team and I were cold – that is to say, I seemed cold, and afterwards everyone said, 'Ah, you're as cold as Bava,' but in actual fact I was filled with fear. I wasn't cold, I was frozen – so I said in a cold voice, 'Let him come here.'

Cataldo said to his guys, 'But no, Benassi is a good lad,' as if to protect me and convince them 'He's trustworthy,' and things calmed down. And we left.

Then one Sunday, at the Adriano cinema, at a demonstration with Michelini, we met up again. They were in the central balcony, on the second or third level, and they began to make noise and to shout at the secretary. We all went there, and as soon as they opened their mouths we began to shout, 'Mussolini! Mussolini!' and the entire crowd screamed at us. No one listened to them any more. Then the demonstration ended and we stood in a cordon along the stairs. They left down the middle, and that's how we accompanied them outside. They were insulting us constantly. Cataldo and the more polite ones called us 'Praetorian Guards! Michelini's White Guard!' but the others taunted us in a cruder fashion, and pushed their way through. Bava didn't want any complications to arise. He just made a sign with his hand to their leaders, moving his index finger in a circle as if to say, 'See you later, see you some other time.'

Stefano, from Catania, was close to me, and took a switchblade out of his jacket and positioned it between Calabrotto's legs: 'I'll cut your ass to shreds,' and the guy jumped back.

Then Bava whispered, 'Put that thing away,' and his eyes were ice-cold. He was full of anger for the rest of the afternoon, until the evening. 'They'll pay for this,' he said.

Two or three days later we went to see them. There must have been seven or eight cars and a small van. All the usual suspects were there. There were some older guys, one even had grey hair. He was a fishmonger, and Muriatico treated him with respect, almost with fear: he was so happy that this guy treated him as an equal. He was taller than me, with straight grey hair combed back like Papà, but his expression was very different from my father's. These men were hard-core, from Bava's early days, and they could be counted on to provide extreme remedies when the situation warranted.

We drove to Colle Oppio. The party office was closed. It must have been around five or six in the afternoon. We hung out nearby for an hour. We went to the bar in front, and the other patrons said, 'That's strange. The offices are always open in the evenings. They're always here.'

'Tell them we passed by,' said Muriatico, and then he asked Bava, 'Should we go to piazza Tuscolo?'

'Let's go. But we won't find anyone there either.' And he seemed tranquil, relaxed now. We had won.

I didn't understand. If it had been me, I would have waited, maybe they would have shown up, who knows? But there wasn't a soul in piazza Tuscolo either. That's where all the former members of the Avanguardia Nazionale would meet. The bar was always crowded. Delle Chiaie was always there sitting on the corner table on the pavement, and that's where people would go to find him. But there was no one there today, and when the guy behind the bar saw us he was worried. The fact is that we hadn't just dropped by. If it were an unplanned visit one could say, 'What do I know? You've caught me by surprise, I wasn't prepared,' and the verdict can always be contested. But there'd been an actual challenge at the Adriano cinema, and Bava had accepted it like a man. He had called and he informed them, 'This is the date when we'll be there,' and they didn't show up. The word had got round, they'd all told each other, 'It's better if no one shows their face for two or three days.' We had got the better of them. When we said goodbye, the fishmonger said to Bava, 'Don't forget, whenever you need us...'

Then another evening – it must have been after midnight, and we had just finished putting up posters – we were behind the offices of *Il Secolo*. We were there chatting, there must have been around ten of us. At a certain point four men approached us, drunk. They weren't totally smashed, they weren't stumbling, but you could see that they were well away, and they started to provoke us. Bava said, 'Let's go,' but they kept following us. They started by telling us they wanted to join the party.

'Join what party?' Muriatico asked them.

'Your party, the Fascist Party.'

'Come back tomorrow morning.'

That wasn't good enough for them, they kept insisting. One took out a trade-union membership card: 'I'll trade you this for membership of your party.' Obviously they were locals, and they knew who we were. They started pushing; they wanted to start a fight: 'Four against four, not all together. Or else one on one: what kind of Fascists are you? Are you afraid of us?'

We weren't afraid, it's just that they were drunk and it was late, and we were standing in the middle of the road and people were looking at the commotion from their windows: 'Forget about them, poor things, can't you see that they're not in full possession of their faculties?' Two of them must have been wrestlers: they weren't that tall, they were dark and stocky, but the muscles on their necks were frightening: their necks were bigger than their heads.

'I saw these guys compete in a wrestling match,' said Bruno, a guy from Prenestino who did karate. We walked away. They insisted. One of them shoved Nero. He gave him a dirty look and was about to respond, but then he saw Bava, thought twice and decided against it. The other one – the bigger, tougher wrestler, maybe he'd had more to drink than his friends – took Muriatico by the arm: 'You Fascists, you're so scared you're peeing your pants.' Muriatico moved away, and also looked to Bava as if to ask permission, and when he saw that it wasn't happening he said to me, 'Give me a chain,' because he knew I always carried one.

I kept the chain with me just in case, like a policemen with his standard-issue pistol: someone like that doesn't go out of the house every morning with the idea that he's going to shoot someone. He keeps it because it's part of his uniform, it's his job, then if something happens, that's another story. I was the same: I hardly left the house in the morning with the idea of having to use my chain on people, not at all. But I always took it with me, because one never knows, and I'd been carrying it with me for months – in the inside pocket of my raincoat, where people usually keep their wallet. It made a lump in my coat because it was so heavy. Piermario had made it as a joke in his father's workshop, with a file and the welding equipment. It was a heavy chain, with big rings, about two feet long, and it had a handle made from a stainless steel tube. I would always keep it with me, but I had never used it on anyone, not even Manrico.

Once there had been another discussion at home, and one word said in anger led to another. At a certain point I said to them, 'Watch out or I'll get you again like that time at the Hotel del Mare.'

And he said, 'Now that's enough, now I'm fed up: let's go to the public gardens.'

More people showed up once we were in the street, a few friends of his, a few friends of mine, some people we didn't know. But gradually the crowd increased in size, and they called others: 'Come here, come see, the Benassi brothers are fighting.'

We got to the gardens, we chose a place, people made a circle around us. I took off my raincoat and I hung it up on a tree branch. He did the same with his white scarf. I felt the chain in my hands, and for a moment I thought, 'Now I'll use it,' but then I thought, 'No, it's wrong to use the chain on my brother. Anyhow, I'll fight with him again, and I can use it then.' But the fight went badly. He was really pissed off; he was all puffed up like a bullfrog. He had some perceived wrong he wanted to put right. So he wrestled me, and at a certain point I slipped on the grass. We fell to the ground, he was on top and I was underneath. Everyone was screaming and encouraging us: 'Go for it!' He began to kneel over me and started to punch my face until he couldn't go on any more, and gave up. Then he stopped and he got back up. So did I. You could see from the expression on his face that he was satisfied and his anger had dissipated. But as I walked through the assembled throng to the tree to get my raincoat, I thought, 'Now I'll take this chain and I'll kill him: why did I just walk away?'

But as I was getting close to him with the chain in my hand and I felt the steel handle in my hand, people came up to us and pleaded, 'Sort out your differences.' So I thought, 'Why should I make myself look like a fool?' It was too late to take out the chain, people would think I was a coward. But I still wasn't fully convinced, I still wanted to take it out, I felt ashamed at having lost. But Manrico came up behind me, took his scarf and hugged me, and he laughed and said, 'Let's make peace, we're brothers, I love you,' and I almost thought the onlookers were going to applaud him: 'Look how good he is, he's so gracious.' Even my friends, afterwards, said, 'But he loves you. Did you see how he came up right away to make peace?' What kind of reasoning was that? If I had won, I would have done the same, what would it have cost me? Anyone can be gracious if they've won; it's when you lose that it's harder to stomach. Anyhow, I wasn't able to use the chain, and it took me years to get over the shame of losing.

So I kept this chain with me without any intention of using it. I had never used it. And even Muriatico, when he said, 'Give me your chain!' didn't really mean that I had to give it to him. He just said it like that, as if to say, 'They would really deserve this,' without wanting to really do anything with it. But what did I know? To tell the truth, I did wonder, 'Why doesn't he attack them?' But then I thought, 'And what if he really means it?' So I took it out to give to him. I didn't want to, but I did, and the chain was in my hands, and already I regretted my actions: 'Poor thing. He may be drunk, but he's nothing more than a loser.' He took it in the head, on the neck, on the cheek and on the head, because I didn't use it in a direct, perpendicular way, from above, but diagonally. He crashed to the ground, flat out. Not moving. I didn't know what to do. Then he lifted his head up a bit, he shook it, opened his eyes with an expression of total confusion, and blood was running down his face. I folded the chain up and I put it back in my pocket.

His friends stepped back, then they put their hands up in a gesture of resignation, as if to say, 'That's enough,' and they bent over him. Bava looked at me as if to say, 'For Christ's sake,' and he signalled us to leave. We got into our cars and left with the headlights out so that they couldn't read our number plates. I was contrite, mortified: I hadn't wanted to do it. Women shouted at us from the windows, 'Fascists!' One even said, 'Murderer!' and she seemed to say it expressly to me.

Before leaving, Muriatico leaned out of the car and shouted back at them, 'But who asked you to come and disturb us?' Then he turned to me. I was sitting next to him. As Pietro drove off with a screech of tyres, he saw that I looked sad, and he started to laugh and slapped me on the back of my neck: 'Don't think so much! I was joking!' and he laughed. So I laughed too.

chapter 7

We lost the elections. In Rome we lost almost eighty thousand votes, and when Manrico saw me he said, 'They lost those votes because of you.' He was joking, but I suspected there was some truth to what he said. Anyhow the elections were over and everyone returned home: 'You promised that you'd go back to school in September,' Bava reminded me. I went back without the chain, at his insistence: 'Give that thing to me, come on now.'

Mamma asked, 'How much money have you got for me?' convinced that one earned a lot of money working on election campaigns. She couldn't believe it when I told her I didn't receive any wages at all. She asked me about it several times, thinking that I was lying to keep all the money to myself: 'I'll let you keep the money, just tell me how much you earned.'

'Nothing, we're not Christian Democrats,' I had to say in the end, and I was almost sorry, because the disappointment showed on her face, so much so that at the time I thought that she'd only allowed me to go because she was thinking of how much money I'd bring home.

Manrico chimed in, 'You must be the only loser in Italy who works on election campaigns for free. I told you I didn't like the look of that Bava guy.'

To tell the truth, at a certain point I got the impression that the others – the ones who had come from out of town, from Genoa and Pisa – had been given 5000 lire a day, and I went to Bava to ask if I could be paid too.

'Who told you that?' and he seemed genuinely surprised. 'Not at all. I already had so much to pay for those lads – their hotel, their meals, their shoes. You were sleeping in a van, with the tramps.'

'But the others?'

'The others have wives and children' – and this was true, they all had families to support – 'and anyhow I'm not giving you all that money.' In the end, before we wound everything up, he gave me 10,000 lire. It wasn't very much, but at that point I had really given up hope of anything. I tried to give it to my mother, but she sniffed with disdain: 'That's not what I thought at all.'

Anyhow, it was the end of June 1966, and the watermelon season was about to start up again, or maybe I'd go to the sugar refinery, or who knows what else: 'Don't worry: I'm going to work,' I told her. But one afternoon – it couldn't have been more than two or three days after I returned – Fabrizio and Mirella dropped by. She was the oldest daughter of Uncle Luigi, my mother's brother who had gone missing during the war, in West Africa.

Mirella was blonde and sweet, like a fairy. She was almost sweeter than Norma. She took good care of me and spoiled me. She and Fabrizio – her husband – lived in Formia. They had two sons and they were expecting another baby: she had a big bump. He was an administrator at the Technical Institute in Formia, and he'd been fond of me when I was little, but he was a bit nosy. He began to chat with Mamma: 'What does this boy get up to?' Then he had an idea: 'I'll take him to Formia with me; he can study all summer and take repeat exams in September, that way he won't lose the year.'

'But the professors, the lessons? How much will this cost?'

'I'll look after everything. They work for me: they have to do as I ask. But he has to be committed.'

My mother couldn't believe what she was hearing. In the beginning, I was enthusiastic too: 'Alright, I'll commit myself: in September I want to sit the teachers' college exams.'

'Teacher's college? But you're crazy,' said Fabrizio. 'I can get you through the course for surveyors – you've already done two years.'

'What about Latin?'

'Latin won't put bread on the table,' and my mother nodded in agreement. There was nothing to be done. They convinced me, and I left right away for Formia. The agreement was clear: I had to obey them in everything, as if it were military service, and study and apply myself. The only thing I was able to get for myself was the possibility of returning home at the weekend. Fabrizio didn't want to grant me even that: he wanted me to lead a totally monastic existence. But in the end he agreed.

It wasn't a bad existence. Mirella took good care of me; she would make saffron rice for me. Every once in a while her back would hurt because of her pregnancy. Fabrizio and I assisted her in household chores: sweeping and washing the floors, washing the dishes. The children didn't disturb us too much; they were the first children that I didn't truly hate. In the mornings, before going to work, Fabrizio would bring me coffee in bed, and he would leave cigarettes for me on the chair. I slept in the lounge. I would wake up rather late, and then start studying. In the afternoons I would go to the homes of various teachers in the blistering heat of July and August: drawing, mathematics, estimates, topography, construction science. Then I would go home to study. I would just go out a little in the late afternoon, then have dinner at home. After dinner I was never allowed to go out: 'That's the agreement,' he said. It only happened once or twice, and only after much pleading from Mirella. 'But why does he have to go out?' he would ask her. 'Who are his friends? I know who he hangs out with…'

Who did he think I was spending my time with? I had sought out my fellow Fascists, I knew them already. I had been to Formia once before for a conference on Europe and nationalism. They were great guys. We would usually meet up in the afternoon with Carlo – a short dark guy who was at industrial college, whose father worked for the railway – and Peppe and Pasquale.

But Fabrizio crucified me. It wasn't enough for him to keep me indoors all the time, and he wasn't satisfied that I was respecting all my commitments, he wanted to give me a thorough brainwashing too: he preached at me all day long. He was a Social Democrat, and he always had some complaint about the evils of Fascism: 'There was no freedom, they did crazy things: we didn't live as well then as we do now.' And he especially hated it when I hitchhiked: 'I've never picked anyone up. How could I let someone with long, dirty hair get into my car?'

'But my hair is short.' As a matter of fact, with the MSI Volunteers, I used to attack lads with long hair in Rome.

'I'm just giving an example,' Fabrizio said, and whenever the weekend came round and it was time for me to go home, he worried. 'At least take the coach,' he would insist. 'Aren't you ashamed of taking advantage of others? You want to make a revolution, to destroy this world of rampant consumerism, and then you rip off poor drivers for a free ride?'

There was no point in showing him that his arguments didn't make sense, he just kept on preaching. He went on and on like a pneumatic drill in my head. I almost longed for my chain. All I could do was say, 'Fine, but now I have to go back to my studies.' That would stop him in his tracks: the important thing was for me to study. So I would sit staring at logarithms and trigonometry trying to be as excited as I used to be with my Latin translations. Sigh. But he watched me like a hawk. As soon as he noticed that I was slightly distracted, or that I'd put away a book, he would start up again against Fascism. He constantly monitored what I was up to. At a certain point even the children noticed that he would make unexpected surveillance visits, and they would laugh when they saw him coming: 'Here comes Papà,' Marta would warn me, and I would go back to my books immediately. It's no wonder I passed all my exams in September. He had made it his personal crusade to get me back on track.

It's not that I wanted to return home every week because I missed my family – not at all. It was in order to get away from my uncle, first of all, and secondly because I enjoyed hitchhiking so much. As it was summertime, I dreamed of being picked up by a woman again. Thirdly, I didn't want to lose touch with the party office. Every once in a while

I would also pass by home to check out what was going on. After the electoral campaign, my relations with the chairman had become somewhat frosty. Lupo had told me that he was pissed off: 'Where did Benassi go? His place is here, not in Rome,' and he said the same thing to me when I returned. 'You didn't used to be like this. You used to listen to me, you would ask my permission.'

The story of the MSI Volunteers really annoyed him: 'So what, we're all volunteers. I didn't get paid, you know.' But basically, what really upset him was that the hierarchy had changed from my point of view: he was jealous of Bava, and every Monday – after my return to Formia – someone would inform him that they had seen more graffiti in Latina reading 'Long live the MSI Volunteers', and he would go mad.

This graffiti was also written all over Formia. They never let me out, or actually just three evenings, and Mirella had to get down on her knees and beg: 'But what fun does he have, this poor boy, all he does is study. Let him go out to the cinema just once,' but those three evenings were enough. We covered Formia with graffiti; we went as far as Itri, Fondi, Gaeta, Sperlonga, Terracina. We covered all the roadsides, all the bridges, the support walls, the overpass. And not just with a spray can: we had pots of thick black paint, behind the fish van that Peppe had snuck out for us. Another time, in the afternoon, we went onto the mountain nearby, to practise using paper bombs with the gunpowder that Carlo had found in a cave where he knew the overseer. I took some of this gunpowder home to Latina, in a paper bag. I would hide it in my drawer in the shelving unit in the lounge, behind my schoolbooks.

But my time in Formia ended in the right way: I finished my exams, I was promoted to year four of high school, and that was that. 'You've done half of your duty,' said Mamma, and I returned home to every-day life: I would always hang out in town late at night, and during the day I would argue with everyone. I argued with my father, who asked, 'When will this end?' and my mother: 'Fabrizio said that you had changed.' What were they thinking?

My fourth year of high school began in September. I was in a new class with different classmates, and in the beginning it was hard to get used to. I really couldn't stay awake for the first two hours. Maybe it's because I stayed out late at night, maybe it's because I'd become used to my wicked ways – maybe because of those pills from Colle Oppio – but the first two hours I felt like sleeping, and when I put my head down on my desk I would fall into a deep slumber. I would wake up in time for break, and that's when my day really began. I would ask my classmates to summarise what little the teacher had explained, and off we'd go. In the beginning the teachers would try to wake me up, but they soon gave up: 'He's a difficult boy,' they said to one another. Yet for better or for worse I was able to keep up even in the most difficult subjects.

I had a few problems with my new classmates. I fought with one of them, in the beginning. He was slight and short, he was repeating the year, he must have been three or four years behind. I don't know what I said to upset him, but something offended him. Maybe more than what I said he was upset by the fact that I would sleep through the lessons when he had taken years to complete his studies. Anyhow, he took offence and we went to the gardens after we were let out. He was furious. I felt like laughing: 'Look at this idiot.' I tried to say to him, 'Come on, forget it. I'm sorry.'

But he insisted, 'No, now we're here, and we have to fight otherwise I'll tell everyone that you were afraid.'

'Alright, let's fight then.' But his first assault consisted solely of rapid and speedy little punches on my legs and arms, without hurting me at all, just an irritation really. I felt like Gulliver against a Lilliputian. After his first assault, I gave him my left hook, but my arm must have been out of alignment, and I heard a 'clank' in my collarbone. My arm weighed heavy along my side, and it was twisted around. I tried to move it but it was impossible. I had to continue fighting with just one functional arm, my right. I didn't even manage to connect with him – the Lilliputian – as he jumped from one side to the other and continued to give me little punches. We continued like this for a while, and then

I started laughing uncontrollably. In the end I said, 'That's it, you've won,' and I returned home with my arm hanging by my side.

As soon as my mother saw me she went crazy. She didn't worry about my arm, or ask, 'What's happened to you?' even though I warned her right away, 'I think I need to go to the hospital.' She started screeching again, 'You can go on your own.' What drove her wild was the fact that I had lost the buttons from my shirt: 'You've been fighting again!' she screamed. 'You can go to the hospital by yourself, and don't come back. You'll be the death of me.'

They put my arm in a cast and told me I would have to keep it on for three weeks. Dislocation of the left shoulder. My arm was bent in two under the cast, and it covered my entire shoulder, back and chest – like a corset – and my hand came out at tummy level. Even now, when it's damp, I can feel a pain in my shoulder, and if I make a sharp movement I always feel that my arm is about to dislocate again. Like Livio Nastri's shrapnel in the leg from the Battle of Monte Cassino. But what hurt more than my arm was the ignominy: I'd lost to a featherweight.

It was 1967. I was seventeen. I felt grown up. On New Year's Eve, as the bell tolled midnight, I was all euphoric. I thought that it would be a fantastic year: seventeen had always been my lucky number. All the comrades from the MSI youth club spent New Year's Eve together. We organised a dinner at the home of a guy called Benito, in Villaggio Trieste. We ate, and then we went out to wander the streets of Latina after dark singing our Fascist songs. But that wasn't enough for me: I wanted something special, to jump into the fountain in piazza della Libertà or maybe even to swim in the sea. But no one else shared my enthusiasm: 'We'll catch cold,' and around 3 a.m., when the group broke up, I returned home and took my bicycle. I rode to the seaside, and I swam in the sea under the Capoportiere pier. Lord knows what I was thinking. The water was freezing. The sea was rough. There were huge waves. I was already numb with cold when I entered the water, and when I dived into the first wave and the water covered my head, I felt almost as if I couldn't breathe, like I'd been hit in the stomach and winded. But then I began to swim for a while. I dressed again, smoked a Nazionale cigarette and went back home on my bike. My hair was wet, I had sand in my socks, and the lobes of my ears were like two ice cubes. I don't know, it seemed to me that it brought good luck. 'You're crazy,' Manrico said when he saw me.

Later in January I began a Fascist study course organised by the MSI. It was the first political preparation course for youth directors, and the chairman didn't want to send me. He said I didn't deserve it because I was too undisciplined. 'Why should we spend money on you?' But they asked for me in Rome, and so I went. Michelini and Almirante told me that I was their hope for the future of the party. To tell the truth, I enjoyed talking about politics, but I did my reading too. Fabrizio and Mirella's house had been full of books: Mark Twain, Steinbeck, Jules Verne. And at home, too, especially those nights when I didn't have anyone to hang out with and I got tired of wandering the streets on my own.

'Why are you wandering about at this hour?' the policemen on patrol would ask me every once in a while.

'That's my business,' I replied, and they made me wait a few hours at the station.

But in the end even they got fed up, and when they saw me they would just say, 'Go home to bed,' and then they would be off. So I would go home and read. I even read left-wing books – Violetta had a lot of them – even difficult ones. Sometimes it was confusing, but I would read. And for an MSI youth member, this was rare.

The course brought together the best of the Italian youth clubs. There were even a few of the Volunteers, from Genoa. We stayed in a hotel, in via Quattro Fontane, but at the other end, near to via degli Avignonesi. The lessons were held in Largo Chigi: economics, history, politics, propaganda techniques, government doctrine. The director of the course was a philosopher, Primo Siena, and there were all kinds of tests. I even remember a little book published by the Ministry of Defence for exclusive use of the military entitled *Techniques for Psychological or Subversive Warfare,* and the author was a certain

Guido Giannettini. When he saw it, Nero was enthralled, and he asked Bava, 'Have you seen the book by Giannettini?'

'Well?!' said Bava. 'Do you remember it?'

Then Nero turned to me: 'Carry on, carry on like that with your studies, and you can be like Giannettini one day,' but it wasn't an insult, he really meant it, with admiration, more for Giannettini – at least for the moment – than for me.

I had a place at the hotel, but I didn't sleep there very often. I would go home at night, and just attend the lessons in the afternoons. In the mornings I would go to school, to keep Mamma happy. I only stayed overnight a few times. At that time the Russian President Podgorny made a state visit to Italy, and Rome was full of red flags. You'll say, 'But they were Russian flags. That's protocol, if a foreign head of state visits, his flags are put up.' Yes, but these were red, with the hammer and sickle, and they were everywhere, even on the lampposts in via Veneto. In the evenings, after dinner, we would go out to take them down: we would shimmy up the lampposts, take them down, and burn them in front of tourists, who looked at us, and people who would make comments and sometimes someone – from the *dolce vita* pavement cafés – would scream, 'Fascists!' We shouted back at them, 'Assholes!' and then fights would start, and the police would come, and we would run away.

But one night – I think it was the same night that Podgorny arrived – I saw Pino from Genoa in the entrance of our hotel at around midnight with a couple of lads, and they were going out. I followed them right away. 'You can't come,' said Pino, but I followed him regardless, right up to the car. 'You can't come,' he repeated, but he was smiling in a way that seemed like he was actually dying to take me along. So I jumped into the back seat of the car, a Renault 4.

Pietro gave me a dirty look: 'Are you mad?'

'What does it matter?' Pino answered him. I didn't know what we were supposed to do, but I had understood that we were involved in some kind of a mission. Pietro drove, and Nero sat next to him in the passenger seat. Pino and I sat in the back, Pino behind Pietro.

We drove for a while. No one spoke. 'What are we going to do?' I asked. No one replied. We drove through the centre of town. We stopped in piazza Vittoria, Pietro parked the car between two fruit kiosks in the dark, there wasn't even light from the street lamps. He and Nero got out, and they put false number plates over the real number plates with wire. We took off again. I still hadn't really understood, but I felt my stomach tightening. The others seemed calm. We returned to the downtown area near the Altare della Patria. Then we drove along Largo Argentino and into via delle Botteghe Oscure, but we turned at the cross street before the Communist Party headquarters. There was no one around; it was a winter's night in January. We turned again to the left immediately, and followed the road along towards Ara Coeli. Then we re-entered via delle Botteghe Oscure from the other direction. We drove slowly. There was only one policeman in front of the main door. Another officer in plain clothes was leaning up against the doorway of a bookshop.

'Give me that thing,' said Pino to Nero – who gave it to him – then he said to Pietro, 'Go now, but slowly.' Pietro turned back to the left as – next to me – Pino lit the fuse. In the meantime he'd opened the window. He waited till it really caught, till it was sizzling. Then Pietro leaned to the left, towards the party headquarters. When we got close to a window, Pino threw the paper bomb. Pietro accelerated. Right away we heard the explosion, followed by the sound of breaking glass, but by then we were already at the end of the road. Pietro drove quickly through the alleyways, then along the Lungotevere, Isola Tiberina, Porta Portese. There we stopped and took off the number plates, then we drove all around the centre of town in the other direction, and then returned to the hotel. We were laughing. All of us. But I remember that at the crucial moment they were white as ghosts. Tense. Like me. I still remember everything as if it were in slow motion: Pino with his arm out, the fuse sizzling, the explosion.

The next day on the TV news it said that we had hit the infirmary of the headquarters of the Communist Party, almost exactly where, more than ten years later, the body of Aldo Moro would be found, in another Renault 4. Bava was quite angry with Pino: 'I said only the three of you. Who gave you permission?'

'I thought it would be good training for him.'

'Your job isn't to think.'

'I told you so,' said Pietro to Pino. But he winked, 'It'll blow over,' and he looked at me as if to say, 'See what you've got us into?' They liked me, they all liked me, and I liked them too.

At the lessons – on the politics course – I always participated, spoke, expressed my opinion. Every time there would be a new speaker as well as the core teaching team, the philosopher Dr Siena as well as Tripodi and Valensise. As soon as the speaker finished and asked, 'If there are any questions…' Tripodi would snigger, 'Benassi of Littoria for sure.' I was their pride and joy, they really admired me, and you could see that Bava was truly rejoicing – it was written all over his face – because it's true that I was the youth secretary from Littoria, but I was there above all as one of the Volunteers, one of Bava's boys, and his expression seemed to say, 'We can do more than just fight.' I was the intellectual of the group.

The Volunteers had grown up; it was an actual section now, present in every party office. It was a kind of police force for the MSI, with its own national directorate, us, and we were named on the letter-head. Later historians – and political scientists especially – wrote that Michelini created it specifically so as not to let anyone try to be more right-wing than he was. There were many groups and divisions, New Order was on the ascendancy, the Avanguardia was still alive and kicking, and everyone measured their level of ideological purity according to what we might call 'activism'. 'Why should I allow others to rip me off?' thought Michelini, and he called Bava in. More-over – again according to the historians – that was a time when the MSI didn't have an active political role, no one took them seriously. The Christian Democrats were in coalition with the Socialists – the centre left – and the Communist Party seemed like the only legitimate opposition. We were 'Fascists', and that was it: what was the point in speaking, who would listen to you anyhow? It's not that he planned to recreate Fascism, corporativism, socialism. Are you joking? They were funded by Confindustria, and he planned a right-wing party, a party of order. In any event he guaranteed the Fascist votes, both on the right and on the left, but obviously that wasn't enough. He wanted mainstream votes, from people who were afraid of Communism and social disorder, people who had trusted the Christian Democrats previously. He said to them, 'The Christian Democrats won't defend you; the Christian Democrats are in agreement with the Communists already. We're your only hope.' So the only strategy was to constantly demonstrate that we were there, whenever the red peril raised its head, to combat it. Us, not the Christian Democrats. Were they demonstrating against the Vietnam War? Then we were in favour. It's so obvious you don't need a political scientist to explain it to you: we were playing a classic Italian game, just at a disadvantage. But no one had ever seen anyone like us; no one had ever had such a dedicated team.

We went everywhere, all over Italy. Bava bought a light grey Volkswagen van and we piled into it. We would leave in the evening, almost always on Saturday, from Prenestino, and we would come back the next day. We spent hours and hours in that van. Nero drove in the daytime, and Pietro at night, because Nero's eyes bothered him and he felt blinded by the headlights of oncoming traffic. We spent hours and hours on the road. I would almost always go behind the seats, at the back, because I was more comfortable there, even if it was a harder seat. Everyone was packed into the seats, there were always around ten of us in a van with space for eight, and our legs were always on top of each other. At least in the luggage space I could stretch out and sleep. We spent hours and hours in the van, with its rumbling motor, chatting. And then we would have fun at the rest stops on the motorways. The motorways were brand new, they hadn't even finished construction. When we went to Parma, I think we left the motorway in Bologna, and after that we had to take via Emilia, because the motorway wasn't finished yet.

Parma had won a gold medal for its resistance movement, and they were all Communists. We demonstrated with banners. Michelini wanted them to know we existed even there. We were supposed to meet up with the boys from Genoa just outside Parma, and we arrived there with our black jackets. There were some coaches from far away. But nothing happened. They allowed us to demonstrate. We didn't see one Communist. We sang 'Giovinezza', and when we went past the partisans' monument we made a Fascist salute. We sang more party hymns. There was a boy from Parma next to me, a comrade, and in the beginning he seemed happy and he told us that he'd come to be with us: 'Are you the Volunteers?' But after a while he became upset, and began to ask, 'But where are the Communists?'

I asked him, 'What's wrong, aren't you happy?'

He replied, 'You'll go back to Rome, I'll be left here alone.'

He ruined my day: 'Look at this coward,' I thought to myself. 'We've come all this way and he's not even appreciative.'

And then I mentioned it again in the van, with indignation, as we were going home, but Muriatico said, 'Well, he's got a point: it can't be easy to keep the faith around here.'

On our way back, we would usually stop in Bologna to eat, always in the same cafeteria. The food was divine: tortellini, ravioli. Bava would pay. He would pay for everything, and when we got back to Rome in the evening or late at night he would always ask me, 'Now how will you get home?'

'I'll hitchhike.'

'Just take the train,' and he would give me two thousand lire. Two thousand lire then was a lot of money. I would say to him, no, I didn't want the money, I could hitchhike. But he would give it to me just the same, and he would give me money whenever we went to Prenestino too, even during the week, even when there was nothing to do. I would just go to be with the others, and he would always give me money and say, 'Come along.' We went to Florence, Trento, Trieste. In Trieste we were attacked. There was a demonstration, a party meeting. The Communists had caused a hullabaloo ten days earlier. There had been a general strike in solidarity with the workers in the shipyards, and various incidents and riots. I lost count of how many police officers had ended up in hospital. They had even made barricades, and they'd dumped a mixer full of cement from the top of a hill. There was cement all over the road, so vehicles couldn't pass. So the next week we made our own demonstration. The piazza was full of local people – it was nothing like Parma – and everyone waved the Italian flag.

It had been an incredible journey for us to get there. Trieste is not just next door and, as I've said, the motorway ended in Bologna. We left early on Saturday afternoon, before dinner. I arrived in Rome after lunch, and I'd brought along two new chains that Piermario had made for me. But these were different, slightly longer. They had the usual handle, and there was a lead ball at the end of the chain with nails melted in, and their points sticking out. Like a medieval mace with a spiked ball. I had wrapped them in paper, for the hitchhiking, but every once in a while the points of the nails would hurt me. I showed them to Muriatico, and we put them in the luggage compartment of the van, but before we left – there were already people on board, seated inside, and Nero was in the driver's seat – Bava also went to put something in with the luggage, and he felt this hard package and heard the sound of metal. He asked, 'What's this?' He unwrapped the package, and as soon as he saw it he went berserk. He wanted me out of the van, he wanted to send me back home: 'You're mad, you want me to end up in prison,' and he made me take them away and place them in the basement of the party offices, and then he stayed mad as far as Magliano Sabina, while everyone else laughed.

'What did you think you were doing?' Pietro asked. 'This isn't the crusades.' And Muriatico laughed and slapped me on the back of the neck.

Then even Bava relaxed: 'But don't you realise that you could kill someone with those things?' To tell the truth, I hadn't thought it through: I just liked them, I thought they were fun. Anyhow, we went to Trieste unarmed.

We travelled through the night, because with all these passengers the van couldn't drive too fast. We stopped a couple of times for coffee and toilets. In Bologna we stopped talking, and anyone who could tried to sleep. When we went through Ferrara I opened my eyes: this is where my mother's family had lived before they left for Agro Pontino. At six or six-thirty – the sun had just come up – we were in front of the Redipuglia shrine, together with the boys from Genoa who'd met us in Mestre. We got out of the vehicles – aching and stiff – and jumped up, reading some of the memorial plaques as we went: 'Look, here's the Duke of Aosta,' 'This is the Third Army'. They had all died for their country in the First World War to reclaim Trieste and Trento, Istria and Venezia Giulia: 'And now they've taken everything away from us.' Then we stood above in a line, with our black jackets, and Bava said, 'Volunteers, on guard!' and we all stood tall. Then, 'Italian martyrs!' and we shouted back, 'Present!' and we lifted our arms in the Fascist salute. I was almost in tears. Then we got down. But everyone was emotional as we got into the van, even the boys from Genoa, even Nero. Only Bava seemed cold. Then we went to Trieste and staged our demonstration, there were speeches in the piazza, and the piazza was full of people, and all the people of Trieste were waving the Italian flag. All around us were police cordons with carabinieri. They didn't have cudgels and jumpsuits like the police, they came in their regular uniform, with rifles. But they were carabinieri and we liked them. During the speeches we chatted amicably with some of them. This time Bava didn't ask us to stand under the stage, but rather on the edges of the demonstration, close to the police cordon.

At the end of the speeches, it was all supposed to end – the police hadn't authorised us to march – but ten days earlier those others had gone mad. If we didn't even march, who would notice us? So as soon as the speeches ended and the music started up on the stage and people lowered their flags and turned around to go home, we lifted our flag and began to push ever so slightly on the police cordon, to open it just where we had made friends with the carabinieri, and we smiled at them and asked nicely, 'Let us through.' We were already at the front of the demonstration. The guys who planned to return home came behind us calmly, marching along, as if to say, 'We didn't realise it wasn't over.' But the carabinieri wouldn't open the cordon. They forgot the nice words they'd said earlier: 'We're with you, we're on your side, the Communists are the enemy.' They forgot all that and began to play tough, they even began to hit us on our legs and backs with the butts of their rifles. Then Bava said, 'Go!' For better or for worse we had to break the cordon, otherwise what were we there for, to be statues? We made ourselves into an arrow formation, like rugby players in a scrum. The people in front didn't have to do anything, not even make nasty faces; actually it's better if they are friendly, as if to say, 'I'm not involved. They're pushing me from behind,' just in case the other side believes you. At most we could kick underneath. Everyone works from behind, they push. All the pushes unite, and although at the back the last guy may think he's not doing anything – he just keeps his hand on the shoulder of the guy in front – but one hand washes the other, and with everyone together, at the front it became a colossal push. It could break down walls, it could break down houses. There's even an explanation for this in physics: it's a 'result'. It's the principle of the Macedonian phalanx.

Anyhow, we finally broke the cordon, we pushed through, and as soon as we made it through we raised the Italian flag, to show the people of Trieste where the north pole was, where the march was heading. But they didn't come. They might have been from Trieste and not Parma, but they must have been fed up with fights and marches. When they saw the confusion, they stayed where they were, they even stepped back, and the cordon closed again. In the meantime, from the wings, other reserve officers arrived running, with their rifles held by the barrel. We attempted to make our way to the exit: 'Get back, get back,' shouted Bava, and we had to make an arrow formation on the other side to break the cordon again and return home. The guys at the back were able to make it, but at the front they started hitting us with the butts of their rifles. Don't think it doesn't hurt, especially when it's done with full force. I attempted to defend myself with my feet and protect myself with my hands. I took a couple of blows on my shoulders sideways, and one heavy one on my back, but straight on, which increased its strength due to the wideness of the surface (in construction science this is called an 'evenly balanced load'). Anyhow, we were making our retreat without losing contact with those behind, who – as they marched back – held us with one hand by the coat-tails and pulled us with them. At a certain point Muriatico fell to the ground, next to me, and the carabinieri jumped on him. They were smashing him with their rifle butts like crazy. They got him in the stomach, on the forehead. He rolled on the ground to cover his face, and they hit him on the back, obliquely. Someone else hit him straight on with the end of a rifle. He lost contact with those behind him. I was the only one there, beside him, but Pietro pulled me away. At a certain point I saw that he was the last one left, and I was almost about to let him go – 'If I stay here they'll kill me too' – when from behind – I was now already on the other side of the cordon, in safety – Bava reappeared. He seemed like a lion, a panther. He pushed the carabinieri away with his hands – with one shove he moved three away – and he leaned over Muriatico and lifted him up, then he gave me a push and he took us to safety. Those guys tried to give him just one shove, but he pushed them aside, as if he had eyes in the back of his head. Then the demonstration broke up, and when we were all together again Bava asked, 'Should we leave right away or should we have something to eat?'

Muriatico replied, 'I don't want to eat here. Let's go as far as Bologna,' and we hit the road. He was hurting all over, and he kept saying, 'Damn those carabinieri, they're worse than the police. I'll kill the next person who mentions their name.' And to me he said, 'I wish we'd taken those medieval maces of yours.'

It was early afternoon, and it was sunny. And hot. It must have been the late spring of 1967. No one spoke, but we'd all been more or less bruised, and when you hurt you're not happy, or at least you're not as happy as when you do the bruising to others. And the local people didn't support us. The next day the papers mentioned 'incidents', and so compared to the Communists basically we were equal, but not with the carabinieri, we had lost to them. And to the people of Trieste.

The traffic was heavy. We took the B-road along the sea. We were moving at a snail's pace. Everyone was in a line. It was boiling hot inside the van. We were all silent. The local people were all enjoying their walks along the seaside, taking a Sunday drive, out for a picnic. We could see children going past with ice cream, people with their car windows open, their radios on, music, and they were laughing, everyone was laughing. And Muriatico sat up for a moment, massaged his back, looked out the window and said, 'Do these assholes give a damn about Italy?' and massaged his back again. Fortune was on our side, and we made it to Bologna, but by then it was quite late and no one said a word, just 'Ciao,' and we all embraced – someone had said, 'To us!' – when the boys from Genoa left us in Mestre. In Bologna, at our favourite cafeteria, we began to laugh in the men's room when Muriatico lifted his shirt to look at his back in the mirror and it was covered in bruises, it was one big blue blotch, and he worried: 'What will I tell my wife now?' Then in the van he moved to sit in the back, because he thought he'd be more comfortable, and he even fell asleep, but every once in a while we'd hear him murmur, 'Ow! Ouch!'

'Poor Muriatico,' said Bava.

'These fucking carabinieri,' said Nero.

We got home very late, it was almost dawn, we were tired and aching, with our legs stiff from all those hours in the van, and we were dying to get into our soft beds. Then, as usual, at the motorway exit in Settebagni, I became sad, melancholy. I had been happier before: 'I'd be happy to set off again,' I said, and Pietro agreed: 'Me too.'

Muriatico disagreed though: 'Not me.'

The sun began to come up. Nero got out at a tram stop: 'I'm going straight to work.' Because he was a municipal rubbish collector, he drove the garbage lorries. Muriatico said, 'No, I'm not going to work, I feel too unwell. I'll send my wife to ask the doctor for something.' He worked for the bus company, in a parking area, where he was a mechanic doing maintenance on the buses. Pietro had started working a short time before at the newspaper *Il Secolo*: he was a typesetter, and he worked nights. Bava also worked in a company associated with *Il Secolo*.

We said goodbye in Prenestino. I took the first train, and I arrived home just when it was time to leave for school. I took back the weapons, I hid them in the vegetable patch behind our home, near the chain-link fence. I thought about going to bed: 'I'd like to sleep now,' but Mamma forced me to leave for school. I slept in class, and when I returned I slept in my bed, and I didn't wake up until the next morning. My back hurt a little.

Then one day the chairman expelled me from the party. I don't remember if it was before or after the Six Day War, I can't quite remember. It was early June 1967, and that month all the Arab leaders were on the TV news issuing their ultimatums, especially Nasser: 'The Jews have to go, for better or for worse. One day we will attack and drive them into the sea.' I don't know how it happened, maybe it was the thought of the six million dead, maybe it was true despite what I said to Violetta. The fact is that I feared they would lose, and I hitchhiked to Rome, to the Israeli embassy, to offer myself as a volunteer to support them in the war. They didn't take me. They said, 'Thank you very much, but we don't need any help. If we do, we'll call for you.'

I would have been happier if they'd accepted me, but I was happy just the same, and this choice to support Israel seemed like a big deal to me. It's true that I was a bit of a hot-head and that I'd already thought of enlisting as a volunteer for some war – with the Americans in Vietnam, or in Rhodesia with Ian Smith – but even with the rest there was something that didn't make sense to me. The Volunteers – my friends, my comrades, my family – they didn't have doubts: Michelini was the heir to Mussolini. He was the modern Duce, and the supreme leader is always right, he never makes an error, by definition. But it wasn't that way for me. For me Fascism was what Bompressi, Livio Nastri and the chairman represented, despite the fact that we didn't always agree: the people, the workers, the national labour state, anti-capitalism, socialisation, revolution. And I had some doubts – about Almirante and Michelini – and now they were growing. I couldn't wait for the opinion of political scientists in fifty years' time. Even with Vietnam: I had gone to all the demonstrations and I'd fought outside the Eliseo theatre, but every once in a while I would still have doubts: 'But if the people of Vietnam want to be Communists, what gives you the right to bother them in their own country? Stay at home and mind your own business,' they said to us at the youth club, especially Wolf and Piermario. 'And why should we help the Americans if we lost the war to them?'

Finally, Manrico added his opinion. He was going to university, he did well in his exams, and he was our mother's pet. He drove me mad. He said that he was a Proudhon-style socialist: 'Who do you take as your example? Give me three names if you can, not including Bava.' He treated me as if I were ignorant, an imbecile. One Sunday at the end of June – there were plans for a concert in the public gardens with the band of the US Sixth Fleet, who were based in Gaeta – I was running out of arguments, and at lunch I replied, 'Maybe I'm wrong, but at least I take action. You're all talk and you never do anything.'

'Alright, this afternoon we'll attack the Americans at the public gardens,' he said, and I didn't have any choice in the matter. I took my bike and went around collecting some mates. But it was difficult: someone had to go out with their family, some of them just said, 'You're crazy,' and after an hour all I could come up with was just Wolf and another guy, Aldo, and I told them to meet me at the concert, because I had a lot to do before then.

When Manrico saw our little group arrive, he sighed in relief, 'Alright, let's forget it,' and Wolf immediately agreed. But for me it was too late: 'Even if we don't have the strength to run them out of town, we can always make a demonstration.'

We found four sticks in the vegetable patch behind our home. We made signs with some of Papà's plywood. We wrote on them with an extra can of spray paint that I'd been saving for a special occasion. The results were 'Yankee go home' on two signs, 'Peace for Vietnam' on a third one, and 'Johnson=Hitler' on the fourth. And while we were preparing ourselves in the back yard, Violetta and Mimì watched us from the window and shouted encouragement: 'Well done, good for you!' And Violetta held up her newborn daughter (in the meantime she had married her intellectual boyfriend, the socialist, and she had left home, or rather she had begun to leave home, because in actual fact she was always at our place, and it was worse than before, because now he was here all the time too and Mimì had to go back to sleeping with my parents, and the baby could be heard crying at all hours and then Violetta would be tearful too). Mamma would only look out occasionally, and she would shout at Manrico, 'Don't encourage your brother!'

By the time the signs were competed, it was five in the afternoon. We went inside and then left for our demonstration. Our sisters were pale: 'Where are you going? Stay here!' – they had thought we were joking – and Mamma also realised that we were serious, and she started shouting at Manrico, 'Leave your loser brother alone!'

Thus we arrived nonchalantly in the public gardens, carrying our stuff on our shoulders, each of us holding a sign, and I had two, one for Aldo, who was supposed to wait for us at the war memorial. That's where they had set up the stage for the band, right underneath the bust of Giuseppe Garibaldi. The Americans must have just arrived, because all we could hear was the sound of them tuning their brass instruments behind the laurel hedge surrounding Garibaldi. But we hadn't even seen the band, and the Americans didn't see us. And naturally, no one saw Aldo. But the police were there, and as soon as Wolf realised they'd seen us, he threw away his sign and began to run. There weren't more than five or six of them, but they came running up to us: 'Where are you going?' and they went to stop me, placing their hands on my chest.

'We'll go where we want,' and I pushed forward. 'It's not prohibited.' But evidently they disagreed. And without even realising it I found myself in the cells. I don't even remember how they wrestled the signs away from me. I only remember one officer, about fifty years old, as he pushed me towards the paddy wagon he held one arm twisted up behind my back, and I thought, 'Just look at this idiot: he thinks he knows judo.'

After having spontaneously offered up his poster, Manrico came along of his own free will: 'I'll come along, I'll come along.' In the cell he was dejected, and he didn't have a word to say. I was ecstatic. 'But why are you laughing?' were the only words he said to me.

At the police headquarters they took away our cigarettes, removed the laces from our shoes, and took our belts before they locked us up. One by one. Time passes in the cells, more quickly than one might imagine. I had just begun to imagine Wolf spilling the details of our demonstration in the piazza when they came to get me for questioning. From the windows in the corridor I could see that it was late evening. The political team seemed to be amused: 'What's happened to you? This is the kind of thing Communists do.' Then they became heavy: 'This time you'll pay for everything.' They looked at a folder full of papers with my name on them; they showed me samples of paint from graffiti written over the past two years, with photographs – 'Long live Mussolini!' 'I love pussy' – and they insisted, above all, that I name my friend who had escaped. I continued to keep my mouth shut, and as they took me back to the cell, Warrant Officer Gibino slapped me, but on the stairs not in the office, because his inspector was modern and didn't like that sort of thing.

Then they took Manrico up. A short time afterwards I heard him come back. When they opened the door to my cell I jumped up: 'Are you taking me to via Aspromonte?'

'There's time, there's time,' and they took me back upstairs. In the office I saw my father with Carmine, Violetta's husband. They were silent. Warrant Officer Gibino continued as before, 'Tell us the name of the other lad. And why were there four signs? Who else were you waiting for? Tell me the name of the one who got away!'

'Mandrake,' I lied, because when I saw my father there I was irritated, it didn't seem right that they had involved him. 'Things will get worse for you,' insisted Gibino. I just smiled. He was annoyed, and lifted his hand, but the inspector said, 'Leave him be,' and stopped him. Then he asked my father, 'You tell us.'

Papà began to cry, bent over a corner of the table. He lifted his head, and his face was streaked with tears, then he put his forehead against mine and held my neck affectionately in his hands: 'Tell your father,' and he began sobbing again. 'You were such a good boy when you were little. Do it for me, then we'll go home to Mamma.' So I told them, but I still feel ashamed about what I did.

Then they transferred Manrico upstairs too, and the inspector went on for a while explaining the charges and the prison sentence we faced: seditious meetings, disturbance of public order, resistance to arrest. 'But I didn't resist,' said Manrico, and he turned to me as if to say, 'He's the only one who resisted.'

'Alright,' the inspector concluded, 'in order to meet your father half way I'll just report you both for offence to a foreign head of state for that sign that read 'Johnson=Hitler'. Then Carmine, our brother-in-law, who had a law degree even though he taught philosophy and – as he was now a fully fledged member of the family – was a few bricks short of a load himself, asked him, 'Excuse me, but could you clarify which is the foreign head of state who has been offended: Lyndon Johnson or Adolf Hitler?'

'You too?' screamed my father in desperation.

'I want all of you to leave,' sighed the inspector.

It was midnight. I was so ashamed for having ratted on my friends. As we walked along the road, Papà tried to embrace me, and I pushed him away gently: 'You made me commit an ignoble deed.' In actual fact, I was truly sad, not just for Wolf, but also because I hadn't been sent to jail this time either. But at home after I had dinner I lay down on my bed and fell into a deep sleep. Manrico tossed and turned, and afterwards he always said that he remembered it as the worst night of his life: tossing and turning in bed, feeling that he was closed in and with the odour of the cells in his nostrils.

The next morning Wolf came to our home to tell me that I had been expelled from the MSI, and he asked me to give back the keys to the party office. At around six in the afternoon the day before, as a matter of fact, Bompressi and the chairman had gone together for a pleasant walk in the public gardens to enjoy the American marine band. As the trumpets rang out and the drums rolled, they saw a policeman come up to them holding a sign: 'Chairman, take a look at this.'

The chairman glanced over and grimaced: 'Those damn Communists.'

'If truth be told,' sniggered the police officer, 'this was Benassi's work.'

He began to laugh, thinking that the cop wanted to joke around, but when he understood that it was true, he had a complete meltdown, and Bompressi had to carry him out: 'Fucking this, fucking that, what's he doing?' And people shouted at him, 'Stop!' and covered their ears.

A short distance away, they ran into Wolf and Piermario, who were hysterical. 'But what happened?' they asked. And when they understood that even Wolf was involved, the chairman attempted to strangle him. He was foaming at the mouth. They had to contact the members of the disciplinary committee and Livio Nastri, who was its chairman. They expelled us. On Sunday. And they appointed Piermario as youth secretary, and he's still there today, and when we run into each other, every once in a while, he still says asks me, 'So which one of us was the true Fascist after all?'

That's it, I don't know if I did it because I had doubts or because Manrico dared me to. But what I do know is that I wouldn't have done it if it hadn't been for Manrico.

chapter 8

At home everyone was pleased. My brothers, sisters and their spouses for ideological reasons, my mother and father as a question of public security: 'At least you won't be hanging around with that crowd any more, especially that Livio Nastri.' But I was very sad, I was convinced that I had suffered an injustice, and I continued to feel that I was more Fascist than ever before: 'How can they kick people out like that?' I was living in a town where you couldn't even leave the house holding a sign: you'd be arrested on sight. Then you wonder why I rebelled.

Most of all I missed hanging out at the party offices, the smell of paper that came from Bompressi's room – full of posters, old newspapers, magazines – it was everywhere. This odour was also tinged with that of the ashtrays full of cigarette butts that no one ever emptied, and the ash on the floor. I missed Mussolini's medallion on the wall in the youth club room. My desk. My typewriter, the Olivetti 70. That's the one I used to learn to type, one key at a time, with just two fingers.

Nonetheless, I wasn't worried: 'Sooner or later the situation will resolve itself,' I thought, and I didn't worry too much. But what I really couldn't accept was the fact that I'd been excluded from the rugby team. The chairman's fury wasn't exactly political-ideological: he was the one who'd taught me to dislike the Americans. He just used the incident as a pretext to punish me: as long as I was working for him I could do whatever I wanted, but the fact that I worked for Bava and that I wasn't his little disciple any longer, this fact drove him mad. He would have kicked me out of the party even if Benito Mussolini had taken my defence – and he would have kicked him out too. This wasn't 'lack of political dignity and collusion with the Communists' as he made Livio Nastri write in the letter of expulsion: it was just a vendetta. In actual fact he even had me kicked out of the rugby team; how did that matter? There were so many Christian Democrats on the team, and one player was pretty much a Communist. Politics didn't count, or at least it didn't count formally.

We'd started the team the previous winter. There was a guy from Rome who had moved to Latina for work, an intellectual, his name was Adriano. He was newly married, he'd read lots of books, and he'd played rugby. He said, 'Let's set up a Fascist rugby team,' because there was already an MSI sports movement called 'the Flame'. And he was the first to say, 'Sport is sport, and politics had nothing to do with it,' and he welcomed everyone who was interested, even Christian Democrats. We'd taken a while to train because rugby is a complicated game for people who only know football, but we had become a good little team. Over time they even sent us a coach, an older guy, sort of a socialist, who would say, 'You're nice lads, but this politics business …' Anyhow, we trained, and I was doing well, it wasn't like the football team at the seminary, where no one asked me to play. Here I got involved; the tackle was my strong point. I wasn't afraid of others; I would throw myself to the ground and fly like an angel. We spent months training and learning the game, and every day we would ask the coach, 'When can we have a real game?' And finally they organised our first match against the merchant marine at the Latina football pitch, and we couldn't believe our luck. But when I arrived in the locker-room and was about to put my strip on – in the hallway I had gone past the chairman as he was leaving, but we didn't even acknowledge each other. I saw that he lowered his eyes, he was all dark in the face, just so that he wouldn't have to look at me, and I didn't say a word to him, and that's how it went on from there. In actual fact we never spoke again (to tell the truth, he told people to tell me that I was an anarchist, a provocateur, and I told people to tell him that he was a dickhead). But when I was about to get changed, Adriano, the founder of the team, the boss, the manager, said to me, 'No, not you.' I felt like shit. It was my right. He apologised, 'I'm sorry, there's nothing I can do for you, it's not my fault.'

'But I'm the best tackler.'

'I know, but he told me that he doesn't give a damn, even if the team is one man down. I can lose a thousand–nil, but you can't play.' That was the biggest humiliation, also because there were a couple of girls in the stands who had come expressly to watch me play, and I'd really had to convince them to come along: 'Now what will I tell them?'

I tried to convince him: 'Alright, let me play this game and then you'll never see my face again.' There was nothing to be done; it was a fully fledged order. Then you ask me why I didn't ever speak to him again. It was more for the rugby team – and for the match against the merchant marine – than for the expulsion from the party: I can understand the MSI, but not the rugby team. They let Wolf play, though. You'll say, 'But he was the prop.' Ah, fine reasoning.

Anyhow, by now it was the summer of 1967 and I had finished my penultimate year at surveyors' college – 'You've done half your duty' – and I was no longer the provincial youth secretary of the MSI. But it was summertime and I had to go to work: 'This year,' I thought to myself, 'I'll really try to get a job at the sugar refinery.' Instead, one day, as I returned home from the public gardens, Signora Visconti stopped me in the street: 'So, when are you coming back to work?' I'd never spoken to her again since our bust-up, and I was totally surprised: 'Now what does she want?' And I told her that I was thinking about working at the sugar refinery.

'But what are you going to do there? That's hard work, it's dirty work, you have to do night shifts. Come to us. We really need someone trustworthy who can look after the bar on their own and all of the beach, and supervise those dreadful lifeguards. We really need someone trustworthy; you're like a family member to us.' I succumbed to her insistence. It's not that I'd forgotten the ignominy of the last time, but those kind words made me change my mind (and this has always been my weakness: I wouldn't touch a caterpillar if you forced me to, but all it would take would be just a few kind words and I'd do anything). She even increased my pay to 2000 lire per day: 'But,' she admonished, 'no days off.' 'Alright,' and the next day I started back at the Hotel del Mare. You'll say, 'How is it that you changed your mind?' What do I know? She must have reasoned, 'This fellow is honest, what do I care about the last time? Let's forget about it.'

But I couldn't forget about it. For a while I worked as I had before: conscientious, I kept everything under control. But she started to act crazy again. When there was something that wasn't right – maybe something to do with the rooms, or in the kitchen – she would go into total meltdown, and you were in trouble if you were anywhere near her, she would scream and tell you terrible things, so I said, 'Now you've pissed me off,' and I made an agreement with the lifeguards. We were partners in crime: so many beach umbrellas for her, so many beach umbrellas for us. We divided the spoils. They thought it was enough to lookout from the terrace every morning, to see how many umbrellas and sunloungers had been rented. But we registered them with a double ticket: one was given to me, and the sunbather gave the other one to the lifeguard, who opened the umbrella for them. But when they left, we would leave everything out, and later – especially for those who came in the afternoon – we would provide the full service: sunlounger, umbrella, even a massage if they wanted, and they paid in full, they even left us tips, and the tickets we sold were the ones from the morning, so the extra went into our pockets. I even changed the prices at the bar, but I did this on my own, without saying anything to the lifeguards. I increased the actual prices: so much for the Hotel del Mare, so much for me, plus tip. You may ask, 'Are you sorry?' No, not at all. Sometimes a client would lose their wallet or would forget to take their change, and I would run after them to give back their money. And the lifeguards were the same. But not Signora Visconti, not her, she had asked for it. It was a kind of cosmic justice. Saint Michael against Lucifer.

Apart from this, work was the same as usual: I was in the bar dressed in my uniform, and outside there were people in their bathing costumes, running in and out of the water, boys courting girls in bikinis and playing volleyball and other games. I would serve fruit juice, ice cream, chinotto and campari soda. Then at around six I would close the bar, go home and have dinner, then I'd go back to the seaside again, hitch-hiking of course. I would walk along the shore with Wolf, staring at the girls who passed by in the eyes, and if they stared back at us, we would ask, 'Can we walk with you?' If only one of them had said yes, but no, it never happened. In the end, we resigned ourselves to our fate and returned home: 'What's the point of trying with them?' asked Wolf.

'Don't be discouraged: sooner or later we'll find someone who says yes. It's a numbers game.'

Then one evening I slept over at the seaside. A couple of my sisters – Norma and Violetta – had rented an apartment to have a holiday at the seaside with their children, and Mimì was with them too, she must have been about fourteen years old then. Around two weeks earlier she had sent me to attack a couple of losers. She complained, 'These guys are talking about me behind my back,' and so I had to do it. I didn't even ask her to explain: 'Alright, but what did you do to provoke them?' Nothing. And she was ungrateful just the same: 'What? After everything you've done, for once your sister asks you something and you're difficult about it? Why are you doing this to me? I'm the only one who always cared for you!' So I had to go out looking for them. I found one of them the next morning, not far from the bar. I jumped the wall and l did what I had to do right away. I couldn't locate the other one; he must have been lying low.

So I had to take a day off: 'I really need this,' I said to Signora Visconti. 'Please: it's a matter of life or death,' and I wandered through all of Latina until I found him and vindicated my sister. Then years later I learned that they hadn't done anything wrong at all. My sister was only fourteen years old, but she was already off her trolley. She would provoke people, then send me to rough them up.

Anyhow, now she had a boyfriend. He was a guy I really disliked, and such a show-off: I should have attacked him, not the others. But she liked him, and one evening she begged me to stay at the seaside and take her dancing with that idiot, because Norma wouldn't let her go alone. So I stayed in that little apartment with all my nieces and nephews around jumping on me from every direction like mini-Vietcong.

I felt like saying, 'Now I'm going to drown every last one of them.' After dinner, I took Mimì dancing.

It was an open-air disco, with thatched bungalows. There wasn't even a band, just a DJ, and they always played the same music. I sat on my own and looked around. There were three sisters sitting at a nearby table, and I began to stare at one of them. She stared back at me, so I invited her to dance. She agreed. We started chatting. In five minutes I filled her head with all kinds of nonsense. She was my girlfriend for about ten days, until the end of the month, when she left with her family. She was older than I was and we talked and talked. She would let me kiss her on the lips, and I even managed to get my tongue in a little. She would let me touch her breasts and her thighs, but I couldn't go any higher, she would close her legs tight. I tried to guide her hand a few times – 'You can touch me too'– but she pulled back with more horror that if she'd just seen a snake. She said that she had a psychological block, some sort of sexual trauma. She liked me, but as far as she was concerned even those few kisses were a sacrifice: she only allowed it as a sort of gesture of appreciation, and she told me, 'One day I'll touch you, I promise: I'll touch you before I leave.' I couldn't believe my luck. But when the moment came, she had second thoughts: 'I'll touch you just on your legs,' she offered.

That was fine for me, actually, very good, because then I began to negotiate: 'Legs? Does that mean thighs?'

'Alright, the thighs,' she agreed, 'but nothing higher than that.' Fine with me, better than nothing.

When we said goodbye, she cried. Not because of the sexual trauma, but because she'd grown fond of me. And I almost felt tears coming on: 'When will I ever find someone else like this?' I felt a gaping emptiness.

One time I went to a brothel, but I didn't really understand what was happening. I had so many spots – I felt disgusting to myself, so just imagine how horrible I must have looked to others – and I would spend ages applying medicinal creams, tubes and tubes of them. But the spots only grew bigger; they didn't seem to mind at all, it's as if the creams encouraged them to grow and to multiply. Then Livio Nastri told me, 'Forget about the creams, you need a good fuck. Tell me: have you ever been with a woman?' I told him yes, but I was lying and it was becoming a problem: 'Dear Lord, I'm seventeen years old.' So one day, in the winter, I took my bike and went to the Mussolini Canal. You'll say, 'You could have hitchhiked.' No, what would I say to people? Could I really ask, 'Please drop me here, I'm visiting the prostitutes'? I went with my bike, one afternoon, with 2000 lire left over from the last time Bava had paid me. There was a girl there, not so beautiful: chubby, a bit past her prime, long in the tooth. 'She could just about be my mother,' I thought. But there was no choice, the moment had come: 'The faster I get this over and done with, the better it will be.' I left my bike in the ditch, and we went on the dyke, surrounded by pine trees. There, on the site of the Anzio landing, where a Barbarigo battalion had died fighting with the Germans against the Americans. As we walked through the trees, I didn't know what to say to her. In actual fact, I didn't even know what to do, not even how to start. So I decided to be frank: 'You know, I don't have any experience. This is my first time.'

'What, a nice-looking lad like you, and it's your first time? I'm sure there are lots of girls interested in you.' Sure, I wish.

'I was at seminary.'

I should have held my tongue. From that moment she couldn't stop talking. It was no good telling her that I'd left, that I wasn't at the seminary any more. As far as she was concerned, I was almost a priest, and I'd only taken off my collar for one moment, just to come here, then as soon as we were done I'd put it back on and go to serve mass. 'A lot of my clients are priests,' she said. 'If you only knew how many of them use my services,' and then she showed me in her purse the holy cards they'd given to her, mixed in with condom wrappers. Finally she got down to work. She asked for the first thousand lire, and she sat down on the ground, with her back against a pine tree. There was a sort of blanket underneath. She fiddled around a bit with her hands and put the condom on, and she lay down: 'Come here.' Then and there I didn't know exactly what to do, but I saw that she'd opened her legs, so I moved in between them. She did everything; I didn't understand what was going on. I just felt a strange sensation in my dick, a sort of tight heat, as if it was being absorbed by a bloodsucker. I think the condom was too tight. I didn't know when we were done. She was breathing rapidly. Then she said, 'That's it. That's enough.'

'Ah, that's it?' I asked.

'Yes, but don't try to tell me that was your first time. You knew what you were doing.' And I even believed her. But she told everyone that. To console them. Then as we were going back to the roadside she said, 'You shouldn't have done this. You've consecrated your life to God.' There was no point in trying to explain to her that I had left the seminary, that I didn't have anything to do with it any more. When I got back on my bicycle, she called out after me, 'Pray for me!'

'What was I thinking when I told her about the seminary?' I reflected during my journey home, and I pedalled like mad, happy and laughing. It was over now. I hadn't understood what exactly had happened – and if I said I enjoyed it, I'd be telling a lie – but I'd done it, and I ran to tell Lupo and my other friends, 'I've done it.' 'Well done.' But I dreamed of her at night, and she really did look like my mother. At a certain point in my strange dream, a huge cock grew out from between her legs, something terrible, monstrous, it was a nightmare. I woke up suddenly and called out, 'Ugh!' But my acne didn't clear up.

In the meantime, Mimì broke up with her idiot boyfriend. Actually, I thought that he had left her, and I wanted to beat him up – not because he'd left her, but because he was such an idiot – but she didn't want me to. Women are impossible to understand. Anyhow, it was August: during the day I looked at the girls who passed by the bar, and at night I tried to chat them up along the seaside. But it was hard, really tough!

At the middle of the month – around the Ferragosto holiday on 15 August – a very tall girl started coming to the bar in the afternoons, she must have been six feet tall. She didn't sunbathe on our beach, she was at the free public beach next door, but she would come over to buy an ice cream cone every once in a while. She came on her own, striding across the sand like a Valkyrie. She walked quickly on her long legs – her high heels clicking away – and she pushed her breasts forward. If you walked in front of her, she would push them in your face. She was from Milan, with long, curly dark hair. She was dark-skinned, and not just because of her suntan, she had an olive complexion. When she came over – just after going for a swim – she would lean an elbow on the bar, and her hair would be all straight because it was wet, and there would be drops of water on her arms and on her neck, it was enough to drive any man crazy. She was statuesque and she was all on her own – she never came to the bar with anyone – and I felt like taking her in my arms and letting passion go wild. She wore a simple one-piece costume, black, and her breasts were big, but also hard, rigid, high – 'Like clay pots,' said the lifeguards – and she had an ass shaped like a mandolin, well-formed thighs, strong and muscular, and very dainty ankles, like a black athlete. She was an ebony statue, the Queen of Sheba. And then her tummy was just slightly rounded, and her costume was tight over her belly-button so that you could imagine its shape and size. She drove me mad. She was an animal, a black panther, and from Milan, too. She had that funny accent. I would start to swoon even when I saw her from a distance.

She was never in a hurry to leave, either. You'll say, 'She would eat then leave.' No, she would hang out there, chatting. But who asked her to? I'd never made any advances on any woman while I was working. I don't know if it's because I considered work something sacred – actually, for years I thought it was, and perhaps it is. But I also felt that I was in an inferior position. Everyone knows that lifeguards score. It's part of their work, that's what they're there for: married women all know about it, when they rent a beach hut and an umbrella, they know that the lifeguards are there to do their bidding. But I never liked this, it felt too much like being a servant. Anyhow, I hated it when someone I knew asked, 'Give me a glass of water,' and I would have to give it to them. No, work is work. Or rather, I felt ashamed: work is work, but mine was servile work, and I would rather look for women in the evening, elsewhere, along the seaside, on even ground. But this girl, she started chatting first, she practically came after me. She would arrive in the afternoon towards the end of the day, a time where things were really dead, there was hardly anyone left on the beach, and the lifeguards were starting to fold up the sunloungers and rake the sand. I was alone in the bar, and often I would be reading. She would show up – 'An ice cream please' – and begin to chat. Her name was Francesca. She had an aunt here in Latina, and she'd come to stay with her and have a seaside holiday. She was a year younger than me, but she spoke in such a way – so grown up, she even said 'shit' and words like that, that girls from Latina would never say – they'd make the sign of the cross if they just heard such language. And she was intelligent, modern, smart (she talked about several writers whose works she'd read). I was left stunned just listening to her.

She came by once, twice, three times. If a day went by without seeing her, I would feel unwell. Then she would reappear. 'Maybe,' I thought at a certain point, 'she's not just coming here for the ice cream. And I tried to ask her out. 'Sure, why not? I have a lot of friends.' And then I discovered that her friends were all my friends. She had met them on the public beach, near a kiosk where they all hung out. She knew Wolf, Giulio, Andrea and lots of others who would go out with me in the evenings. That night I met up with them. We were all lads, she was the only girl. They all followed her around, and she said, 'We're all friends.' Apparently she had a boyfriend in Milan, but we never heard much about him. Naturally, we didn't want to look like horny, retrograde Southerners: 'Of course we're all friends,' we said, 'what's strange about that? Do you think that we're only interested in girls for one thing? Of course we can be friends, just friends.'

To tell the truth, this didn't convince me: 'It's hard enough for me to be a friend to other lads, now I have to make friends with a girl? I'm not crazy.' And I told her so too, because I don't like unclear situations. 'Bread for bread and wine for wine,' as Father Cavalli used to say. Of course I didn't say this to her the first time, otherwise she'd have run away. I waited for a while. Until we went for an evening stroll.

But when I realised that she liked talking with me more than with the others – we walked around all over Latina, because it's true that she could stride, but so could I, and I was a good walker after all those miles of hitchhiking, walking between one ride and the next, and we would walk side by side. Finally, I put my cards on the table: 'Friendship is fine, but only up to a certain point.'

And she nodded: 'I agree: up to a certain point. We'll see how things develop.' What was I supposed to understand from that? Then she said that it was my fault. She added, 'Anyhow, we're friends.' And I continued to be her friend.

But it must also be said that she was a left-winger, but not just in generic terms, as if to say simply 'left'. She was a card-carrying member of the Italian Communist Party – even if some say that the party was moving to the right. Her father had fought in the resistance, he'd been a partisan. Her mother, too – she was from Bologna, but she went to Milan after the war, and that's where she met her husband – had been a partisan as a child. She would take notes rolled inside the handles of her bicycle, she would cross the bridge of boats in Mesola, on the Po, back and forth on her bicycle with the excuse that she was going to sell eels, and she kept connections between the people in Codigoro and Porto Tolle. The Germans stopped her numerous times, but only to steal a few eggs or maybe an eel. Francesca's father had really fought, he even used a gun. He was injured in a clash and tortured by the Black Brigades, by the Koch Band, and he just missed being killed and strung up in piazza Loreto with the rest of them. This is why later – she said – when they killed Mussolini, they took him there and strung him up from the shelter of a petrol station so that everyone could see him, together with all his cronies. It was to vindicate those whose blood was still fresh on that site – at least that's what she said – and to make them suffer as others had suffered. When she spoke about these things her face would go red. She was already dark because of her suntan, with that hair and those eyes dark as coal, but when she got heated up she would be like burning coal. She wasn't so much Venus as Minerva in all her fury, or Diana the huntress, a war goddess, even more beautiful than when she was at peace. And my soul became emotional. Because of her beauty, but above all because I feared that she would dump me, that she wouldn't care what happened to me.

In actual fact, when I had told her that I was a Fascist – because I still considered myself one – she hadn't liked it, she shook her head: 'I thought that you were an intelligent person,' and for a few days she didn't come back to the beachside bar. But I couldn't wait to see her again, and I wondered how I could repair this disaster one day. At the end of the day, there was a time I had been on the point of converting to Protestantism for the sake of true love. When I finally saw her again – drenched, stepping out of the waves like Aphrodite – I thought, 'Ah, a sign of interest.' It was only a momentary thought, and I really should have reflected more on this to exploit the moment, use this opportunity, but no, instead I began to rationalise, differentiate, analyse: 'Yes, I am a Fascist, but I supported the Vietnamese, I demonstrated against the war and I was even arrested' – and already this gave me a hundred points – 'and then I'm for the workers, against capitalism: I'm for socialisation, corporativism, the European nation.' She didn't truly understand this last point – the European nation – but with regard to all the rest she said, 'So what kind of Fascist are you then? You're a Communist like me.'

I almost had a stroke: 'How dare you?'

In actual fact, for some time, when I found myself chatting in the gardens with Wolf and the others, every once in a while we would say, 'But the Communists really defend the people, the MSI is just in cahoots with Confindustria. Shouldn't we join up with the Communists?' but we would say it as a joke, just to test the ground, to see how others might respond. And talk is cheap: that expulsion had changed our lives. We were used to hanging out there, at the party office, and putting up posters. We no longer knew what to do. It seemed to us that life without politics wasn't much of a life – 'How do others manage? – and so, in order to overcome this abstinence crisis, we even considered – as a joke – becoming Communists.

In August we ran into the Volunteers again. I was at the bar over-looking the beach, and suddenly Nero and Muriatico showed up: 'Two coffees, please.' They were as shocked as I was when they recognised me: 'You disappeared, what happened to you?' They were all staying together at a camping site along the seafront; it was their paramilitary 'summer camp'.

That evening, after I finished work, I went there to say hello to the others. They welcomed me warmly, even Bava – although in the beginning he was rather cold – and we spoke about the expulsion. He said that there wasn't a problem: 'I know that guy from the disci-plinary commission: I'll speak with him and with the secretary,' and we agreed that he would write a letter asking for an appeal, saying that I had nothing to do with the anti-American demonstration, I had only been there to defend my brother, I wasn't at all interested in Vietnam. No one would believe it, but that didn't matter, he would look after things.

'You're a right idiot,' laughed Muriatico, and Pietro and Nero were kind to me. I slept there that evening, in their tent, and the next day I went back to work. I returned to visit them a few more times, but more out of a sense of duty than for pleasure. I went to visit them because I thought I should, that it would look bad if they didn't see me again, but it wasn't like before, when I would travel from Latina – hours and hours hitchhiking – to meet them in Prenestino. Maybe I had already moved on, maybe things weren't yet clear to me, but maybe I just no longer felt like I was one of them. Or maybe, who knows, it might have been that they were on my turf now – in Latina – and they were enjoying the beach like everyone else, swimming, playing games and having fun. With one thing and another I started to make myself scarce. It's not that I made a conscious decision. Actually, every week I would say to myself, 'Next week I should go to see them,' but I never did. I even wrote the appeal letter – as Bava had suggested – to the national disciplinary committee, and I posted it, and spent months living in anxiety, waiting for them to call for me, to clarify everything and return to the ranks of the MSI.

On 1 October, school started again: I was in my last year. When I arrived on the first day, there was a new student. He came from Belluno, up North. He sat in the back row. I said to him, 'This is my place.' He looked for somewhere else to sit, then came back and took a place next to mine.

'Why do you have to sit beside me?'

'Because I've sized up all the other students and you seem kind of weird... You know, I'm kind of weird too.'

'Alright, sit down,' I said to him, 'but don't bug me for the first two hours.' I crossed my arms on the desk, put my head down and slept.

He didn't disturb me at all; when the teacher took the roll call in the second class, he said to her in a quiet voice, 'I believe he's present.'

'Ah, yes,' she replied, after craning her neck to look at me, and everything went on as before.

His name was Serse, and no one else could stand him because he was rather full of himself. He treated everyone like they were idiots. He said that they were underdeveloped Southerners. Even I – if truth be told – was rather full of myself, but everyone liked me: I amused them, I made them laugh, so at the end of the day I was accepted. But Serse was really horrible, he didn't do anything to be accepted, and then he had this silver medal, which he wore hanging from his trousers, with a portrait of Palmiro Togliatti. I was a Fascist and almost all of our classmates were Christian Democrats: they could just about accept my views. But he was a Communist. And this was Latina, not Reggio Emilia, where the reds were in the majority.

Serse's father had been a partisan too. He was a doctor from Naples, and the Fascist regime had him imprisoned under house arrest in a little town in the Dolomites. When war broke out – and then the town was taken – the resistance began, and he was there, as a medical officer in the Garibaldi Brigades. He named his son after the wartime moniker of a friend who had died next to him in a valley just above Canale d'Agordo. There was nothing he could do to save him. They'd been best friends. Three shots to the stomach. All he could do was stay with him as he died. The agony lasted for more than an hour under a pine tree high in the mountains where he had dragged him, with the dying man asking him, 'Remember to visit my mother,' and requesting a last cigarette. They smoked and he replied, 'But we've had some good times, we've had fun,' as the Germans continued searching the valley below. After the war Serse's father stayed there, in the Dolomites, for a while he'd served as a medical officer in the army, then he had moved on to work for the National Insurance. Now, having almost reached retirement, he had asked for a transfer to Latina, to be closer to Naples, and he was the head physician at the National Insurance office.

Serse couldn't decide if he was from Veneto or Naples. By birth – and for his entire life up to this point – he was from the Veneto, from Belluno, in the mountains, but he said that he felt Neapolitan and didn't have much to say for the good citizens of Belluno: 'All they think of is family and the Church, they're all Christian Democrats! To tell the truth, he always spoke ill of everyone, he couldn't stand anybody, except for the Russians. He said that Russia was better than America, that they were the first in space, that they had the most powerful missiles, and that it was a just country. He was a little bit annoyed with Khrushchev and the current regime: 'If Stalin were still with us, who knows where Russia would be today.' But he wasn't a member of the Partito Communisto Italiano, and he'd never joined any left-wing trade unions: 'Full of assholes,' he explained. Even his father had left the party, he was a dissenter. He didn't approve of Longo: 'Too far to the right.' He was still nostalgic for the days of Pietro Secchia: they had been really close friends, and now he was just in contact with Terracini. He said that they'd sold out the resistance: 'What did our fallen comrades die for, so that the Christian Democrats could take power? They died for their love of socialism!'

Serse's father was rather gruff and taciturn. He was always to be found sitting in his easy chair at home with a book in one hand and a cigarette in the other. He smoked Superfiltro. Serse's mother smoked Esportazioni without filters, the ones in the short brown packet and the three caravels with flags a-flutter. She was very sweet and kind.

When I was with him in his room, she would always bring us tea and biscuits or make us coffee if we wanted. As soon as you entered their apartment you could smell this strange odour that I'd never smelt at home: it was a consolidated smell of stale cigarettes which had impregnated everything: the furniture, the books, even the TV set. They all smoked in that apartment. She was a very elegant lady. Serse said that she was from a family of Neapolitan aristocrats, and he told me that his father's family had once been very rich, but it had all been frittered away – first by his grandfather, then his father – in bad investments. But they still lived well: every Sunday they would go out for lunch, they took holidays, they went to the seaside, and to parties and concerts in the evenings. They hadn't been in town more than two months, and already Serse knew the names of every restaurant in Latina and the surrounding area: 'The food there's excellent!' In my entire life, the only restaurant I'd seen was at the Hotel del Mare, and there I'd only ever been in the kitchens.

Serse always had money and cigarettes. We would share our cigarettes, at least two of us would smoke each one, but he was always disgusted by this: 'I don't want to put something in my mouth that's been in someone else's mouth.' And rather than letting you take a drag on one of his, he preferred to offer everyone a single cigarette each. Whenever he walked into a bar he would order a coffee, sometimes a cognac. But he was generous too; he would pick up the tab for anyone who was with him. In the end, although they couldn't stand him, even our classmates would let him come along for the evening stroll through the gardens, because he would pay when we went to the bar, and he offered them cigarettes.

I don't know if I was more struck by him, or by his father, or by their lifestyle. Serse had everything I didn't: his own room, a record player, records – everything by Adriano Celetano, the Platters, Elvis Presley, the Beatles – a Ronson lighter, lots of books, every back issue of *Urania* (he was a science fiction fan). And he was intelligent, funny, at times sarcastic. He didn't do well at school at all, he was a first-class dunce, he just knew a little Italian and history and some maths, but he didn't know the first thing about construction science or topography. He was two or three years older than me, and it was hard to figure out how many different schools he'd tried: classical lyceum, scientific lyceum, technical college. He'd always failed. In the end his father sent him to a boarding school in Sicily, where in one year they were able to get him through the entire programme for the first four years of surveyors' college, but he admitted that he'd only passed the exams because his father had paid, otherwise he'd still be there. He was often mentally absent. When the teachers explained things, he was lost in a dream world. I could see him next to me doodling in his notebook. From far away it looked as if he was taking notes, but he was actually drawing lines and arrows: space battles. For the entire scholastic year I had to do all his assignments for him.

When his father saw me at their home, he barely greeted me. He didn't even lift his head; he just looked at me with an expression as if to say, 'Who is this? What is he doing in my home?' Francesca's father was the same. You couldn't get a word out of him, not even under torture, not even if you were the Black Brigades. At a certain point I wondered, 'Are all partisans like this? What did they teach them in the mountains?' His face was always inscrutable, pensive, as if he was still reflecting on what he'd seen in his life. They never laughed – permanently damaged – as if a smile could cause them to lower their guard and the enemy could break through a chink in their armour. As if they hadn't won, as if they'd lost. 'That's not the reason,' said Carducci in one of his poems – and even Francesca's father seemed to feel that this wasn't exactly the Italy he'd dreamed of and fought for.

It's not that I saw him very often – only once or twice at most – but she was always talking about him. In August and even at the beginning of September before she went home, she kept asking me, 'Please visit,' and then we wrote each other two or three letters every week. They were always letters 'between friends' in which we'd write about inconsequential matters just to fill the pages, just to have an excuse to write to each other. She kept insisting, 'Come and visit.' Of course it was just rhetoric, it wasn't like now, when I can just say, 'I'm going to Milan,' and no one bats an eyelid. Then, when someone went to Milan, people would go to say goodbye at the station, the entire family would be there, the grandmother, the aunts and the cousins' boyfriends, and mothers would cry and everyone would wave white handkerchiefs, until the train was as far away as Cisterna, and people would say, 'Who knows if we'll see him again.' It wasn't like now, when you just leave, go, and come back the next day. But she kept saying, 'Come and visit.' How was I to know that it was just a rhetorical flourish? It's taken me a lifetime to realise that people don't ever say what they think. They say one thing and they think another, then it's my fault for taking them seriously: 'I didn't really mean it,' like that time with the chain. But what did I know then? At the end of September, shortly before school began again, I arrived in Milan.

However, it's not that I did things secretly. I knew that I just had to try my luck. There were a few other lads who were writing to her – 'just as friends' – and at the end of the day I had accepted this chivalric tournament, so before I left I told everyone, 'I'm going to Milan. Who wants to come?' as if it were the north pole. And I left. You'll ask, 'But what made you do it?' I don't know. Of course I was in love, and what more can one add? She was beautiful, intelligent, elegant, and above all Milanese. Milan: the North. It seemed like a magic place; Jung wrote several books in which he maintained that man is oriented to the north, everything that he knows about the north is positive. That's where Good lives, Evil resides in the south. If Evil is where you live, you have to move, you have to leave. There's no comparison between North and South, you have to go north: to Milan.

I had saved a bit of money – from the tips and the profits off the beach umbrellas – and late one afternoon, after I had spent several hours sleeping, I set off. I made it to Rome, then took the motorway, and from there I headed north. Two or three rides, but it was the first time, I didn't know the way. There were signs at the toll booths that said that hitchhiking was forbidden, and the staff would shoo you away, so when the cars were leaving I had to jump out quickly. I'd ask them to leave me on the side of the motorway, and I would raise my thumb to everyone who passed by, just as if it were a normal road. Back then it wasn't much different, it was just wider, more spacious, and especially straighter. There weren't even guardrails in the middle, you could cross wherever you wanted to. And there wasn't the traffic that there is today. A car would pass by every once in a while, then the occasional lorry, but there were never traffic jams, and at night you could even stand there for thirty minutes without anyone going by. Anyhow, I made it as far as Bologna, it was the middle of the night and there was no one around. An Autobianchi Primula stopped – it looked just like an Innocenti JM3 but inside it was more beautiful, the seats were very comfortable, and there was a kind of rubber that wasn't smooth but irregular, a bit like bubble wrap – it was fantastic. They were two brothers from Pesaro not much older than me, both had gone to industrial schools, and they were planning to visit the electronics trade fare. They took me as far as Milan. At a certain point they started arguing and they asked me to adjudicate. I tried to be wise like Solomon.

When we arrived, it was still dark, and they began looking for Idroscalo Park: 'Let's sleep there, then we'll go into town when it's daylight.' There was a strange, sickly sweet smell everywhere. I asked, 'What is it?'

'That's smog,' they said with looks of disgust.

'I like it,' I said, and we fell asleep. They didn't believe me, but I really did like it. I understood right away that I would like everything about Milan, even the disgusting aspects.

As soon as it was light they drove me into the centre of town: 'Thank you and goodbye,' and I called Francesca. 'You're in Milan?' She couldn't believe it. But she seemed happy. We met up. She took me home. I ate with her family (it was the only time, except for one other time with Serse), and that's where I met her father. He had a little workshop on the outskirts of town where he did metalwork and carpentry. He was a self-employed welder, and he'd done well with the post-war economic miracle. He arrived home for lunch with *L'Unità* tucked under his arm, and then he went back to work. At six he'd come home for the evening. He wore this contrite expression on his face, not angry but contrite, and his expression when he saw me seemed to say, 'Who is this? What's he doing in my home?' And moreover, 'What does he want from my daughters?' What did he think I wanted? You have a daughter and you don't know what's going to happen to her sooner or later? He had two daughters, one more beautiful than the other. The other sister was a bit older, but not that much, and indeed over time the others moved their attention onto her, but Francesca was the best, she was a dream girl, and he was a fool to wonder why boys buzzed around her like flies. He disliked us more than he disliked the Christian Democrats; I couldn't wait for him to leave and go back to work. I liked their apartment. I could have spent my entire life there; I would never have left again, because they treated me so well, I felt spoilt. Even her mother. Only at a certain point her sister asked, as if I wasn't in the room (maybe she thought I couldn't hear), 'But isn't this one the Fascist?'

'Yes, but only a little bit,' was sweet Francesca's reply.

'Perhaps it's better we don't tell Papà,' and she went back to listening to her albums. She liked the music of Jannacci and Fabrizio De André. I hadn't even known that they existed, I learned about them from Francesca and her sister. They were crazy about De André, even though they said he was a liberal. I liked Jannacci better. I liked everything about Milan; I wanted to be Milanese too.

I stayed three days that time. I had money then, and I stayed in a pensione. School hadn't started yet, and their father had a lot of work, so Francesca had plenty of time for me. We went everywhere: on foot, by metro, by tram. What can I say? To me the trams seemed even better than in Rome – more beautiful, faster, more airy, even the rattle of the wheels on the tracks and the accelerations of the motor of the Milanese trams were more musical. There was no comparison: it was something completely different. Francesca introduced me to her friends and classmates. She showed me off to them. Proudly. We walked arm-in-arm, but always as 'friends'. Nothing had changed by the time I left. Yes, the usual: 'I care for you; I care for you as a brother, even more than that. But we're friends! Let's see how it goes.'

'Friends like everyone else?'

'No, how could that be: a bit more than that.'

And that 'bit more' caused me all my problems. If she had told me earlier how things stood, I would have said, 'Thank you and goodbye,' but instead I started travelling back and forth – Latina–Milan– Latina. Hitchhiking. But what was behind it all?

The fact is that this story never ended, it went on for a few years, on and off. For the rest of the year – at least until June – we were never apart more than two weeks. Sometimes I took Wolf with me, sometimes Serse, and other times I went alone, but I was always back and forth on the motorway.

We would leave on Friday night to be there by morning – we would miss school on Saturday – then maybe we would go back on Saturday night, or the next morning, so that we could sleep a little on Sunday and be ready for school on Monday. Sometimes we would go even if the weather wasn't very promising: 'Who knows? Maybe it's sunny in Milan.' And actually, when we arrived the sun would come out. We would arrive at her school early in the morning, before classes started, and we would wait for her. She would arrive without expecting us, she would see us from far away, or her friends would see us, and they always said to her, 'Tell them to come more often, they bring good weather.' Every time it seemed as if there had been nothing but rain and fog until the day we arrived, and the Milanese would think, 'Lucky Southerners.' We would arrive and the sun would come out.

One time a friend of Francesca's actually said, 'This morning when I opened my shutters and saw that the clouds had cleared, I thought, "I bet that the boys from Latina will be here today!"' They would always say, 'Rome! Rome!' (the Coliseum, Saint Peter's, Villa Borghese). But as far as I was concerned, nothing was as beautiful as Milan. Maybe it's because whenever I was there it would be sunny, as Francesca said, but Milan is beautiful in the sun. Those wide avenues. It almost seemed like Latina. Those gardens. The trees. The buildings. The trams. Even the traffic that was always so fast, even corso Sempione, even via Monti, where you had to be careful when you crossed, because they would run you over. And then everyone spoke with that accent, the shops with their dark signs – the black glass, over the door, with white letters. In the latteria you could even have something to eat, not just buy milk, like back home.

But you have to get to Milan, and it was a long journey, it would take all night, sometimes even longer. The worst part was the ring road around Rome, at the beginning of the trip. It wasn't like it is today, with twenty-four lanes. It was a normal road, and it didn't even encircle the entire city of Rome. You could only go as far as via Cassia. Stop. End of the road. If you wanted to go any farther, you had to go back, and it was just like a normal road. From via Pontia to via Appia we would travel on a road lined by umbrella pines, but no one drove there, especially not at night. On more than one occasion we had to walk all the way to Laurentina, and it was uphill. It would be rare for us to find a lift all the way. It would usually take several rides and lots of hours sitting on the guardrail waiting at the Salaria junction, with the RCA factory below: I've spent days there, months, years. I can still remember the stains on the steel barrier, the rust, the cracks in the asphalt. When we finally made it to the beginning of the motorway, we felt like we'd reached the doors of paradise: 'Now we're here.' You could almost smell the air of Milan. You could smell the smog. Idroscalo Park.

From there everything was easier, the rides were longer. It's not that people were eager to stop; they weren't falling over each other to pick us up. Actually there weren't very many who passed by, but every once in a while someone would stop. There were a lot of hitchhikers, and sometimes there was even a queue, you had to fight for your place: 'I saw him first,' 'He stopped for me.' There were foreigners with backpacks who held pieces of cardboard indicating their destination: 'Milan', 'Florence' or 'Rome' on the way back. We didn't have signs, just our thumbs. When cars stopped, we would run up and ask, 'Are you going to Milan?' but we were happy even to go part of the way:

the important thing was to be on the motorway, after that it was done. The first couple of times I would get out on the carriageway, but they drove too quickly, it was too dangerous, and one time the highway police stopped and sent me away to the toll booth. So I would have them leave me there, even if the toll operators complained. Anyhow, the toll booths were all quite different. There were some where you could only stay for a few minutes, then there were some that were truly jinxed.

The worst ones were Arezzo and Florence North. In Arezzo one afternoon we waited for eight and a half hours and no one stopped. There was a huge queue of hitchhikers, and only two French girls managed to bag a ride. There were dressed totally in black, with black jeans, but they were as ugly as sin. One was tall and heavy, a lump of mountainous proportions. But they were picked up right away. A car screeched to a half, braking suddenly, and we – Wolf and I – tried to run after it, and he was adamant: 'I want that one.' They hopped on board without rushing, and Wolf shouted after them, 'Sluts.' The fat one wanted to get out and hit him, her friend had to restrain her. So we waited there for eight and a half hours. There was a road sign – a big arrow, with the word 'Arezzo' – and someone had written 'shithole' underneath with a felt pen. Never was a truer word said. At least as far as hitchhiking was concerned, it was a shithole, it would be better to walk. But that time we were on our way back, so I didn't let it bother me too much. Florence North was worse one night on the way north. I must have arrived there at midnight. I said to myself, 'By seven at the latest I'll be in Milan.' At nine in the morning I was still there. As soon as I arrived, it began to rain lightly, then the rain became heavier and heavier and it didn't stop. The toll booth operator even kicked me out from under the roof. Cars passed, they slowed down, they would enter the queue to take their ticket and I would ask, 'Are you going to Milan?' with the water dripping from my raincoat – the same dark grey one. The water was dripping from my head, all my hair was flattened, and the water ran in rivers into my neck. I was soaked to the skin. I spent the entire night in the rain begging for a ride, and no one stopped.

As day gradually broke, I wondered, 'When will I get to Milan?' and by 9 a.m. the rain showed no intention of letting up and no one was stopping. Then – right along the pavement – an old Prinz pulled up, a 750, and I heard it coming from far away with that strange high-pitched whistling sound. It was a ridiculous vehicle, and it was packed to the gunnels: husband, wife and two kiddies (they seemed like the Holy Family). They didn't even give me a chance to ask for a ride, they rolled the window down and called out, 'We're going to Rome.' I was just about to say, 'Sorry, I'm going to Milan,' but then I thought, 'Where the fuck do I think I'm going?' It was nine in the morning, I was wet to the bone, I had to travel all that way and come back for school the next day, and I was completely numb, I didn't have any strength left, and this bloody Florence North was getting on my nerves more than Arezzo, because at least that time it had been sunny, so I said, 'Alright, thank you.' They didn't even make me sit in the back, crushed between the children: she went in the back, the wife, and she made me sit in front. She even gave me a dry handkerchief, because mine were soaked.

As soon as we left and got to Florence South – we hadn't even left Florence – the sun came out, damn it, and I almost felt like saying, 'Let me out, I want to try again,' but I was physically and mentally drained and I fell asleep. They didn't wake me up. They spoke quietly, and told the children, 'Sssssh, don't make any noise.' I slept until Settebagni, and it was still sunny, and then I could see the road was dry. When I arrived home everyone had just finished lunch: 'Home so soon?' my mother asked. I was completely destroyed, but not because of the rain, because of Florence North. And the fact that I hadn't made it to Milan.

But three or four times I managed to find rides all the way from Rome to Milan. Once I was picked up by a man with an Alfa Romeo 2600. He was taking contraband cigarettes to Rome from Switzerland. He was on his way back, with the car empty, and he was racing like Fangio: four and a half hours to Melegnano, the closest village. You went slower with lorries: at that time they were slower, and if the road was steep, like in the Apennines, they went at a walking pace, with their motors churning. But they were great trips. It was warm. Comfortable. They would chat, they would tell stories. Hitchhikers were company, obviously. They would always buy you a coffee or a cappuccino at the roadside service area: there was no point in you insisting, even if we didn't insist very much, because – after that time I slept in a hotel – I didn't have much money left. I was able to leave for Milan with no more than two thousand lire in my pocket, just enough for cigarettes, a couple of sandwiches and tram fares, what more did I need?

Once – all we had left was about twenty-five hundred lire for the two of us – Serse decided to play the big guy. We were with Francesca and some friend of hers who seemed interested in Serse. At a certain point it came out that she loved to ride bumper cars, and so did Serse. I'd never cared for them much, and neither did Francesca. But he adored them: whenever he went to Naples with his father they spent all their time at the Edenlandia fun park; even his father loved it. Those partisans. Anyhow, at the junction of via Venti Settembre – the time before, when I was alone, Francesca climbed up on my shoulders and with a felt-tip pen she added to the marble street indication, in Roman numerals, 'IX', and now it was via Venti*nove* Settembre: who knows if it's still there? We used indelible ink. At that time, at the junction, in the middle of the public gardens, there were rides, and that idiot spent all our money on tokens for the bumper cars. I could see that he was going back and forth to the desk, and as soon as he'd finished one ride he started another. He even gave some tokens to us – a few each – and Francesca had fun. When we bumped the other cars, she would hold onto me. I touched her leg with my leg, I put my arm around her shoulders, and she would laugh, 'Let me drive,' and I would let her drive. When we bounced her hair would cover her face, and I would brush it away, and as I brushed it away I would brush against her cheek. But I did ask Serse, 'So what about our money?'

'Don't worry,' he replied, so I didn't. But after several more rides – when he came back with more tokens – I asked him again, 'What about the money?'

'There's nothing left,' and he started to laugh. I thought he was joking, because he was laughing, and we took the girls back and they were totally happy. We walked along arm-in-arm. 'When are you coming back?' they asked, and we each gave the girls a couple of kisses, even if they were only on the cheek, but more than usual with the simple excuse that we were leaving. And we were both happy, me and him: 'It went well this time, didn't it?' But when I then realised that he really had spent all our money on the bumper cars, and we didn't have even one lira left for the return journey, I became angry. I couldn't believe it.

'But didn't you have fun?' he continued to ask me for the entire trip home.

I complained, 'How could you? From Milan to Latina without so much as a sandwich: we haven't had a thing to eat since lunchtime, the entire night on the road, till tomorrow, without even cigarettes, without the money for a coffee.'

'But didn't you have fun?' he asked.

The strange thing is that on the way there, every time, I couldn't wait to get there, but as soon as I could see the Melegnano toll booth I felt a bitter sensation. I don't know if it was the anxiety about how things would go with Francesca, like when you're about to take an exam, or on the way back because the trip was ending. Then as soon as we got out – near piazzale Corvetto or Metanopoli – I could feel my anxiety lifting: there was Milan, the trams, the cathedral, the roundabout in piazzale Cordusio. More often than not she would skip class and we would hang out. We went to Boden Bar, nearby, where they had booths and a jukebox. Then I would take her home: corso Magenta, the Sforza Castle, piazza 6 February, the Fiera, via Domodossola. Every time we walked through piazza 6 February, she would show me, 'This is where they shot and injured a lady' in the film *Bandits in Milan*. It must have happened not long before. In the afternoon I could only see her for two or three more hours: either she had to study or her mother wouldn't let her out, or her father was around. Sometimes she invented excuses – that she was going to a friend's house to study – and then we could meet up. Otherwise I would have to spend hours wandering the streets of Milan on my own, going back and forth past the cathedral or waiting near her house on the benches in the public gardens. One time it even happened that she had to go to school because she had an assignment, and once she was off school, at home. I waited there in front of the school for her to show up, and when I called she was unwell, she just came down to the front door of her apartment building and she said hello and then went back upstairs – I didn't get invited in very much. On several occasions I would go all the way to Milan just to see her for one or two hours: 'Wait. I'll be right down to get some milk.' I felt like Gianni Morandi, who would sing, 'Ask Mamma to send you out to buy milk.' But even when everything went well I would have to spend hours waiting for her: back and forth, Fiera, cathedral and Central Station. Sometimes, when Serse was with me, we were so desperate – you never know – that we would chat up passersby, like at the seaside. But without much result. It was a numbers game anyhow.

Then I would call her from a phone booth and sing to her, and she would laugh and laugh, 'Here I come.' And we were always friends, just friends, nothing more. At a certain point we had an argument. I don't even remember why any more: 'That's it, we can't continue like this,' and we stopped writing. But I'd met one of her friends, a girl called Angela – not a close friend, just a girl she knew – a blonde as sweet as candy, and she would also write me every once in a while. So I returned to Milan to see Angela, just her, and we got on well together. We were also just friends, but it was a warmer, more tender friendship. It certainly seemed more promising. When Francesca found out – you'll say, 'But you did it on purpose:' of course, what do you think? I'm no fool – she went berserk. She wrote, and that's not all. She didn't just write to me, she wrote to Wolf and Serse and everyone. So I called her: 'She must be interested,' I thought to myself, and I told her so.

'No, I'm just disappointed in your behaviour,' she mused, but then she admitted, 'You're right, it's not just friendship, there's something more. But give me time to decide.'

'Alright, but you have to decide one way or the other.' Instead things went on like before for a long time. Every once in a while, just to keep me sweet, she would give me just enough to let me dream, and so I kept on travelling back and forth to Milan. At night I'd sleep in the waiting room of Central Station. It wasn't the most pleasant atmosphere. The benches were made of wood, and it was full of tramps and strange people, the kind of people who spent their nights wandering the station, and imagine what they were like in a big city like Milan. There were rent boys, who looked us up and down, even offered us their wares. We would shoo them away. And there was an old man with white hair; he wore a country-bumpkin-style hat and a brown sheepskin jacket. He fell in love with Serse. We ran into him two or three times. He had a strange manner: he was arrogant and seemed like a mafioso, even though he was Milanese. Once, the last time we ran into him, he sent a guy to tell us, 'He wants you both, but especially him,' pointing to Serse, 'and he'll pay good money.'

I tried to encourage Serse: 'Go for it.' What did I care? It was good money.

But I started to laugh, and he told the messenger, 'Just get lost.'

The guy looked at us in a menacing way: 'You don't know who you're dealing with.' And it was cold in Milan in the wintertime, truly cold. The waiting room was heated. As soon as you opened the door to go inside you would be overcome by a wave of warm air, and everyone inside would shout in unison, 'Shut the door!' Inside the hot air was thick with a pungent smell. And it was full of rent boys. So much so that in the end we went to sleep downstairs in the entrance on the marble benches at the foot of the stairs. It was freezing cold, and there were drafts of cold air swirling around everywhere, but there was nothing I could do to convince Serse to go back to the waiting room.

Serse was interested in Francesca's older sister, but it was a futile campaign. She was a know-it-all, and once she declared, 'I'm a Marxian atheist existentialist.' I can still remember the exact moment: we were on a street corner of piazza Cordusio near a bank in front of a florist's display on the pavement. I can still remember every detail because I almost fell down – I loved that sentence so much. It changed my life, it turned my entire existence upside down, and for a moment I fell in love with her even more than with Francesca. For months I'd been reading *Urania* – all those back issues at Serse's place, he would buy a new issue every week – and I'd become a science fiction fan. I read them all, every last one, and when she said 'Marxian' – a word that I'd never heard before in my life, not even from Violetta and her husband, they just said 'Marxist' – she said it with her cute Milanese accent, with a soft, lispy 'x' that sounded like 'sh', so that I understood she meant 'Martian', a citizen of Mars. She was all serious and convinced, and I thought, 'She's impressive,' because even though we believed in extraterrestrials we would only talk about it between ourselves, we were never so convinced as to make it our political manifesto, and this girl instead could stand there in all seriousness and say, 'I'm a Martian, I'm waiting for them, I'm on their side.' To me she seemed even more of a heroine than Garibaldi's wife Anita. But then we clarified the misunderstanding and I didn't want to say too much, because I was afraid I'd look like some kind of cretin. But Serse started laughing right away about the 'atheist existentialist' part, and he understood what she was trying to say.

We changed topics, and he moved on to other girls, anyone he could find, but his luck was as bad as mine. The closest we got to getting laid was at night at Central Station. I can still remember her saying 'Marxian' to this day, and even now, long after the fall of the Berlin Wall, I continue to declare myself a convinced 'Marxian'. I'm a much more fervent supporter of Mars than of Marx. But not an atheist existentialist, no, that made me laugh.

Anyhow, we would always hang out in the daytime like zombies, due to sleep deprivation. I only truly woke up when it was time to see Francesca, otherwise I would walk as if in a trance, like at that time when I took pills in Colle Oppio. As soon as I sat down on a bench I would fall asleep, one time she even found me there asleep, on a bench on via Venti*nove* Settembre, where she lived. I liked to hang out in piazza Cordusio best of all, I don't quite know why: 'What's so special about it?' she would ask me. She preferred Boden Bar. Wolf told me, a few years later, that it had to be closed because of drugs: I'd never noticed any. But the strange thing is that as soon as it was time to go home I didn't feel sad. Maybe I'd been aware of it the entire time I was there, because things with Francesca didn't seem to be progressing. She'd been effusive when we said goodbye, and as I waited for my tram for piazzale Corvetto, but when it was time to go back, as soon as the tram had made its way along corso Lodi to its destination, and we arrived in piazzale Corvetto at the end of the line, any sadness had already lifted. Maybe it was the thought of the trip home. All I had to do was get off the tram, stand on the corner of via Marochetti, and then another adventure would begin and I'd feel exhilarated.

Now there's a horrible overpass system, but back then the road was flat, it was almost a normal junction, and there was a hedge on the corner, a tall hedge, with wide, large leaves. Behind there was a garden for two or three yards and then a block of flats, covered in a kind of green majolica tile that they used to use in Milan, and the windows of the flats seemed to balance on the hedge. You could see into the windows of the kitchens, and as you hitchhiked you could see the lights on and the mothers cooking and people eating. I was totally in love with that hedge, it seemed so different from the ones back home, and I would play with the leaves as I waited for a car to come into view from the other side of piazzale Corvetto, sitting on the kerb. When I went by there the last time – a few decades ago – I tried to see if it was still there, but it was impossible: the taxi drove too quickly over the horrible overpass.

Sometimes it seems to me that all this travel back and forth to Milan didn't really have anything to do with Francesca. Perhaps I was actually more in love with Milan than with her. And in love with the journey.

chapter 9

It was 1968. The world was changing everywhere, except for Latina. In Latina everything was calm, even calmer than before, seeing as we weren't Fascists any more – or at least we weren't official Fascists with membership cards – so there was no one to spray graffiti on the walls, put up posters or burn stuff. It was more peaceful than the Sea of Tranquillity on the moon.

In January – as well as turning eighteen – I finally received a letter inviting me to the appeal hearing of the MSI national disciplinary committee, to review my expulsion. I'd been waiting for months, and I couldn't wait for it to arrive. But when the day finally came, I didn't show up. I'd been planning my defence up to the day before: 'I'll tell them this, I'll tell them that.' But when the day suddenly came – it was a Friday – the sun was shining and I said to myself, 'When will there ever be another day like this? I'd rather go to Milan.' I don't know what happened; I just know that when I got there and saw Francesca, I told her, 'I'm not a Fascist any more.'

She was delighted: 'Does that mean you're a Communist now?'

'No, an anarchist.'

'It's a start.'

Anyhow, the chairman had always said, 'You're all anarchists,' and he didn't know how right he was, even if he only started to say if after Bava came on the scene. Anyhow, I was no longer a Fascist. I don't know when it happened and I don't even know how – if it was a gradual process, one thing today, another thing tomorrow, or if it was actually something sudden, a bolt from the blue, an epiphany that caused everything to change without me realising. What I do know is that if lightning had struck, I must have been daydreaming – I missed it completely. It wasn't anything like Saint Paul on the road to Damascus, when he fell off his horse. I didn't even fall off my bicycle. Maybe, though, it was a case of the straw that broke the camel's back: first Vietnam, then Serse, then Francesca, as well as the Jews, Manrico and Milan. What do I know, it was like a love affair. First you want one woman, then you see another, and suddenly she's the one you want and you don't give a damn about the one you loved before. And 'anarchist' only meant that I was fed up with politics: 'That's it, I want to be like normal people. I want to think about women, money and having a good life. I'll leave it to others to worry about what's happening to Italy.' What did I care? I had to go to Milan.

But it wasn't as if we could always be travelling on the motorway. Actually, I had to spend most of my time at school in Latina. I would always sleep through the first two hours – then in the afternoon I would hang out, have something to eat, and hang out again in the evening until late, walking under the porticoes in the centre of town talking about women and Martians. Then I'd go home, read some science fiction and back to school again. Total boredom. Plain vanilla. No wonder that straw broke the camel's back.

Then chaos started breaking out everywhere. We didn't quite understand what was going on. We just saw the TV news images of students running amok on American university campuses, then in Paris, in Germany, in Czechoslovakia, and then it started in Italy, first in Rome and Milan and then in Naples and Pisa, then everywhere. They went on strike, they occupied the university buildings, they clashed with the police: urban guerrilla warfare. None of this affected daily life in Latina: everything was tranquil. We wondered, 'Is this the only quiet backwater left?' If we'd still been MSI members – if we still had our official membership cards – we would have turned the city topsy-turvy, but what could we do on our own? Could I really put up a poster proclaiming a general strike and sign it 'Accio Benassi'? In Rome there was more chaos every day, and when they burned a police van in Valle Giulia we heard that it was the work of a group that was also active in Latina. They met in via Oberdan, above the premises of Banco di Santo Spirito.

This place was a kind of drop-in centre set up by the Cassa per il Mezzogiorno, a community centre for depressed areas. They offered photography courses, there was a library, a stamp-collecting club, you could play chess or watch films, they organised hikes; but it was all managed by left-wingers. When Violetta was younger she would always go there the few times she left the house, and my father was opposed to it, he said that it was full of Communists, but my mother would plead, 'She studies so much, poor thing,' and he would let her go. That's where she met Carmine. So my father was right after all. We'd been there before – just a couple of times, when they were showing films, to make a hullabaloo when they showed films starring Ugo Tognazzi. We'd never gone back.

One evening we showed up. There must have been four or five of us: me, Wolf, Serse, some others. Wolf had grown a beard and he'd become stocky, enormous, he'd even competed in Graeco-Roman wrestling. He glowered at everyone, and he still had that Bergomi-style unibrow. His hair was in a crew cut, black, and now this ginger beard. You may well ask, 'How could he have black hair and a ginger beard?' I don't know, but that's how he was. I had a moustache, but otherwise my face was the same, Serse still had his smile of superiority, and then there was Wolf, with his black hair and ginger beard and this whopping unibrow.

When we arrived, the room was half full. There must have been around thirty of them, they were all sitting facing the table, with their backs to us. There were three or four of them at the table. Someone was talking; a philosophy teacher we'd always known was a card-carrying PCI member. Next to him sat Vittorio, who studied physics in Pisa and had been one of Violetta's admirers when she was younger. He would come to our home sometimes, and he was always nice to me, maybe to ingratiate himself, but Violetta wasn't interested. One time, he even gave me a present: a biography of Che Guevara. We entered from the back of the room, and the philosophy teacher was talking, but when he saw us arrive he stopped talking, and everyone turned in their chairs to see who we were and they didn't say a word. After a moment he spoke: 'What do you want?' He didn't go back to his talk, he spoke to us: 'What do you want?'

Then and there I felt badly intimidated, and I stammered, 'They told us that this is where the students are meeting.'

'Yes, but what do you want?'

'What do you mean, what do we want? We're students,' and then the misunderstanding was clarified, because Cristina – she was all skin and bones, very petite, she'd lived near us when we were small. Her father was a well-known Communist, but she'd gone to the convent kindergarten in my class and she stayed on to study with the sisters and the Daughters of Maria until recently. She went to all the summer camps and on all the pilgrimages. I remember she had a devotion to the Sacred Heart, and she would pray with her hands clasped around a candle. Cristina turned to the students sitting next to her and whispered in an agitated voice, 'They're Fascists, Fascists.'

'We're not Fascists,' and I started to laugh: they were all afraid that we'd come to attack them. They let us stay, but they weren't really sure they could trust us, and every once in a while they would look at us – as if to say, 'Do I dare?' before they made any remark that was even slightly provocative. But they started up their discussion again; they tried to go back to where they were when we'd arrived. Vittorio spoke after the teacher had finished, and then someone else took the floor.

I don't exactly remember what they said. They would use the word 'Fascist' every thirty seconds. Everyone was a Fascist: the Christian Democrats, the police, schools, institutions, society, the socialists, the unions. Even the community centre itself came under fire. They were all Fascists. And then they used a lot of words like 'education', 'student proletariat', 'middle-class proletariat' 'platform' 'class analysis' – stuff like this, but most of all 'education'. Whenever someone talked, they would use the word at least a hundred times, and they would drone on and on for ever, and everyone would quote from their favourite authors: Mao, Marx, Herbert Marcuse. I didn't understand anything, but then neither did my friends. At a certain point Serse asked, 'Fine, but when will these guys start talking about the strike?'

So I asked for the floor: 'We can facilitate a strike in our school, even tomorrow. If you give us a hand we can get the art college to strike as well.'

The teacher replied in an ironic tone, he was making fun of us, 'And how exactly do you intend to organise a strike tomorrow without any preparation?'

'What does it take? We stand outside and we block the entrance.' They all started laughing. 'Don't you believe us?' I asked.

'We believe you, we believe you,' but they kept on laughing.

'We've done it before.'

'We know, we know,' but they stopped laughing because they saw that I was getting agitated, and the teacher began again, calmly, speaking slowly as if he was talking to a retard. He was very careful not to be aggressive with me, because I wasn't just retarded, I was dangerous: 'That's not how we want to strike, not by force. People have to be convinced of what they do, they have to agree.'

'Alright, we're all agreed. Tell him to go fuck himself and we're all agreed.' They started laughing again, even that girl Cristina. I'm not sure if I'd liked her better when she chanted, 'The Fascists, the Fascists.' They started laughing again, and I really became angry: 'Now you've pissed me off,' and I was about to throw my chair, but then I saw that next to me Wolf and Serse were laughing too, so I did the same. 'Why am I laughing?' I asked myself, and that know-it-all started up again: 'You can't do that: if you want to strike, first you need an inquiry, a platform. You have to know what you want and what you're asking for. If people ask you why they have to strike, what will you tell them?'

'I'll tell them: for solidarity with the students in Rome.'

'Right, for solidarity...' And they all looked at me as if I were an imbecile, even Wolf and Serse, I could have killed them. Wolf and Serse, that is, not the others. And then the teacher started up again: 'First you need an inquiry, a class analysis. Then a platform and especially education, education of the masses. Only after this can one think about striking, not before,' and everyone nodded in agreement. And they looked at me, turning around in their chairs, with an expression that seemed to say, 'What will it take? Even children know that.' Even Wolf and Serse.

We stayed a bit longer. The others continued to discuss according to the terms that they knew. No one mentioned strikes. Maybe, if all went well, within two months it might have been possible to produce a flier, just maybe. 'It reminds me of spiritual exercises when I was a seminarian,' I said to Wolf.

'You're right,' he replied, but very quietly, and he looked across at Cristina, they smiled at each other.

When we left, the philosophy teacher said to us in a condescending tone, 'Come back any time,' but it was obvious that in his heart he wished for the exact opposite. He just said it for good manners, and all the others said the same, even Cristina: 'Come back any time,' but with the same tone of voice as the teacher.

Still, Wolf insisted I was wrong: 'No, they really meant it. Cristina was smiling at me, she was really smiling.'

Serse: 'They were all smiling.'

'Sure, it was a smile of relief: they smiled because we were leaving,' I tried to explain, and I didn't want to go back again. What was the point of going back: to amuse them? To be an object of ridicule?

In the meantime, Manrico had suddenly left home. Until then he'd been a model student – 'half your duty' – he did well on his exams, he studied every evening. Every morning he would take the train and go to Rome for his lessons, then in the afternoons he would work with Glauco, who was a sales rep for a drinks company and had a bar near the courthouse. He did the books, and sometimes he would run the bar. My mother thought it was wonderful: 'If only you could be more like him.' But from one day to the next he left home and we never saw him again: he just phoned once.

I wasn't worried about it at all, actually, it was better for me: there was more space in the bedroom. I didn't even ask myself, 'Who knows what happened to him?' What did I care? I had my own worries, especially the fact that I still didn't have a girlfriend. I had to travel as far as Milan, and we know how well that was going. Once, by chance, I met some of Manrico's friends, and they told me that they had gone to see him in Rome, I think he was living in the student residences: 'He always has women following him around,' they said. 'He is definitely getting laid.' And this annoyed me: 'He always falls on his feet,' I thought. But my mother was worried, and my father sighed, 'This is all we need.'

Then one day Uncle Carlin came to our house – he was always stirring up intrigue in the family – one morning when he knew my mother would be at home alone. He showed her an article cut out of a newspaper from the week before, with the news of four arrests in Rome, and Manrico's name was there, Manrico Benassi. She was so devastated that the atmosphere at home was funereal. As usual, no one told Papà anything, but at that time Norma was staying, with all her family, and her husband – the socialist who couldn't stand me – said, 'Alright, let's go to see what the situation is,' because Uncle Carlin hadn't even left the article and he hadn't been able to explain things clearly to Mamma. He just came, stirred things up, and left. So my brother-in-law wanted to take me along, to get more information from Uncle Carlin.

Mamma shook her head: 'Don't take him with you,' and so did Norma. I didn't even want to go, but he insisted.

As we were driving there in the car, Norma tried again: 'It's better if he doesn't come along.'

I thought to myself, 'I wish I could be at home just reading.' (Serse had just given me a new issue of *Urania*.)

Her husband disagreed: 'What are you saying? Can't you see that he's older? He's calmed down.'

'Maybe,' she replied, and when we arrived I almost thought about refusing to get out of the car.

'It's better if I don't come.'

But he insisted: 'You're his brother,' and so I had to go.

We went up the stairs, and I was still dubious. We rang the bell. My uncle didn't even let us in: he started shouting as soon as he opened the door. My brother-in-law said, 'Alright, just explain,' and my uncle screamed at us, 'Shame on you! You'll be the death of my sister.'

My brother-in-law insisted, 'Just explain,' but it was no use, all my uncle did was yell.

Then I spoke up – I was standing behind Norma and my brother-in-law, and my uncle was at the door. I said to him, 'Now you've made me angry, Manrico is still my brother, and before you went to upset our mother you should have taken time to think what you were doing. You've been causing trouble for as long as I can remember. You could have spoken to us first.'

He didn't reply to our arguments. He just screamed louder, 'Shame on you!' and then he threw himself past the other two and attacked me, he tried to grab me by the neck. I hit him twice in rapid succession, and then we were at it, both of us trying to shove the others out of the way – my sister and my brother-in-law – because there wasn't enough space to fight. Then we heard a 'boom', and at that point I didn't realise what it was, not until the door in front opened on the other side of the hallway and out came Uncle Piero with his wife, Aunt Daria, who had her arms around his waist and was trying to pull him back inside. He was dragging her behind him as she screamed, 'Come inside, Piero, come inside.' He must have made a superhuman effort to get out of the house with that dead weight around his body.

When I saw him I breathed a sigh of relief: 'Thank goodness, now he can try to calm his brother,' and I even smiled at him. But Uncle Piero took it out on me, and he started shouting too: 'Shame on you!' And then he started taking everything out on me: 'It's your fault! How dare you come here to attack your uncles!' and he began to hit me too. So I hit him back. They were my uncles, and they were a little mad; but I was crazier than they were. It was a fine match, with my sister and her husband behind me, pulling me away down the steps, one by one. My uncles were still coming after us, taking advantage of the height of the stairs and the difference in our positions. Aunt Daria remained attached to Uncle Piero's waist, dragging him back from the stairs. I still can hardly believe that he was able to hit me with all that weight behind him. Uncle Piero was a big man. I was giving my hooks right and left to both of them. A fine match. If my brother-in-law hadn't intervened, we'd still be there fighting in that hallway.

'I told you not to bring him along,' said Norma when we were back in the car.

Then Mamma sent Otello to Rome to find news of Manrico, to discover what had happened to him: 'Bring my boy home,' she ordered him, as if he were her knight in shining armour.

He tried to suggest, 'Let me take Accio.'

'Aha, so you really want to kill me.' In the end, they didn't tell me anything, not even that he was leaving on a special mission, just in case I ruined their plans.

Otello wandered the streets of Rome. He hung out at the student residences, he visited all the occupied university buildings, he asked questions of hippies with long hair and strange clothes. Nothing. He wandered through Termini Station, checked out the benches at Villa Borghese. Nothing, no one had heard of Manrico. Then one evening he went to the Faculty of Education, which had just been occupied. There were student guards at the entrance. He asked, 'Do you know someone called Manrico Benassi?'

'Never heard of him. Now get lost,' because they thought he was a cop.

'No, I'm his brother, he's missing, my mother is desperate.' Now it seemed like a real-life mystery, so they felt sorry for him.

'What did you say his name is?'

'Manrico Benassi. He's tall, thin, light brown hair.'

'Never seen him. Never heard of him.' They asked around: 'Never seen him, never heard of him.' Then they asked more students inside. 'Never seen him, never heard of him.' In the end they got fed up and went back to whatever they'd been doing before. Then just as he was saying goodbye – seeing that Otello was on the brink of tears one guy said to him, 'I'm really sorry' – someone came to ask, and it was really at the very last minute, the last instant, 'What do you mean you've never seen him? He always wears a scarf around his neck.'

'A white scarf?' called the other one.

'Yes, a white scarf.'

'You should have said so before, we call him White Scarf! Hey, there's someone here looking for White Scarf!' he screamed, and in thirty seconds Otello was admitted into his presence.

He was more powerful than Strelnikov in *Doctor Zhivago*: he had become a sort of supreme commander, everyone knew him, they all respected him. But he wasn't an ideologist, one of those guys who takes the floor in political meetings and then never shuts up, telling the story of the world since Adam and Eve every time, going over everything that's ever happened and re-examining it in light of the sacred texts by Marx, Engels, Lenin, Mao Tse-Tung. Every time they would drone on for hours and hours, and the people in the auditorium would yawn, everyone would go in and sit down only when their leader spoke; when the other leaders spoke they would make noise and go out to chat in the hallways. He was different. When he spoke at meetings, people would say, 'Scarf is speaking, Scarf is speaking,' and they would even tell people outside, so that they could rush back in. He didn't speak much, never more than fifteen minutes, and at the end everyone would applaud, no matter what their political allegiance, because he wasn't an ideologist, he was a technician, a military leader. He was the *lider maximo* of the student movement in Rome. How on earth this had happened, I really don't know. All I could remember was that time when we demonstrated against the band of the Sixth Fleet and he was scared to death, and now he'd become a sort of Italian Che Guevara. I can hear you saying, 'That's life!' I know, it's true, one never knows. Maybe – who can say? – it was in our blood, like a sort of hereditary disorder.

Anyhow, they allowed Otello in. Manrico got up from the table, came over, and they embraced – while his lieutenants turned to look at them – and Manrico said, 'I don't have time to speak to you now because I'm busy: come back tomorrow.' Otello obeyed, and the next day he went back, but Manrico was in a hurry again; he told him, 'Walk with me,' and they left the Faculty of Education building. They got into a couple of cars – Citroën 2CVs – and drove to the centre of town. They made him get in the car behind, not the leader's vehicle.

When they got out, Otello called to him, 'Manrico!' and he replied, 'Come with me.' They arrived in a little piazza near Campo de' Fiori. There was already a crowd in the centre, and police were standing around their vans on the other side of the piazza, but everything seemed tranquil. Someone was speaking into a megaphone. Then Manrico asked, 'How are things at home?'

'Fine.'

'I'm glad. Now let's have some fun, but please watch these guys for me,' and he pushed a girl wearing a Mexican poncho towards Otello, and winked as if to say, 'She's all yours; you can do as you please,' and he disappeared.

Two minutes later all hell broke loose. There were small groups attacking the police. They fought back with truncheons. Molotov cocktails were thrown at the police vehicles. Other vans began to drive after the fleeing mob, with police leaning out and swinging cudgels. The students fought back, throwing more molotovs. They turned parked cars over in the middle of the road, and set them on fire, and gave the market stalls the same treatment. It was madness; Otello didn't know what to do, and this girl was holding on to him for dear life: 'Oh my God, the police!' as a group of cops moved towards them. He ran away with the girl by his side. He protected her, he held her tight, he took her home, and then he took advantage of her: 'What was I supposed to do?' he shrugged. When he came home – a few days later, because Mamma had given him plenty of spending money – he told her, 'He's fine.'

'But isn't he coming home?'

'I don't think so.'

'What do you think I sent you there for? Didn't you tell him to come home? What have you been doing all this time?'

'But Mamma, all I did was…' But she was practically ready to start dressing in black to show her mourning. She was desperate: 'I've lost him. I've lost another child.' (I don't think this referred to me, but rather to that miscarriage brought on by Father Pio.)

And Papà shook his head: 'It's as if my home has been taken over by the Devil himself.'

Mamma took it out on me: 'It's all your fault. You were a bad influence on him.'

'Me? But he's older than I am.'

'No. You were a bad influence, that time that you got him arrested. He was so good, so well behaved. He would never think of doing anything like this. You showed him these things, it's all your fault.' That's life. Poetic justice. Manrico was leading the revolution, turning cars upside down on the streets of Rome, then setting them on fire, and it was my fault.

Later he told me that in the beginning, when the university was first occupied, the Fascists were with them: they were in occupation together, and they would have political discussions at the assemblies. Everyone expressed their opinions, but they were in it together. It was – how can I explain? – a generational struggle: youth against the older generations. The 'global left-wing struggle' started out like that, because it had become impossible to live in Italy: you couldn't say anything, you couldn't do anything, you didn't have any rights. If you weren't already someone, you counted for less than zero, the professors could expel you just because they felt like it, they would fail you unless your father was a wealthy, powerful man. You could only dream of a university career if your father was already a faculty member, otherwise forget it. The truth is that Fascism didn't fall on 25 July, and it didn't fall after the resistance either. Its name was gone, but it still existed. Society wasn't Fascist yet – they were right about that at the community centre – and unfortunately not social revolutionary Fascism, popular, for the masses. All that existed were the remnants of the Fascist sense of order, authoritarian, rigid, hierarchical: the Fascism of the Christian Democrats, who were stealing as much as they could lay their hands on. This wasn't 'public service'; people got involved in politics so they could advance themselves and their own interests. There were scandals every day, over backhanders on tobacco and bananas, simple items like these. And you couldn't even protest:

if more than three people met on a public street, it was a 'seditious meeting' and the police would break it up. You couldn't speak out, and they were free to steal. I hear you saying, 'Alright, but is it any different now?' What does that matter? Now we're used to it; before we weren't. The young people felt that something wasn't right, and they had decided to stand up and be counted. They were out on the streets, everyone. Even the Fascists. In the beginning everything seemed beautiful: together, discussing, parties, 'imagination in power', and the girls stayed out all night. Nothing like this had ever been seen before.

Then the police created a cordon in Valle Giulia, where the Faculty of Architecture was. It began calmly, there wasn't anyone in sight with a truncheon or with a motorcycle helmet, this was yet to happen. But the police began to attack, and in the beginning all the students did was take it and then run away on the stairs. The police went after them with their vans – like *Battleship Potemkin* – and they ran away, they didn't even think of fighting back. But the Fascists were there with them too at the demonstration. Stefano Delle Chiaie from Avanguardia Nazionale was there, and so were Mantovani and Franco Papitto. They knew that there were some tactics they could use, and they did. They began to resist, to fight back. When the lefties tried to run away and find safety in the gardens or on the stairs, the Fascists and Delle Chiaie stayed in the road, to fight the aggressors head on; together in small groups, they met their attackers straight on, and they over-turned a couple of vans. Then it would seem that Manrico, standing on the stairs with his scarf stained with blood, stopped the withdrawal, exhorting the students to fight back: 'Onwards, comrades!' he shouted, with his bloody scarf flowing in the wind – I don't know what came over him, maybe it was some kind of defective gene in our family – 'Onwards, comrades!' and he guided them on to victory. The students followed him, they joined in the struggle and they drove the police away. At the end of the battle – the police vans still had smoke rising from them – there were hugs and kisses with Mantovani and Delle Chiaie and their boys. The De Luca brothers were there, two rugby players, possessed by the Devil; and the Cataldo brothers. It almost seemed like they were about to break into song, those Fascist hymns again.

Michelini was not pleased with this episode, and neither were the Christian Democrats. Maybe even the Communists were unhappy: they'd always had a monopoly on opposition. Anyhow, our heroes got along very well together up to a certain point: 'I'll occupy Humanities and you can have Law.' Everyone attended political meetings, no matter who organised them, they shared food and resources, and they worked together to provide guards to look after the entire university campus: it was a honeymoon. But one morning the MSI Volunteers showed up. They arrived in war formation. Everyone was there, from all over Italy, the only person missing was me. The MPs stood in front of them, Almirante front centre. Michelini had forced them to go: 'If I don't do something soon, I'll lose all of them.' He didn't have anything against the left – he didn't give a damn – he was thinking of himself: 'If they start collaborating with the left, I may as well close up shop and go home.' He had to scare them, he had to divide and conquer. All the blackshirts were in the Law building – Avanguardia and the others – and until the night before they'd been cheek by jowl with the reds. But now, as soon as they saw them marching in formation, they knew something was up.

As soon as they arrived at the fountain, the Volunteers turned right. Things began to get serious, and they launched an attack on the Faculty of Humanities, where our boys were waiting for them fully armed. Actually, all they had were truncheons and motorcycle helmets, nothing more. They started to equip themselves after Valle Giulia – they'd learned that lesson – and everyone called them the 'Katanga brigade', because the year before, in the summer, there had been another coup in Zaire, the former Belgian Congo, that later failed, but the mercenaries had become famous. They were encircled more than once by substantial enemy forces, but every time they had broken through, routed the regulars and hidden somewhere else: they may have been mercenaries, but they were invincible. So that's what ours were called, and now they were standing on the threshold of the

Faculty of Humanities – where Paolo Rossi had died two years before – waiting for orders from Manrico.

They tried to move up the staircase. The MSI Volunteers who had come from out of town were alone. All the other Fascists, the ones who were university students, remained to one side. Mantovani stayed inside the Law building, his boys didn't come outside. But Avanguardia came out, on orders from Delle Chiaie. They lined up on the other staircase, the big one in the centre of the main administration building, behind the statue of Minerva. They stayed there throughout what happened next, because they were strategically located between Humanities and Law. Of course Delle Chiaie was a man of honour – at least as far as I knew him – but that was the biggest error of his life. He shouldn't have stayed neutral, he shouldn't have limited himself to saying, 'It's nothing to do with me.' A strategist can't allow anything to pull on his heart strings – he has to decide with his head. He should have lined up with his men, fought at our side: a pact had been written in blood at Valle Giulia. On that day, in front of Humanities, the generational front finally broke: it was the beginning of the *anni di piombo*, with a wave of bombings and shootings.

Almirante and the Volunteers tried to go up the stairs outside the Humanities building. They had long truncheons and chains, but they were pushed back, overwhelmed, broken and chased away. They sought refuge in the Law building. They didn't really flee: after the first violent clash on the stairs of the Humanities building and the red counterattack, they just ran away to the Law building: 'Every man for himself.' Almirante was isolated, surrounded. The guards had to protect him; Manrico himself saved him, because the students were baying for his blood. Manrico even exchanged a few blows with Bava, who, as he stumbled back, looked at him strangely, as if to say, 'I know I've met you somewhere before, but where?' Manrico was almost tempted to explain, but there was no time. Then, as everyone knows, it was all-out war, and our boys surrounded the Law building: they wanted the aggressors. They were still Fascists deep inside, so the Volunteers thought they couldn't lay a hand on them. Law was surrounded, under siege. The students responded with everything they could lay their hands on: tables, chairs, desks and blackboards rained down from the windows of every floor. Oreste Scalzone was seriously wounded. Then the police arrived, and Almirante and the Volunteers were escorted to safety. It was a military disaster, but a political victory.

Throughout the student movement, from that day forward, the division was sharp. It was as if we'd gone back to 25 April 1945, the day the Resistance triumphed. 'Dirty Fascists, go back to the gutters you crawled out from!' they shouted. In actual fact, after the retreat of the Volunteers, even Avanguardia had retreated to defend the Law faculty and Almirante. Then one group, commanded by the Di Luiz brothers, gave birth to the Popular Struggle movement, and defined themselves as Nazi-Maoists, but they didn't have any real influence at the end of the day. There was no more chance of mediation, only clashes, each more violent than the last. That meant victory for Almirante and Michelini, not the Fascism of the social republic. They were the defenders of the state, of the status quo, of the Christian Democrat government; they were the White Guards of the capital.

Anyhow, we were still in Latina, and we missed out on all this fun. We went to Rome one evening, finally, when the television news said that the next day the police would clear out the university buildings: 'There'll be a battle; let's go and join in.' But when we arrived, there was no one in sight, everything was closed, tighter than a drum. The assemblies had decided to demobilise, and everyone had gone home; the last to leave had cleared out just a few hours earlier. 'We always arrive when the party's over,' said Wolf, as if it were my fault, but I had wanted to go to Rome for a while; the others insisted we should just go to the community centre. In the end they'd even convinced me: 'There are lots of girls.' That much was true. We would go to meetings and pretend we understood, but in order to be noticed by the women it wasn't enough just to be there, we had to talk. So we had to study *Letter to a Teacher*, four or five sentences from Mao and Marcuse and books by Lenin: *The State and Revolution, Imperialism* and *What is to Be Done?* We even had to read *Psychology of Sex Relations* by

Theodor Reik. Whenever Wolf spoke, he didn't address the assembly, he would just look at Cristina, as if he were speaking solely for her benefit. But now – after the way she smiled at him before, 'Come back any time' – she would always turn away. He would approach her silently from behind, and as soon as she saw him she would jump and run off: 'She's madly in love,' he explained.

'Yes, but not with you,' we told him.

'What do you mean? She's like that because she's in love with me and she doesn't want anyone to notice.'

We went there, we spoke, we flirted with the girls and they encouraged us, but they didn't allow anything more. They didn't really consider us part of their crowd. I know, I can hear you saying, 'Alright, but you had been Fascists.' I understand, but we hadn't killed anyone. And what about Serse? Serse was hardly a Fascist: he wore a Togliatti medallion and his father had been a partisan. You say, 'Yes, but he was your friend.' OK, now I understand.

Only once did they treat us like real comrades. There was a guy who came to the meetings, and once he started talking he would really drone on. He was short and blond. At first glance he might seem innocuous, but he was worse than a dog with a bone. I had known him since I was small, we'd been at kindergarten together. He was one of those lads who hung out at the Don Bosco youth group when my father would send me there; he was Father Russo's pet, his favourite. He tried to encourage him to become a priest, but he wasn't interested, even though he was always hanging out at the San Marco parish centre. He studied at the classical lyceum – he always had top marks and seemed as saintly as Domenico Savio. Now he had a bee in his bonnet about coming here to the community centre with the student movement, and it's not that he came in the spirit as us, as converts, with our tails between our legs ready to learn all the new concepts. He wanted to preach his own ideas, from the Catholic Action youth group, and he was always taking the floor and speaking for hours on end. He was a smart fellow, no idiot: sophisticated discourses and reasoning. He was a fine orator; he would take every sentence written by Marx – he'd read his books more than our little philosophy teacher – and he would twist them around. Sometimes it would come out as if it had been written by Saint Augustine, other times it would come out as if it had been written by Saint Thomas Aquinas.

At a certain point one evening, as we were going away, the teacher and Vittorio – Violetta's ex-admirer – came up to me and Wolf: 'Let's take a walk together.' I was immediately suspicious. Then – one thing led to another – Vittorio said to us, 'We have to get rid of him.'

I thought this was strange: 'Why don't you just tell him not to come back?'

'Well, we can't really do that, someone has to make him understand.'
'Us?'
'You.'

That was all we needed to hear. The next day we took him to the public gardens. Wolf and I stood on either side of him. We started in a roundabout fashion. 'Why do you hang out at the community centre? Don't you think it's just a waste of time?' There was nothing to be done, he still wanted to hang out there. 'We don't want you there.' This was even worse, he began to play the martyr: 'It's my right.' We went on for an hour, and he continued to insist that he wanted to come to the community centre. So I thought, 'I'll look like a fool with Vittorio and the teacher.' I didn't want to, but at that point I felt I had to. I took my knife out of my pocket – I may have forgotten to mention that since Bava had taken away my chain I always kept a switchblade in my pocket, but just a little one, not that big, those ones that everyone carries with them, with a blade barely two inches long – and I began to pretend to clean my nails. 'It would be better if you stopped coming,' I said to him. 'It would be better if you never came back again.'

He didn't bat an eyelid: 'Do you think you can frighten me?'

So I jumped him – we were sitting on a bench, he was in the middle, and I was beside him. I didn't want to, and it was just a joke, but I did jump up, I stood in front of him, and he was still sitting there. I bent over him and placed the point of my blade on his neck. I looked at him sternly and said, 'Don't come back.' Even Wolf had to make an effort not to laugh. He knew I was joking, but not the other guy. This time he did go white and said, 'Alright, I won't go back,' and he never showed his face there again. But he complained to Father Russo, and Father Russo went to the philosophy teacher. He made a big deal out of it – 'The only reason I'm not reporting you is because I'm a priest' – but actually it was because there were no witnesses, Wolf and I weren't that stupid. Anyhow, the next evening Vittorio and the little philosophy teacher took us to one side: 'What have you done?'

'We did what you said. Aren't you happy? He's never coming back.'

'You're crazy. We only asked you to talk to him, not to threaten him with a knife.'

'If it was only a question of speaking with him, why didn't you do it yourselves? You told me to convince him at any price.'

'But what did you understand by that? Now you're making it sound like it's our fault.' How could I have misunderstood? They were like my mother: it was always my fault. Then they started to treat us a bit better. Not exactly like comrades, but slightly better. They started – what can I say? – to trust us. Anyhow, that little teacher had been a secretary at the Communist youth organisation, and he had been there when we went to the PCI meeting at the Chamber of Commerce to shout 'Long live Mussolini', and that old guy told me, 'Apologise to the assembly, apologise to the assembly.' Then a few days later there was a meeting at his house, at the little teacher's house. In his lounge there were bookshelves full of books, and as the others were speaking I leafed through one. He came up to me – it was *Gargantua and Pantagruel* – and asked me with surprise, 'Do you like it?'

'Yes.'

'You can have it. It's a gift.' Who knows what he was thinking.

Teorema was published at about that time. I liked it. I had already read *Ragazzi di vita* – Violetta had it – but I liked the films more. Then one evening, as we were going to Milan, a Mini stopped at the start of the ring road around Rome. I don't remember if it was a Mini Minor or a Mini Cooper, but it was green, I remember that much. It stopped far away, with a screeching of brakes, because it had been going fast. The driver backed up to come closer to us, and this was rather strange, because usually people would stop and wait for you, they didn't come towards you, they left you to run. He came towards us, and as soon as I leaned down to the window of the car I recognised him. It was Pier Paolo Pasolini himself. He took us as far as Arezzo.

Wolf sat in front and I was behind. First we talked about *Teorema,* and then we realised that we hadn't understood it at all: I didn't realise that the angel does the father, too, at the end. Everyone else, yes, but not the father.

'Of course the angel does the father,' said Pasolini.

'How could you fail to understand? It's so obvious!' echoed that cretin Wolf, and I almost felt like saying to him, 'Ah, yes? So why didn't you tell me so when we left the cinema? Can you tell me now?'

And Pasolini: 'You blocked it out, you didn't want to see it.' Not the father, no, good God, did he have to sodomise the father as well? But Pasolini was gentle, sweet. He wanted us to call him by his first name, but I couldn't. He asked us what we did, about our lives. We were seduced by him. From one moment to the next, we expected him to make a proposition, because his tastes were well known. I was also curious to see how I would react – after all, he was the great Pasolini. Poetry. Culture. What did anything else matter? Maybe we would have been up for it, maybe even Wolf. As a matter of fact, usually I sat in front, but this time he pushed me into the back seat, he wanted to sit in front at all costs, next to him.

Anyhow, at a certain point we began to talk politics, and Pasolini went wild. He shrieked with his sharp voice that sounded exactly like Uncle Carlin's voice; he seemed violent like my uncle too, he seemed more violent than us. I screamed even louder, and we argued about everything. He didn't like us, the student movement: 'You're all priests, you're red Fascists,' and the more he said, the more I became angry, so I was really shouting loudly. Wolf was taking his side: 'Well, yes, if one looks at it like that…'

Pasolini went on: 'Red Fascists!'

Then I screamed: 'You're the priest!' louder and louder. So at a certain point I thought, 'Who knows where we'll end up,' and I was even sorry, because he was the embodiment of Culture. 'But I don't give a fuck about culture,' I thought to myself. 'If you're looking for trouble, you've found it.' After a while, however, we fell silent; it must have been around Orvieto. After two ear-splitting screams, no one said anything more. We continued driving, with the headlights shining into the night and the hum of the engine.

He offered us cigarettes. We lit up. More silence. Then – we were almost at the exit for Arezzo – he stopped at a petrol station, to fill up. But he didn't need very much: it must have been just an excuse to stop. He handed over a 10,000 lire note, and the attendant gave him change; he couldn't have put in more than 1500 or 1600 lire. He drove off still holding his change in his hand, and when he drove back onto the motorway he gave it to Wolf, for us. We tried to protest: 'What are you doing? Forget it,' but he insisted. Now he was almost smiling, and just as we arrived, Wolf said, 'One day I'd like to visit the city of Arezzo.'

Right away he said, 'It's very beautiful, you must visit it.' I wasn't so convinced, because I still remembered the eight-and-a-half-hour wait, and that comment 'shithole' written on that sign, but I said, 'Alright.' Pasolini had given us money, could I disagree? When we got into Arezzo, he let us out in the piazza and said goodbye to us in a gentle, sweet way, affectionately, as if nothing had happened.

We couldn't believe our windfall, and we wandered around Arezzo by night, we saw almost everything there was to see. Then Wolf mentioned, 'I've never seen Florence either.' I'd been there with the Volunteers, and anyhow the idea of going back to that cursed toll booth didn't even occur to me: 'Let's go to Florence,' I said, and we took the first train. I thought, 'Let's take a look around, and then we'll leave for Milan.' But Wolf really wanted to see everything, and we spent the entire day there: 'We'll go to Milan another time.' By afternoon, we had a fight about how to get home. Wolf wanted to take the train – 'Now we have this money from Pasolini' – but I disagreed: 'Why should we waste it like that?' It seemed like blasphemy to me.

We divided the money and said goodbye: it was the first time we'd ever had an argument. Wolf went to the station, and I went to the Florence South toll booth. If only I'd gone with him. There was a queue of hitchhikers; it was busier than a job centre. Soon it was night, late at night. I was finally able to get a ride, and I was dropped off at the first roadside restaurant – that big, tall one suspended over the motorway – and I started to feel stomach cramps. I tried to take a crap but it didn't help: I had intestinal cramps that seemed to twist my innards in two, a real abdominal colic that lasted the entire night. Then a lorry driver took me as far as Rome. It was almost daylight, and the pain didn't stop. It suddenly stopped when I got to Pomezia: at a certain point I didn't feel it any more. I got home at eight-thirty: 'Now I'm going to bed,' but my mother forced me to go to school. It was Monday, and the more I insisted – 'I've been ill all night' – the more she insisted: 'So what? You can stay out all night when you're sick, and you won't even go to school now that you're feeling better?' It was impossible to reason with her. I had to go.

Then one evening – only a few days later – I saw Wolf out for an evening stroll, we'd already made up. As soon as he saw me from a distance, he began to shout, 'Did you see that Pasolini wrote to you? If you only knew what he said, he really hates you,' and everyone turned to look. I thought to myself, 'He's lost it,' but he pulled out a copy of the *Corriere della Sera,* and there was an article about 'red Fascists'. He made me read it, and I said, 'He's not angry with me, he's speaking in general, my name isn't in there.'

But Wolf insisted, 'So you expect him to include your name? These are the same identical words that you said to each other the other night, take a look: it's a reply to you specifically,' and he indicated the various points contained in the article with his finger.

'Maybe,' I shrugged, but when I reflected on it a few years later, it all seemed so clear: that's why he gave us the money. When we got home, no one believed us that Pasolini had given us money and hadn't even made us do anything for it. That was Pasolini, he was Poetry. But he did give us the money, and it was my mistake to share it with Wolf, because it was mine, I had earned it: he paid for my idea. That's why, before, near Orvieto, he was still furious to the point that if I'd said to him, 'Stop the car and let's fight,' he would have left the car in the middle of the motorway. And then afterwards, gradually, silently, as he drove, his kindly smile returned, and he offered us cigarettes. The idea of the article had come to him – 'Now I'll write about this stuff' – and he paid me my copyright.

There was a period of resurgence of student activism both in Rome and throughout Italy, and we started to go to the community centre less often. The last few times had been taken up with a discussion of *entrismo*. We didn't even know what it was at the beginning. We were revolutionaries, and our overall views on the parties were quite negative: even the PCI, which claimed to be for the workers, was revisionist. It wasn't Communist or revolutionary any more, it was more – objectively, as they said then – for the status quo there was no point trusting the counter-revolutionaries. The party was just another instrument at the service of the employers, to be thrown out together with the entire system. This was our opinion, everyone felt this way. Then people started talking about *entrismo*: 'Let's enter the Communist Party en masse, and let's change it, we can use its structures to create the revolution.' It was an unsuccessful line, it was a slogan, but some functionary had invented it. At a certain point, Wolf said, 'Alright, but then we may as well enter the Christian Democrat Party. Those guys are in government, and if we enter we'll do well for ourselves, and then it won't be at all difficult to make the revolution.' He said it like that, neutrally. I can hear you saying, 'Alright, but this is reckoning without your host.' I agree, but you only realise that afterwards. The reasoning itself seemed to make sense, and anyhow it's not certain that things would have gone better inside the Communist Party. It's not that they were any stupider.

Anyhow, Wolf joined the Christian Democrats, at the section close to his house. They were all excited, and they made him youth secretary right away: at the end of the day we'd still learned a few things during all those years. We had – as one says – a basic professional ability already. He wanted me to join too, but I wasn't so convinced, not from a logical point of view, because I repeat there wasn't anything to laugh at there. It was just a gut feeling that the thing wasn't right for me. It was – how can I say? – an aesthetic sensation. I would go with him to the party offices sometimes, and I went to a couple of meetings about *entrismo* into the Christian Democrats, and I supported him. 'You owe me,' he said. 'I supported you lots of times.' But Serse didn't want to get involved at all, not even from a distance. When he invited Cristina, she made the sign of the cross and ran away as he shouted after her, 'I was counting on you.'

But this didn't go on for long, just as long as the elections. He found a candidate in Rome who had a lot of money and no supporters in Latina. He didn't even know how to put up posters. 'I'll look after it,' Wolf told him, and we overcharged him (but then he did get elected, which gave him an opportunity to rip off others). He was one of the worst. 'They're all equally bad,' said Wolf. 'Even Marcuse says so.' The three of us charged him 8000 lire a night. But he was happy. The three of us looked good – they need background – and we routed the teams of the local candidates, a lot of people. We went out last – we would leave home at midnight, when the others were returning – and we covered all their posters. However, at a certain point I saw that the guys who were still involved in the MSI were putting up posters with the flame symbol, and I felt a moment of nostalgia. They didn't even say hello to me when we were all together. When they were on their own, though, they always said hi. They were younger than me, you could say that they were the ones that I brought into the party. One time I even ran into Carlo and Peppe, the guys from Formia, and Carlo said, 'You made me into a believer,' and he was amazed how much I'd changed.

Peppe said to him, 'Let's go, otherwise I'll rough him up.' His face was sad too.

'You'd be better off dead,' they said.

I replied using the words of Mussolini himself, to tease them: 'You hate me because you still love me.'

'That's right, that's right!' they said as they left.

I felt nostalgia for those posters with the tricolour flame, and I went back to Ghersevich one evening to look for Livio Nastri and ask him – please – if I could go and put some up. He refused: 'First you have to recant,' and I never spoke to him again. Thank you and goodbye, that was the end of that. But that hesitation wasn't rational. From a reasonable point of view now there weren't any more doubts, I was an anarchist-marxist, an anti-Fascist; but on a sentimental level, I was a bit less certain. I still liked all my old friends, and the symbol too, the flame. Nostalgia, that's what it was, and thank God Livio Nastri said no; if he'd said yes, I'd still be there.

The electoral campaign ended, and so did Wolf's *entrismo* stage, as soon as the money ran out. Then we had our final exams at secondary school. It was the last year, and for better or for worse one day I'd be a surveyor. But Serse had to wait until September, because in July he only passed four subjects: topography, estimates, construction and law. I told him that he couldn't continue like that: on the day of the exams I almost fell asleep in class, but I couldn't pass him the answers, so I don't know what he wrote. But he didn't seem worried, it wasn't his concern, more his father's; he sent him for private lessons with the surveyor who was the facilities manager where he worked. He would test resistance of materials in the laboratory, he went with us to building sites and the public gardens for topography, with all his instruments – theodolite, spirit level, tachymeter – and he would take measurements. Serse couldn't stand him. Naturally, the surveyor felt the same about Serse, because he would make little barbed comments, and he didn't understand anything. Once he told him to centre the bubble of the tachymeter, and Serse dropped it on the floor with the entire trestle. He looked like he could kill Serse, it cost a lot of money. But his father had already spent so much money on him that summer, for his private lessons. Serse didn't really care. He continued reading science fiction, and in September he passed the exams. But the fellow told him, 'I never want to see you again.'

That summer we spent mostly at the beach, trying to chat up girls. I didn't go to Milan, and Francesca didn't come to Latina. The last time I'd been to see her, she had written to me the week before. She had already been sending me sweet letters for a while, and reading between the lines I could tell that she was offering something more than just friendship. She stopped writing to the others, she just wrote to me. But I still continued to write to her girlfriends – to hedge my bets – and she didn't like it. She sent me photos of herself too. Once she even sent some sexy photos that she'd asked a girlfriend to take of her. In one of them she was wearing a hat like Zorro's, with a rose between her teeth, and all she had on was a shirt, which just covered the tops of her thighs. In another one she was reclining on a sofa as if she were a figure from a Roman fresco: she was wearing a bikini, and her hair was in ancient Roman style, with a wide headband and her hair piled up above in curls. You could see her belly-button. She looked like a dark Pauline Bonaparte. At this point I thought, 'Here we go,' and after the next steamy letter arrived, I called her on the phone.

It wasn't like it is today, when everyone has mobile phones and they call each other all the time. Once upon a time, telephone calls would be made only on rare occasions; it just wasn't a regular occurrence. You would only call to say, 'So and so is in a critical condition in hospital, so and so has died,' and you would never call from home – my mother would have had a stroke – so you would have to go to the telephone company offices. I don't even remember if you could direct dial at that time; anyway, it cost more. So I went to the telephone company and I placed the call – you would ask the operator to dial the number for you, and she would connect you to a phone in a booth – on a Friday, and she said, 'Alright, I'll be your girlfriend,' and then, 'I love you,' and things like that. I would have done a cartwheel if I hadn't been in the booth. I wanted to leave right away: 'I'll be there tomorrow.' But she had something on, I don't know where it was her father had to go, but he wanted to take her with him: 'Come next week,' she told me. Just imagine, nothing could have stopped me, not even an earthquake. Not even hail or snow, not even if the motorway was closed. I would have gone to Milan on foot.

It was the longest week of my life. I couldn't wait until Friday came, and every night I would dream of Francesca wearing her Zorro hat, and those thighs. Finally Friday arrived, and I even had some money in my pocket from putting up the Christian Democrat posters. Late one night I got a ride in a Fiat Giulia as far as Bologna-Borgo Panigale – a big roundabout by the toll booth, with an enormous lamp in the middle. I listened to the music on the car radio – a late-night station was playing Adriano Celentano, and I felt like all my dreams were about to come true. I got a ride as far as Modena, and then it only took a moment from there to the Brennero junction. I was picked up by a Lancia Flavia that dropped me off in Milan, right at piazzale Cordusio. It was a little before four-thirty in the morning.

I didn't wait at Cordusio; I went straight to her apartment building in largo Domodossola. It was still dark. I waited until dawn broke. I thought to myself, 'She's still sleeping, she's in her nice warm bed, under the covers, and maybe she's dreaming of me.' Then I went around a corner to wait, so that her father wouldn't see me when he left for work, but when the time for our appointment arrived, I began to worry that maybe her mother was at home. So I went back to piazza 6 February. 'And what if she goes the other way?' I started to pace back and forth, wandering around the building at least twenty times. Finally there she was. My heart was beating fast, and I could hardly breathe.

We walked hand-in-hand all the way down via Monti. We saw via Venti*nove* Settembre again, then passed by the North Station, the Stella supermarket, corso Magenta, via Meravigli, piazzale Cordusio. Then we went to Boden Bar and chatted all morning. We were always hand-in-hand, or else I would have my arm around her shoulders as we walked. To tell the truth, I wasn't too interested in going to piazzale Cordusio and Boden Bar. I would have preferred to go to the gardens around the Sforzesco Castle, where we could have some privacy on a park bench or maybe behind a bush. But she insisted. 'No, let's go to Boden: we'll have more privacy, there's not anyone there at this hour of the morning.' I tried to convince her, it was a sunny day. As we walked along I would try to kiss her on the mouth every once in a while – 'Oh my God,' I thought – but she would draw back. 'No, not now,' and then she would laugh and laugh.

So we went to the damn Boden Bar, and we stayed there all morning. I had my arm around her, and I kept trying to kiss her, and she would always say, 'Not now.' I tried to put my hand on her thigh. She would push it away and laugh, then she would move my hand onto the table and say, 'Be serious,' and she would carry on chatting. 'Oh my God,' I thought again. Then at around eleven I said to her, 'Alright, that's enough, now give me a proper kiss,' and she moved away from me. Her face turned darker than it already was – if that's possible – it seemed like death had fallen on her shoulders, and she whispered, 'There's something I have to tell you.'

'This is it,' I thought to myself. 'Could it really be possible for everything to go well? I knew that there would be a glitch, I should have realised.' I thought that at the very least she was about to confess that she wasn't a virgin, that she'd already been with another man. What can I say? I wasn't pure either. She was Milanese, she spoke in such a knowing way, it was logical that she might have already had some experience: 'Girls in Milan don't just sleep at night the way girls in Latina do.' It's not that this made me happy, not at all: now I had to content myself with someone else's seconds. It's true that I was from Latina, but it was still disappointing. I prepared myself: 'Better than nothing. What can I do about it now? I'll still have her despite this.' So I was all ready – but I had been ready before I left home, I'd been ready for months, I'd been ready from the first time I'd seen her at the bar, when she emerged from the waves like Aphrodite – so I decided to be generous: 'What does it matter? This is the twentieth century. I can accept that.' And I looked at her as if to say, 'Tell me,' and she did: 'I have a sexual problem.'

'Again?' and I thought about that girl I'd met at the seaside, the summer before. 'Holy shit, why does this always have to happen to me?' But I wasn't too worried, and so gave her the look again, as if to say, 'Tell me.' And she did.

She said that she had a sexual problem. I don't quite understand what, and she didn't either, but she had it. She said that she had never kissed a boy, that she'd never allowed anyone to touch her. 'This is much better than I'd expected,' I thought. 'What a relief.' But I said to her, 'So all those boyfriends you told me about, all those love stories of the past, your open attitude to relationships, what was all that about?'

'It was only a facade.'

'And that other boyfriend?'

'I never had one. One time I tried to kiss a boy, but he had just finished eating something with mustard, and as soon as I smelt it, I felt like vomiting.'

'Alright,' I said to her, 'but I haven't eaten mustard. I'll never eat it again. In Latina, they've never even heard of it, have you ever seen me eat mustard? All I've had is a coffee,' and as a matter of fact I still had the empty cup on the table in front of me. 'Maybe I'll taste of coffee. Does coffee disgust you too?' and she started to laugh. But there was nothing to be done; she wouldn't let me kiss her. She said that it reminded her of the mustard experience, and she felt like vomiting. We even tried a few times to put our lips close together: 'I promise I'll keep them closed,' I said. 'Don't worry, I'll keep them closed,' and, to be fair, she did try. She closed her eyes and she put her lips close to mine, but her hands were tight fists. With one fist she gripped the table tightly – I remember it was made from Russian pine, light in colour, with dark grain and knots – she held herself against the table and moved her face forward, that devilish face, with her pursed lips offered up in sad resignation. Then, when she got close to my face, she would suddenly move back: 'I can't do it,' and she began to break out in a sweat. Just once we were able to touch lips, but they only brushed very slightly. She drew back: 'I can taste mustard.'

I should have told her right then and there, 'Just fuck off, you and your mustard phobia,' but I didn't. I loved her, I was willing to be her boyfriend even as things stood, what did I care? I was happy just to be close to her, listen to her, look at her, know that she was mine, know that she loved me. And I told her, I told her all these things, I told her this over and over, and she was happy, content, radiant: 'Really you don't mind? Really it doesn't matter to you?'

'Of course not, why should it matter for us?'

Now she was all relaxed, she was almost ready to burst into song. Her hands weren't clutching the Russian pine any more, and she reassured me: 'Don't worry. With time it will pass, slowly, you just have to be patient. Can you wait for me?' And she didn't even give me time to respond, she continued, 'Already today we have made huge steps forward.' She was giving her heart to me.

I was in seventh heaven. When it came time we went to wait for her girlfriends, who were finishing school. She wanted to show me off, we had to stand there embracing, and walk together with her friends through piazzale Cordusio along via Meravigli hand-in-hand.

I took her home. I carried her books. We laughed. We joked. I went with her right to the door: 'I'll be back at three,' and she smiled as she kissed me on the cheek.

I had a sandwich at the latteria. By two-thirty I was already waiting for her outside her building. Then it was three. Three-fifteen, three-thirty. 'I'll be there,' she'd said. Then it was four. Four-thirty. I know what you're thinking: 'How stupid could you be?' No, that's what I'm like: if someone says to me, 'Wait,' I wait. I'd wait for eternity. I'm like those fanatical Japanese soldiers, I had been a Fascist, and I don't move until someone gives me new orders. But perhaps it's also down to Father Cavalli's training.

Anyhow, by four-thirty I was fed up. I went to a phone booth and I called her: 'Maybe something has happened,' I thought. But nothing had happened, her sister told me: 'Francesca is here,' and I could hear her insisting, 'Come here, don't be stupid.'

'Bloody hell,' I thought.

She came on the line. and said, 'I'll be down in a moment,' but her voice sounded angry, dark, as if I had offended her in some way.

I waited five minutes, and still no sign of her. Ten minutes. Twenty. Thirty: 'How long does it take to come downstairs?' Forty minutes, fifty. An hour. It was five-thirty. I called her again. She told me, 'Listen, there's no point wasting any more time: I apologise for bothering you, but I don't want to see you again. Go back to Latina. Thank you and goodbye.'

'But you're crazy,' I said to her. 'What's going on?'

'No, there's nothing to be done. It will never work out between us, there's no point trying any longer. Ciao,' and she hung up.

I called back right away. The phone rang and rang, and no one replied. In the end her sister came back: 'Look, there's really nothing to be done, she refuses to change her mind. She's sorry, but she doesn't want to speak to you again, not even on the phone.'

'But you're as crazy as your sister. Tell her to come downstairs right now, or else I'll come up to your place.'

'No, please don't come here: our mother is in, our father will be home soon…'

'I don't give a damn. Tell her to come downstairs right now, or else I'll come up: I'll break the door down; I'll destroy everything you own. Don't you realise I've come all the way from Latina to see her? I've travelled hundreds of miles to see her. Do you think you can send me away just like that? She has to tell me to my face.' And then I realised that she was there, listening to her sister speak to me, so I shouted, 'Hurry up and come downstairs, or else I'm coming up.'

She came downstairs at last, but they came downstairs together. Her sister was in front, and she was hiding behind, and her sister said, 'Try to understand where she's coming from.'

'Why don't you get lost,' I told her. 'Let me speak to Francesca alone,' because I still thought we could resolve things. 'This is just a temporary crisis, now we'll talk and she'll get over it. We were so happy this morning,' and the two of us stood there alone. I mean it's not as if we were completely alone, but once I had pushed her sister out of the way Francesca did face me. She stood on the bottom step, her expression angry, petulant: 'Alright, now I'm telling you to your face: I don't want to see you ever again. I'm sorry, but I want you to leave.' She turned around as if to go back upstairs.

I grabbed her arm and pulled her towards me: 'Where are you going?'

Her sister was afraid – 'Our father will be here soon' – and she convinced Francesca to leave. She'd been watching us from a distance.

But there wasn't anything more to be done. Francesca had made her decision; nothing could convince her to change her mind: 'You frighten me. We're not right for each other. I have sexual difficulties.'

'I told you that I don't mind.'

'Well I do. You upset me. You make me feel uncomfortable.'

'I make you feel uncomfortable? But this morning you said that you love me.'

'I lied.'

'You made me come to Milan.'

'I'm sorry.'

'You're sorry?' Actions speak louder than words; she was like the princess with the pea, pretending to say 'Sorry,' but really thinking, 'Stop bothering me!' I couldn't believe I'd travelled all the way from Latina to be treated like this. 'Fuck off, you Milanese bitch,' I said to her. 'If you have sexual problems, you shouldn't play the tease. I didn't come after you, you came after me. You were like a slut, the way you looked at me. You invited me here, you sent me sexy photos, and now you're telling me you don't want to see me because you have sexual problems?'

'I'm sorry.'

'I don't care about your problems.'

'I'm sorry,' that's all she would say. I was furious, but there was nothing to be done; I could say anything to her, she wasn't going to be convinced. She was like a marble statue. Ebony. As inanimate as a statue. A marble statue, or maybe a pillar of salt. I tried everything to defend my position, I fought tooth and nail. But I gradually realised there was no point. She was upset too, I have to say. She didn't shed a tear, but you could see that she was upset. For herself, not for me. Even if she told me she was sorry.

I gave up. I walked with her in silence. As we stood at the entrance, as she began to go up the stairs, she said, 'Ciao,' and there was so much more in her eyes, there was everything, total abandon.

It was dark. I walked back. When I got to the cathedral, I said, 'No,' and I took the tram to Corvetto, then continued to the train station. I had some money with me: 'I'm going to take the train.' I didn't feel like hitchhiking, there was such a heavy weight on my heart. 'I'll take the train, and at least I can sleep. I don't want to think about anything, I just want to drown in my pain.' I was furious.

The next train wasn't going to leave for a few hours. I wandered around the station. I bought a sandwich and a coffee. I tried calling her again, just in case she'd changed her mind. I decided to give her one more chance. But there was nothing to be done; she wasn't interested, so I started to insult her. I kept telling her, 'Remember everything I've done for you,' and she didn't even say 'I'm sorry' any more, just, 'My father is here,' and she couldn't wait to hang up. 'You can never repay all I've done for you,' I told her, but in my heart right up to the end I hoped she would reconsider. I prayed to Our Lady and all the saints, just like when I'd been a seminarian. But none of them could help. Francesca was through with me.

'Now what will I do?' I wondered. You're thinking, 'Alright, but it wasn't the end of the world.' Well, there you're wrong, because for me it really was the end of the world: I loved her; I had never loved anyone as much as I loved her. I wanted her always, for the rest of my life, how could I really stop loving her and find someone else to fall in love with again? How could that ever happen? So I sat at a table in the bar and I wrote her a very long letter, full of terrible insults: not just everything that I'd already said to her – just in case she might have forgotten – but all the things I hadn't been able to think of then, the most horrible, nasty things. I made her seem worse that Messalina, worse than Lucrezia Borgia. I insulted her entire family.

I know, you'll say to me, 'One mustn't do that.' Sure, fine advice, what would you really do if you'd been in my place? You'll say, 'But that poor girl, just think what must have been going through her head, think how she must have felt panicked.' Really, that poor girl? And what about me? Wasn't I a poor boy? Doesn't anyone ever feel sorry for me? You may well say, 'But she had problems.' Problems? I had problems too, lots of them. Don't my problems count for anything? 'But she had sexual problems,' you say. So what kind of problems did I have then, mathematical problems? I'd still never seen a woman in my life, I'd been jerking off since I was twelve years old, and now I was eighteen. Don't you think this is a problem? Every once in a while, I would still think about that cute boy at the seminary. So now you're thinking, 'She had sexual problems, try to understand: who knows what might have happened to her as a small child?' To her? And so, don't you think anything had ever happened to me? Things happen to everyone, don't you know? I didn't give a damn about her problems, I had my own. Every once in a while I still found myself thinking about the cute boy at the seminary: 'Maybe I'm gay? Could I really be a faggot?' Doesn't that seem like a major problem to you? And then what about that time with Pasolini? If he hadn't been such a shit, maybe I would even have been willing, at least to see what it was like. And then you say to me, 'That poor girl.' She wasn't a poor girl at all, I was a poor boy, she led me on, she was a tease. That's not right. 'I have a problem.' I'll give you problems.

Anyhow, I wrote this horrible letter to her, I put it in an envelope and posted it, and I felt better right away: 'Just fuck off!' And then I asked myself, 'The train? Am I crazy?' and I left the station and went to piazzale Corbetto. When I got close to the hedge it began to rain. I hummed a little tune, but I was starting to feel better. 'She'll regret it,' I thought to myself. 'She'll come back to me sooner or later,' and then a car stopped and my travels began. It's not that it didn't matter to me any more. I was still very down, but I had begun to turn the corner – it was manageable, I could live with my pain. At least until I got home.

chapter 10

The summer was like all the other summers before: I tried to pick girls up at the seaside. It was the only way to forget about Francesca, there was no other solution. But I wasn't successful, so I kept thinking about her. All I did was talk about her with my friends and tell them how much I was suffering. 'Not again,' they would sigh.

I didn't work that summer. I'd finished school, and I had my surveyor's diploma, I could hardly go back to the Hotel del Mare. 'I need a rest,' I told my mother. I just planned to go to the country-side for the wine harvest in September. The Russians had invaded Czechoslovakia, and an emergency meeting had been called at the community centre. They told me to come along: 'Someone has to organise the protests.'

'Now?' I asked. 'Where can I mobilise the masses now: at the beach?' They dropped it. We also really told them where to go, because – if truth be told – we weren't that convinced ourselves. Maybe it was Serse, maybe it was Serse's father, but we weren't convinced that you had to take a position. You may well say, 'You're just like Michelini.' Well, sort of. And Russia may well have been revisionist, but it was still Russia, and if they'd invaded Czechoslovakia then there must have been a reason. We didn't exactly say that, but Serse gave this impression, and Cristina looked at Wolf with even more indifference. 'She's in love with me,' he would say.

'Maybe,' we shrugged. And everyone went their own way.

I began to look for work. Naturally, I didn't just decide to. My mother sent me out. She threatened me with a hairbrush one morning when I was still in bed, and said, 'Get out and find a job, we're fed up

with feeding you for free.' You'll say, 'She wasn't entirely wrong.' Fair
enough, but she could have been more diplomatic.

I started looking for work, and I even found a job. I began work
as a surveyor in a firm of architects, but it wasn't a real job, just something to do for the time being. I kept on sending out letters every day
to all the factories, and especially to the major construction firms
working in Africa. I wanted to go there to work as a surveyor. I even
wrote directly to Kinshasa – it was still called Leopoldville back then
– to the Congo government: 'Do you need a surveyor?' I was obsessed
with the Congo – ever since I'd been a seminarian – and I was even
convinced that I could earn a lot of money there: 'If they pay mercenaries so well, just imagine what they give surveyors.' I continued
to work in the firm of architects as I waited for a reply from Africa.
The boss told me, 'You're not my employee, you're an assistant,' and
he paid me 50,000 lire a month, ten less that I made the year before
working for Signora Visconti as a waiter. But I'd begun my ascent of
the career ladder, I was an assistant, a surveyor-assistant, and he was
a socialist, he would tell me, 'We're comrades.' If only! Thankfully he
would usually come to the office late. I had the keys, and at eight-thirty
I would open up. As soon as I'd opened up, I would go to sleep. He
wouldn't show up until midday. Then we closed at one and didn't go
back until three. He only worked in the afternoons, until five, five-
thirty: 'See you tomorrow.' He knew Otello; they had often played
billiards together. He knew Bar del Corso better than he knew his
own office. But he was a comrade, on the left. He said that he was a
Lombardiano: 'I'm for the revolution too: society is unjust. Have you
seen how much the Christian Democrat architects make? And here I
am busting my ass from dawn till dusk…'

Then the guys from the student movement came looking for me.
The usual suspects: Vittorio, Violetta's ex-admirer, and the philosophy
teacher, the one who'd given me his copy of *Gargantua and Pantagruel*.
They came looking for me at home: 'Bring the others with you.' The
battle over the salary zones had begun. At that time, throughout Italy,
workers were paid on different rates. If you worked in Milan or Rome

you earned so much, a little less in Florence, even less in Viterbo, and if you worked in the South, in Latina, then you would hardly earn a thing. For the exact same job. As if people in the South or Latina worked less or the cost of living was lower. That's the way it was. But now, in the autumn of 1968, the workers had begun their struggle to remove salary zones, so that all workers would be paid the same throughout the country. You'll say, 'Alright, but how did this concern the student movement?' What do you mean? If we wanted to make the revolution, we couldn't do it without the workers, could we now? What kind of proletariat dictatorship would that be? Oh yes, and salary zones were unjust, and we wanted justice and equality for everyone. But that isn't the point. The student movement in Latina had already held meetings to discuss these matters, and they never invited us. Several strikes had already begun in local factories, organised by the unions, and they participated on the picket lines and did all that investigation, analysis and education that they loved. They even started to take little groups of supporters to Rome.

We had thought that there was only one student movement. But in actual fact it had splintered into a thousand groups: Continuous Struggle, Workers' Power, Workers' Unity, People's Struggle (Nazi-Maoists), IV International (Trotskyites), Marxist-Leninists of various shapes and sizes: Black Line, Red Line, Situational Anarchists and the Anarchical Revolutionary Groups. There were as many groups as there were South Seas islands. We didn't even know that they existed or that they were coming to Latina. You can imagine, they were in Rome, and Latina – the closest location affected by the zones and therefore the salary struggle – was just a stone's throw away, it didn't take much effort on their part. When they didn't have anything to do, they would come here to do their investigations, analysis and education. Suddenly they came and called us – 'There's a meeting tonight' – and we went, at around nine (they couldn't hold it at the community centre because they wouldn't let them have use of the meeting room: they had moved too far to the left, and the Communists weren't happy with this. So we went to the PSIUP – the

Socialist Proletariat Unity Party – where they were supporters of Red China).

The meeting was to discuss picketing the Goodyear tyre factory. It was a new factory, they had opened it three or four years earlier. One thousand workers. They were all former farmers and builders who used to commute to Rome for work. They'd all been hired on the basis of re-commendations from the parish priest and the Christian Democrat Party, under the command of a former Republic of Salò production manager who was a slave-driver. If you got on the wrong side of him, you'd face the sack immediately, and the pay was minimal, but you could earn extras in cash if you were willing to spy for him. They were all furious, but they didn't have the courage to go on strike. There was a little group that had contacted some unions and the student movement, but very few. Everyone else was too afraid of the production manager. We had to organise a picket line somehow. They'd picketed a few days earlier, but they'd been overwhelmed by a group of thugs (apparently it was the MSI Volunteers themselves, hired by Goodyear), and everyone else – the workers who were trying to see which way the wind was blowing – as soon as they saw that it was blowing this way, ran into work. So this time they would have to show up in larger numbers, also because those guys were waiting for us. That's why they'd called on us, not for any other reason. 'Thanks for believing in us,' we said to Vittorio, and I almost didn't want to go, I felt like supporting Goodyear. But the workers were being treated unfairly. And it would be fun.

We showed up at the PSIUP. Right at the door, but even more just inside, in the entrance, we could still see all the signs – black walls, blackened door jambs and window sills – of the fire we'd started there a few years previously. Actually, Wolf, Piermario and I had thrown a paper bomb, but it didn't look like we'd done a very good job. We left it in the entrance, close to the door. We lit the fuse and ran away before it exploded, but nothing happened. All we could hear was 'ffffsss', and there was a flash of light. We didn't go back to see what had happened. The next day we asked around: only the door had caught fire, nothing more. The lady who lived opposite had heard the 'ffffsss' and saw the flames, and she called the fire department. But when they arrived, the flames had already died down into embers; she had put it out with buckets of water from her kitchen. Now, in the entrance, Wolf and I elbowed each other, and Serse didn't understand why. We laughed, 'This is our handiwork.'

All the leaders of the Roman splinter groups were present at this meeting. All of them complained about the others. Manrico was there too. He barely acknowledged me, and just said, 'Ah, ciao,' before he continued on with his friends. He moved from one side to another, he whispered in someone's ear, then in someone else's, then he lifted his hand and interrupted the person speaking. He had plenty of irons in the fire. Now his group had become the Union of Communist Italians (Marxist-Leninists), and they didn't agree with the nihilism of the other groups. Actually, they couldn't stand Vittorio and his sidekick, the philosophy teacher, they considered them to be bandits, too spontaneous, adventurers, Trotskyites, and certainly counter-revolutionaries. But they were pure Marxist-Leninists of the highest category, of pure Chinese derivation – Maoists – and so they were Stalinists, as Chairman Mao himself had taught. The lefties in Latina were already favourable to Continuous Struggle (or rather Workers' Power, as it was still called at that stage, like the newspaper they published in Pisa: it was only some months later that they changed their name to Continuous Struggle and the others became Workers' Power, but it really doesn't seem that important to me). Even they claimed that they were Maoists and Marxist-Leninists, not Stalinists, which – as everyone knows – is a contradiction in terms. They were very spontaneous: there were no plans, no intellectual discipline, no logic. But we didn't realise any of this until much later. For us – I mean me and my friends – they were still all the same, there was no distinction, we were all comrades: 'Aren't we all on the same side?' But Manrico didn't think so: he fought with everyone, and all the leaders.

At around one in the morning we went to stand outside the factory and wait for the shift that started at six. There was quite a crowd. At least two or three hundred people. It was freezing, and everyone was wearing parkas, but all I had was the grey raincoat. We stood on the road all night waiting for the workers to arrive. The actual main entrance of the factory wasn't there: there was a gate opening onto the street and a fence, a sort of parking lot. Further along – at least a hundred yards beyond – were the real gates, with the porter's lodge and the armed guards, but we had to remain on the road, we couldn't go past the first gate, because it was private property and there were a couple of vans filled with carabinieri who had been sent there to observe. We had to stay outside.

It was impossible to breathe the air; you had to always keep a handkerchief to your mouth. The workers said that they sprayed ammonia, they had flooded the piazza with it just to keep us away: it hit you in the face and burned your nose and your eyes. Every once in a while it would dissipate, gradually, as the wind blew the fumes away. But then we would see them behind the porter's lodge, spraying us again. Jets of ammonia came across the piazza.

For better or for worse, the night went by, with all these people warming themselves up in front of a camp fire – we'd collected some old tyres and set fire to them – and we sang Communist hymns this time, like 'The Red Flag'. Everyone waited for the scabs to arrive – 'They'll come a bit earlier, they won't come right at six' – but the atmosphere was upbeat, as if to say, 'This time we'll teach them. Where can they run to?'

A few of them arrived, they wanted to go inside. They insisted. We tried to convince them by reasoning. Then they would turn back in their cars, park at the street corner: 'Let's wait and see.'

A few others were tougher nuts to crack. They insisted, and began to drive forward in their cars, towards the gates. They would push very slowly, with people sitting on the bonnets of their cars, with their legs hanging over the wheels. Others would start to bang on the roof of the car and try to shake it. Then they'd give up. They'd reverse and wait with the others.

Then someone arrived who couldn't be convinced at all. He was driving a Simca 1000. He went through everything the others had suffered: protestors sitting on his bonnet, banging on the roof, shaking the car. But it was all an act: could we really give him the satisfaction of playing the hero? No fucking way, I'd rather go to hell. Actually, afterwards Manrico even said, 'You see? It's all your fault,' and he showed off to his friends: 'It's the fault of my idiot brother,' and Wolf said, 'But he arrived after you.' His friends, those other scabs who'd also played it safe.

Anyhow, that night no one got through. As soon as we saw them arriving, we would stop them, far away from the gates, and if they were even slightly hesitant we would pull open the car door and drag them out and beat them up. That's how the first strike happened at Goodyear, and after that they never had to strike again; we had to use violence to get them back to work.

The struggles over the salary zones went on for several weeks. Almost every night we had to picket at various factories. There were a lot of female comrades, and sometimes – in front of the bonfire made from tyres – while the others were singing, you could make out if you were lucky.

Manrico came home. Well, sort of: as he was active in the area, we would see him every once in a while. He'd sleep at home and bring lots of friends over. My mother was delighted. She would make him pasta e fagioli with home-made tagliatelle, and he would bring all his friends for meals. Every time they ate with us, he would tell them: 'You're sitting right where Bava did when he ate here,' and he would look at me as if to say, 'What were you thinking!' and then my mother would look at me in the same way.

'That's the truth,' I would say. 'There've been plenty of losers at this table,' and I would look pointedly at his friends, because it seemed to me that they were a little too full of themselves. Alright, so Bava was on the wrong side, but he'd never been as arrogant as they were.

One morning we came home from picketing at around eight in the morning and we ran into my father, who was leaving the house. He was in a bad mood: 'I've had enough. You're treating our home like a hotel!'

Violetta – because Violetta was still living in the 'hotel', with her husband and children – said to him, 'But they've been helping the workers.'

'Oh really? Now the workers need their help? These are losers who make the factories close, they don't help the workers.'

'They've been helping the workers!' decided my mother, and so he took his bicycle – he was the only actual worker in the family – and went to work. 'Why don't you come to help me instead?' But she took Manrico's side. She certainly would never have stuck up for me like that.

Then there were some terrible fights between various groups as the conflict gradually came to an end. The unions had never liked us. The workers did, they would come looking for us, they would come to our meetings at the community centre – when they allowed us to hold then – or at the PSIUP offices, they called us to picket, but the unions didn't. They wanted to reach agreement, where you never get a hundred per cent of what you're asking for, you're happy just to get half, then you can try for more later. Not us, we wanted revolution: either you give me everything or that's it. The workers were with us, and we began to have fights, sometimes with the union leaders. But we weren't even that united internally – the Latina student movement and the supporters from Rome – we were open to anything. Manrico's people, the Union, were Stalinists, and they didn't negotiate on any-thing: imagine them doing that, with their principles. When they became a minority they went back to Rome: 'Bandits! We'll see you on the day of the revolution.'

I didn't quite understand, I even tried to ask him, 'But aren't we all on the same side?'

'What do you mean? Those guys are bandits,' and he disappeared.

One evening he was home, and Mamma was running a bath for him. He said, 'I'll be right there.'

'The water's getting cold.'

'Don't worry, I'll be right back,' and we didn't see him again for four or five days. A few days before, however, he'd asked me, 'The

Union is sending me to Milan, I have to reorganise things: didn't you tell me that you knew some girls there?' I gave him Francesca's number.

We continued to go on the picket lines, and the union negotiated their agreements, and gradually the struggles ended, with all the salaries lowered. The workers were furious. Or rather, those who'd gone on strike were furious; they'd fought with police outside their factories and spent entire nights on the picket lines. But the scabs – the ones who jumped the fence round the back in order to get in hidden from view – were all happy, and their pay had been increased. We went back to the spiritual exercises at the community centre and at the teacher's house. Once they put us – just us – with someone from Rome, an ideologist, I think his name was Goffredo, who was supposed to give us a sort of advanced course, because, as Vittorio said, 'We still have some gaps in our knowledge.' He explained to us about class struggle, historical materialism, exploitation through capitalism. He explained that all of history had been determined by struggles between social classes: the few dominated the many, the subordinate classes. They tried to redeem themselves and rebel against their oppressors. It was this pendulum that determined history. We became courageous, and Wolf asked, 'So Mussolini was right: corporativism eliminates class struggle, everyone collaborates – labour and capital – for the common good, for the state, for the collective.'

Our lecturer went white as a sheet: 'But then…' He got up from the table and began to wander around the room; he took out the handkerchief from his pocket and mopped the sweat from his brow, and the teacher came into the room just as he started to scream, 'What am I doing here? Is this some kind of a sick joke?' and the teacher laughed.

I was about to become angry, but I was also deeply ashamed, I felt like some kind of an idiot, and I must have looked at Wolf as if to say, 'What were you thinking?' Then I realised, 'Alright, now I'm fed up. Maybe we've said something wrong, something stupid, but then please sit here and explain things to me, otherwise what's the point,' and the teacher agreed with me. Mr Ideologist sat back down and begged my pardon, and he began to explain. But he stopped almost right away – at the first counter-deduction that we proposed to him, I think it was about education – and he said, 'Look, I really don't feel like it today,' but in my opinion it was because he didn't know how to respond. He acted like such a big shot, but if you led him away from the few things he knew, he would lose himself like Hansel and Gretel. What an ideologist.

At that time I only ran into the chairman once, in piazza San Marco. We didn't even look each other in the eye. But when I met Bompressi he would say hello, even if I were on the other side of the road, even if – maybe – I pretended not to see him. He would call me from far away – 'Benassi!' – and he was always smiling, or even laughing. He would enjoy himself, he would ask me, 'What are you up to? When will you get your act together? That's right, you wanted the revolution, and these guys are really doing it, not like us. Stay in touch, study, be a good boy.' I almost felt embarrassed.

Now it was 1969. Everyone remembers 1968 with so much nostalgia, but for me 1969 was an even better year. It was winter. One morning I didn't feel like going to work. I wasn't paid very much, and I didn't learn anything, I was little more than the office receptionist, what was the point? So I spent the morning in bed and started to go out every night to hang out with my pals. I even started to go to the community centre less often. The last time I went there, they said to me, 'Your father was just here.'

'What did he want?'

'He wasn't looking for you; he was looking for Manrico and Mimì.' Manrico had left home again months before, and now Mimì had started to hang out at the community centre sometimes. My father couldn't stand the community centre. As far as he was concerned, it was the home of the Devil, full of Communists, they'd ruined his family: first Violetta, then Manrico, and now even Mimì. I was the only one who hadn't fallen into their clutches. 'Accio may be crazy,' he thought, 'but at least he's only a Fascist.' They hadn't told him yet.

Anyhow, he'd been there. They were in the conference room with the table in the centre. They were all standing around it, and some of them were leaning on the walls. He came in: 'I'm looking for my children.'

'They're not here.'

It's not as if he left it at that; instead he started making one of his scenes. They didn't let him speak at home, but when he was out and about he had plenty to say. For years I couldn't stand him because he was a Christian Democrat, he gave his vote to Tasciotti, who was also the chairman of the San Marco choir. To me he seemed too passive: 'Stand on your own two feet!' I felt like saying. But at the choir he was a sort of dictator. He had established it during the Fascist regime, and he ran it like a military organisation. A long time after 1968 – when they would travel by bus to concerts – he'd still make the girls sit in front and the men behind, and you were in big trouble if you changed places. He woke up every morning at five-thirty to go to the early mass at San Marco. Then ten hours of work – two hours of overtime every day, his entire life – then he would come home, have dinner (two hard boiled eggs and salad), take his bicycle again and go back to San Marco for benediction, and then choir practice. He would come home at ten and go straight to bed. Every once in a while he would get up in the night to go to the toilet, without turning on the light – he was obsessed with lights, he couldn't bear to see them on, he said they used too much electricity – and that's how, in the dark, sometimes he would bump into his children and speak freely with them, without anyone interrupting.

He didn't leave, he continued with his sermon: 'Do you know who I am? I'm a Christian,' and so on like that. 'You represent evil, Communism, but you can still convert your hearts and be saved.'

They listened to him for a while, but then they got fed up, and they said to him, 'Yeah, sure, but we have things to do now.'

But he continued, and they started to roll their eyes. Then he said, 'Ah, what I'm telling you is boring you, is it? I touched something in you then,' and someone started to snicker. He put a hand in his pocket:

'But I came armed,' and everyone froze, they were glued to the walls. Mauro still got upset just telling me about it, and the others teased him and he said, 'But he was right beside me, he touched my shoulder with one hand, and as he spoke he gripped me harder. So then I thought he'll start by killing me first.'

My father loved the moment of suspense he'd created. He put his hand in his pocket and asked, 'What were you thinking, that I would come unarmed into this lion's den? Here's my weapon,' and everyone froze as he took his hand out of his pocket, clutching something, and raised it above his head. 'This is my weapon against the Devil,' and he opened his fist to display a rosary and a crucifix. The philosophy teacher got up, went over to him, spoke gently and calmly, and walked him out of the room, then down the stairs, finally out onto the pavement where he had left his bicycle. When they told me, I wanted to die from the embarrassment, and I ran home to tell my mother what had happened, and we confronted him over his actions, but he didn't seem to care, indeed he was proud: 'I would do it again,' like the holy martyrs, like I'd been with every stupid adventure I'd had. He was clearly a few bricks short of a load. Clearly my problems did not originate exclusively with the maternal branch of my family.

Anyhow, I stopped going to the community centre, also because the student movement had splintered in Latina as well. Wolf, Serse and the others agreed with me – we didn't belong to any group, we were 'stray dogs'. We kept to ourselves, actually, and we decided to make our fortunes. It's not that I really believed we could, but Serse had almost convinced me: 'I don't think this revolution is going to happen, and sooner or later we'll have to find jobs: we may as well try to get good ones.' He always had grandiose ideas. There was another guy from the student movement – another anarchist – who was studying to become an architect, he only had about one more year to go until he graduated, and his designs were something else. We set up a firm called Polistudio, because we did everything – it was Serse's idea – design, construction, sales of building materials, contracting, everything. We could build an entire city from start to finish. It was a good idea, but a bit ahead of its time. Serse was a little like the old lady who goes to market to sell her eggs and has already started to dream of the money she'll make, and the new house she'll build for her family, then suddenly trips and falls, and all she has is an omelette. Serse said, 'We have to give a good impression to our clients, they have to be able to trust us,' and we ordered new furniture, gigantic design tables, the latest models of all kinds of technical equipment. We bought it all on credit. But then we had to start working, and I didn't really want to go to every building site in the area with a bag full of samples to ask if they wanted to buy some skirting boards, or parquet flooring, or a lift. I did it a couple of times, and then I started sleeping in every morning. We would stay until late at night in the office making calculations of how much we would earn. Then we would go out for a pizza – 'These are business expenses,' said Serse – and we would even take prospective clients out for meals, to give the impression that the business was flourishing: 'You have to spend money to make money,' he insisted. Sometimes I would worry, but he seemed to take it easy: 'A big job will come in soon.' A few jobs did come our way – an illegal development near the seaside – but with what we were spending, we needed a contract as big as the Messina bridge.

Anyhow, to make a long story short, at a certain point we found ourselves overextended, and at that point along came someone who sold heating fuel in Rome. He had a warehouse on via Appia and offices in San Giovanni. He provided fuel for furnaces in apartment buildings, convents and kindergartens. He needed someone to plan his new systems, and especially to transform and maintain the heating systems. This was just at the time when the anti-smog legislation was coming in, and they needed to transform all the old coal and combustible oil systems. So I went to work for him. I think I made a hundred and twenty or a hundred and thirty thousand lire every month. That was a lot of money at the time, almost 30 per cent more than my own father earned. But I had to pay eighty thousand to the firm – to Serse – as my share in the investment. I only gave my mother thirty for room and board, and she was scandalised: 'Not even the most miserable pension.'

'If you want the money, it's all I've got.'

In the beginning the work was difficult; I didn't know what I was doing. But I studied and worked hard, and the client was pleased. Except he wasn't pleased with my timekeeping: 'Take the bus,' he said, 'and I'll pay your travel pass.' There was nothing to be done, I had always travelled from place to place hitchhiking, and so naturally I couldn't say exactly when I'd arrive: sometimes I'd be there at nine, sometimes at ten, sometimes at eleven. I'd make the time up at the end of the day. I didn't stop for lunch, and so I worked right through the day, when the others went out for something to eat. I would stay on my own working, or I might sleep with my head on my desk, but he wasn't to know that; when he arrived back in the office he would always find me working efficiently. Let's just say that my schedule was elastic. 'I wouldn't mind,' he sighed, 'but what are the others going to think?' The other staff. 'What do I care?' I thought. 'That's your business.' But he was pleased with my work. He was a good man, from Carpi, near Bologna, I think, and he paid me well. His deputy would crucify him over my timekeeping, and one day he said to me, 'I don't know how much longer I can keep him calm.' And I invested the money I earned back into the firm.

Then it was summertime, August, holidays. And Mimì asked me, Will you take me to Bari?'

'Bari? Sorry, I want to go to Milan.' I'd been there a few times over the winter with Serse to visit some other girls we knew there. Once I'd gone on my own to see Angela. But Francesca found out about it. (I know, you're thinking, 'You did that on purpose.' Of course I did.) She wrote to me: 'I understand, I can hardly criticise you, but you could have at least said hello when you were in town, I'd like us to be friends,' and that was it, I was still in love with her. But it was never like before, and I only went to see her a few times that year. They were starting to put the steel guardrails in the middle of the motorway between the two carriageways, not the cement walls they have today.

But Mimì wanted to go to Bari. Her boyfriend had been transferred there. She was sixteen. He was thirty-two. He was a big union boss;

he'd been a leader of the student movement at the Faculty of Architecture in Rome. He was a bit crazy. The Union had sent him to Latina shortly after the salary zones issue to establish party structures and support the workers. He'd opened the new party offices. Manrico had brought him home a couple of times to eat pasta e fagioli, he'd introduced him to Mimì, and he'd turned her into a Marxist-Leninist. Mimì was a beautiful little flower, and she was crazy too. He fell in love with her and she fell in love with him. Anyhow, they had Manrico's blessing (but when she wanted a lesson shown to someone, that's when she'd come to me).

His name was Gilberto. He was also a talented architect. He knew Marx and Lenin practically by heart. And he had ginger hair. He had a huge handlebar moustache and glasses like Gramsci used to wear. He was a likeable fellow. He was very down-to-earth, and in a short time he brought together a good group of workers from Campo Boario and a few students. Mimì always hung out there, at the party offices. One time – a few months after his adventure at the community centre – when she left the house in the afternoon, Papà followed her on his bicycle. He did it on the sly, without her noticing. He cycled for part of the way, then he got off his bike and held it as he hid behind a corner, and then he would continue forward only when the coast was clear. He thought that she was going to the community centre: 'This time I'll catch her there,' but when he saw that she was going towards Campo Boario – the most dreadful neighbourhood, the worst area in Latina – he became even angrier. 'What is my daughter up to?' He saw her turn the corner and go into the office. He ran after her. Fortunately, right at that moment another friend of ours, Paolo Forte, met him on the doorstep: 'Your father's here.' She was like an eel, a snake. She slipped into the toilet, jumped up on it and slipped through the tiny window – it was so small that a cat would find it hard to slip through – then jumped down and ran like the wind. He walked in.

The office was made up of two rooms on the ground floor in a shabby hut built shortly after the war. The windows were rusty, and so were the shutters, broken glass covered by cardboard. Gilberto and the others were standing around the table. He marched in: 'Where's my daughter?' he asked furiously.

Gilberto tried to get away with it: 'Who are you looking for? There's no one here.'

'What do you mean there's no one here? I saw her come in.'

'Can't you see there's no one here? Take a look around.' And they even opened the toilet door for him to look in. Papà looked everywhere in the office, under the tables, in the toilet, but he wasn't satisfied: 'I know I saw her,' he roared. It's not that he suspected Gilberto; he wanted to save his daughter from the Communists, and Gilberto understood. Earlier, when he had arrived, he had felt uncomfortable, because he was guilty, then when he saw that it wasn't a question of the age of consent, but rather only of politics, then he became more courageous, he became haughty, arrogant: 'Leave us alone! Now I've let you look around. Stop disturbing us.'

'Where is my daughter? I saw her,' he roared again, not at all intimidated, actually he was even angrier. And I forgot to say that he had one hand in his pocket. He'd had his hand in his pocket since he arrived. That's when Gilberto's patience ran out – maybe he was even afraid to lose face in front of the others – and he replied menacingly, 'That's enough! Please leave. I'm fed up with you now. And who do you think you're trying to frighten with your hand in your pocket?' Obviously Mimì had told him about the rosary incident at the community centre. 'Come on, show me, I'm tired of this farce, show us what you've got in your pocket.'

So Papà showed him my number 26 tyre iron. He began hitting Gilberto. He even broke his glasses. The others tried to hold him back, but when it was a matter of protecting the virtue of his daughters Jesus Christ couldn't hold my father back, nor could Mamma. It took several men to carry him out of the room. He was still brandishing the tyre iron on the pavement, and they were never able to prise it out of his hand. He took it back home and put it back in its place in the storage cupboard, arranged according to size with all the other tyre irons, lined up nicely on top of the vice. Ready to be used at any time.

He didn't know that Mimì had a boyfriend. And he was twice her age, that pervert. But this time my mother said, 'You've done half your duty.'

Anyhow, they sent Gilberto to Bari to reorganise the party there, and my sister wanted to go and visit him: 'Tell Mamma that I'm going with you to Milan, then I'll go to Bari on my own.' I agreed, fool that I am, but in those days – the sexual revolution, women's liberation, equality for everyone – I could hardly give her a lecture on morality, telling her, 'No, you're too young.' She already complained that I was oppressive, a male chauvinist. I'd even been a Fascist, so how could I say no to her? Good God, she would start preaching to me about the liberalisation of sexuality. I thought to myself, 'Why are other guys always so lucky?' I'd never run into any girl as sexually liberated as my little sister. Some guys have all the luck.

We left. Mamma was delighted: 'What a nice lad he's become, so generous, now he's even taking his sister on a holiday.' We took the train and went to Termini Station in Rome. It was night-time. I put her on the train for Bari and went back to hitchhiking: 'Maybe I can come to pick you up, otherwise we'll organise something by phone.' It depended on how things went in Milan; I still had a glimmer of hope. But things didn't go well: 'Why did I come here?' I asked myself, as I walked along via Monti with Francesca. She was kind, affectionate, but quiet. She'd lost her sparkle; she seemed like a little old lady. She was a year younger than I was, but without dreams, illusions, joy. Instead of laughing, at most she would make a grimacing smile, even when I tried to tease her, even when we walked past the sign for via Venti*nove* Settembre. It was over; there was nothing more to be said. We spent the entire day together, then went out for dinner with friends of her sister. One of them let me stay at his place for the night. The next morning he made breakfast for me.

I went out again. It was a sunny day. Trams would pass every once in a while. There was no one around. Everyone was away on holiday. We had planned to spend more time together; I was going to stay for a few days. But when I saw her at piazzale Cordusio I changed my mind. She seemed sad, even sadder than the day before. We walked to the station. I felt like I was with a cadaver: 'I know we'll never see each other again, that you'll never come to visit me again,' and she seemed distraught.

'What have I done wrong?' I asked her.

I sent a postcard to Mamma, with a picture of the cathedral, and I forged Mimì's signature on it. She kept that postcard until her dying day. Then I boarded my train for Bari, and I called out to Francesca from the window, 'If you change your mind, you know where to find me. But I'll come back one day, because I'll always love you.'

'Me too,' she said.

'You surprise me.'

'It's because of my problem!' she cried out as the train was leaving – she was referring to the sexual problem – and I went to Bari a little earlier than expected, to meet my sister. I'd asked Francesca if she'd heard from Manrico: 'Yes,' she replied. 'I gave him a couple of addresses and then I never saw him again.'

The train trundled on, everyone was dozing off in their compartments. The atmosphere was very boring, and if you tried to strike up a conversation, they would look at you as if to say, 'Please leave me alone.' It was nothing like hitchhiking. I decided to nap like the others.

I slept more or less all the way to Bari. When I arrived it was late at night. I looked for them. I found them. They let me sleep in a loft above the kitchen in an old apartment. I lay there in this tiny, low-ceilinged, dingy loft, on a cot that was too small for me, with a chair at the end so that I could rest my feet somewhere. Mimì was happy, in love. 'Good for her,' I thought.

We stayed there for three or four days. I was bored stiff. Bari wasn't of much interest to me, and the comrades were boring too. They spent most of their time preaching their ideological rhetoric to me, Gilberto most of all. Equality, exploitation and workers were all things that I agreed with, but they had a newspaper called *Serve the People*, and I didn't much like this idea of service: 'Didn't I serve enough at the Hotel del Mare? Am I supposed to be a waiter for the rest of my life?' Then they were all obsessed with the *Little Red Book*: 'Chairman Mao says...' and then they would start reciting from memory. Even when we would go out for a meal, at Osteria del Buco, in the historic old town of Bari, in the evening, if you so much as stained your shirt with a little bit of sauce from your orecchiette, they would say, 'The revolution is not a gala dinner.' I felt like I was back at the seminary, when every time the wind blew Father Tosi would solemnly pronounce, 'The Old Testament says that...' or 'The Gospels, the Acts of the Apostles, the Book of Revelation.' They were right about all the rest, and I even admired them, because they had dedicated their lives to the revolution – they weren't like me, with my capitalist dreams of making money, and I even felt guilty about it – but that smell of incense and prayerbooks disturbed me a little: 'Maybe Pasolini was right after all.'

Anyhow, we went home: 'Thank you and goodbye.' Mimì wanted to stay longer, but I was totally fed up, and I didn't have much holiday time, I had to go back to work. It was early August. Before we left, Gilberto told me, 'You're a good person.'

'Sure I am,' I thought to myself. 'I let you have my sister.' But I didn't say anything.

'At the end of the day, you're just like us,' he continued. 'When the revolution comes, we'll be side by side.' I felt like the good thief being crucified next to Jesus Christ.

I went back to Rome to deal with the furnaces, the boilers, and all the other heating paraphernalia. That was just as boring, I may as well have stayed in Bari. Every evening we would walk along the seaside trying to pick up girls, even if our efforts were always futile. Serse said, 'We'll still be doing this when we have beards and grey hair.' It seemed like a bigger problem than what Francesca had to deal with. We didn't even go to the office any more, partly because of this problem, and also because there was nothing to do. Just pay the bills that arrived at the end of every month. I said to Serse, 'I can't do this any more.'

He replied, 'Too bad.'

Then one day in Rome, one morning, a complicated project was required urgently for a block of flats. The owner wanted to take it at any cost, to be able to fill it with fuel for all eternity. He could see that

I was having problems concentrating in the office, so he said, 'Why don't you work from home? That way you can be more at ease, and we'll have it all done by tomorrow. But take the bus,' and he walked with me to the bus station in piazza San Giovanni. He bought a ticket for me, and he waited for the bus to leave. I had taken everything I needed with me in one of those professional-looking blue cases: the files, the drawings, the plans, the tracing paper, all the blueprints, pens, ruler and compass. I entered the bus looking like Pier Luigi Nervi.

I saw two girls sitting together and – with a reflex like Pavlov's dog – sat opposite them and put my blue case down next to me. For a while I acted cool. I saw that there were other men eyeing them – but they were a bit older than me. I even pretended to open the case and study my documents a little. I pretended not to notice the girls. I just looked at them from the corner of my eye. Then the bus left, it drove past the outskirts of Rome and onto via Appia. I noticed they were speaking English. After a few miles, I made my move: 'Parlez-vous français?' Back then we still used to study French at school, and thankfully so had they. We began to chat with our stilted French – one word at a time – but we still managed to converse.

One was tall, the other short. I preferred the short one, but the tall one had studied more French, she spoke almost all the time. I learned that they had hitchhiked from England to Italy; they had only bought a ticket for the ferry across the Channel. They were on their way to Sperlonga. Some of their girlfriends had been there the year before, and when they came back it was all they could talk about: 'Sperlonga this, Sperlonga that.' It seemed like the most fantastic place in the universe, so they decided to see for themselves. 'How long does it take to get there?' they asked. 'Is it really as beautiful as we've heard?'

I began to denigrate Sperlonga more than a Christian would have denigrated the Emperor Nero: 'Why on earth are you going there? It's disgusting, and the water is polluted.'

They looked at me wide-eyed: 'Really?'

'It's the Gospel truth,' and I continued telling them horror stories as far as Velletri. I practically told them that it was infected with the plague and all the inhabitants were paedophiles. But they insisted that they wanted to go to Sperlonga: 'At least to see with our own eyes,' they said. 'We've come this far…' At this point I had almost lost all hope, when – looking up on the luggage rack and seeing that all they had were two sleeping bags – a brilliant idea came to me: 'Where do you plan to stay? Do you have a tent?'

'If only,' said the tall one. 'We lost it at the beginning of our trip. We'll sleep outdoors, on the beach.'

Then I made my move: 'I have one, I mean my friend can lend one, and the seaside in Latina is a hundred times better. If you want, feel free, you can stay here tonight, we'll lend it to you, and tomorrow you can go on to Sperlonga.' I certainly didn't expect it when they agreed. I was only taking my chances. Then I remembered: 'It's a numbers game.' It's a science, not a game of chance. I had convinced them to stay in Latina.

'What about the tent?' they asked.

'Let's go,' and we walked together. They carried their backpacks, and I carried my blue case for the project. I almost forgot it on the bus; the girls had to remind me to take it with me. When they stood up I got a better look at them. The tall one seemed even taller, and the short one seemed even shorter, but they were both well built and nicely proportioned, with attractive breasts, nice asses and small waists. The tall one was called Joan and she was blonde, the shorter one was Sarah and she was darker, but very attractive.

We arrived at Serse's house; it must have been three in the afternoon. I rang the entry buzzer, and his father answered in an angry voice because I'd woken him from his nap. I could hear him say, 'What a time to drop by,' to his wife as he passed the phone to Serse.

'Come downstairs – I'm with two English girls.'

He started to laugh, he couldn't believe it, but he came downstairs, and when he saw them he still couldn't quite believe his eyes: 'Where did you find them?'

I asked him about the tent right away: 'Do you really have one?' because he always talked about this tent that he'd used with hundreds of girls when he lived in the Dolomites.

'Of course I do, of course I do.'

'Then get it right away.'

'Later, later,' he replied.

And the girls began to ask: 'What about the tent?'

'Later, later,' I said. 'Let's go to the seaside now, and I'll show you that it's much better than Sperlonga.' And we walked towards the traffic lights outside the football stadium to start hitchhiking. I whispered under my breath to Serse, 'This one's mine,' indicating the short one, Sarah. But for whatever reason I always found myself walking next to the tall one. 'Serse,' I asked, 'what game are you playing?'

He looked embarrassed and moved back to his girl: 'They're the ones doing it,' he said.

'Do you think I'm some kind of an idiot?' I replied.

We hitchhiked from the junction, but as there were four of us and the first car that stopped only had two places, I sent him on ahead: 'We'll meet you at the rotunda.' When he was inside he motioned to Joan, the tall one, to get in with him, and I also pushed her a little, putting my hand on her shoulder to guide her. But she turned around, grabbed her friend – Sarah, the short one – and pushed her into the car. Serse started to laugh, the car moved off, and Joan and I were left on our own. She looked delighted.

We met up again at the rotunda on the seaside. Serse was laughing. I was furious. I wanted the other girl. I even tried walking next to her, but Serse advised, 'Forget about it, let's go with what they want,' so I resigned myself.

We walked onto the private beach at the Hotel del Mare. We rented a changing cabin, a sunlounger, an umbrella. The same lifeguards worked there as before, and they told me, 'You don't have to pay,' but I insisted on being a gentleman.

The girls went to get changed. Before, they'd been wearing jeans, and now here they were, wearing bikinis. Now that I could see them undressed, I began to like mine better, Joan; she was tall and blonde, and her tummy and belly-button were just as I liked them. Sarah wasn't bad, but this one looked better in a costume. Then we smoked, chatted, ice creams, coffees, Coca Colas. Money was no object. Every once in a while they would ask, 'What about the tent?'

'Don't worry, later.' In the meantime we got to know each other better. It was obvious that they were enjoying themselves, and then they suggested going on the pedal-boat. We rented one, and soon we were pedalling out to sea, and then they wanted to swim. Serse stayed on the pedal-boat: 'I don't know how to swim.' But I went in the water with the girls. I didn't swim very well, but I managed to stay afloat, even though it was hard without flippers. The girls were very athletic. They swam quite a way out from the pedal-boat: 'Viens!' said Joan, and I followed her, floundering. The sea was choppy, I was afraid, and it was cold. I was trembling. The girls looked back and forth as if possessed. I stopped and held on to the pedal-boat for a moment. Serse saw my blue lips, and the terror in my eyes, and said to me, 'Come on out.'

'I'd rather die.'

Fortunately Joan also noticed, but I wouldn't leave the water until she did. We went back to the shore. They pedalled. In the beginning we had tried to do it, but the pedal-boat didn't move an inch, it just zig-zagged. 'This is making us look bad,' said Serse.

'At least I jumped in,' I said.

But it was time to cut to the chase, the girls kept asking, 'What about the tent?'

'Let's go for a walk,' and we began to stroll – one couple in front, the other behind – towards the public beach. After a while – each couple went their own way – we walked over the dunes, through the tamarisk bushes.

As we sat together on the sand, under the bright sun, I held her close to me. Then I kissed her. She didn't resist. Actually, the more I touched her, the more she touched me, and as soon as I put her hand on my trunks, she began to take off her bikini. I was shocked, and wondered, 'Now what should I do?' I said to her, 'No, no, someone could come by, they can see us from the beach,' and as a matter of fact, from a short distance away, someone did walk by along the beach, and glanced over towards us, and she looked at me as if to say, 'My God, you're so intelligent.'

She reached down inside my costume to caress me, and I couldn't believe it, and then she said, 'If only we had that tent.'

'My God, we have to deal with this tent business,' I thought to myself.

The sun was beginning to set. We went back. We showered, then we got dressed and hitchhiked back to Latina. 'What about the tent?' I asked Serse.

'Don't worry, we'll manage somehow,' but he still hadn't formally admitted that it even existed. Theoretically I was still convinced that sooner or later we would go to his house to get it, then we would return to the seaside and pitch it somewhere on the dunes. And the girls would be happy.

Anyhow, we took them to Latina with all their possessions – the backpacks and my blue case – and we took a walk in the centre of town, showing them off to everyone, friends and enemies, and I was more and more in love with mine. Serse's girl began to look rather ugly to me. My only regret was that every once in a while Joan would look sad and say, 'What a shame that we have to leave for Sperlonga tomorrow.'

We took them out for a pizza. We spent almost all the money I had with me. They had fine appetites, first a pizza, then a plate of spaghetti, and finally they asked for a cappuccino to wash down the pizza and the spaghetti. After the spaghetti they had some antipasto. Serse reflected, 'It seems like they haven't had anything to eat in days, these two,' and he laughed with that air of aristocratic arrogance, like the princess and the pea.

It was ten. Then eleven. Serse's girl was yawning, and both of them kept asking, 'What about the tent?'

'There is no tent,' said Serse. 'It was a lie. Let's try to take them to the office.' His idea was for them to sleep there on the floor. But when we arrived, it was a mess. The girls took one look and asked, 'What's this?' 'We just wanted to show you our offices, our drawing boards, our desk,' said Serse, and he realised that it wasn't such a good idea, especially because he didn't want problems with the other investor, because he was all we had left. So we left the office – it must have been midnight or even later – and the girls were yawning.

Our office was located in the Banca Nazionale del Lavoro building. It was just one room and a toilet on the top floor. The Hotel Europa was right opposite, the best hotel in Latina, super-luxurious. The girls asked again, 'What about the tent?'

'Look, it's right in front of you,' said Serse. We walked across the street and walked into Hotel Europa: 'Two rooms please,' said Serse, ever the Neapolitan aristocrat.

'How much will this cost?' I asked.

'Don't worry.'

'What do you mean, don't worry?' I remembered that time in Milan with the tokens and the bumper cars. Joan asked me: 'Qu'est-ce qu'il y a?'

'Rien, rien.'

Finally, when we got into the lift, Serse said, 'Tomorrow morning I'll ask my father for some money, or I'll make a withdrawal from my savings account,' and I breathed a sigh of relief. First we went to their room, and then we said goodbye because our room was on a different floor, then Joan and I went up, to the seventh or eighth floor, and we entered our room. I was tense, and I kept thinking about the project I had promised to complete. As we went up in the lift, I had fleetingly thought I could finish it before going to sleep.

She took a shower; I could hear the water running. The bathroom was on the right when you entered, then down a little hallway was the room, with twin beds. There was a little table in between them with a lamp. I sat on the bed and waited for her to finish; in the meantime I opened my case and started looking at the paperwork. She came into the room, smiling, in a nightie. I went into the bathroom to freshen up. When I returned, all the overhead lights were turned off, just the bedside lamp was left on. The room was tidy, she'd folded her things and put them away in the wardrobe, together with her knapsack, and she had even put my papers back into my case on the table. She was tucked up in her bed, next to the window. She was lying prone, looking away from me. I had put my trousers back on. I'd spent five minutes after my shower trying to decide, 'What should I wear? How do I want to look?' and in the end I opted for the trousers but no shirt. Deep down inside I secretly hoped I would find her asleep.

But no, she was still awake. As soon as she heard me come out of the bathroom, she turned to me – just her face. I came close. I sat on my bed, by the table, near her. I think I must have had an idiotic smile on my face. At this point I didn't know exactly what to do, I was afraid of making a wrong move. She smiled at me, so it felt natural to push back her sheet ever so slightly and put my hand on her leg, by her knee, then I moved it up towards her thigh. I felt her nightie, I'd expected that. I put my hand underneath and kept moving upwards. I expected to feel her panties, but to my surprise she wasn't wearing any. I felt her ass, her buttocks, then in between. No panties. I felt dizzy: 'Pauline Bonaparte!' Then I don't remember anything else, I just remember that I was on top of her, in the bed, and we were naked and she grabbed me with her hand and pulled me inside. And she groaned. And I followed her. And I guided her. My heart was beating like mad, and at one point I thought I was about to die, but I kept going. Happy. And I laughed. I was making love, and I laughed. I laughed and laughed.

The alarm went off at six. I still had to deal with the flipping project. I had agreed with Serse that I would go to Rome and come back to meet them in the afternoon at the seaside: he was supposed to watch over them, and if they really insisted on going to Sperlonga, we would go with them; who wanted to let them go? Even Joan – when I said goodbye and left – didn't seem to have any intention of letting me go: 'A cet après-midi. Mais fais bientôt.' 'You're telling me,' I thought, and I grabbed my blue case. But the porter wouldn't let me leave. He wanted money. There was no point insisting that the others were still upstairs.

'Precisely,' he said. 'But they'll pay when they check out, my friend will deal with it.' He didn't flinch: 'If the first one to leave doesn't pay, imagine what the others will try. Here the first one to leave has to pay: your room is 5000 lire.' All I had were a couple of thousand in my wallet. 'Bloody hell,' I thought, and I went back to Serse.

They had a double bed. They were still in bed leaning against the headboard, sitting up with the sheets pulled up to their necks. I didn't even notice – when I entered the room – that they didn't look too happy, I had enough problems of my own with the porter: 'Who does he think he is?' I asked, and they laughed, and Serse started to look through his pockets to find any money he had, but we still didn't have enough, Sarah had to give me some, and we just made it to five thousand plus enough for my bus fare. Just as I was about to leave, I asked Serse, 'So, how did it go?'

'A disaster,' he said. 'She didn't want to go all the way. What about you?'

I didn't go into details, I just answered in a vague tone of voice, 'Fine, fine,' and he said, 'I can tell you scored just by looking at you,' and he laughed. He was genuinely happy for me: 'But don't worry. I'll still look after them for you until this afternoon.'

When I got to Rome it was a disaster. It was the first time I'd ever arrived so early in the office at the same time as all the other staff, but – instead of being pleased – the boss was furious. He didn't really yell at me like an employer, more like a father – why do I bring this out in people? – because the day before, at a certain point he had called me at home to ask something or other about another job I was working on for him. And no one knew where I was: 'He hasn't come home.'

'What do you mean? He left by bus hours ago,' and they kept calling back and forth until late at night: 'Who knows what's happened to him, who knows where he is?'

'Shit!' I said, and that made him even angrier. 'Just let me get to work now, please,' I said.

And then he started to pace in the hallway, he went into all the offices – except for mine – and harassed everyone: 'Now what will I say when they arrive and ask for the project?'

Anyhow, I completed it – very badly – and I gave it to him in the early afternoon, then I asked him for another payment, and I said, 'I'll be back in three or four days.'

He looked suicidal: 'What about the urgent projects?' he asked me.

'I'm in love with an English girl,' and I went back to Latina. I couldn't believe how good it felt not to have to worry about that damn blue case any more. I dropped by at home to say, 'I'm alive,' and change my shirt. I took the cashmere pullover, because I'd been cold when we were out walking the night before. It wasn't mine, it belonged to Manrico actually, but I didn't know where the hell he was and I liked it: it was smooth and soft and caressed the skin. Then I left for the seaside.

They were at the rotunda, waiting for me. When they saw me get out of the car – I'd hitchhiked, of course – they came over to meet me and Joan ran into my arms. She really seemed happy. And I was even happier, because until then I had spent the entire day worrying that they might have gone to Sperlonga after all without waiting for me, and maybe I wouldn't see Joan again. But there she was. Proof that God does exist. Things were going my way at last: cosmic justice. And it looked like Serse and Sarah were getting along well too. Serse confided, 'After you left, she finally gave in.' She must have thought it over.

I didn't want to go back to the Hotel Europa, with that asshole porter again, so we went to the Hotel del Mare, en-suite rooms, lunch at the restaurant, breakfast in bed, and all the staff would wink at me, and Anna, the chambermaid with kids, would say to me, 'Do you remember when you tried to seduce me on the ladder?'

We spent a lot of money in four days: the payment from the client, everything that Serse had managed to get from his father, and the entire balance of his savings account. But it was money well spent, and we didn't have any regrets. We went to all the best restaurants in the area. We ate tortellini alla panna, and the best cuts of meat and fish, and cappuccinos. The girls didn't drink any wine, just cappuccinos with lots of sugar. Serse laughed, 'They've never had a holiday this good.' Nor had I. But we never went to Sperlonga. It was only twenty miles away, and they'd travelled all the way from England, but it just couldn't compare with Latina. Why should they go there anyhow? I don't know about Sarah, but Joan was really in love. I think she truly loved me.

We didn't spend all our time eating, drinking cappuccino and copulating. Despite all of our raging hormones, it just wasn't possible, every once in a while we would pass the time chatting. After a while you finish the standard topics and you have to talk about yourself and about life in general. I told Joan that I didn't like the world, that it was ugly, that it was full of injustice, the atomic bomb, that we're born to die: 'Life is suffering. For every fleeting moment of happiness like I have now with you, there is so much suffering before and after. It would be better never to be born at all.' And then I told her that I never wanted to have children, that I would never condemn a child to live this life. She started to cry. We were lying on the dunes between Fogliano Lake and the sea, surrounded by sunshine and tamarisk, with a view to the Circeo cliffs, and she cried. She cried for me.

Then she begged, 'Promise me that you will never say these things again, that you will never think them again. Promise me that you'll be happy.'

I promised. With all kinds of mental reservations, and without being convinced at all, but I did it and then she was happy again.

She cried again the night before she left, our last night together. She said, 'We'll never see each other again.'

'Yes, but let's not think about it,' and I tried just to enjoy the moment. We left the bedside lamp on, so that we could look into each other's eyes. I put my cashmere jumper over the lampshade – Manrico's soft, silky jumper – so that the light in the room was delicate and romantic.

The next morning we were awoken by a burning smell. The cashmere jumper had scorched, and was about to burst into flames. That wonderful jumper. I was never able to find another like it, and when Manrico came home and looked for it I didn't say a word. My mother consoled him: 'Who knows where you left it.'

'No, I'm certain I left it here.' I kept my mouth shut. I'd pay anything to get it back. To have it again.

She cried again after breakfast, as she left the hotel with her back-pack on her shoulders. We listened to 'Aphrodite's Child' on the jukebox – 'Rain and tears are the same' – and she cried.

Then we went to Latina, to the Agip petrol station. That's where the pavement ended and the ditch along the road began. Our last kiss. The final tear. Serse and I went back about twenty yards, otherwise no one would stop for them. As soon as they lifted their thumbs a Mercedes stopped. I felt almost jealous. They left.

Serse laughed. 'I'm desperate,' I told him. 'I'll never get over this.'

'You should thank God they've left,' he said. 'We don't have a lira left to our names.'

'But I'm in love.' And I was worried for the girls: 'How will they get back to England?'

'They won't have any problem. Those two know what to do with their pussies.' But I didn't want to listen to him, I really was in love. The next day – or maybe the day after – Serse felt some discomfort, more than an itch. His father found it all very amusing, and kept slapping us on the shoulders with pride and delight.

There's a poem by Salvatore Quasimodo: 'Ed è subito sera.' Everything in life has its price.

chapter 11

I was fired.

Not right away: it took another two weeks, but I could feel there was an atmosphere. In the end I asked him, 'What's the matter?'

'Enough is enough. Either you arrive in the office on time like everyone else, or this is the end.'

'Fine. This is the end,' I said. And I went back home, where I waited to leave for the Congo. Now it was called Zaire, and Leopoldville had changed its name to Kinshasa. They had replied to my letter. They needed a surveyor. There were a few more details to finalise, just formalities. This was my mother's only consolation when I left the position in Rome. She liked the idea of Africa: 'Let's hope he leaves soon,' I heard her say to Papà. I think she even liked it better than the job in Rome. She was probably thinking, 'If only it were farther away.'

Anyhow, to pass the time we also began to hang out with the Union of Italian Communists (Marxist-Leninists). Summer was ending, and autumn was on its way, with the renewal of all the national labour contracts. Every day there were strikes in the factories, and we would stand outside – with red flags and Mao Tse-Tung badges – to sell *Serve the People*.

I don't exactly remember any more how it was that we would go there, if Mimì would take me or Wolf. He was still in love with Cristina from the student movement (later Workers' Power, now Continuous Struggle) and he followed her around like a puppy-dog. The more he followed her around, the more she mistreated him. She started taking an interest in him and going out with him when things became heated and a couple of Fascists started harassing her. He couldn't believe his good fortune. We encouraged him: 'Go for it.' He wanted to take his time. Finally he decided, and he told her he was in love with her. She looked ill: 'There's no way.'

'What do you mean, don't you love me?'

'Not at all,' and the closer he moved towards her the more she would pull back, as if he were Satan. 'Just the idea of physical contact upsets me. Don't be offended, but you're too big, enormous, grotesque: I'm terrified of you.' She just wanted a bodyguard. He was pissed off, and so he moved on to the Union of Italian Communists, and kept asking us, 'How much do you weigh?' And he was always measuring his height, the circumference of his wrists, the dimensions of his hands, and he concluded that in the final analysis he was smaller and better proportioned that we were.

Serse consoled him: 'Maybe it was your beard.'

'What difference would that make? All she had to do was tell me, and I would have shaved it off.' But in actual fact she was very petite, even if she was very spirited – they seemed like David and Goliath. Who knows what he saw in her. Anyhow, we started to hang out at the Union of Italian Communists too. At the end of the day, if you're going to participate in the revolution – or even just cause a disturbance – one party is as good as another.

But we weren't special any more; we were just anonymous foot soldiers. We were even less than that: extras. We weren't even in the Red Guard, just 'party members'. A couple of guys from Rome had taken over from Gilberto, then there were a handful of workers and a few students. Mimì was in the Red Guard, but we weren't, we still had a long way to go. We waved flags outside factories, handed out fliers, sold *Serve the People* and studied the *Little Red Book*. Labour. When there were 'critique and self-critique' meetings, the party members – the guys from Rome – always listened to us with smiles like the philosophy teacher's the first time we went to the community centre. Sometimes I would wonder, 'Wasn't it better when we were stray dogs?'

Then towards the end of September, the national organisational conference was to be held in Rome, and they asked for volunteer security guards. They sent me and Wolf. Serse didn't want to come: 'No, I'm afraid of getting hurt,' and then he still spent time at the Polistudio office: 'One never knows,' he would say. 'Just in case the revolution doesn't happen, at least we can make money.'

We showed up at the party headquarters in Rome. It was in Prenestino – things had come full circle – and there was still some giant graffiti at Porta Maggiore, 'Long live the MSI Volunteers', that I'd written years before. We showed up in a huge, enormous basement room that was carved up with temporary room dividers: 'We're from Latina; they sent us here for security duty.'

'Over there,' and they pointed to a room.

There was Strelnikov, Manrico. He was looking over some plans, surrounded by ten members of his cabinet. Rumour had it that as soon as the revolutionary government took power – the theme of the organisational conference was 'Onwards towards the construction of the revolutionary workers' government, for the peasants and the workers, elected and controlled in the people's assemblies' – he would be the minister of defence.

When he saw us he was happy – it was the first time he'd ever been happy to see me – so much so that I even wondered, 'Has he mistaken me for someone else?' He told his men, 'Ah! The elite squadron is here,' and came all the way around the table to give me a hug, and he even kissed me. 'He really has mistaken me for someone else,' I thought. And right away he put us into the Red Squad, his elite troops.

Ordinary service was provided by two brigades: an effective brigade of fifty comrades armed with pickaxes who always stood alongside the vehicle entrance along via Prenestino, above and below the ramp and on the corners of the nearby roads. Then there was a reinforcement brigade, comprising fifty more men, chosen from the conference delegates, but they would only be mobilised in case of emergency. They feared a Fascist attack, apparently it had been promised, and their hegemony in the neighbourhood was at risk: 'Who's in charge here?' But all these troops – especially the brigade in effective permanent service – as well as guaranteeing the normal functioning of the conference, were mainly there to make a point, and actually Manrico had told them not to blend in at all, but to show themselves with their sticks and flags all over Prenestino. They had even given them some helmets – just a few – so that passersby would take them seriously: they had to be seen, and counted one by one, and then they could make all the attack plans they wanted.

We were three blocks behind, inside three cars hidden among those parked there. We were in contact with walkie-talkies, and we were ready at all times to swoop down like unexpected falcons.

The squadron had the best mercenaries in all of Italy; there were even some guys from Milan. One guy from Gaeta – he was enormous, a giant – they say had spent time with the Brazilian Tupamaros, in the middle of the Amazon forest. He wore an American watch that had the crest of the Green Berets engraved on the back, but if you asked him where he got it he would be vague, and you got the impression that he didn't want to reply. We took it for granted that the legitimate owner hadn't exactly given it to him as a gift – war booty – and maybe he was buried in the jungle now. The commander of the Squadron was Alfredo C. (at that time we all used first names and initials in the Union – I was Accio B., but only Manrico was Scarf and nothing else – because we had now entered the pre-revolutionary stage, and vigilance and confidentiality were fundamental, especially with surnames and on the phone: every militant had to always consider that all telephone calls could be recorded). Manrico was formally the leader, but when he wasn't there Alfredo was in charge. He was a little bit older than me, but he was cold, decisive, he always hung out with Pino the Monster. Apparently the year before, armed with just pickaxes, they had won all the fights with Fascists in front of Roman schools, they were mythical heroes for junior high school students. Then there was Giulio from the Anarchist Revolutionary Group, and he would always wear black. The ARG was famous too: there weren't many of them, but they were real 'knights of nothing'. They weren't afraid of anything, they never backed off. Once the battle began, they wouldn't turn around even if Our Lady appeared to them. It didn't matter if they lost or won, the important thing was to fight and keep moving forward. 'Anyhow,' said Giulio, 'sooner or later we all have to die.' Now he was a Maoist, and he was in the Union, and Manrico liked him. I liked him too. You felt at ease with him, certain that he would never abandon you – but despite that there were problems, because they didn't want to understand this question of tactics and strategy. When Manrico said to them, 'That's enough,' he would pretend not to hear, he would stay, pacing forward like he had when he was an anarchist, and they would have to take him away by force. Then in the critique and self-critique meetings they would put him in the middle: 'You're undisciplined, an anarchist, you endanger the life of the party' – I think it was the chairman – and he would self-critique, 'You're right, I won't do it again,' and he seemed ready to swear on a copy of the *Little Red Book*. But the next time he was leading a squadron of twelve men.

There were five of us in each car – three cars: two Alfa Romeo Giulias and an Ami-8 – three behind and two in front. We all wore helmets and motorcycle glasses, and we all had a kerchief ready to put over our faces and a baseball bat to hand. The passenger in front held a huge fire extinguisher between his legs, he had to be the first out, he would only use a weapon after he'd finished spraying. The fire extinguishers were filled with ammonia – we had learned from Goodyear – and the orders were clear: go for their faces, for the eyes.

We'd done a period of training in the countryside near Monterotondo with a lot of members of the ordinary brigade. It was theoretical-practical training in combat with batons. The rule was categorical: it wasn't enough to win the immediate battle, we had to definitively place our adversaries in conditions where they could no longer harm us. So an adversary on the ground – if that were possible – had to have his knees, his elbows or at least his wrists broken. I didn't like this, I was used to doing things another way. I'd been taught that the important thing was to win, then when the adversary is on the ground, you're finished. But no: 'These are the remnants of your Fascist past. Results are what counts, you have to think not only of yourself and the fight you're having at that moment. You are the embryo of the Popular Army, you are at the service of the people, you have to think about the masses. If you leave your adversary and let him go, tomorrow he could attack a student, or a worker, or maybe even you, and if you fall in front of him he won't take pity. Once you have him you have to render him innocuous, at least for a time.' The places which were best for these purposes – because they take the longest to heal – were the joints: elbows, knees and especially hands and wrists, which are full of tiny bones. Wolf said to me right away, 'Of course, that makes sense!' I tried to disagree, and Manrico got angry: 'Remember what our father used to say: when you start a job you have to finish it, you can't leave things half done,' so he convinced me, and I started to practise on mannequins, giving them blows to the knees with the baton, and on the wrists and the hands. At a certain point, I don't know how, we were able to bring Serse along too, but after this training he was horrified, and when it was time for the next session he excused himself because of a hand injury. He'd broken a finger – or so he said – and he went back home. Then, when it was over, he would always ask us, 'How many wrists did you break today?'

We spent entire days like that, sitting in the car and waiting for orders, then in the evening when the conference ended we accompanied Aldo Brambillari home to Monterotondo, and we would go back to pick him up in the morning. He was our supreme leader. He was from Milan. He was the leader and the founder of the Union. At the end of the assemblies, or in the parades and at the demonstrations, we would chant various slogans: 'Long live Marx!' 'Long live Lenin!' 'Long live Mao Tse-Tung!' or 'The workers must be in charge of everything!' or 'Long live the revolutionary government!' but one of the favourites was: 'Stalin! Mao! Brambillari!' He was the man who would save Italy, the future leader of the revolutionary government. They said that he had been to China, and that Mao Tse-Tung had been impressed by his scientific analysis. Enver Hoxha, in Albania, admired him, and that's were he got some of his financing. He had charisma; he knew what he was dong. He had imposed collectivism: every militant had to give everything he owned to the Union. I think I'd already heard this somewhere else, maybe from Father Tosi or Father Cavalli. Anyhow I was poor, I didn't have anything, what could I give them? But there were a lot of people – intellectuals, aristocrats, people from wealthy families – who sold their homes to give the proceeds to the Union. Brambillari received the profits from every film by Lou Castel. We had become a fine organisation, with thirty thousand militants throughout Italy, and they weren't triflers or dilettantes like Continuous Struggle: we were a Stalinist, military organisation, you paid for your errors and they controlled your private life too. You'd be in trouble if you took advantage of a female comrade, you had to marry her, and you'd be in trouble if they found out that you engaged in strange sexual practices. But that was Aldo Brambillari, our leader, and we were his bodyguards, us, the Red Squad. Now he's with Berlusconi, actually with Formigoni. Aldo Brambillari. Life is strange. And we would sleep at night in the headquarters on American military cots – the wooden ones that you could fold up, with canvas, from the Second World War – purchased in the flea market at Porta Portese.

In the morning, Manrico – or should I say Scarf? – would give us each 10,000 lire in those old notes, the big ones with the portrait of Michelangelo: it was a lot of money. But every evening we had to give them back. They were just for emergency use: 'One never knows when the time will come that you have to go to the mattresses.' We weren't supposed to do it – he insisted – because the time had not yet come, it would cause huge problems. 'But one never knows: if the moment comes, you might have to go to the mattresses, run away to Paola in Calabria.' There was a 'red base' there, the entire local population was behind us, all you had to say was, 'I'm with the Union,' and they were all willing to hide us; Manrico had managed their peasant revolts, a road blockade, and another one on the railway lines. But every evening we would have to give the money back: 'It belongs to the people.' Just once – I was driving with Pino the Monster and Giulio – we ran out of cigarettes, and so we used the cash reserves, and as long as we were spending petty cash we decided to order cappuccinos and croissants too, and Pino the Monster laughed, and when it came time to pay he let me use my 10,000 lire note. 'It's better: you're his brother,' but he gave me a lecture worse than anything I'd ever heard from Mamma, it was a critique and self-critique meeting that lasted an hour, and everyone laughed. Wolf took Manrico's side: 'You can't just do that: Chairman Mao says so,' because he hadn't been in the car with us. If he had, I know he'd have ordered a cappuccino too.

Manrico wasn't that fraternal with me: 'Good morning;' 'Good evening.' He would smile at me, to show the others that he was a good brother and – in his own way – he was proud of me, and he always liked it when I would tell him stories about when I'd been a Fascist: 'Listen to this, listen to this,' he would say to Alfredo, but we never talked about more personal matters. He avoided being alone with me, he always had to show how busy he was. It was only at the very end, one evening, that he came in the car where I was sitting – the others were standing outside – and he said, 'Let's talk,' and he told me that he had always loved me, not just now that I was a comrade, he'd always loved me, and actually I was his favourite sibling.

'I never noticed,' I told him. 'Are you kidding?' And he hugged me.

'You're the one I love the best.'

'Maybe,' I thought to myself, but I was happy. 'Imagine that! Who would ever have thought?' and I warmed up to him a bit. I loved him too. The minister of defence. I would do anything for him.

That was about the time that the final letter arrived from the Congo – I mean Zaire – with the signed contract, with a regular pay cheque at the end of every month from the Ministry of Public Works. All that was left was to sign it and send it back. But he asked me, 'What will you do in the Congo? The revolution is just around the corner, and you want to leave for Africa?' He convinced me, and we laughed and joked like we never had before.

At a certain point I asked him, 'Did you ever meet up with my friend Francesca in Milan? Poor thing,' I whispered sympathetically, 'she has some real sexual hang-ups, she's totally frigid.'

'That's not the impression I got.'

'Really? What do you mean?' I asked sharply.

'Nothing, nothing, what are you thinking? It's just the impression she gave me. She doesn't look like she has any hang-ups at all. But what would I know? I only ever saw her once,' and he started laughing and slapped me on the back of my head. 'What were you thinking? You'll never change.' Then he hugged me and he said, 'But that time in the garden, I kicked your ass.'

'I slipped, and I had the chain in my pocket but I didn't use it. And when we were at the Hotel del Mare I whipped your butt,' and he laughed. 'Do you want a re-match?' I challenged him again.

But they never called on us during the party conference. Well, just once, but it was a false alarm. There was a car that wanted to park right in front: four arrogant bullies. We were there in a nanosecond, one car in front and another behind them, and we all piled out wearing our helmets and sticks, handkerchiefs over our faces. They were shocked – 'Are you crazy?' – and they jumped back into the car and peeled away with a squeal of tyres. But when the conference ended, on the last day at the closing session, when it came time to say good-bye, Aldo Brambillari wanted us to leave our posts, come into the room and walk on the stage in front of all the national delegates, and he said, 'Let's salute the Red Squad, the embryo of the future Popular Army.' And everyone jumped to their feet: 'Long live the Red Squad! Long live the Red Squad!' and we began to sing our Communist hymns, and Manrico raised his fist, and tears were streaming down his face, the way he would be whenever the Internationale was played, but we were all on the verge of tears ourselves, even Pino the Monster and Wolf. Actually he was almost as far gone as Manrico – but when the conference ended and all the delegates went home we decided to teach the Fascists a lesson: we needed to clarify the situation in the neighbourhood once and for all. As far as we were concerned, Prenestino was another 'red base', just like Paola in Calabria. We could hardly leave it to the Fascists, could we?

They had long since abandoned their offices in via Gattamelata, with the basement and the spiral staircase. They had moved to the other end of Prenestino, a dilapidated former military installation that had served as an air-raid shelter during the war. It was in the middle of a field full of brambles and bushes. They had installed a gym for boxing. It was huge, paid for by Caradonna. They called it the boxing academy, and it was the bastion of the entire region.

One evening we equipped ourselves. Manrico had sent the Red Guards out in pairs to distribute pamphlets throughout the neighbourhood. They walked the streets two by two, handing out fliers with nonchalance. He even sent one pair – a boy and a girl – to the boxing academy to give them to the Fascists, to the Volunteers. We watched from a hiding place far away. The first one who saw the hammer and sickle printed on the pamphlets gave the girl a slap in the face and called for his pals. Everyone came out of the gym. In the meantime the girl – and her partner – left crying, while the alarm was raised on walkie-talkies. The Fascists came after them. They were shouting and chanting. They even threw a few stones.

It was dark. We were waiting under the last streetlight before the open countryside began, with brambles and thorny bushes. The two Red Guards joined us. Manrico barked, 'The ones with the helmets in front,' because we didn't have many helmets, and there were others there from the ordinary brigade. We walked out in formation, and in the dark we could see the shadowy figures of Fascists in front of us.

I was slightly nervous. I asked myself, 'How do I get into these situations? No one forced me. If I leave now, that's it. I'll never do this again as long as I live, no matter what happens.' I almost felt like taking my helmet off, giving it to someone else, telling them, 'You take my place,' and returning home. I think I was even shaking – I knew that the Fascists would crucify us – but I think the guys next to me knew that too: from the terrified expressions on their faces, even Wolf, even the Tupamaros. Then Manrico, in front, issued the command: 'Long live the words of Mao Tse-Tung!' and we were off. We followed him in formation, with batons held on our chests, chanting in unison at the tops of our voices: 'Long live the words of Mao Tse-Tung! Long live the words...' and we marched forward, fearful no longer.

The Fascists had rushed out to challenge us, and there was no turning back now. They had to keep moving forward. The battle began in the dark. They rushed at us, but they came from the left and from the right, disorganised. They hadn't had time to mobilise properly. I saw a big shadow approaching me. I only recognised him at the very last minute, I could hardly see, it was Pietro. He was breathing heavily after having run towards us. I dodged to the left, he lifted the baton with his right hand to get me, I ducked and turned around, then hit him from above, aiming right for the head. At the last minute he had jumped, it's as if he'd taken flight, and I got him on the shoulder. I heard his collarbone crack. He dropped his baton, leaned forward and fell to his knees. I remembered what I'd learned during all those hours of training, and I told myself, 'Now I have to break his wrists, his knees,' but I just couldn't, I stood there looking at him until someone grabbed me by the arm and we ran off together. Manrico shouted, 'Retreat!'

'Shouldn't we follow them?' asked Wolf.

'No, it's too dark, this is their home turf, they know the area better than we do: we've won, that's enough.' Then he started chanting again, 'Long live the words of Mao Tse-Tung!' and everyone followed him, it was like a victory hymn. We had won on their home turf; we'd whipped them in front of their own bastion. But to tell the truth, it was a bittersweet moment for me. Of course, in this world everyone has to follow his own road, right to the end. Pietro had been like a brother to me. I was fond of him. I still am today. If it had been up to me, I would never have done it. I really didn't want to.

We ran into them a few evenings later at largo Prenestino after seeing a film, it was the late show. We were in the stalls, and they were in the balcony, but we were only separated by a partition wall, because the balcony was on a raised dais. There were about fifteen rows of seats between us. Pietro was wearing a cast. He was eating a packet of crisps. They got up to buy ice cream. They were having a good time. So were we. Everyone minding his own business. We'd said all that had to be said, and done all that had to be done.

Then everyone went back home – 'For now the work of the squad-ron is temporarily suspended' – and they greeted us like usual in Latina: red flags and copies of *Serve the People* to flog. That's how the Union worked: the military apparatus just served a PR purpose really. Politics was what really mattered – analysis, planning, class consciousness, firm principles, theoretical ability – we weren't of any importance.

It was now the end of October 1969, and the national labour contracts were being renegotiated again. It was a big deal in Latina. The unions couldn't stand us. Up to that point they'd always been in charge of the factories with their internal commissions: elections every once in a while from predetermined lists of candidates, and they could pretty much do as they pleased once they were in. But now people wanted control, and that was our platform: 'Delegates elected and controlled in mass assemblies', soviets, direct democracy. There was nothing worse for a union, they think that once you've joined you're their personal property. They couldn't stand us. And then perhaps I should admit that we weren't very diplomatic. When we arrived in front of a factory, if we saw others, maybe from Continuous Struggle, we would start arguing with them too: 'Don't listen to them,' we would invoke the workers. 'They're soldiers of fortune.' If you consider all the trade unions and all the parties that hated us, it practically seemed like we would find more sympathy from the Fascists themselves.

Anyhow, a general strike was called at the end of October. It was the first general strike that had ever been held in Latina, unilaterally proclaimed by all three unions. There'd been open hostility between them until almost the day before, but now they were uniting. One of the conditions that they had agreed – in a written contract – was that there couldn't be any banners, symbols or flags of political parties, just of the unions. We spent the last two nights writing graffiti all over town. We used endless spray cans: 'Long live Lenin! Long live Stalin! Long live Mao Tse-Tung!' 'Power to the working class!' We made cardboard cut-outs, along the lines of Gutenberg, so all we had to do was hold them to the wall and paint over them to leave an enormous hammer-and-sickle motif: 'Onwards to the formation of the revolutionary government' on every wall in the city, even the police station. And maybe we ruffled a few feathers.

When morning arrived, the demonstration was off to a promising start. Thousands and thousands of workers invaded the city. There was a parade that seemed to go on for ever. We were almost at the end, close to the supporters of Continuous Struggle. We shouted our slogans and walked along with everybody else. At a certain point I noticed Otello under the porticoes in piazza San Marco. I hadn't seen him for months – he'd got married and moved to Anzio, where there were a lot of gambling houses, and he didn't come to see Mamma very often, but even if he did drop by he never ran into me. I ran over, smiling, to say hello. He gave me a harsh look: 'Where's that other loser?' he asked, referring to Manrico. 'You'll be the death of our mother.'

I didn't know what to respond: 'Please, I just came over to say hello.'

And he continued preaching: 'If you cause anything to happen to her, I'll show you.'

All I could respond was, 'What are you doing here, are the pool halls on strike too?' and I went back to the parade.

He screamed after me, 'I'm a union member too!'

'Shame on you!' shouted the supporters of Continuous Struggle.

When we arrived in piazza del Popolo it was almost full. A sea of faces. I'd never seen anything like it. Guglielmo – the intellectual from Rome who was our leader – had always maintained, 'Latina is a Fascist bastion.' Now he was delighted: 'This is like Red Square! Let's go get our flags!' We tried to explain that it might not be a good idea, that there had been an agreement, that it could cause problems, but he insisted: 'No, this occasion is too important. We have a duty to politically orient the masses, otherwise this could finish as nothing more than an economically based movement. Let's go and get the flags!' What could we do? He was in charge.

We ran to Campo Boario. We grabbed the flags. We rushed back. The others were waiting for us on the corner outside the municipal offices, near the citizen's centre. We arrived with twenty flags. One red flag each, with a long wooden flagpole. People were still pouring into the piazza from the other side. Standing up on the stage, the union leaders told them to enter and take their places in the piazza, the proceedings were about to begin. The stage was in the middle of the piazza as usual. People kept pouring in, and soon it was packed. Guglielmo began to scream, 'Parade! Parade!' and we followed him with all our red flags, and we started to parade around the piazza, towards the Town Hall, under the tower. From the stage there were shouts of, 'Stop, stop, the parade is over!' but the workers came behind us, they came behind the red flags and shouted, 'Parade! Parade!'

Guglielmo turned towards us and started laughing gleefully: 'Do you see? Do you see? What did I tell you?'

'Do you see?' echoed Wolf. Even the Continuous Struggle people were following us.

We arrived in front of the Town Hall, then we kept moving forward. The first assault came just past the corner from the CISL union with their workers, Christian Democrats. They started jumping us and trying to get our flags away. They divided us from each other and isolated us: each of us was surrounded by about twenty from the other side. They were screaming, 'Drop the flags!' and pushing us from all sides. We had to give up a couple – I think that Guglielmo handed his over voluntarily – and we tried to hold on to the few remaining. There were only two left, but now our hands were free, and we began to defend our flags. We counter-attacked, overcame them, then ran away, and we held the last two remaining flags aloft – they were billowing in the wind – and we began to shout again, 'Parade! Parade!' And we took off again, with the workers behind and the comrades from Continuous Struggle singing 'The Red Flag', 'Onward people to the insurrection', as they made their way around piazza del Popolo.

The second attack came in front of Bar Poeta, from under the porticoes. This time they were Fascists: there were five or six of them, and I knew them all. They'd all been under my command once upon a time. They didn't even get close to the flags: little clashes, immediate, swift, us against them. The parade started up again. The third attack came on the next corner. They rushed out from under the porticoes. Fascists again, but there were more of them this time. Not just my soldiers from the old days, but others who'd come from Bar di Russo. They'd never been involved in politics; the only time they'd ever darkened the door of the party offices was that time for Zone B. But now they were out in full force, they ran out from the porticoes, they seemed like flag bandits, it was obvious what they were after.

These fights went on a bit longer, then a few of the CISL guys from before entered the fray – there was one they called Carnnera, built like a house. At this point the procession stopped, the workers took a few steps back: 'You'll have to deal with this on your own.' Montanari was there – a guy from the council estate who was a municipal dog-catcher and a PCI member – and he implored his comrades, 'Come here, come here, the red flag is being desecrated!' It was no use telling him that it wasn't a flag from his party: 'It's still the red flag!' He must have been about fifty years old, and I saw him throw a punch. But the scuffle was almost over. One guy jumped out in front of Wolf and punched him right in the face: now he had a bloody nose. It looked like Serse had given it to three of them, one after another, but he couldn't even remember what had happened afterwards, he just said, 'I'm against violence, I'm afraid.' Anyhow, the fight ended, and we were left with one red flag. The other one had been lost, but at least this one was left. We lifted it again: 'Parade! Parade!' we shouted victoriously, and we left again. But this time only the Continuous Struggle supporters followed us. And Montanari, the municipal dog-catcher. Cristina was with our group, she was next to Wolf, and she wouldn't let him out of her sight. He was thrilled. But the masses – the thousands of workers – had stayed a safe distance away, like cars on the motorway stay back from a lorry sliding out of control. We made it to the Town Hall at last, then our effort gave out: entropy. The masses had started listening to the union meeting, and we left singing 'The Red Flag'. We left them behind.

We marched straight back to Campo Boario, passing the police station on our way. There were two squad cars outside, nothing more.

They observed us as we walked by, and we stared back at them: four police officers, nothing more. We arrived at the Church of Our Lady, then carried straight on to the party offices. We opened the shutters, put away our last, glorious flag, and began the critique and self-critique meeting, to analyse in minute detail – and learn from – our experience. Cristina came along too. 'It can't hurt,' she must have rationalised.

Manrico was waiting for us. They had come from Rome – him and the regional secretary – to monitor the situation, because Latina was still a crux of the revolutionary process, especially because of its rapid industrialisation. They must have said to each other, 'Let's go and see.' They arrived late, when the piazza was already full, and just as the attacks began – they saw us, or rather they heard us from far away – they left and went to wait for us at the party office, because their visit was semi-clandestine, they were senior leaders and the Union could not risk losing them: they were under direct orders to avoid any risks. They waited for us there, and the meeting began. There was a heated atmosphere, everyone had something to say, everyone had praise for their comrades, and Guglielmo especially praised the foresight of the institution, and was critical of us again: 'Once more today I saw an example of your lack of faith in the party and in the party leadership. But the most serious point, as Chairman Mao would say, is that you showed a lack of trust in the masses.' We looked at the floor and felt contrite.

I don't know how long the meeting lasted: half an hour, maybe an hour, I don't know. I hadn't looked at my watch since early that morning, actually I wasn't even wearing it – it had been broken in the first attack – and I had put it in my pocket. I don't have any idea what time it was. I just know that it was morning, late morning, maybe midday. We were there – still immersed in our discussions – and at a certain point I heard a bang on the window. I went to look out. It was a young lad on a bicycle, a local kid. He was still standing astride his bike, he hadn't even got off, he was there on the pavement, knocking on the window: 'Go! Go! They're coming to get you.' I thought that it was a joke. I looked out, checked to the left and to the right, but I

didn't see anything – I thought he meant that the police were coming
– and I went back inside: 'Piss off!'

But he was insistent: 'Go! Go!'

So Serse went outside and looked down the road and he called
all of us outside. We could see a cloud of dust in the far distance. Just
a cloud of dust, but a big one. We couldn't even see the apartment
buildings, just this cloud of dust.

We ran inside to get the pickaxes and distribute one to everybody
there. Wolf and I spontaneously took command. We lined up behind
the offices, we were decisive and focussed.

Someone else arrived on a scooter: 'Go! Go!' Serse looked out again.
So did I. Manrico and the regional secretary got back into the car. He
didn't want to go, but his comrade insisted: 'It's a direct order.' They
told Mimì and another girl to get inside – 'They're too young' – and they
sped off in the direction of Rome. It was a red Ford Cortina.

The cloud of dust was getting closer. Now it was at the Church of
Our Lady, then it came closer. There were so many of them, it was
hard to believe, we could see them now marching along in the cloud
of dust, every once in a while we could see that they were holding
long, tall pikes.

Others arrived on scooters, but they weren't coming to warn us
any more, they were advance troops on a reconnaissance mission. We
hit a couple of them right away with our batons. Guglielmo asked,
'Can you manage?' We nodded yes, but he wasn't convinced, he con-
sulted with Serse: 'What do you think?'

'I think we'd better run.'

Guglielmo couldn't believe it; he didn't even let him finish: 'Let's
go, let's go! Run! It's an order,' and he started to set an example, and
Serse was right behind him.

We felt like crying. 'But we're outnumbered,' said Serse. What did
we care if we were outnumbered? We weren't courageous, we were
worms. What the hell did we care if we got into a fight, but we couldn't
run away like cowards, no. We couldn't just abandon the party office.
We could live with a few bruises, that passes, your body heals. But

shame is something that you never recover from. Shame stays with you for the rest of your life.

Now they were about to arrive. They came around the corner from the main street in Campo Boario. We were now the rearguard cover; we were covering the others as they fled, so we felt as if we were counterbalancing that feeling of shame. We were about twenty, thirty yards from the mob. The others had run down via Milazzo, and then turned at the corner of via Lepanto. Serse came back. He saw us, and he turned back, he didn't want to abandon us: 'Hurry up,' he cried. The Fascists were arriving. We saw them crowd around the office, in front of the shutters that we had closed. Gradually some broke away from the main group and came after us. It was a small group, but they weren't in any hurry, they walked towards us shouting insults: 'Come out if you dare,' 'Come forward.' We were dramatically outnumbered, even by this small group. We gradually retreated. We got as far as the corner of via Lepanto, and we turned. They came after us. Now they were at the corner and we were further on, half way down the street. But at a certain point we saw little groups fan out, run along via Milazzo and overturn a red Ford Cortina and then, next to it, a Fiat 1500. We could see clearly, it was one of the guys from Bar di Russo. And then we could hear people shouting. There'd been some screaming earlier, but now it was more and louder. The little group following us stopped. They turned around. One of them put his hands in his hair, and we could see smoke rising from behind the houses, a plume of smoke coming from the direction of the office.

There were hundreds of them. They weren't all Fascists. Of course some of them were Fascists, the militants, my soldiers, but the guys from Bar di Russo were with them, and everyone from the piazza. There were people from Latina who didn't give a damn about politics, they may even have been Christian Democrat voters, but they couldn't stand the sight of the red flag. At the end of the union demonstration they stayed behind. They gradually trooped into the piazza. They came out from the bars and began to comment. They followed a couple of Continuous Struggle supporters who they saw go by far away. They

chased Paolo through the public gardens, but he played football, he
was fit, and he got away. He said that as they ran after him they were
shouting, 'Lynch him! Lynch him!' I don't know if it's true, but that's
what he said, maybe they were joking. The fact remains that at a
certain point a large crowd had formed – everyone from the piazza,
everyone we used to see taking an evening stroll – and the Fascists said,
'Let's go after the Chinese,' and they followed along.

They went straight down corso della Repubblica of their own
accord. Their numbers swelled because they were joined by people
who didn't give a damn, but when there's major public mayhem like this,
a lot of people think, 'Let me go and check out what's happening.' But
what do you know? These observers add to the numbers in the crowd,
and, depending on how the wind blows, if they can take out their
frustrations and attack someone with no risk of retribution, sometimes
they'll think, 'Why not?' Then they become truly ferocious.

Along the road, as they came after us, they grabbed the pikes used
to support the little trees planted along the pavement by the council,
and that's how they went along, without anyone saying a word to
them, right past the police headquarters. Maybe the officers from the
political groups thought, 'It's time this happened.' By the time they
got to Campo Boario the crowd had become a mob.

Manrico didn't feel like going straight to Rome, nor did he want
to drop Mimì off at home. He wanted to watch the show. So he
turned back in the car. He thought that we were still maintaining the
defence of the office, but he saw that the mob was too big and that it
was an impossible mission: 'I have to go back and warn them, they
have to get out,' and he turned back.

'What are you doing?' his comrade asked, but Manrico was on a
roll by then. He arrived in front of the office – coming from the other
direction, past the Church of Our Lady – he saw that we had left, and
he breathed a sigh of relief, but by then the mob had surrounded the
car and they were thumping on the bonnet and the roof. He worried:
'Someone will recognise us here.' He slammed the gearstick into first
and screeched away through the crowd at full speed. Mimì saw them

jump onto the bonnet and then start banging on the boot. The next day the newspapers said that fifteen people had been injured – 'it could have been even worse' – and two were in a critical condition. The Fiat 1500 followed them along the road to the train station. They continued for a while, until they understood that he was crazier than they were and they stopped.

Meanwhile the others were dumbstruck looking at all the people who'd been injured. There was blood. Who knows how many risked their lives. This is why the ones who came after us – after me and Serse, because at a certain point Wolf made Cristina his priority: 'Wolf, I'm afraid, take me home' – stopped following us and turned back. They prised open the shutters and got into the office and destroyed everything, they threw all the furniture out the window. They used our spray cans to write graffiti on the walls – 'Stalin's a pig', 'Mao's a clown' – and they even drew an erect phallus. Then they set fire to everything, inside and out. The apartment upstairs even went up in flames. Alright, you may say, 'They were angry.' I agree, but if Manrico hadn't arrived in his Ford Cortina, the culprits would have made it home scot-free: 'Those responsible were never apprehended...' The mob had come after us and the others who followed, then wanted to be entertained: they had to show them what they were capable of. The fire brigade and the police arrived after an hour, by which time all that was left of the office was blackened embers.

We didn't know anything of what had happened: we just saw the smoke rising behind the houses, and people stopping and putting their hands in their hair. We kept on throwing rocks for a while. At that time the roads in Campo Boario were unpaved, and full of pot-holes, and you could find as many stones as you needed. Then we saw that all of our people were safe. We turned round and left ourselves. We dragged our weapons behind us: 'Lord knows what happened,' mused Serse.

'What do you think happened?' I replied. 'We lost and ran away,' and I felt like I'd hit rock-bottom in my life. I'd never felt so grim. Not even when Francesca dumped me.

We walked along. The battle was over for us, too – 'Everyone go home' – but we walked along alone, not running, but walking at a brisk pace. We left our batons on the roadside, so as not to attract attention, and every once in a while we would look behind us to check: it was over. Then on the corner of via Legnano we saw a crazy coming towards us, and another nutter about ten yards behind. The first guy looked like he was out of his mind. He was a guy who'd only moved to Latina a short time before. He had tears streaming down his face, he was having a full-blown hysterical crisis, and he screamed deliriously, 'Murderers, what have you done! Murderers, what have you done!' and he threw himself at Serse, who was just in front of me. Serse grabbed him by the neck and threw him to the ground (he always said that he didn't like violence, but when the situation warranted he knew how to use force).

The other man was Bompressi. He was about ten yards behind, and he was screaming and gesticulating in the same way. I didn't understand what he was saying, but he had his arms up in the air and was flailing them about. Then we found out that he had come after the other guy to stop him, but how could I have known? He was screaming and waving his hands, and he came towards where Serse was with that other guy, and he looked at me as he shouted. I took a few steps forward, and went towards him. I punched him in the stomach. He doubled over, then fell to the ground, he stepped back and to one side, he tried to grab a garden wall to support himself. He slipped down almost to a sitting position, then he leaned over to one side towards the ground, bent double, and he wasn't holding his stomach, but his hands – both of them – were on his chest, clasping his chest. He started to foam at the mouth. He looked right up into my eyes.

I whispered, 'Sorry, I didn't mean to.' Immediately I realised that it was his heart.

'He shook his head: 'Eh! That's what you say!' Then he sort of smiled, and he was dead.

We ran. At full speed this time. The other guy – the madman – leaned over his body, shouting, 'Signor Bompressi! Signor Bompressi!'

and every once in a while he would shout after us, 'Murderers! Murderers!' A gate opened as we ran down via Marsala: 'Come here.' We ran in. It was the home of Renato, a worker comrade, he was a marble-cutter. Inside we found Guglielmo – the supreme leader – and another couple of comrades. We stayed there until late at night. I didn't say a word to him. Once in a while – every thirty minutes or so – we would start to leave, and Renato would look outside, to monitor the situation, or else he would send his wife out to ask the neighbours for news. Nothing doing. 'They're making a house-to-house search,' said Renato, and in actual fact, from a small hole in the shutters, once in a while we could see small groups of Fascists with tyre irons and batons patrolling the streets, going back and forth. 'This is civil war, this is civil war!' exclaimed Renato in semi-disbelief. But it wasn't civil war yet – that came later – even if the more he said this the more we were all convinced. But to tell the truth, as I lay in the corridor on the floor, with my shoulders resting against the wall waiting for time to pass, I was more concerned for Bompressi than for the civil war.

A few days after, I heard that the church was full at his funeral. There were people outside, and the piazza was full. Almirante and Michelini came too, and Romualdi, and they sat in the front pew. There was a tricolour flag with the MSI flame on top of his coffin. But inside, his wife had put his San Marco brigade beret on his heart. Apparently for years he would always tell her in the evenings, as they lay in bed drifting off to sleep, 'When I die, bury me with my beret.' It reminded him of his glory days as a warrant officer for the social republic.

But I didn't want this to happen, not at all, he was my friend. But it was his fault. If you have heart problems, you stay at home, you don't go out looking for trouble. Hadn't his wife always told him so?

chapter 12

The Union sent me to Bari. It's not really that I was at risk; they just thought it was better for me to be out of sight and out of mind. Anyhow, Latina wasn't important to them; they had definitely erased it from the revolutionary map, eliminated it: 'It's a Fascist city. A black bastion. We'll deal with them later.' To tell the truth, we wanted to do something right away: 'Let's mobilise the Red Squad and we'll come in full force from Rome, thirty or forty at most. We'll start with Bar di Russo, then we'll go to their party headquarters and set it on fire.'

'That's a military response, we're a political organisation, it's ideology that really matters,' pontificated Guglielmo, the mighty leader, and he convinced them. There was no point insisting, 'This is the only language they understand. If we destroy them on a military level it's a political massacre as well, and we can take over the city.' As a matter of fact, Wolf and I were even still convinced that we might have been able to win that day if we hadn't been forced to run away. All it would have taken was to achieve a victory over the first few troops, then the others would have run away in fear. Our desertion – and the arson attack on the office – weighed heavily on our hearts; we felt like we had been personally violated. We even requested Guglielmo's expulsion from the party: 'The whole thing was his fault, he was shitting himself, he's not worthy to be a party member.' Instead, we were sent into exile, to Bari of all places.

I didn't like it. If only they'd sent me to Milan. But I had to obey my orders. I left like a good little soldier. This time they gave me a room with two other guys, and I even had a real bed. We lived in this apartment in a building in via Carulli. Gilberto wasn't there any more, they'd sent him to Naples, and they sent a guy from Naples to Bari. His name was Francesco. Things were always on the move within the Union.

There were about ten of us. I was the lowest by rank, together with another guy from Palermo who was also wanted by the police because he had tied a Fascist up with barbed wire and left him on the beach. We were almost all men in that apartment, with the exception of two married couples and a girl who cooked for us. We all got along well, and sometimes we would clown around. But it was usually about as dynamic as a monastery. We were party executives, professional revolutionaries. That's all we were supposed to think about, and we had to live like the masses: 'A communist has to be like a fish in the ocean of the masses,' said Chairman Mao.

The office was in via Quintino Sella, about a twenty-minute walk from where we lived. Political work was tiring, we were always on the go: standing outside the factories of Bari, hanging out with agricultural workers in various towns throughout the Puglia region: Andria, Cerignola, Corato, Foggia, Taranto. The Italsider steelworks had just opened in Taranto. There were seven thousand factory workers, and two of us would stand outside the gates selling copies of *Serve the People*. I truly hated selling newspapers, I felt ashamed. It was like begging for alms: 'Would you like to buy a newspaper?' But the union disagreed, they said that if people don't pay for things they don't appreciate them, if they didn't buy the paper, they wouldn't read it, they would just throw it away. I can hear you saying, 'It doesn't matter.' Of course it doesn't matter, but I still felt ashamed. 'So why did you do it?' What do you mean? It was my duty. I was a foot soldier for the party.

Then I had news from Latina that the police weren't looking for me any more, there was no danger, I could return whenever I wanted: Bompressi had died of a heart attack, and no one cared any more, maybe not even the chairman and Livio Nastri. They were all looking for the driver of the red Ford Cortina. Apparently every police force in Italy was looking for him, but they still hadn't been able to identify who exactly they were looking for.

The danger was over, and I wanted to return home, but the Union wouldn't allow it: 'What's the point of going to Latina? That's a black zone. Stay in Bari and work for the revolution.' Once more I obeyed. Actually, they even sent Wolf to me, although in the beginning he refused. He only agreed when Cristina dumped him again. We enrolled at the university, but only to avoid military service. We signed up for degrees in agriculture, but we never went to the campus. We would just go past on the train on our way to Taranto.

So we became party members, professional revolutionaries. I was the director of the 'Central Propaganda Brigade' for Puglia, but basic-ally Wolf and I were it. We would travel throughout the region from dawn to dusk. We spent two or three days a week in Taranto because of Italsider; we slept in the local office. We purchased two cots and sleeping bags. It was on the third floor, and there was no bathroom. There was just a toilet that was always blocked and a tap for water. We had to wait for nightfall to take a crap: then we would creep outside behind the office towards the buttress by the drawbridge, down a flight of stairs next to the wall, by the sea, in wintertime, in the freezing cold, to take our craps; there with seagulls who seemed none too pleased whenever we showed up. Sometimes in the evening, when we were in Bari – walking back home in the evening from our office – a girl would look at me, and I would look back at her, then Wolf would yank me by the arm before anything could happen: 'Be serious, we're revolutionaries.' There was no point in reminding him that I was the director of the brigade, because I was never quite sure if he might report me.

Anyhow it was 12 December 1969, and a bomb exploded in the Banca Nazionale dell'Agricoltura in Milan. Sixteen dead. On the same day, almost at the same time, another bomb exploded in piazza Vittoria in Rome, and they found another one in a bank that didn't detonate. Now everyone knows how the story unfolded: the autumn unrest had continued into the winter, but there was even more unrest than before. The metalworkers couldn't agree on a new labour contract. The workers weren't allowing the unions to boss them around like before, and no one could rein them in. They wanted everything, they wanted all they'd asked for: salaries, justice, democracy, liberty, assemblies. It seemed like no one could control them any more. But that bomb started to put things back into shape, and the contract for the metalworkers was quickly agreed, and everything was supposed to return to normal. 'The extremism of the opposition will never end,' declared the Christian Democrats, and they were right. After the first bombs there were more. On trains. In public squares. You may well ask, 'But who planted those bombs?' What kind of an idiot are you, who do you think planted them? The Christian Democrats, the democratic state. You'll say, 'No, the secret service.' You really don't understand a thing. Have you ever heard anyone admit to the existence of the 'secret service'? Services are secret by definition, in every country of the world and at every era of history. If they weren't secret, then everyone would see them: they would just be normal police acting in the clear light of day. If they're 'secret' that's precisely because they work outside the law, otherwise what kind of secret service would they be? It's their job, it's a specifically designed apparatus between all the structures of the state; as a mater of fact it's the apparatus linking designed to protect the 'security of the state'! They were just doing their job, what their commander asked them: 'What are you doing?' the minister would ask, or someone on his behalf. 'Get a move on.' And that's what they did: they planted bombs everywhere, they killed people, and then blamed it on the 'extremist opposition'. Now the status quo was guaranteed and the 'silent majority' could finally go back to work. It was all taken care of.

That day we were in Bari: we followed the news on the radio, on TV, we were still uncertain how things were, exactly how many had been killed. After dinner we returned to our office to prepare a press release and make copies to hand out the next day at the factory gates. It must have been ten or ten-thirty at night when the police arrived. They broke in by force. They searched everywhere. They took everything apart. Then they took us to the police station. We found the others there; they'd been taken from the apartment. They kept us overnight, and at the same time throughout Italy they made hundreds and hundreds of searches and arrests. They even went to my home in Latina and to Wolf's parents'. It was the middle of the night, two or three in the morning. They arrived on the doorstep with automatic weapons, as if they were looking for bandits, but all they did was wake up my father, my mother and Mimì. They told me that Papà wept tears of shame. They had automatic weapons. They were looking for me, not Manrico: they didn't even know who he was back then. They looked everywhere – who knows what they expected to find? – and they ended up seizing my poems. Maybe they deserved to be seized, but not for any other reason than the fact that they weren't very good. Anyhow, that's what happened. They planted a bomb in Milan and used that as an excuse to come and arrest me in Bari. And you're asking if I could have been responsible? It's not that the idea had never crossed my head: I'd thought about it often, and I even told Serse and Wolf, a long time before, that I had an overpowering urge to go and plant a bomb in Milan. But outside Francesca's house, not in a bank. Anyhow, the next day they even threw an anarchist out of a fourth-floor window at the police headquarters – up north in Milan – but they claimed that he fell, that he committed suicide: 'Because he regretted planting the bomb,' they said. His name was Giuseppe Pinelli. And that's what life was like in Italy in 1969.

A few days later some boxes of pamphlets arrived form Rome. It was a special edition of *Serve the People*, just one page, but big, with the headline 'Against Repression', because as well as hundreds of searches, dozens and dozens of arrests and the anarchist who committed suicide from the fourth floor, there had also been seventy thousand official complaints made all over Italy. The pamphlet cost only 20 lire, but that was a nominal fee. They told us in Bari, 'Distribute this, even for free.' We left for Taranto with five hundred of these pamphlets. When we got there it was cold, but I wasn't comfortable with this idea of giving them away for free, not this time. 'What is this: I'm here to serve you, they're killing us, they're reporting us, and I even have to beg you to read this? If you want to know what's going on, then pay.'

'They should at least thank us, these ungrateful assholes,' added Wolf. But standing outside the Italsider plant – out of more than a thousand workers going in and coming out as the shifts changed – we sold maybe twenty. 'Now do we have to take all these pamphlets back to Bari?' complained Wolf. So we went into the piazza, where everyone was taking their evening stroll, and the longer we stood there trying to sell these pamphlets to people who weren't interested the more furious we became. We were angry with the passersby – 'Oh, good for you! Here I am fighting for your rights and you're out taking an evening stroll?' – and we started to feel aggressive. All I could think of were the deaths in Milan, the exploitation of seasonal workers, injuries in the workplace, but I thought of Joan and Francesca too – who knows where they were right now? – and I thought of Massa Carrara, and I started going up to people in a belligerent way, yelling in their faces, 'Twenty lira against repression!' And they shouted insults back at me.

Wolf was shouting even louder than I was. We yelled in their faces with anger, bullying them – 'Twenty lira against repression!' – and we sold all of them. When we went back to Bari they couldn't believe it, we had to show them the money to prove that we were telling the truth. They even called Rome to inform them of the 'splendid triumphs' of the Central Propaganda Brigade of Puglia.

So we carried on as before with our political work: you never really notice when a sea change in history occurs. No one woke up in the year 476 AD one morning to say, 'The Western Roman Empire has just fallen.' They didn't notice a thing, every day was just like the one before: you were born, you took your sheep to graze, and then you died. Who knows how many years had to pass before someone reflected, 'You know what? Do you remember back in 476 when such and such happened? Well, I think that must have been when the Roman Empire fell,' and that's how it was for us. We didn't realise that history had changed, that the bombing in Milan was a turning point. For us it was a serious matter – of course – but it didn't change much in terms of the questions, and then the next day we went back to work like 'fish in the ocean of the masses', exactly like all the workers, exactly like the farmer who – even if his entire family died during the night – the next morning wakes up early and goes to the stable to milk the cows and feed the animals. What's he supposed to do, let them die as well?

Then I don't quite understand what happened. In the middle or towards the end of January – 1970 – the Union began to splinter. There was a breakaway movement in Rome, a big one. Almost all of Rome – which was one of our major centres – broke away: 'Thank you and goodbye.' We were in Bari, what did we know? They sent me on a special mission to Rome: 'Go and speak to your brother,' because he had left with the splinter group. 'He's an honest bloke, if you go you can convince him,' and I left immediately. 'How could this happen?' I wondered. 'Has he become a counter-revolutionary?'

I arrived early in the morning at the station. I went to the new office – they were in charge in Prenestino, and it would cause problems if I showed up there – near largo Argentina, a squalid office with four empty rooms. I found only three people working there. I asked after Pino the Monster, Alfredo G., Guilio. They had all left, they were with the counter-revolutionaries. But it was a real problem finding Manrico, I had to wait until it was dark, it was dangerous to go there, I had to find a way to be able to speak to him privately. I thought, 'Alright, I'll wait.' That morning there had been a strike of railway workers, and they had prepared some pamphlets, but there was no one around to distribute them. 'But we need to show that the party is with the workers,' said Brambillari, and he looked at me.

'Trust me,' I said, and I took the pamphlets and left with another loser. We found the demonstration at the Ancient Forum just where it's about to turn into via Cavour. We went over and began to distribute the pamphlets, starting from the front of the crowd. But the atmosphere had changed, and they didn't seem to appreciate our presence. The union security team gave the demonstrators a knowing look, and they all said, 'No thank you.' Then, in one way or another, they pushed us almost to the back, to the margins. I felt truly depressed; it had been such a bad day. The weather reflected my mood, and the sky began to darken. But I was there now. I couldn't just abandon the masses, so I continued to follow the demonstration, with this package of pamphlets under my arm, and every once in a while I would try to hand one out, even to people who were watching as we passed by. At a certain point I had dropped back about twenty yards from the end of the demonstration, and I rushed to catch up, but suddenly I turned round, because I felt that there was someone standing behind me. And I was right. It was Muriatico. Like a shadow. Who knows how long he'd been following? He was wearing a dark wool jacket, and he had his hands in his pockets. He gave me a surly look, from head to toe. He didn't say a word. I was truly taken aback, first on a personal level – meaning I was surprised to see him myself – then on a collective level: I wondered if he was about to attack the demonstrators. I turned to look around, and see if I could spot some of the others, maybe on the street corners. I didn't see anyone: 'Who knows where they're hiding?' So I asked him, 'What do you want? Get lost before something happens.'

'That's what I want,' and he pointed at the pamphlets: 'Show me what's written on those.'

'You can't have one. Get lost!'

'Why won't you give me one?' he cried out, and he grabbed the package of pamphlets from my arms. I resisted, I defended myself, and I screamed as well. People turned round in the back of the demonstration. Security came running over: 'What's happening? What's going on?' they asked me. 'The Chinese again.' They looked at each other knowingly. They seemed aggressive.

So I cried out, 'The Fascists, the Fascists! He's a Fascist, I know him,' and I pointed to Muriatico. They left me right away and went for him.

Now it was his fault, and he tried to play the part of the innocent passerby: 'I'm no Fascist! I'm a conductor on the trams, a worker; I'm on your side. I work at depot number 8.' It's true, I'd forgotten that.

Someone said, 'That's right, I've seen him at depot number 8,' and he seemed to gain confidence, and said, 'I know you, your name is Paolo, I'm Giulio's friend, I'm a conductor.'

'Yes, that's right,' and they let him go. Then he began to shout, 'He's the one you want, what's he doing here with us? Fucking asshole!' and they started to look at me with suspicion again.

I was fed up: 'You can all go to hell,' and I began to collect the pamphlets that had fallen to the ground in the scuffle, and then I went back to the office.

'How did it go?' they asked me.

'If you only knew!' I didn't even feel like seeing Manrico any more: 'What's the point?' And I felt disgusted by the way I'd been afraid when I saw Muriatico. Not to mention calling my comrades 'fucking assholes'. I felt – how can I describe it? – a sense of shame. At this point Manrico was the least of my worries. The only consolation was that even Muriatico at some point must have given up on Fascism: 'I'm no Fascist!' he'd said.

They took me to see Manrico later that evening. A guy called Emilio took me in his Citroën 2CV, to Monteverde nuovo. Manrico was working behind the counter in a bar. When we arrived he was laughing and joking with the boss and a couple of customers. He was always the life of the party, as suave as Paul Newman. As soon as he saw me he smiled, but when he saw Emilio standing behind me his expression changed. Manrico said hello, and then, 'Wait for me outside.' We saw him take off his white coat, say a cheery goodbye to his boss and come outside, but as soon as he came over to us his expression changed: either he took off his mask or he put it on, I'll never know. To break the ice, I asked him, 'Do you work here?' and pointed to the bar.

'It's the only job I know how to do.' He was depressed, negative, there was no way of talking to him. Emilio tried every way, but it was just impossible, the more we tried to understand, the more stubborn he became.

In the end I said to him, 'So basically you've become a counter-revolutionary.'

'A counter-revolutionary?' he shouted, and he seemed very upset, his hands kept shaking and his head twitched, and he looked like he was on the verge of tears. 'They're the real counter-revolutionaries.

They're criminals, opportunists, self-interested bourgeoisie; all they think about is looking out for themselves at the expense of the masses.' He seemed like a nutter. There was nothing to be done. The trip had been utterly pointless. He pleaded with me: 'Come on, why don't you come with us? Don't let them keep on taking advantage of you: they'll never stage the revolution. Go to Africa, to the Congo, to be a surveyor.'

'Now you want me to leave for Africa? Now that the contract has been withdrawn? I wish they'd killed you – why couldn't you tell me this before? This is just like seminary all over again. First you dragged me into the place, then you leave and tell me the story of Darwin's theory of evolution! What do you take me for, your little puppy-dog? Just fuck off, you and the whole Congo!' I went back to Bari, and it was all I could do not to teach him a lesson he'd never forget, to give him what he deserved for that time in the gardens – because it's true I had slipped – and those comments about Francesca that hadn't left me with any illusions about what really went on. For months, once in a while, sometimes at night when I was squatting in the bastions of Taranto next to the seagulls, it would come back to me. 'This is all adding up,' I said to myself. But then Emilio separated us, and when we left he wanted to embrace me: 'Come here, give your brother a kiss.'

'Sure, like Judas,' I said, and then he laughed for the first time that night.

'Come with us,' he tried to convince me. 'We'll really make the revolution happen.'

What do I know about what happened? Something had happened. Now I don't really remember, and I don't think that I quite understood at the time. But – as I later saw – they really were serious. They would say, 'So you want to shoot me? I'll shoot you.' But the Union was moving back from its positions. Four months earlier they had given their word to the revolutionary government, and now that the 'paper tiger of capitalism' had shown its true colours with the Milan bombing, now they wanted 'unity of action' with the other groups, and they even wanted to enter the union structure. 'We'll be the red line of CGIL,' said Brambillari, so that one day, as we were returning form Taranto, Wolf said, 'As far as *entrismo* goes, then my idea was better,' even if he then laughed. We were an organisation with thirty thousand militants: 'the steel nucleus', as Brambillari would say. Once – before the office was burned – Serse had an idea, and we went to Rome to tell Manrico, the minister of defence: 'If there are thirty thousand of us and we're so well organised, why are we wasting time waiting for the masses to be educated? Let's act, let's prepare a good plan, and we can mount a *coup d'état*: all thirty thousand of us, at the same time, we could easily seize power. Then we could educate the masses after the fact.' Manrico even liked the idea, he found it amusing, but he said that it would be impossible: 'No, no, we need the masses.'

But at that time we hadn't really understood fully: we were from Latina, and we were always the last to arrive. We remained in the Union, in Puglia, and we did our duty, we looked after things, and when finally – but it took almost a year – we threw in the towel, we were still convinced that they were right – 'Stalin! Mao! Brambillari!' – even if they were starting to say that it would take longer than expected. In actual fact, we were just fed up. We couldn't stand the monastic atmosphere in the apartment, selling newspapers and always trying to agitate the masses. We didn't feel like 'fish in the ocean', we felt like members of a religious brotherhood, and all around us normal people, students, trade unionists, the Continuous Struggle supporters, the Lenin Circles throughout Puglia were enjoying a little bit of freedom after 1968. There'd been a sexual liberation, and girls started staying out after seven in the evening, and everyone now was getting laid – especially my sisters. We were the only ones living like monks. All that was missing was for us to start flagellating ourselves in the evenings when we got home from Taranto or Cerignola.

We continued for almost a year, but in the end we couldn't stand it any more. We'd always been stray dogs, and they had us on a very short lead. Too short. 'I can't take it any more,' said Wolf one evening as we walked back from the office to our apartment in Bari. We were in front of Standa, and I had turned to look at a blonde girl passing by. Instead of reproaching me, he said, 'I can't take it any more,' and I understood that the moment had truly come.

'You're telling me,' I replied. If only there were the slightest chance of the revolution coming sometime soon, I could have held out. But now that it seemed farther and farther away – who knew when it would happen? – and politics had just become a power trip for some people, there didn't seem to be much point in waiting patiently for the masses to be educated. We risked wasting our youth in a project that was going nowhere fast.

We kept walking, and I told Wolf, 'The problem is, who can you explain it to?' We had tried a few times at meals to express doubts, but the others hadn't been very receptive. We were simple lads from Latina, they were all intellectuals; they twisted your words every which way, and they quoted from a thousand books, and in the end it was easier just to agree with them. Once they had brainwashed me to the point that I made a self-critique and – because Wolf had been encouraging my doubts – I asked for his expulsion: 'I am very sorry, but he must be expelled immediately because he's a dangerous counter-revolutionary.' He looked at me with his jaw on the floor, and all the others started laughing: 'Let's not exaggerate,' they placated me. If we didn't leave right away, we risked spending our entire lives on their leash.

Wolf suggested, 'There's no need to tell them anything,' and so that's what we did.

We went home, to via Carulli, had dinner, like every other evening, laughed and joked like everything was normal, then we discussed the political work of the day with our comrades and made plans for the next day: 'Will you be in Taranto tomorrow?'

'Of course.' Then the two of us went off to bed without saying another word. The next morning we got up, made our beds, drank our caffè latte and left: 'Ciao.' They never saw us again. 'But that's desertion,' I hear you say. Maybe that's how you see it, but I couldn't stand it any longer. We were stray dogs, we couldn't live like that. You'll say, 'But desertion is desertion.' Sure, I understand, but then what would the Volunteers have made of us?

We went home to Latina. My mother couldn't believe it. First she was happy to see me, but then she wondered, 'Will he be moving back home?' It would have been different if Manrico had come back; she hadn't seen him in ages and she would still remind me, 'It's all your fault, you led him astray.'

*   *   *

Months passed, then years.

We enrolled in political science at the University of Rome. Wolf took it very seriously, he would go to class every day, study, take his exams, and he managed to graduate in five years, but he stopped going out in the evenings. I would go to class occasionally, just to say, 'I went,' or to pick up girls. I took the minimum course load to stave off military service – that was the last thing I wanted to do. 'I'll wait and serve in the Popular Army when the revolution comes.' I would do a bit of work for Serse in the office. He took me on again, but I was dead weight. I'd lost my lust for life. The Central Propaganda Brigade of Puglia had taken it all out of me. I didn't feel like doing anything, just reading until late at night. Then every evening, before I fell asleep, I would say to myself, 'Tomorrow I'm going to leave for England,' to see Joan. But then when I woke up I wouldn't feel like it any more: 'Such a long way ...' Then in the evening I would start to think about it again: 'Tomorrow I really will leave,' and of course I never did.

I'd stopped masturbating, and I began taking drugs, but not always, just sometimes. You're shocked: 'You just mention it casually like that, as if it were something normal?' And how should I tell you then? Should I prostrate myself in shame? Do you really think that someone who does drugs has a life filled with problems? How stupid can you be? If someone's on drugs, he doesn't have problems when he's high, it's when he's not high that there's a problem. And then the problem becomes someone else's concern. But what the hell do you care? It's not so different from cigarettes.

I would get laid occasionally, but it wasn't like before. Girls were pretty willing, but it seemed like they had sex just for the sake of it, not because they really wanted to. And I felt the same. I don't know if it was because of the drugs – or maybe because of the experience in Puglia – but sex was about as exciting as jerking off; there was no particular satisfaction if you took love out of the equation, so at that point I preferred drugs. I wasn't able to fall in love any more. In my head – and in my heart – all I could think about was Francesca. Not Joan from England. Francesca. I had started to write to her again, and sometimes she would right back. She always said, 'Come and visit me.'

'What's the point?' I'd reply. 'I'll only come to Milan if things are clear between us, if I have some kind of a chance.' I wasn't seventeen any more. You'll ask, 'Fine, but then why did you write to her?' Because I couldn't help it. Because I loved her.

It was all over with politics. We never wanted to have anything to do with Continuous Struggle. Wolf would go to their meetings occasionally, on the off chance of bumping into Cristina. 'Will you never learn?' we tried to convince him.

I tried to find the guys from the Red Squad, I looked them up when I was in Rome – Pino the Monster, Giulio, Alfredo – but they had all disappeared, they'd gone underground. The government had cracked down. There were bombs exploding all the time: in the piazzas, on the trains, men, women and children were dying. They would take the train and go to their death, so people began to be fearful – 'Have you seen what the Communists have done? Have you seen what's happening?' – and everyone voted Christian Democrat because they were living in fear. And those who'd gone underground weren't so different: 'A military attack requires a military response: we have to guarantee the masses some freedom of action.' At the end of the day, they'd learned their lessons from Brambillari, not just from Mao Tse-Tung. And then judges were being kidnapped and senior managers were being kneecapped. Even the Fascists started shooting, and then they started to shoot each other, and more bombs exploded. So they stopped knee-capping and began to shoot higher, and there were casualties on both sides. More and more. Like a vortex. It was civil war. Before piazza Fontana no one had ever used a gun, just their hands or maybe a truncheon or a chain, never guns. That all happened after piazza Fontana: 'Are you going to shoot me? Then I'll shoot you.' Civil war.

Anyhow, in the beginning I looked them up, for old time's sake. A man needs his old friends. But their lives had changed direction, they'd gone underground. I never found them again, I arrived too late, and they had already left. If I hadn't gone to Bari I would have left with them. But now it was too late: 'Goodbye and thank you,' also because I didn't want to go underground myself. I hadn't escaped from Bari to find myself in a different kind of prison. Living underground is almost worse than living in a monastery: 'Call me when it's time for the revolution, but until then leave me in peace, because I'm going to the Congo,' I told Manrico when I was able to locate him.

'But why, what are we doing wrong?' he asked.

'Of course you're in the right, and I admire you, I respect you, and I even feel guilty that I'm not with you, I feel like scum, but I can't take it any more: I'm fed up. Call me when the revolution starts.' He gave me a gun – 'One never knows' – and some telephone numbers. He told me that he would give me a signal at home if necessary, and then I was to call him back form a public phone booth. But it only happened a couple of times, just to find out how Mamma was doing, and for little errands in Rome, nothing much.

Time went by. Then one day I received a signal. The password. I called back. The person who answered gave me another number – in Milan – and he said, 'Come here. And bring the gun.' I don't remember exactly what his words were, if I was supposed to take the gun to give it to him, or for my own protection, I was unclear at that time. I left, I took the train. I arrived in Milan early the next morning. The appointment was at ten in piazzale Cordusio, at the tram stop. I walked there from the station, and I still had plenty of time, two and a half hours before we had to meet. I went to Boden Bar. The usual table, where Francesca and I used to sit. I asked the owner if she still came by. He hadn't seen her in months.

At a certain point, as I was waiting there, I heard someone call out my name: 'Benassi!' It was Lombarducci, a Fascist from Aprilia who worked at the stock exchange, and when I saw him my blood ran cold: I put my hand over the gun in my pocket, and I pretended to be relaxed and happy to see him, because he seemed happy to have run into me. The last time we'd met was in piazza del Popolo in Latina during the demonstration, that time that they burned the party office, but obviously all that was water under the bridge, and he seemed genuinely happy to see me. Or maybe he was just lonely in Milan and had reached the point where he was grateful even to run into his worst enemy. He wouldn't let me go: 'Why don't we meet up during my lunch break? We can have a bite to eat together. But no, why don't I call in sick and we can spend the day together.'

I didn't know how to stop him; I told him I was waiting for a girl – 'As a matter of fact she's running late, I think I should give her a call' – and I pretended to get up and go to the phone.

'Then I'll let you go, I'm off,' he said, and just as we were saying our goodbyes he whispered, 'Come back to our side.'

Now I'd got up from the table and I was at the phone, so I decided to call Francesca. I woke her up, but she was happy to hear my voice, she wanted to see me. 'I have an appointment at ten,' I told her, 'in piazzale Cordusio.'

'With Manrico,' she said, it was a statement of fact.

'What is it with you and Manrico?'

'No, nothing, that's all,' but I felt that something was up. She said, 'I'll be right there, wait for me, I'll meet you both there just before ten.' I wanted her to meet me at Boden. 'No, Cordusio's better. I'll be there at nine-thirty.'

I don't remember if I was high, I really can't remember, sometimes there's too much going on and you get information overload. But at nine-thirty I was in piazzale Cordusio – this much I do remember – on the corner with via Broletto, next to a florist. Everything was tranquil, that is to say everything was the usual confusion: traffic, noise, trams, people bustling along the pavement. But Francesca wasn't there, and by nine-forty-five she still hadn't shown up. Francesca wasn't there but – I have to say – it didn't worry me that much. I waited for her.

Ten o'clock. The tram stop – on the other side of the road – was chock-a-block. The tram arrived from corso Magenta. A lot of people got off, and pushed their way through the people trying to get on, and then they wandered away. Then I saw Manrico. He didn't get off; he was just standing there on the step, his scarf wrapped around his neck. I saw two office workers – wearing suits and ties with newspapers under their arms – on the other corner, by via Meravigli, then suddenly the newspapers dropped to the ground. Manrico stepped out of the tram, turned, and came towards me. The man is holding a gun; he shoots. In my direction.

I hear the florist fall to the ground next to me. He drops between roses and daisies on the wooden shelves. He was holding a gun too. It all happens in a split second.

A squad car comes around the corner from via Meravigli.

Manrico takes another step. The office workers shoot. He takes another step.

A carabiniere jumps out of a squad car onto the pavement. He has one knee on the ground. I see him take aim.

I don't hear the shot. But Manrico is on the ground, face down, five yards from me. His gun slides away and lands in the gutter.

Traffic stops. People scream.

The carabiniere gets up. He doesn't run. He walks calmly and coolly towards us, or at least that's how it seems from far away. When he gets closer, though, I can see that he is shaking – as if he's having convulsions – and his face is white as a sheet under his black beret. He looks at the florist lying splayed among the daisies – probably a colleague of his – and goes over to Manrico. He kneels down again, with just one knee, the other knee is bent, and he is balancing on the heel of his boot, I can hear it clicking against the asphalt as he taps it. He leans over Manrico and asks him, 'Now what do you have to say for yourself, eh?' and he puts his gun to the back of Manrico's neck.

'Fuck you,' says Manrico. And he shoots. And this time I do hear the shot.

Squad cars come from every direction. Sirens blazing. I didn't move a step, I was frozen, I couldn't move. I was blocked like that from beginning to end. Panic. Total panic. I couldn't even move my arm, I could barely breathe. Then suddenly I could move again, and I thought, 'They're going to kill me next.' I turned and left. Worse than Judas, worse than Lord Jim.

I just walked and walked. My legs felt like wood. I was afraid they'd give out, afraid I'd crash to the ground, afraid they'd find me. I ordered my legs to keep moving, and they did. I looked around to see if Francesca was anywhere in sight. I was worried for her. But Francesca was nowhere to be seen, so I went to Boden Bar: 'She'll be there.' But around there – from a distance – I could see that the carabinieri were milling around: 'Here, too?' I turned towards the stock exchange. There were people standing outside, they had come out to see what was going on. In the doorway, on the stairs, I saw Lombarducci, the Fascist from Aprilia. He saw me, and he must have understood what had happened. He gave me a nod, as if to say, 'Do you need anything? I'm here to help you.' I shook my head, no, and continued walking, one step after another, in a conditioned reflex; I needed to get as far away as I could. Farther and farther. Without thinking. Autopilot. The only thing I could think – and I felt it more in the depths of my stomach than in my soul – was, 'What will Mamma say?' But then another thought came to me: 'If they'd let me study at the classical lyceum, none of this would have happened.'

Mimì told me later that they had been having lunch in the kitchen. They were eating pasta e fagioli, with home-made tagliolini. The television in the lounge was off, so they didn't hear the news: 'Terrorist killed in police shoot-out. Police and paramedics did what they could to save him, but he couldn't be saved. An officer disguised as a florist is wounded, but not in a critical condition.' But Signora Elide upstairs heard the news, and she opened her window, put her hands to her face, and scratched her skin with her nails, then she pulled out clumps of hair and put her hands to her head again and screamed, 'Signora Lììì...they've shot your son!'

Mamma ran out into the garden, hysterical: 'Which one?' she shouted back.

'Manrico!' And all the neighbours ran out into the courtyard to comfort her.

'No! Not Manrico, no!' And she collapsed into the arms of the first person who came to her side.

But my father put his spoon down, and before shedding a tear he made the sign of the cross and prayed: 'Pater noster qui es in coelis.' He was already sobbing as he recited the words, 'Sicut et nos dimittimus debitoribus nostris.' Then he went out and put his arms around my mother, and said gently, 'Come inside, your pasta is getting cold.'

I walked all day back and forth along the streets of Milan. In a trance, like a sleepwalker. I don't remember anything of where I walked, I just knew that I had to keep walking and act like nothing had happened. Police and carabinieri drove past with their sirens screeching. All I knew was that I had to keep walking and avoid crowds, the station, the cathedral, public squares. My legs were numb, but I kept walking, that's all I did, I just walked and didn't think of anything, not even Francesca – just for a moment I wondered, 'Did he seduce her then abandon her?' – and I can't bear to think of it now. Who knows? But someone had to have tipped off the carabinieri that he would be in piazzale Cordusio. Someone must have told them.

I began to return to my senses by the evening. I had to leave Milan, I had to get away. There was no question of taking the train – with all those controls at the station and then during the journey, where could I hide? I bought a pint of milk and a sandwich in a supermarket, but what I really wanted was the plastic bag. I walked all the way down corso Lodi. When I saw police cars I would put my hand in my pocket and touch the gun under my grey raincoat. But they didn't look at me twice. I just looked like another anonymous person walking by.

I arrived in piazzale Corvetto. It was dark. I sat down on the little garden wall in front of the hedge. I ate my sandwich, drank my milk, smoked a cigarette and waited a bit longer. I thought about Manrico, who was no longer with us, his white scarf stained with blood on the asphalt in piazzale Cordusio, and Francesca, who had called the carabinieri, then how he'd seduced her and – to tell the truth – I almost felt like crying. When there was no one around, I pulled the gun out of my pocket and wrapped it in the plastic bag. I dug a hole in the ground under the hedge, between the hedge and the wall – tight between the trunk and the bricks – and I put the gun there and covered it up. I pressed the dirt down on top and put a rock on top. It's probably still there, if the hedge and the wall still stand.

But now I knew what to do and where to go. I got up and stood along the side of the road waiting for a car to pass. I thought to myself, 'Terrorists don't hitchhike.' I went to Siena. I arrived there the next morning. I went to see Father Cavalli, at the seminary in via Piccolomini, where he was the Superior now. He welcomed me in right away, without saying a word, without asking me anything, just, 'Have you killed someone?'

'No' (I didn't feel like dealing with Bompressi, I thought: 'We can discuss that later'). And he welcomed me.

I slept downstairs, in a little room near to the coadjutor brothers. I participated in all the liturgies, because otherwise they would have disapproved, but I kept to myself without attracting attention. I usually ate on my own. I didn't speak to anyone; I was in my own world. I spent months working in the garden. I hoed and I dug, even where it wasn't necessary – around the oak trees where I'd already hoed. I hoed and hoed. Sometimes I think I can still feel the calluses on my hands.

Father Cavalli didn't say anything: 'When you're ready to talk, you come to me.' He didn't even pressure me to make my confession or to take communion. In the evenings he would give me a paper to read, when he thought that there was something that might – in some way – concern me. That's how I learned that Serse had died. They waited for him one night outside his home, and ambushed him with an iron bar. It was the guy he'd clashed with that day – he'd remembered Serse's face but not mine. He didn't know if I was tall or short, he didn't remember me at all. But he knew who Serse was. Apparently for a while, when they would run into each other in the piazza during their evening stroll, he would even say hello, as if they were friends. And Serse would say hello back. Then one night they waited for him outside his home, just when business had started to go well for Serse. Polistudio had really taken off, Wolf told me that he was doing very well and was making good money. Nonetheless, after he died his father received a lot of letters from creditors.

Bava died in Genoa at a meeting organised by Almirante. Only the Volunteers were there to hear him speak. They lined up in front of the stage to protect him, to allow him to take the floor. All around him everyone was hostile. They even threw things at him; someone aimed a bottle at his head. He spent six months in a coma; he didn't want to die.

I kept hoeing, hoeing around the oaks. I spent the day of the Palio horse races hoeing, and I had completely forgotten about my drug habit. I would wake up in the morning at dawn, and I would go to bed very early, as soon as I'd finished supper, with my body aching. I would fall asleep as soon as my head hit the pillow, like a baby in a crib. Hoeing is the best medicine.

Then Father Cavalli had to go to Rome for a meeting, and he dropped by Latina to see my parents. By this time things had calmed down, and no one was looking for me any more. Well, the only ones looking for me were the army recruiters, because I hadn't been there to do the paperwork to postpone my military service for another year. If I didn't show up right away there'd be trouble. So I left to do my duty, and I grew up in the infantry – it was nothing like the Popular Army – and it was a few months before they gave me leave. When I finally returned home I saw my mother on the balcony. She saw me at the entrance to our building, wearing my uniform, and she came towards me. I smiled and tried to make a joke: 'Bad pennies always turn up.'

'You've done half your duty,' she said, and she embraced me.

But the night before I left Siena I went to Father Cavalli's room and I said, 'I want to make my confession.'

He understood that it was to make him happy, he realised that I didn't believe in it the way I had before, but he was glad to nonetheless:

'It won't hurt.' He put on his stole and said, 'Kneel down.' I told him everything, from A to Z, without hiding or leaving out any details, including all my faults and everything I'd done wrong. I even told him things I'd never admitted to myself. And at a certain point I began to cry, and he put his hand on my shoulders paternally, and I kept crying and trying to talk, talking and crying. I cried for myself, I cried for my brother. But I also cried for Bompressi. For Serse. For Bava. It was late at night when Father Cavalli finally gave me absolution.

I don't know if he really had the power to absolve me, but I do know that he was able to find me peace, and the next morning – before he accompanied me to the station, after I had finished my caffè latte, as I stood in the entrance just as we were about to leave – I asked him in all sincerity, 'Father, give me your blessing.'

He made the sign of the cross, and put a hand on my head – he had to reach up because now I'd grown much taller than him – and he said, 'Benedictio Domini Nostri Jesu Christi descendat super te et maneat semper.'

My train was waiting at the station. He said goodbye: 'Praised be Jesus Christ.' Then he gave me another blessing on the track, and turned to get the bus before it left him behind. In front of me, on the wooden seat opposite mine, there was an old man, a farmer. He was wearing a beret, and he had a little portable radio: 'Do you mind if I listen?' he asked.

'Not at all.' He turned it on to a station that played old hits. Betty Curtis was singing full throttle, just like she used to when I was a boy.